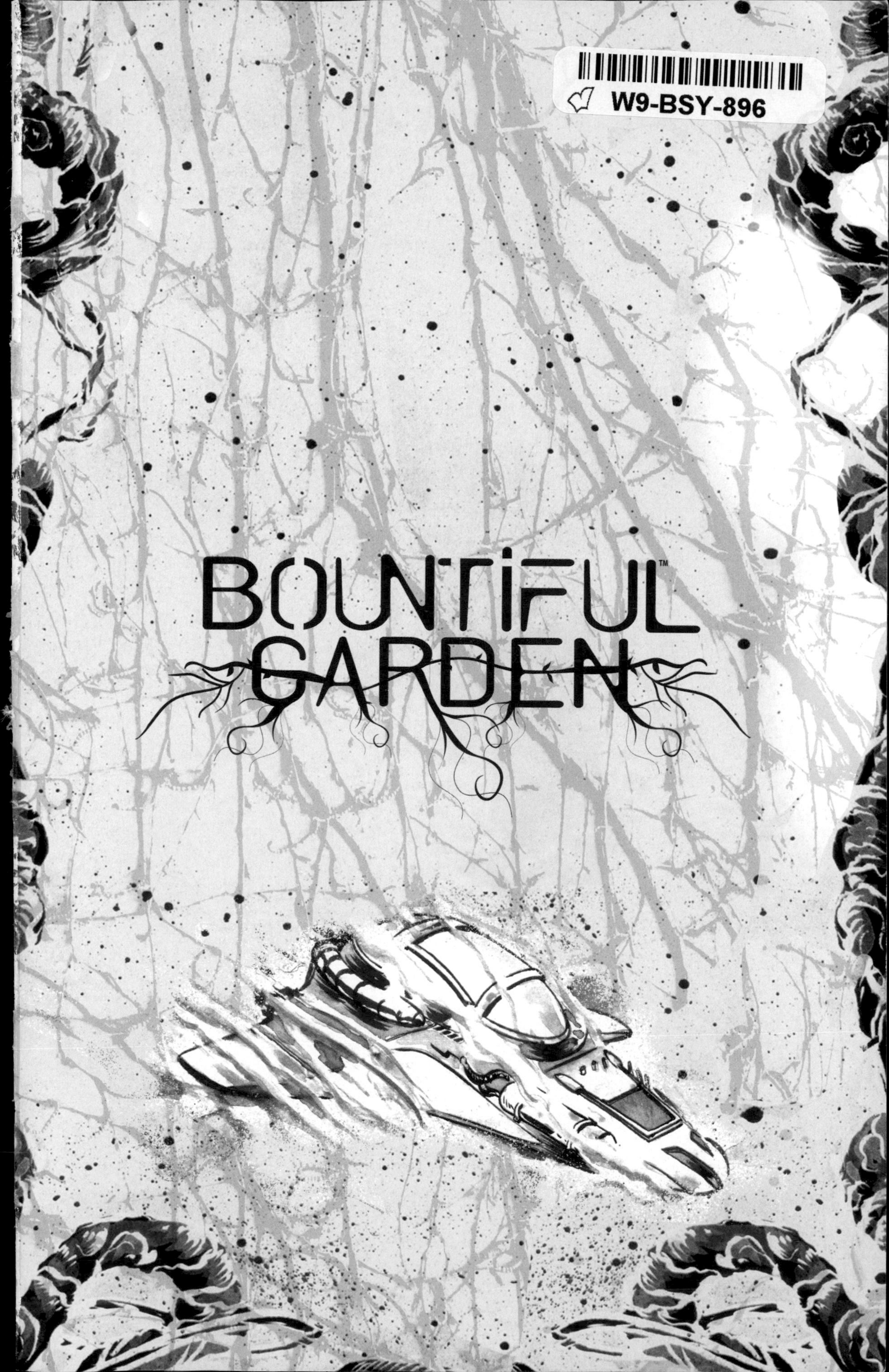
BOUNTIFUL™
GARDEN

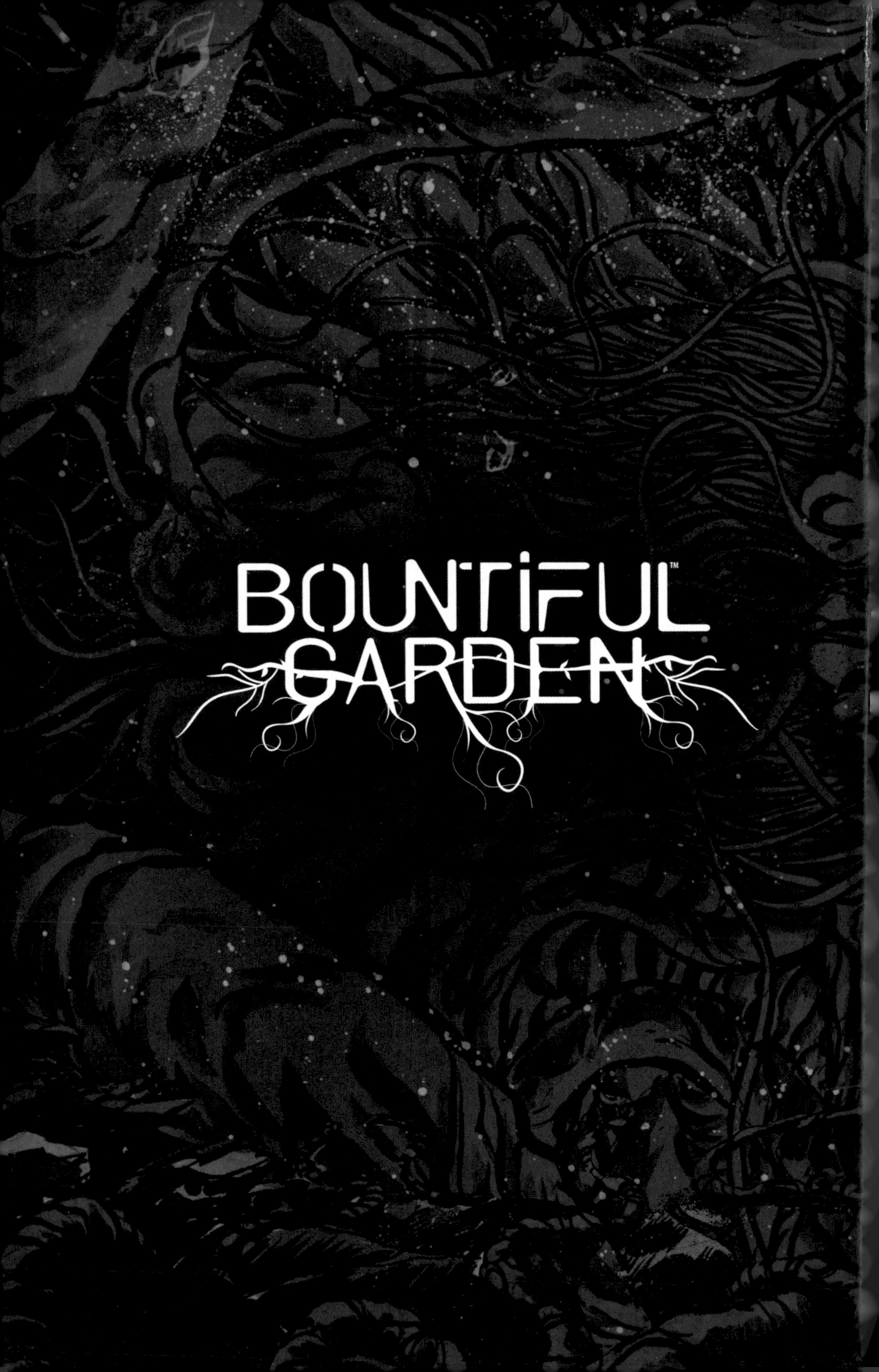
BOUNTIFUL™
GARDEN

IVY NOELLE WEIR
WRITER

KELLY WILLIAMS
ARTIST

GIORGIO SPALLETTA
COLORIST

JUSTIN BIRCH
LETTERER

STEENZ
EDITOR

DIANA BERMÚDEZ
LOGO & BOOK DESIGNER

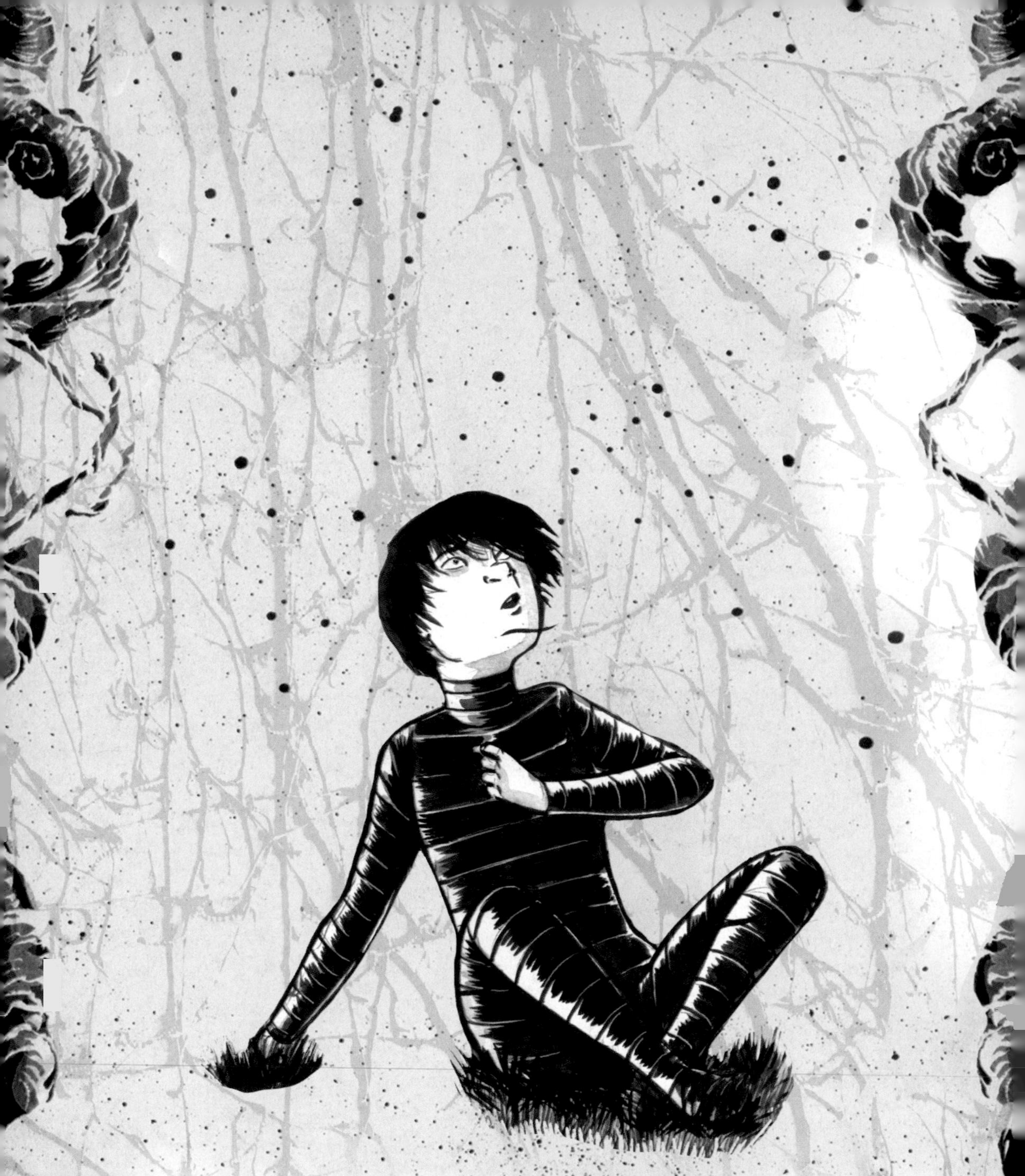

LAURA CHACÓN FOUNDER • MARK LONDON CEO AND CHIEF CREATIVE OFFICER
MARK IRWIN VP OF BUSINESS DEVELOPMENT • CHRIS FERNANDEZ PUBLISHER • CECILIA MEDINA CHIEF FINANCIAL OFFICER • ALLISON POND MARKETING DIRECTOR
MANNY CASTELLANOS SALES & RETAILER RELATIONS • GIOVANNA T. OROZCO PRODUCTION MANAGER • MIGUEL ANGEL ZAPATA DESIGN DIRECTOR
CHRIS SANCHEZ SENIOR EDITOR • CHAS! PANGBURN SENIOR EDITOR • MAYA LOPEZ MARKETING MANAGER • BRIAN HAWKINS ASSISTANT EDITOR
DIANA BERMÚDEZ GRAPHIC DESIGNER • DAVID REYES GRAPHIC DESIGNER • ADRIANA T. OROZCO INTERACTIVE MEDIA DESIGNER
NICOLÁS ZEA ARIAS AUDIOVISUAL PRODUCTION • FRANK SILVA EXECUTIVE ASSISTANT • STEPHANIE HIDALGO OFFICE MANAGER

FOR MAD CAVE COMICS, INC.

Bountiful Garden™ Trade Paperback Published by Mad Cave Studios, Inc. 8838 SW 129th St. Miami, FL 33176 © 2022 Mad Cave Studios, Inc. All rights reserved. Contains materials originally published in single magazine form as Bountiful Garden™ (2021) #1-5.

First printing. Printed in Canada
ISBN: 978-1-952303-17-3

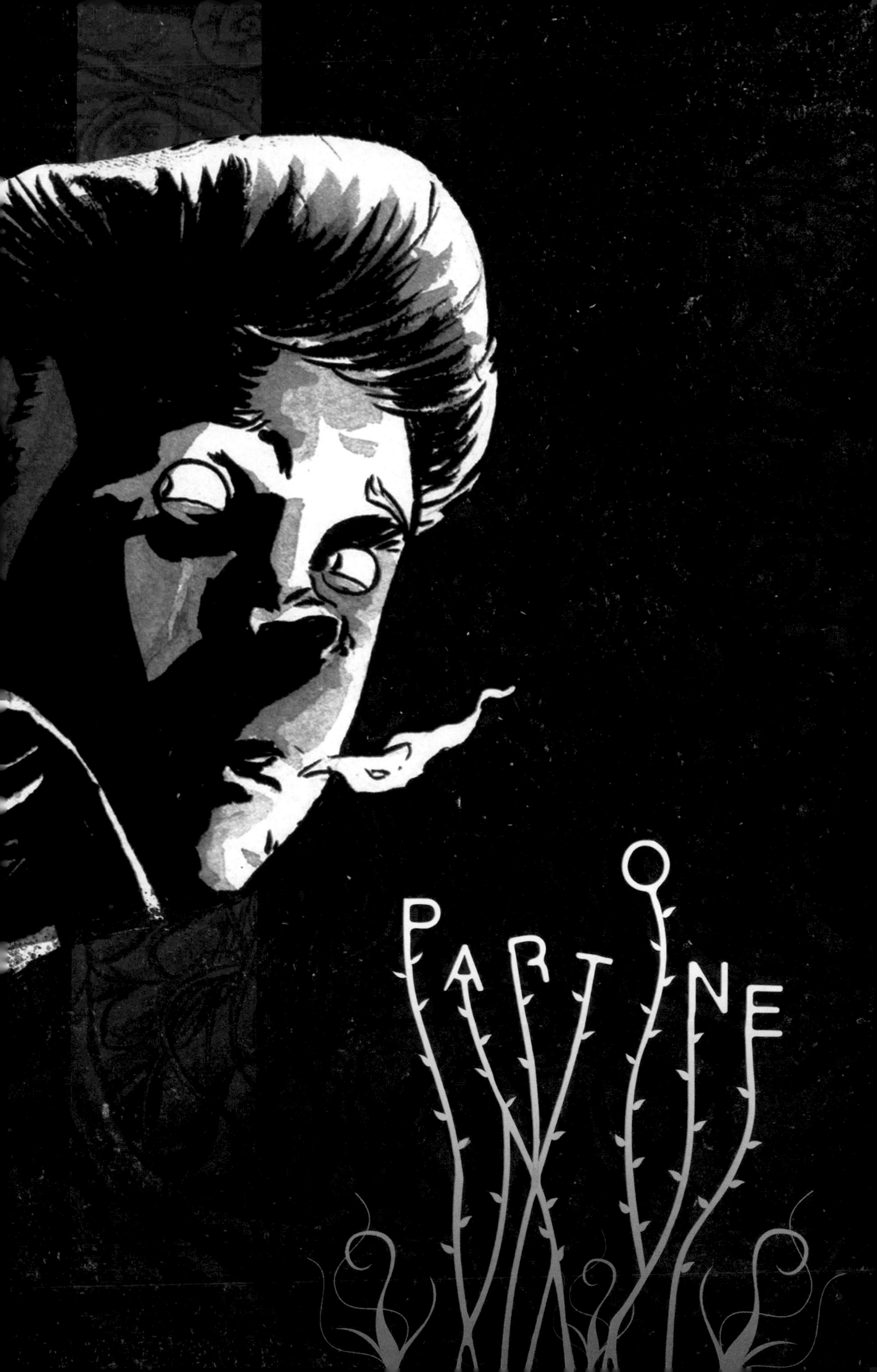
PART ONE

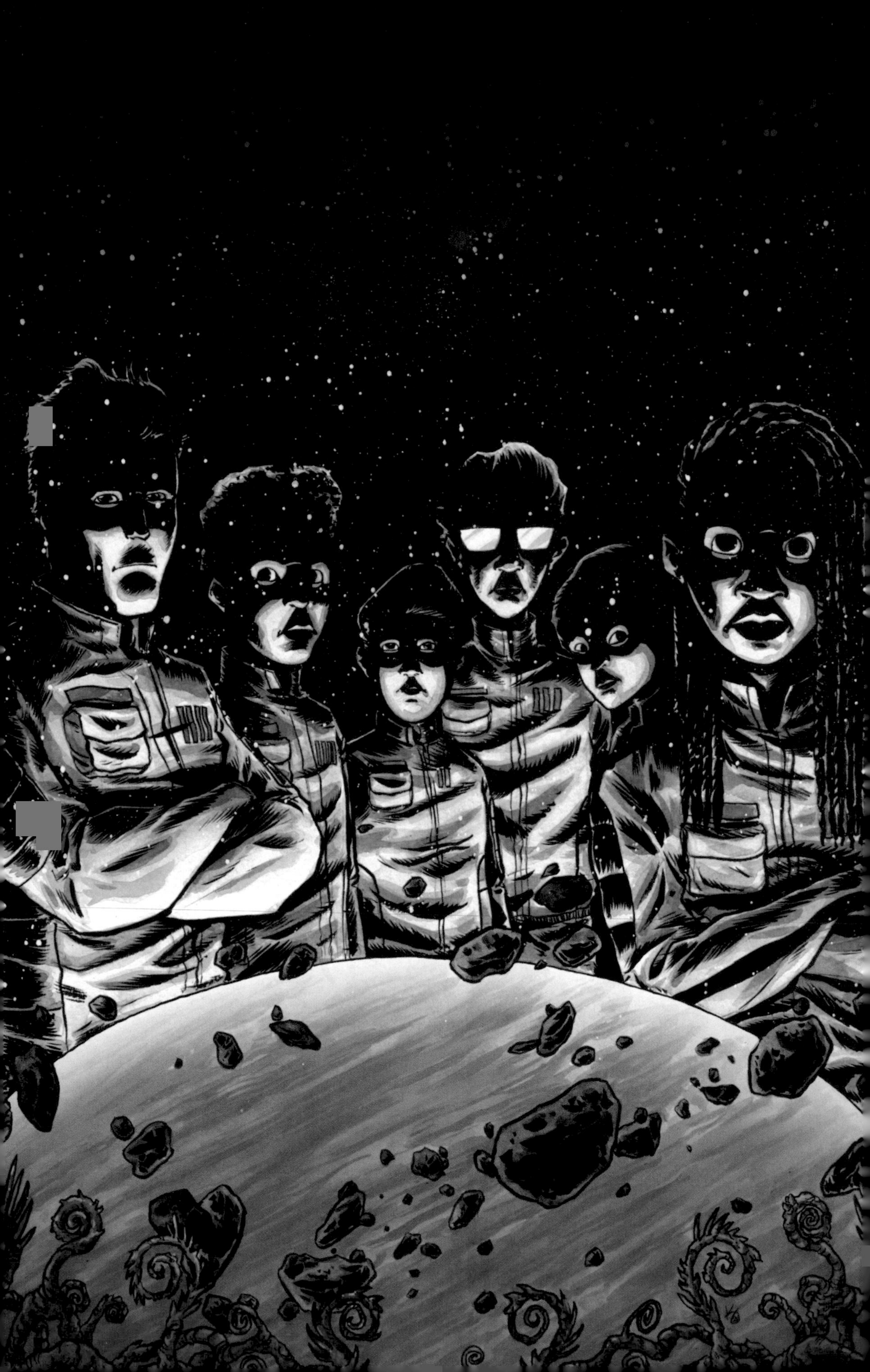

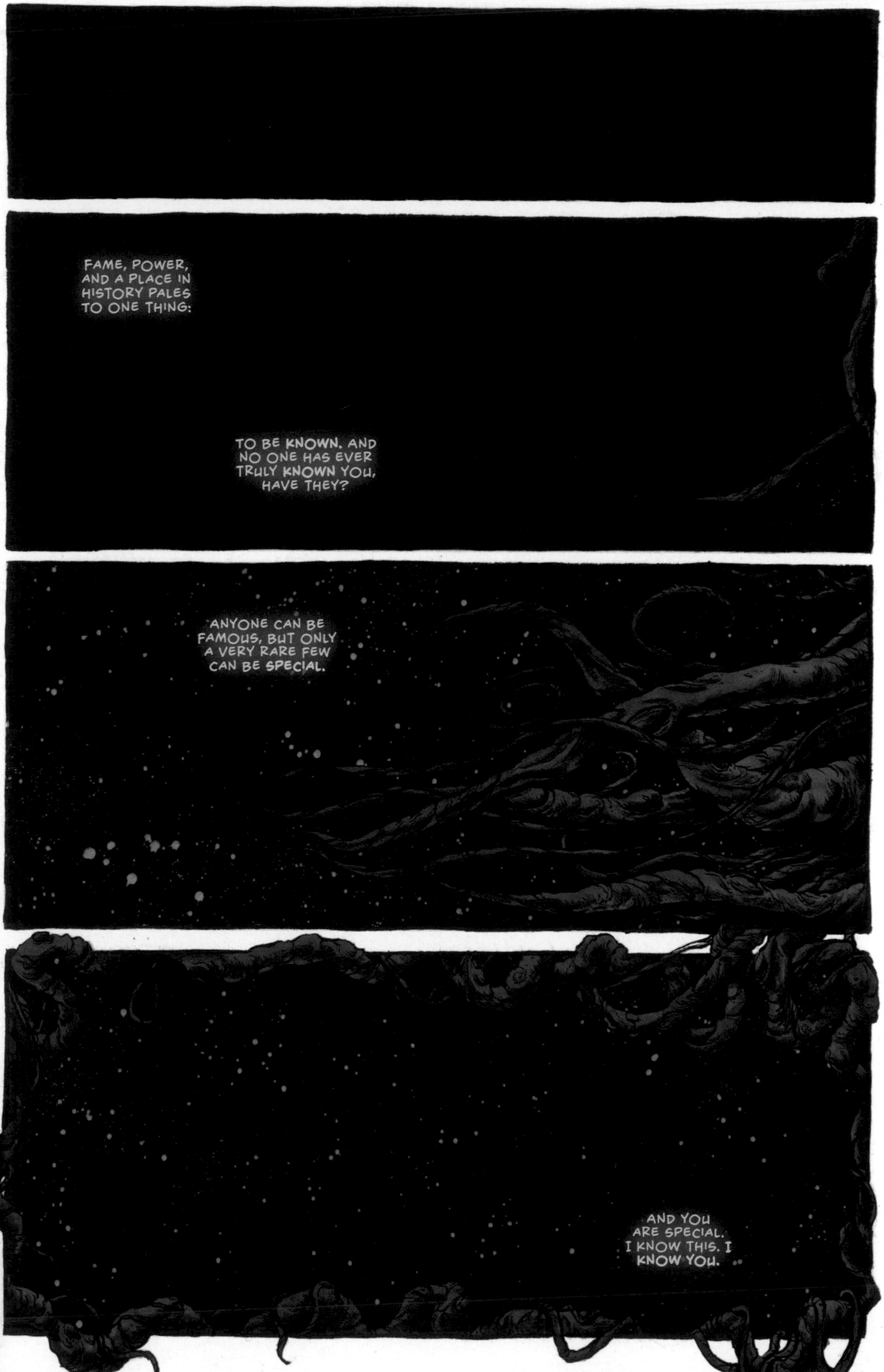
FAME, POWER, AND A PLACE IN HISTORY PALES TO ONE THING:
TO BE KNOWN. AND NO ONE HAS EVER TRULY KNOWN YOU, HAVE THEY?
ANYONE CAN BE FAMOUS, BUT ONLY A VERY RARE FEW CAN BE SPECIAL.
AND YOU ARE SPECIAL. I KNOW THIS. I KNOW YOU.

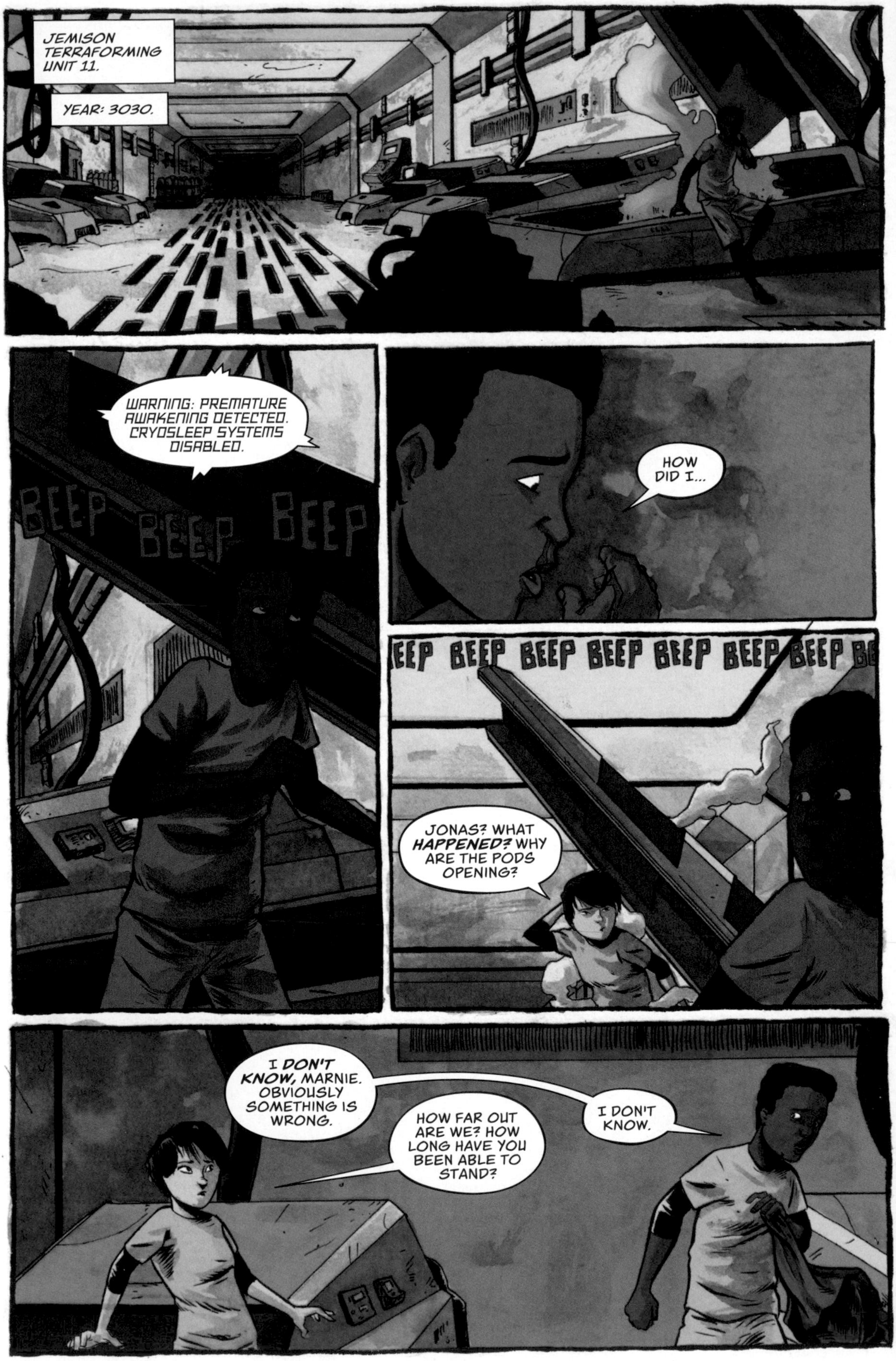
JEMISON TERRAFORMING UNIT 11.
YEAR: 3030.
WARNING: PREMATURE AWAKENING DETECTED. CRYOSLEEP SYSTEMS DISABLED.
BEEP BEEP BEEP
HOW DID I...
BEEP BEEP BEEP BEEP BEEP BEEP
JONAS? WHAT HAPPENED? WHY ARE THE PODS OPENING?
I DON'T KNOW, MARNIE. OBVIOUSLY SOMETHING IS WRONG.
HOW FAR OUT ARE WE? HOW LONG HAVE YOU BEEN ABLE TO STAND?
I DON'T KNOW.

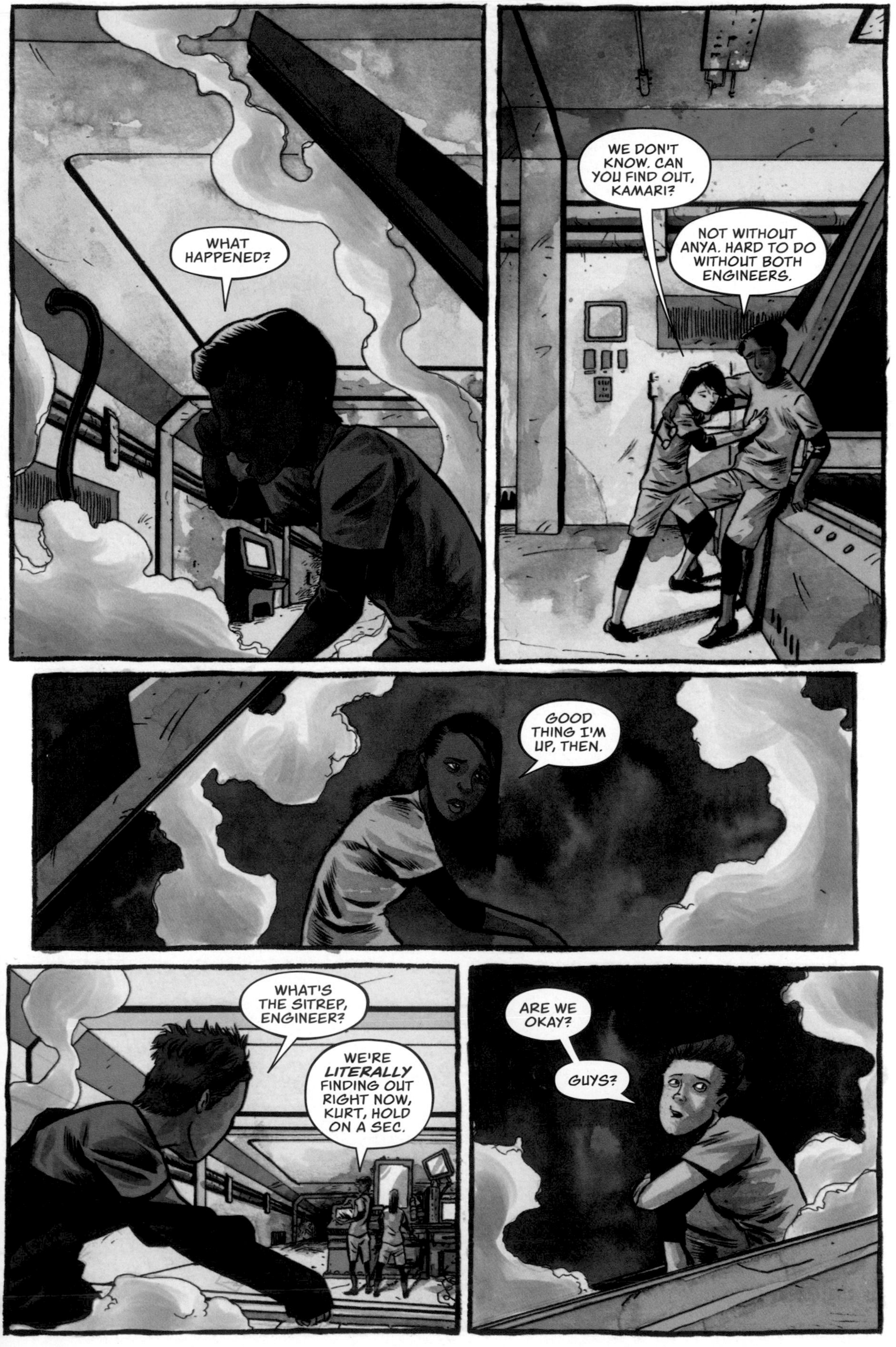
WHAT HAPPENED?
WE DON'T KNOW. CAN YOU FIND OUT, KAMARI?
NOT WITHOUT ANYA. HARD TO DO WITHOUT BOTH ENGINEERS.
GOOD THING I'M UP, THEN.
WHAT'S THE SITREP, ENGINEER?
WE'RE *LITERALLY* FINDING OUT RIGHT NOW, KURT, HOLD ON A SEC.
ARE WE OKAY?
GUYS?

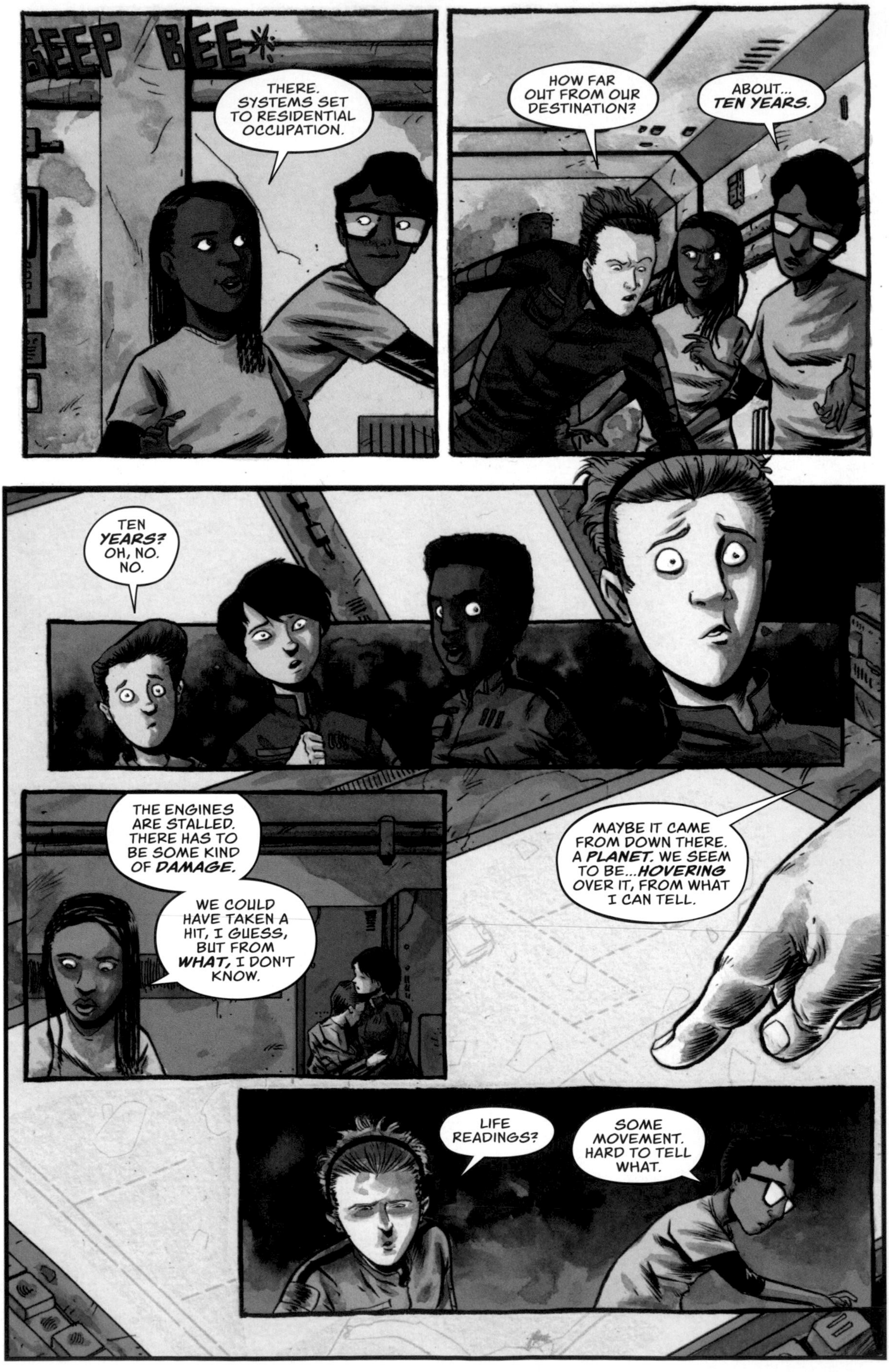
BEEP BEE
THERE. SYSTEMS SET TO RESIDENTIAL OCCUPATION.
HOW FAR OUT FROM OUR DESTINATION?
ABOUT... TEN YEARS.
TEN YEARS? OH, NO. NO.
THE ENGINES ARE STALLED. THERE HAS TO BE SOME KIND OF DAMAGE.
WE COULD HAVE TAKEN A HIT, I GUESS, BUT FROM WHAT, I DON'T KNOW.
MAYBE IT CAME FROM DOWN THERE. A PLANET. WE SEEM TO BE...HOVERING OVER IT, FROM WHAT I CAN TELL.
LIFE READINGS?
SOME MOVEMENT. HARD TO TELL WHAT.

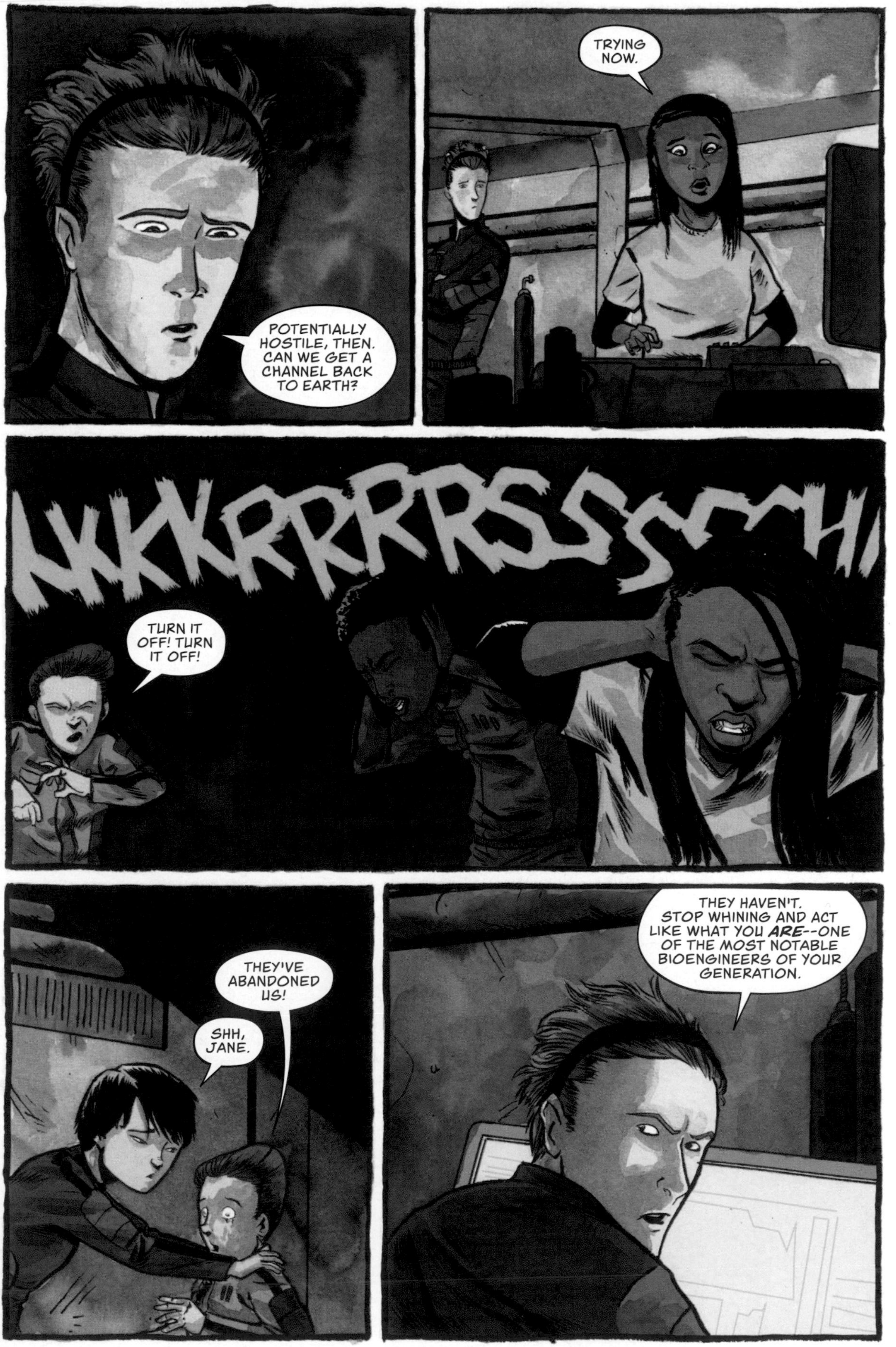
POTENTIALLY HOSTILE, THEN. CAN WE GET A CHANNEL BACK TO EARTH?
TRYING NOW.
NKKRRRRSSSSHH
TURN IT OFF! TURN IT OFF!
THEY'VE ABANDONED US!
SHH, JANE.
THEY HAVEN'T. STOP WHINING AND ACT LIKE WHAT YOU ARE--ONE OF THE MOST NOTABLE BIOENGINEERS OF YOUR GENERATION.

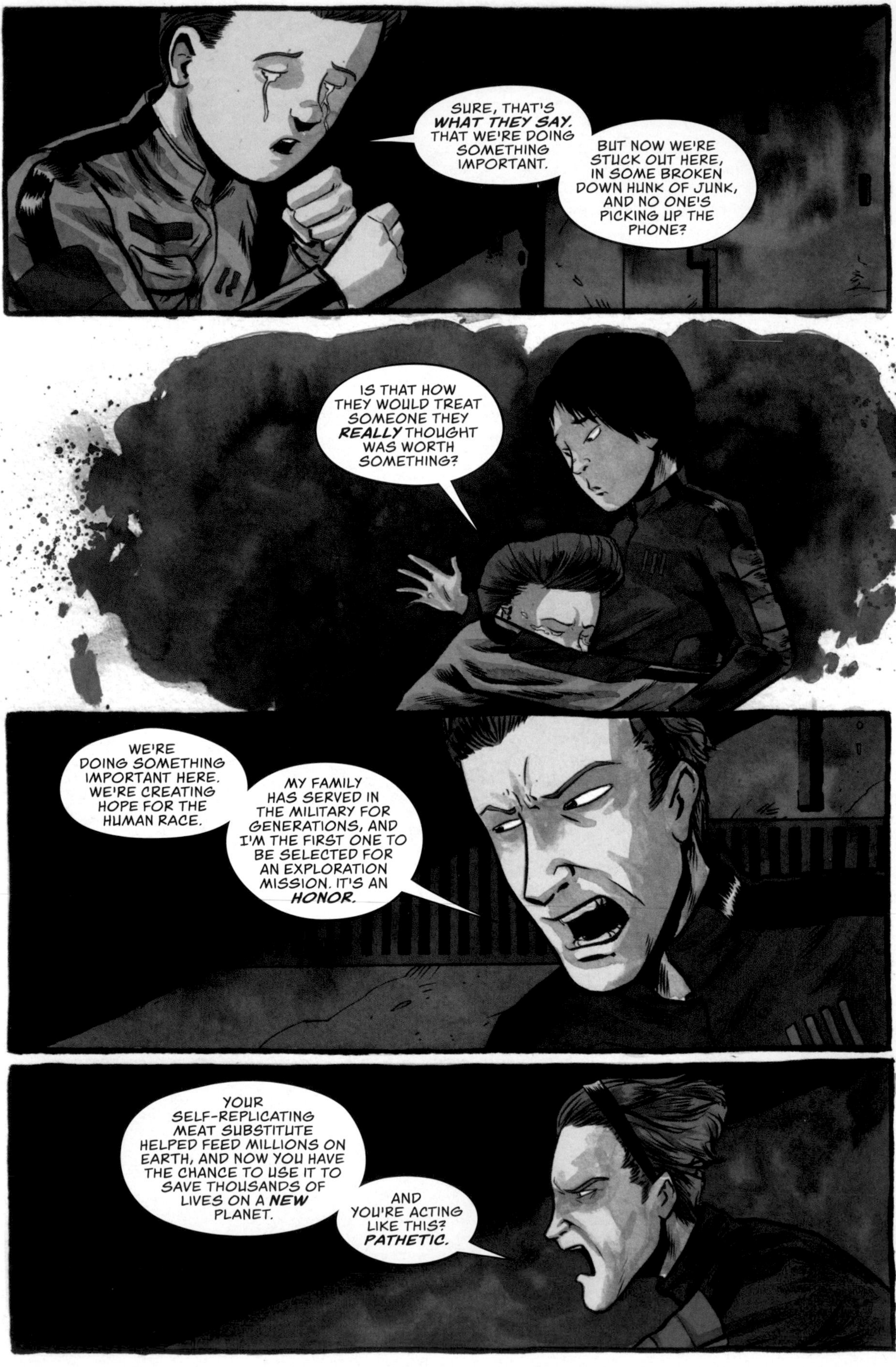
SURE, THAT'S **WHAT THEY SAY.** THAT WE'RE DOING SOMETHING IMPORTANT.
BUT NOW WE'RE STUCK OUT HERE, IN SOME BROKEN DOWN HUNK OF JUNK, AND NO ONE'S PICKING UP THE PHONE?
IS THAT HOW THEY WOULD TREAT SOMEONE THEY **REALLY** THOUGHT WAS WORTH SOMETHING?
WE'RE DOING SOMETHING IMPORTANT HERE. WE'RE CREATING HOPE FOR THE HUMAN RACE.
MY FAMILY HAS SERVED IN THE MILITARY FOR GENERATIONS, AND I'M THE FIRST ONE TO BE SELECTED FOR AN EXPLORATION MISSION. IT'S AN **HONOR.**
YOUR SELF-REPLICATING MEAT SUBSTITUTE HELPED FEED MILLIONS ON EARTH, AND NOW YOU HAVE THE CHANCE TO USE IT TO SAVE THOUSANDS OF LIVES ON A **NEW** PLANET.
AND YOU'RE ACTING LIKE THIS? **PATHETIC.**

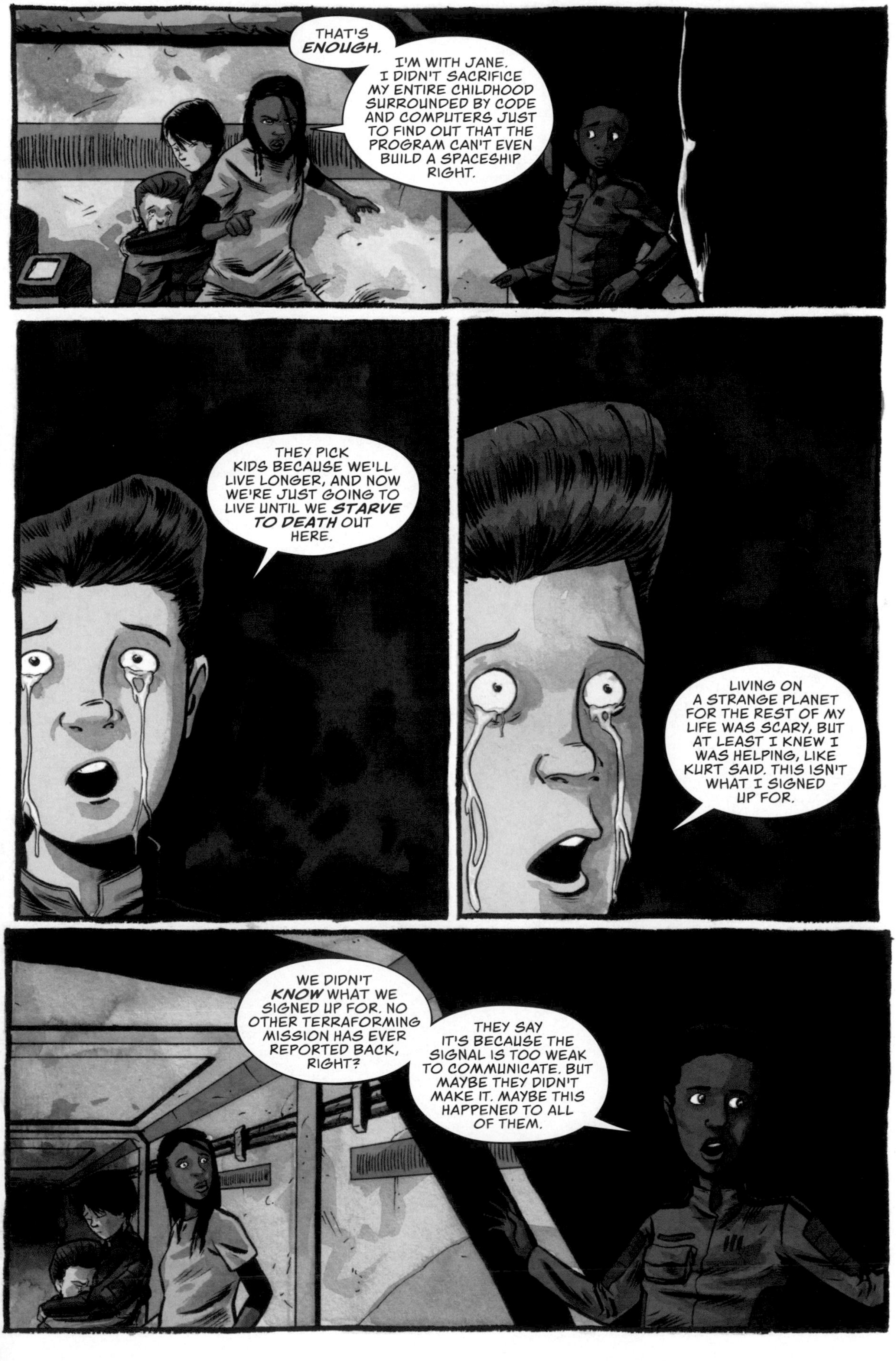
THAT'S *ENOUGH.*
I'M WITH JANE. I DIDN'T SACRIFICE MY ENTIRE CHILDHOOD SURROUNDED BY CODE AND COMPUTERS JUST TO FIND OUT THAT THE PROGRAM CAN'T EVEN BUILD A SPACESHIP RIGHT.
THEY PICK KIDS BECAUSE WE'LL LIVE LONGER, AND NOW WE'RE JUST GOING TO LIVE UNTIL WE *STARVE TO DEATH* OUT HERE.
LIVING ON A STRANGE PLANET FOR THE REST OF MY LIFE WAS SCARY, BUT AT LEAST I KNEW I WAS HELPING, LIKE KURT SAID. THIS ISN'T WHAT I SIGNED UP FOR.
WE DIDN'T *KNOW* WHAT WE SIGNED UP FOR. NO OTHER TERRAFORMING MISSION HAS EVER REPORTED BACK, RIGHT?
THEY SAY IT'S BECAUSE THE SIGNAL IS TOO WEAK TO COMMUNICATE. BUT MAYBE THEY DIDN'T MAKE IT. MAYBE THIS HAPPENED TO ALL OF THEM.

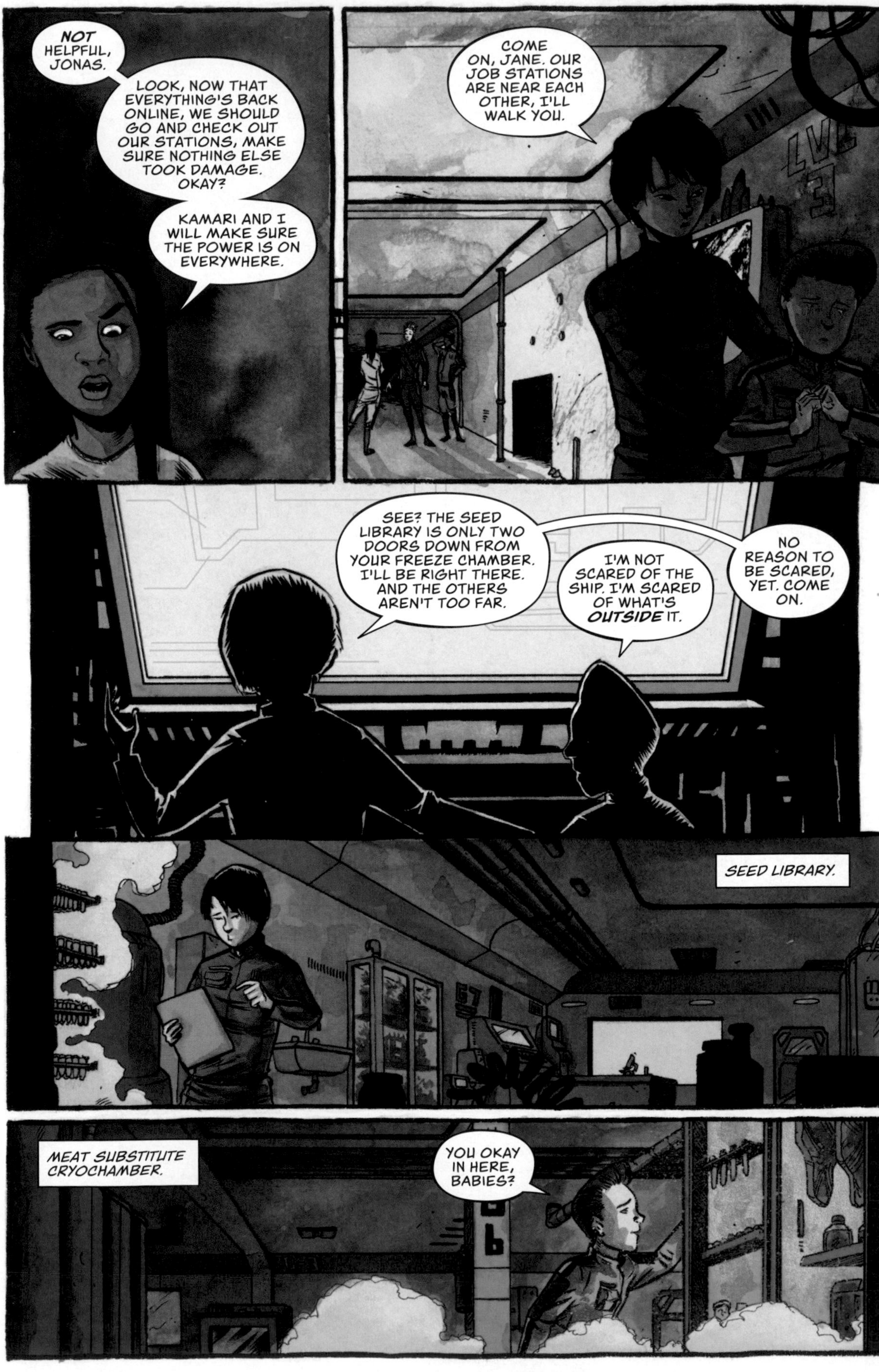
NOT HELPFUL, JONAS.
LOOK, NOW THAT EVERYTHING'S BACK ONLINE, WE SHOULD GO AND CHECK OUT OUR STATIONS, MAKE SURE NOTHING ELSE TOOK DAMAGE. OKAY?
KAMARI AND I WILL MAKE SURE THE POWER IS ON EVERYWHERE.
COME ON, JANE. OUR JOB STATIONS ARE NEAR EACH OTHER, I'LL WALK YOU.
LVL 3
SEE? THE SEED LIBRARY IS ONLY TWO DOORS DOWN FROM YOUR FREEZE CHAMBER. I'LL BE RIGHT THERE. AND THE OTHERS AREN'T TOO FAR.
I'M NOT SCARED OF THE SHIP. I'M SCARED OF WHAT'S OUTSIDE IT.
NO REASON TO BE SCARED, YET. COME ON.
SEED LIBRARY.
MEAT SUBSTITUTE CRYOCHAMBER.
YOU OKAY IN HERE, BABIES?

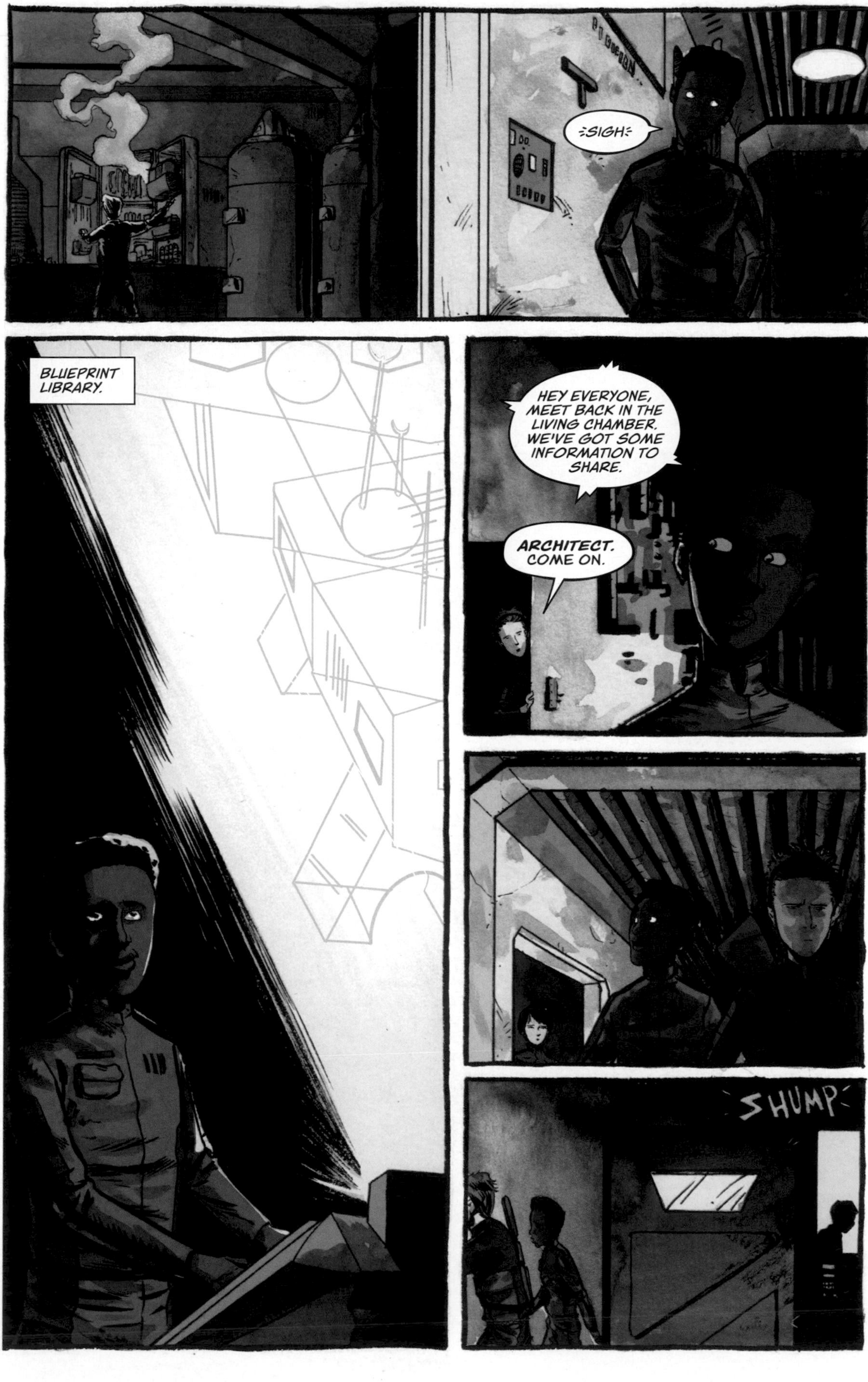
SIGH
BLUEPRINT LIBRARY.
HEY EVERYONE, MEET BACK IN THE LIVING CHAMBER. WE'VE GOT SOME INFORMATION TO SHARE.
ARCHITECT. COME ON.
SHUMP

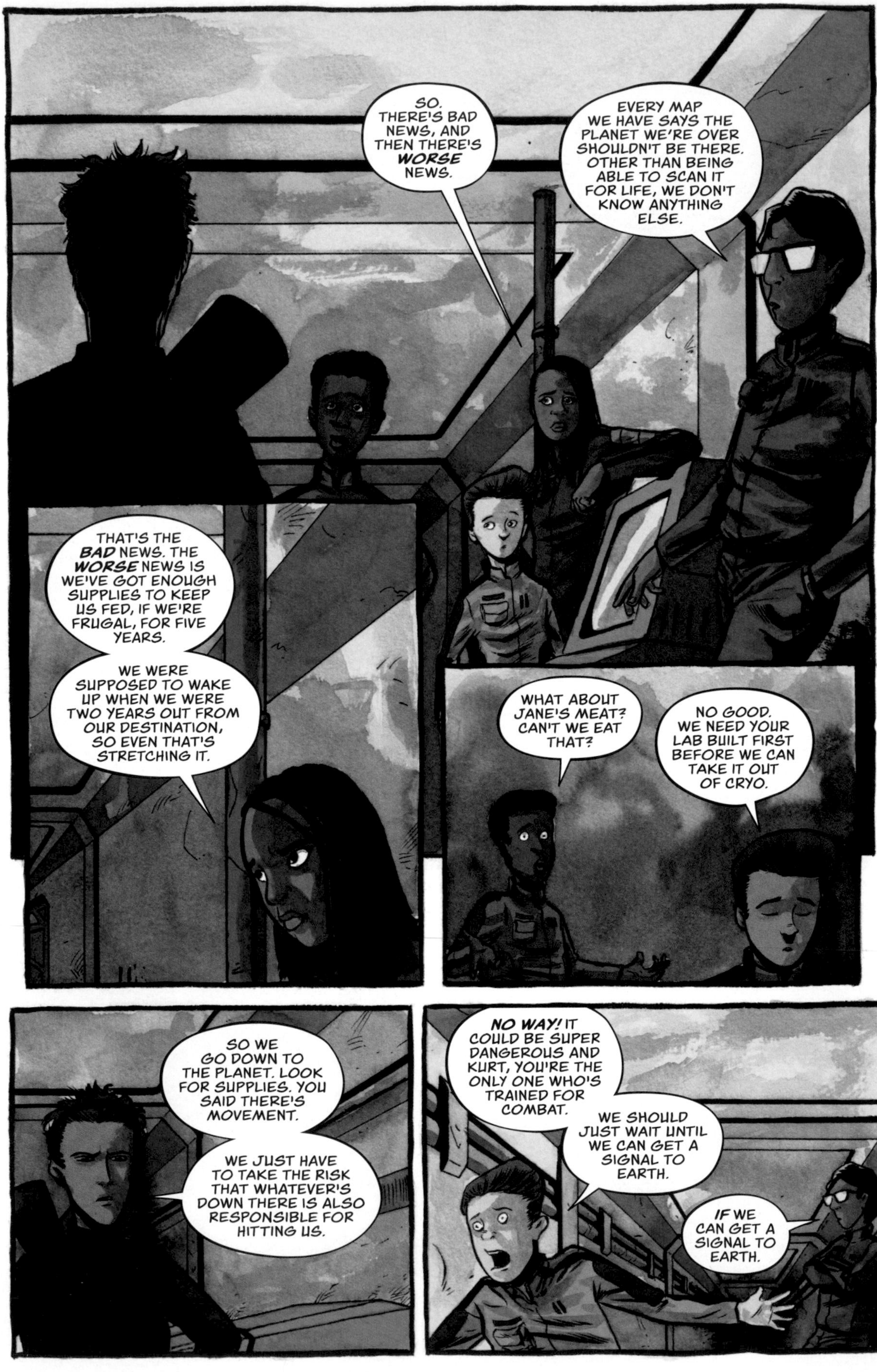
SO. THERE'S BAD NEWS, AND THEN THERE'S WORSE NEWS.
EVERY MAP WE HAVE SAYS THE PLANET WE'RE OVER SHOULDN'T BE THERE. OTHER THAN BEING ABLE TO SCAN IT FOR LIFE, WE DON'T KNOW ANYTHING ELSE.
THAT'S THE BAD NEWS. THE WORSE NEWS IS WE'VE GOT ENOUGH SUPPLIES TO KEEP US FED, IF WE'RE FRUGAL, FOR FIVE YEARS.
WE WERE SUPPOSED TO WAKE UP WHEN WE WERE TWO YEARS OUT FROM OUR DESTINATION, SO EVEN THAT'S STRETCHING IT.
WHAT ABOUT JANE'S MEAT? CAN'T WE EAT THAT?
NO GOOD. WE NEED YOUR LAB BUILT FIRST BEFORE WE CAN TAKE IT OUT OF CRYO.
SO WE GO DOWN TO THE PLANET. LOOK FOR SUPPLIES. YOU SAID THERE'S MOVEMENT.
WE JUST HAVE TO TAKE THE RISK THAT WHATEVER'S DOWN THERE IS ALSO RESPONSIBLE FOR HITTING US.
NO WAY! IT COULD BE SUPER DANGEROUS AND KURT, YOU'RE THE ONLY ONE WHO'S TRAINED FOR COMBAT.
WE SHOULD JUST WAIT UNTIL WE CAN GET A SIGNAL TO EARTH.
IF WE CAN GET A SIGNAL TO EARTH.

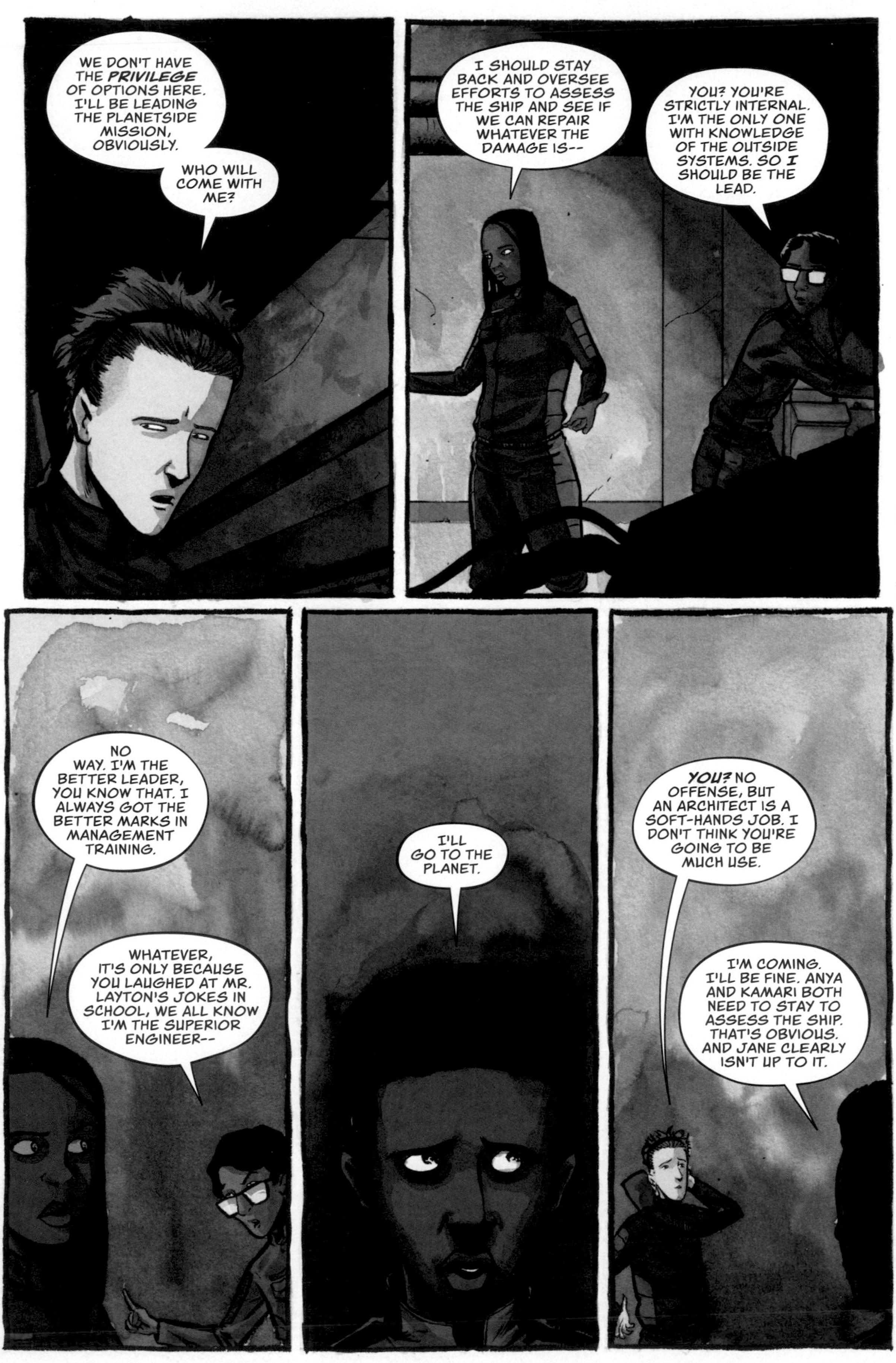
WE DON'T HAVE THE *PRIVILEGE* OF OPTIONS HERE. I'LL BE LEADING THE PLANETSIDE MISSION, OBVIOUSLY.
WHO WILL COME WITH ME?
I SHOULD STAY BACK AND OVERSEE EFFORTS TO ASSESS THE SHIP AND SEE IF WE CAN REPAIR WHATEVER THE DAMAGE IS--
YOU? YOU'RE STRICTLY INTERNAL. I'M THE ONLY ONE WITH KNOWLEDGE OF THE OUTSIDE SYSTEMS. SO *I* SHOULD BE THE LEAD.
NO WAY. I'M THE BETTER LEADER, YOU KNOW THAT. I ALWAYS GOT THE BETTER MARKS IN MANAGEMENT TRAINING.
WHATEVER, IT'S ONLY BECAUSE YOU LAUGHED AT MR. LAYTON'S JOKES IN SCHOOL, WE ALL KNOW I'M THE SUPERIOR ENGINEER--
I'LL GO TO THE PLANET.
YOU? NO OFFENSE, BUT AN ARCHITECT IS A SOFT-HANDS JOB. I DON'T THINK YOU'RE GOING TO BE MUCH USE.
I'M COMING. I'LL BE FINE. ANYA AND KAMARI BOTH NEED TO STAY TO ASSESS THE SHIP. THAT'S OBVIOUS. AND JANE CLEARLY ISN'T UP TO IT.

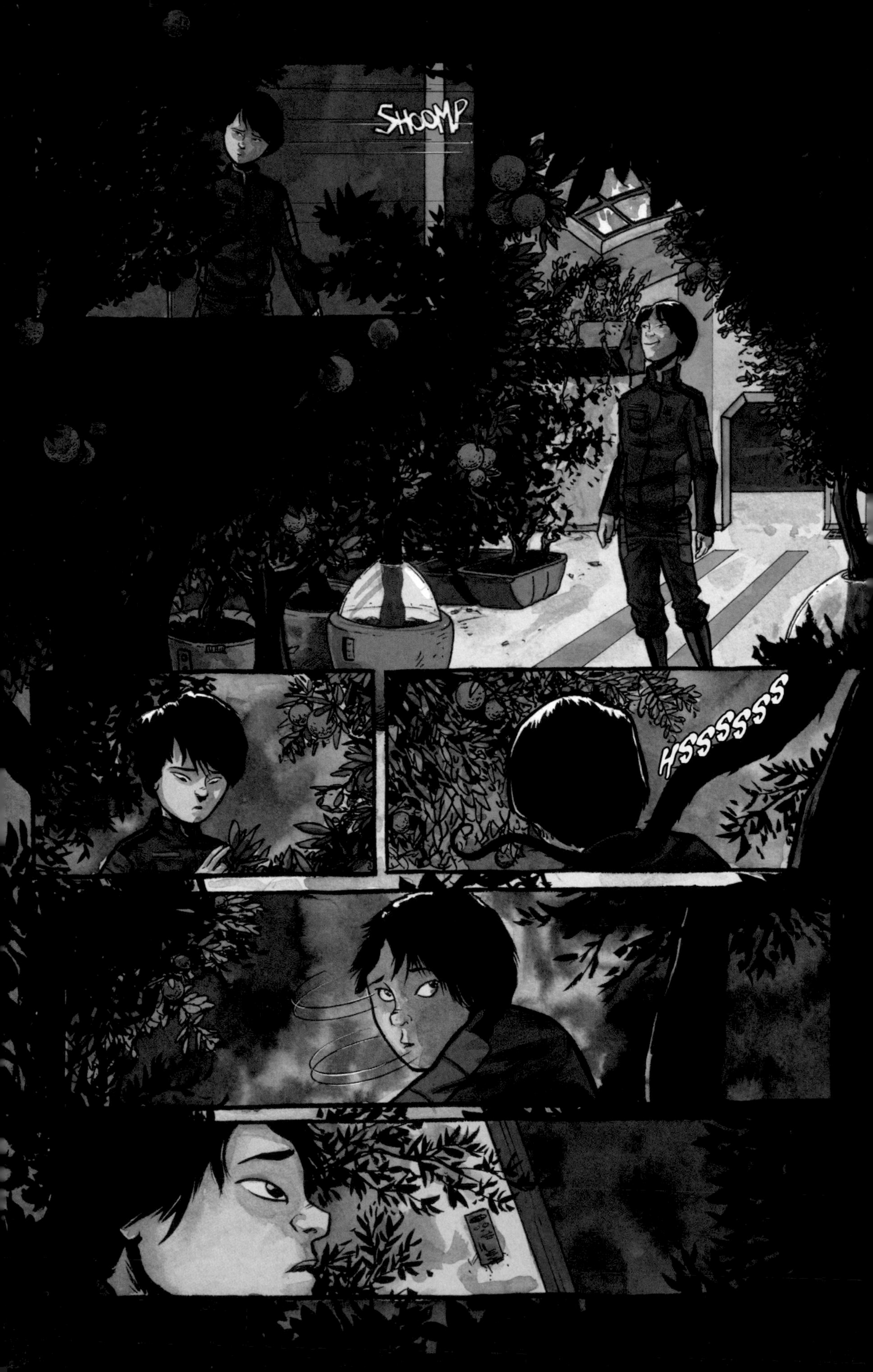
SHOOMP
HSSSSSS

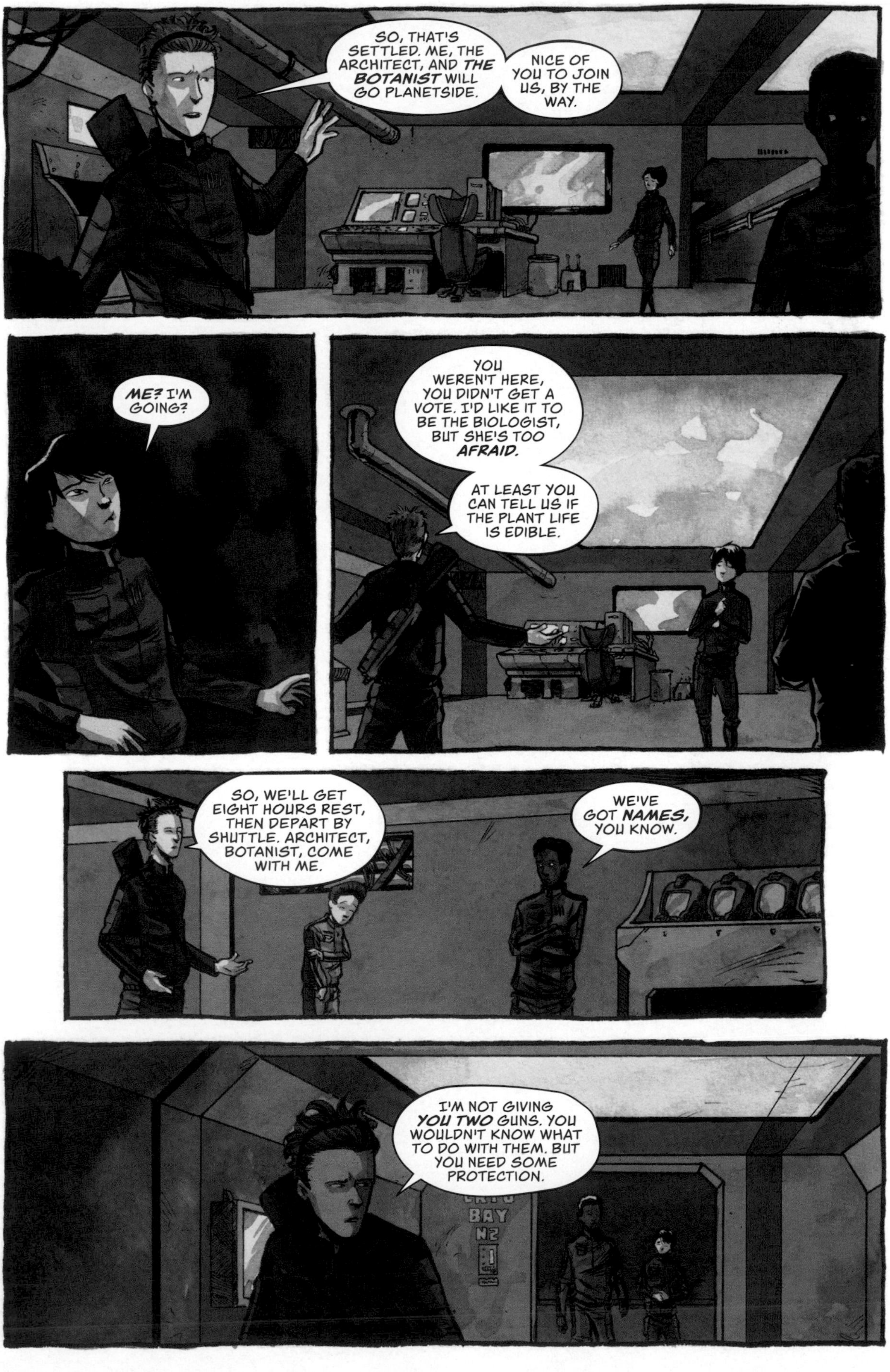
SO, THAT'S SETTLED. ME, THE ARCHITECT, AND THE BOTANIST WILL GO PLANETSIDE.
NICE OF YOU TO JOIN US, BY THE WAY.
ME? I'M GOING?
YOU WEREN'T HERE, YOU DIDN'T GET A VOTE. I'D LIKE IT TO BE THE BIOLOGIST, BUT SHE'S TOO AFRAID.
AT LEAST YOU CAN TELL US IF THE PLANT LIFE IS EDIBLE.
SO, WE'LL GET EIGHT HOURS REST, THEN DEPART BY SHUTTLE. ARCHITECT, BOTANIST, COME WITH ME.
WE'VE GOT NAMES, YOU KNOW.
I'M NOT GIVING YOU TWO GUNS. YOU WOULDN'T KNOW WHAT TO DO WITH THEM. BUT YOU NEED SOME PROTECTION.
BAY
N2

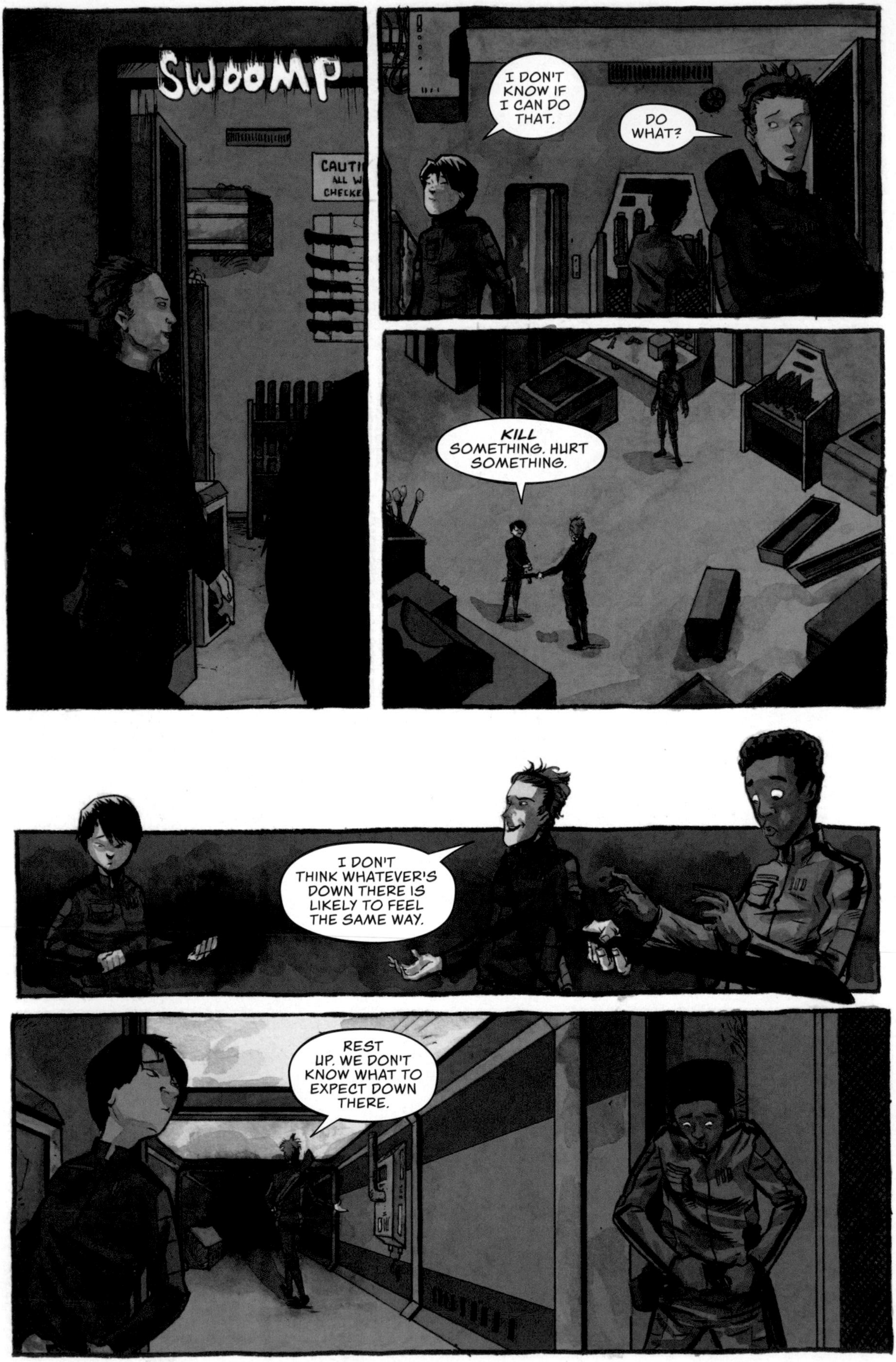
SWOOMP
CAUTI
ALL W
CHECKE
I DON'T KNOW IF I CAN DO THAT.
DO WHAT?
KILL SOMETHING. HURT SOMETHING.
I DON'T THINK WHATEVER'S DOWN THERE IS LIKELY TO FEEL THE SAME WAY.
REST UP. WE DON'T KNOW WHAT TO EXPECT DOWN THERE.

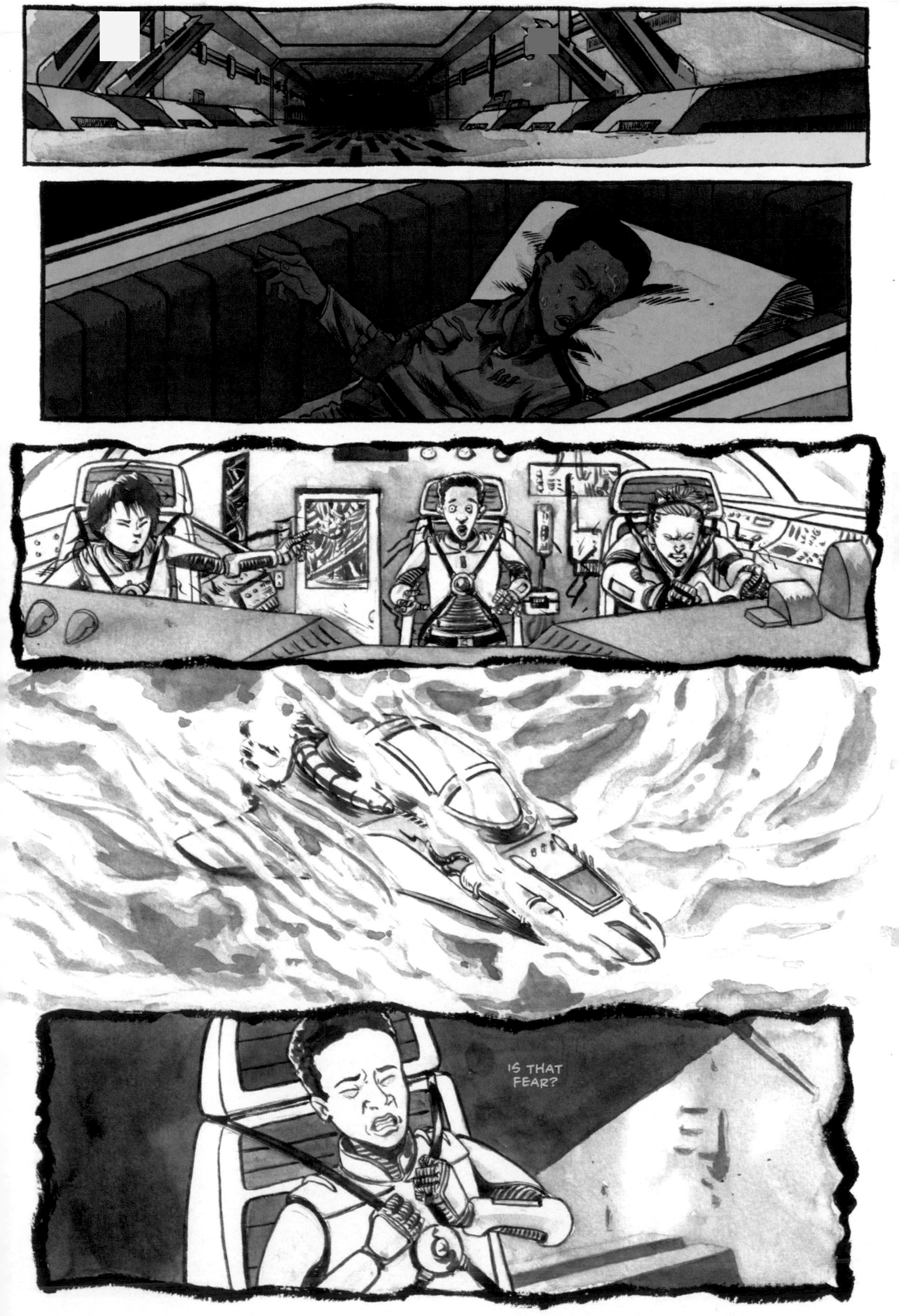
IS THAT FEAR?

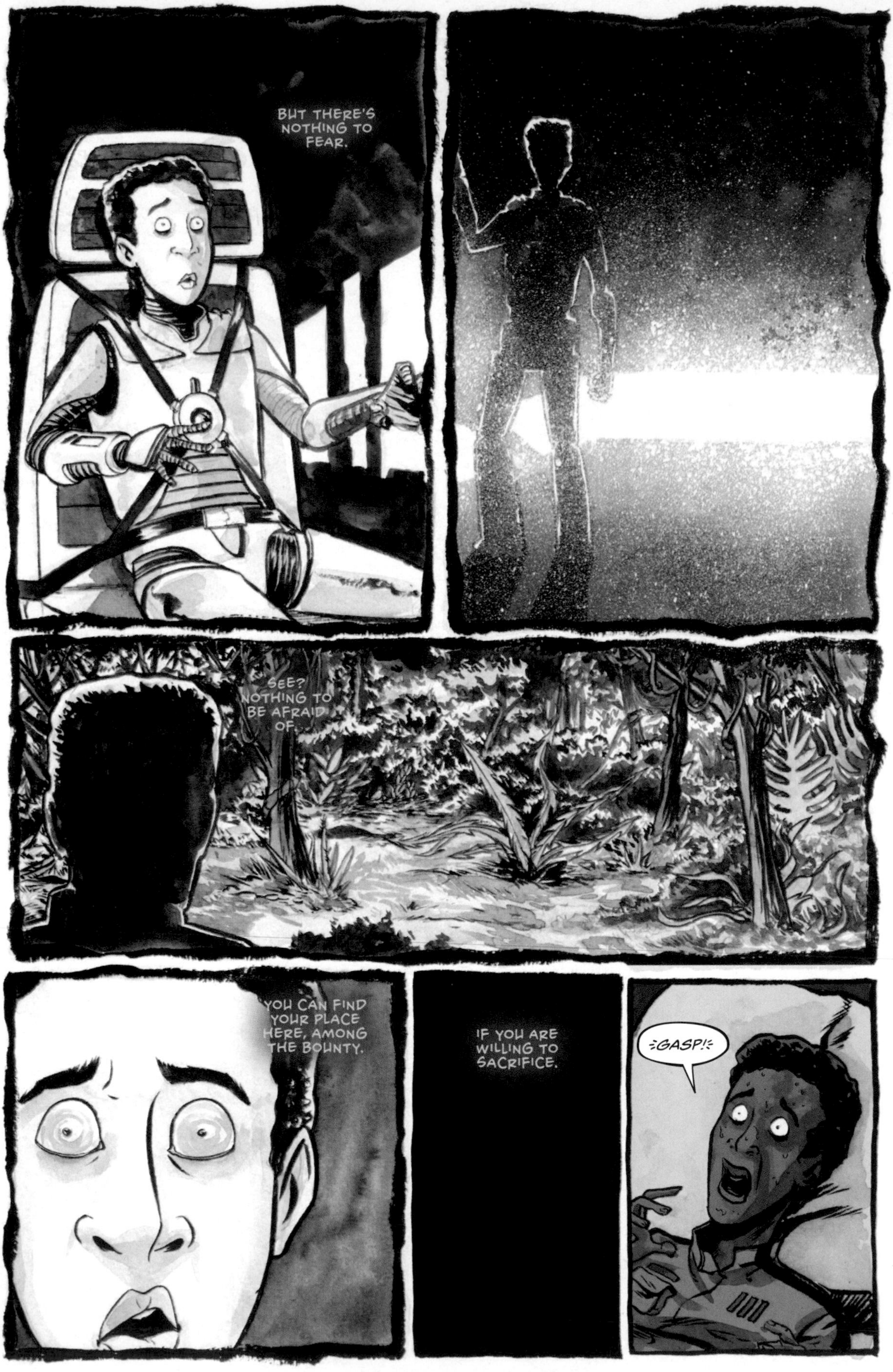
BUT THERE'S NOTHING TO FEAR.
SEE? NOTHING TO BE AFRAID OF.
YOU CAN FIND YOUR PLACE HERE, AMONG THE BOUNTY.
IF YOU ARE WILLING TO SACRIFICE.
GASP!

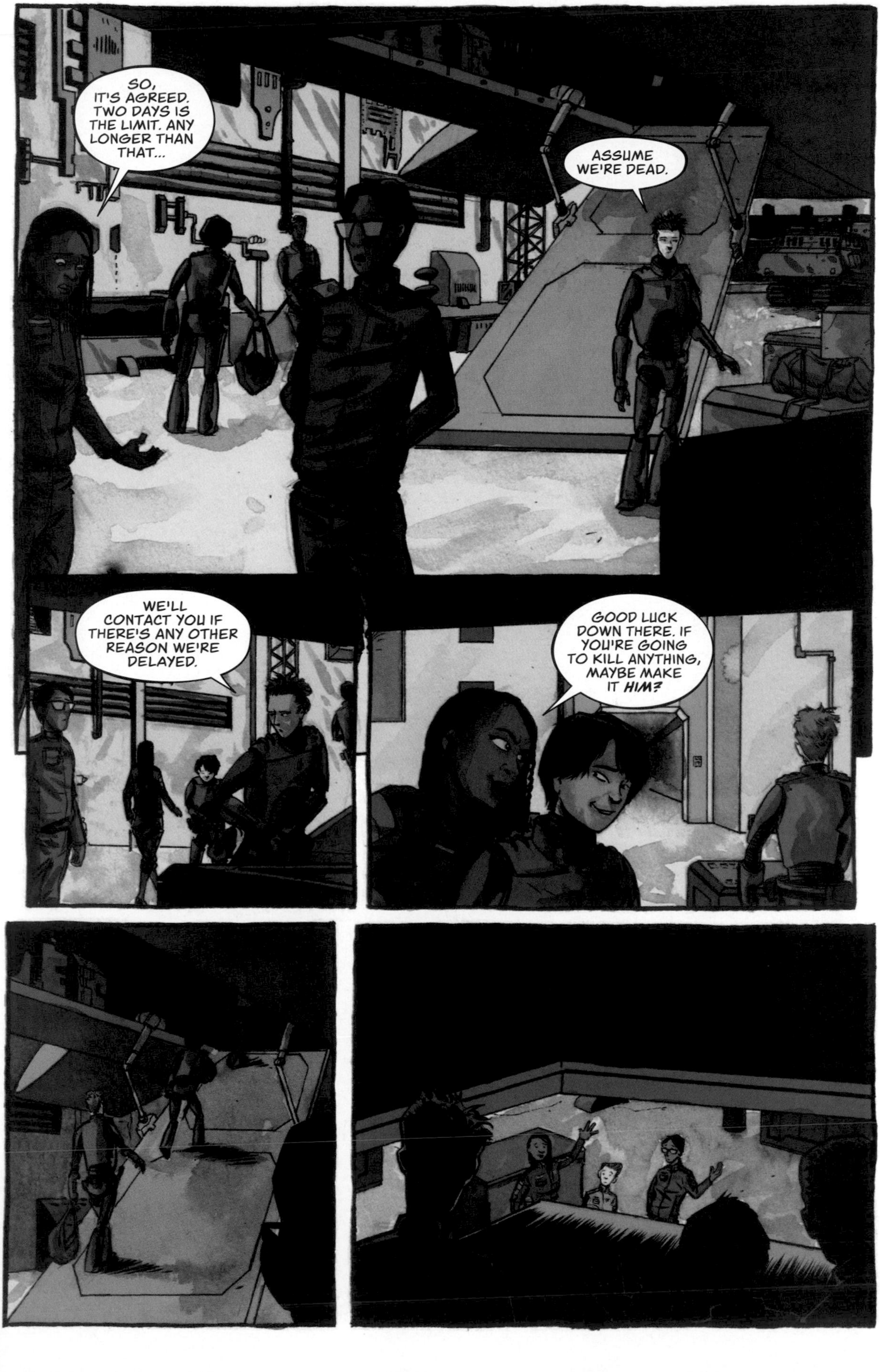
SO, IT'S AGREED. TWO DAYS IS THE LIMIT. ANY LONGER THAN THAT...
ASSUME WE'RE DEAD.
WE'LL CONTACT YOU IF THERE'S ANY OTHER REASON WE'RE DELAYED.
GOOD LUCK DOWN THERE. IF YOU'RE GOING TO KILL ANYTHING, MAYBE MAKE IT *HIM?*

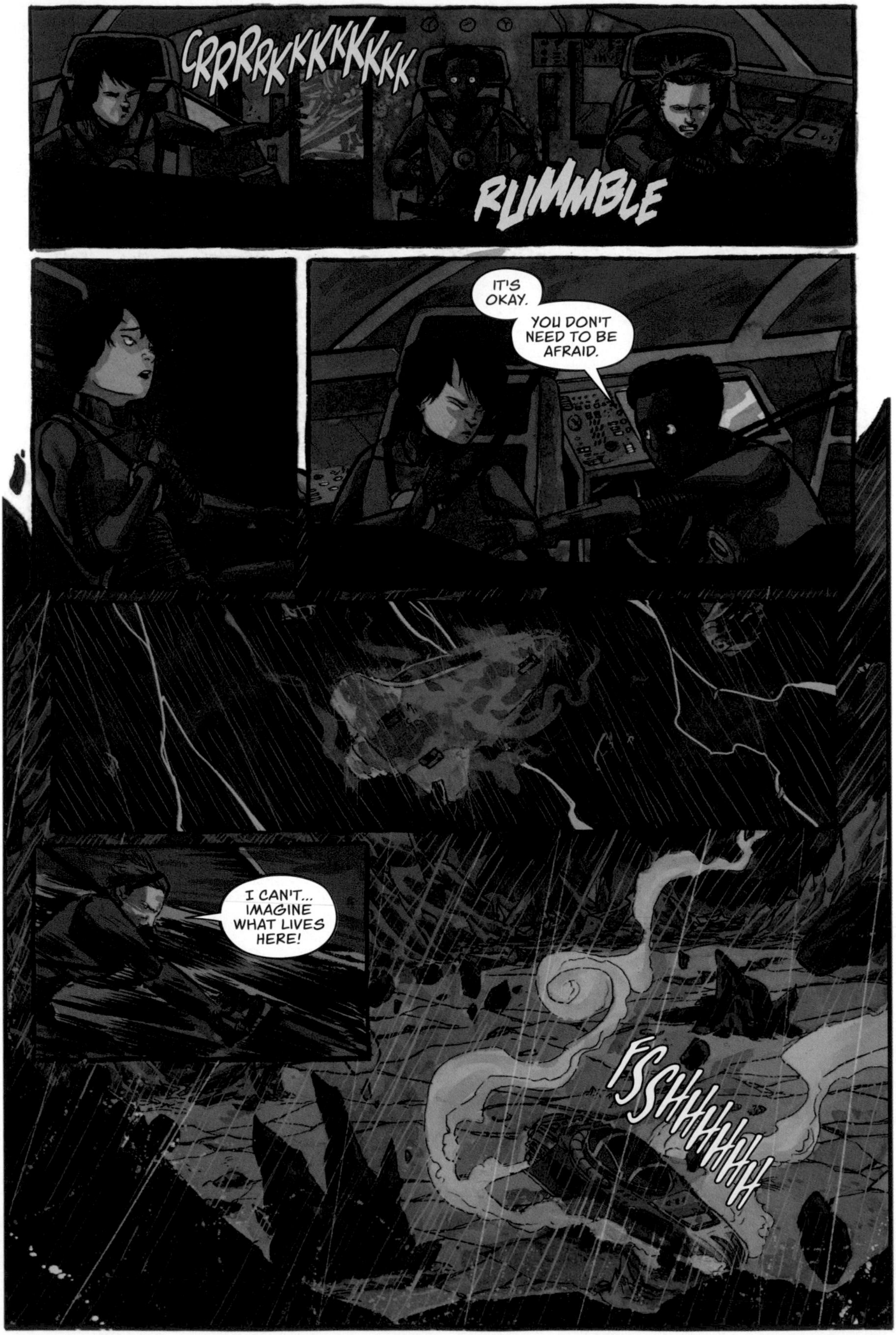
CRRRRKKKKKKKK
RUMMBLE
IT'S OKAY.
YOU DON'T NEED TO BE AFRAID.
I CAN'T... IMAGINE WHAT LIVES HERE!
FSSHHHHHHH

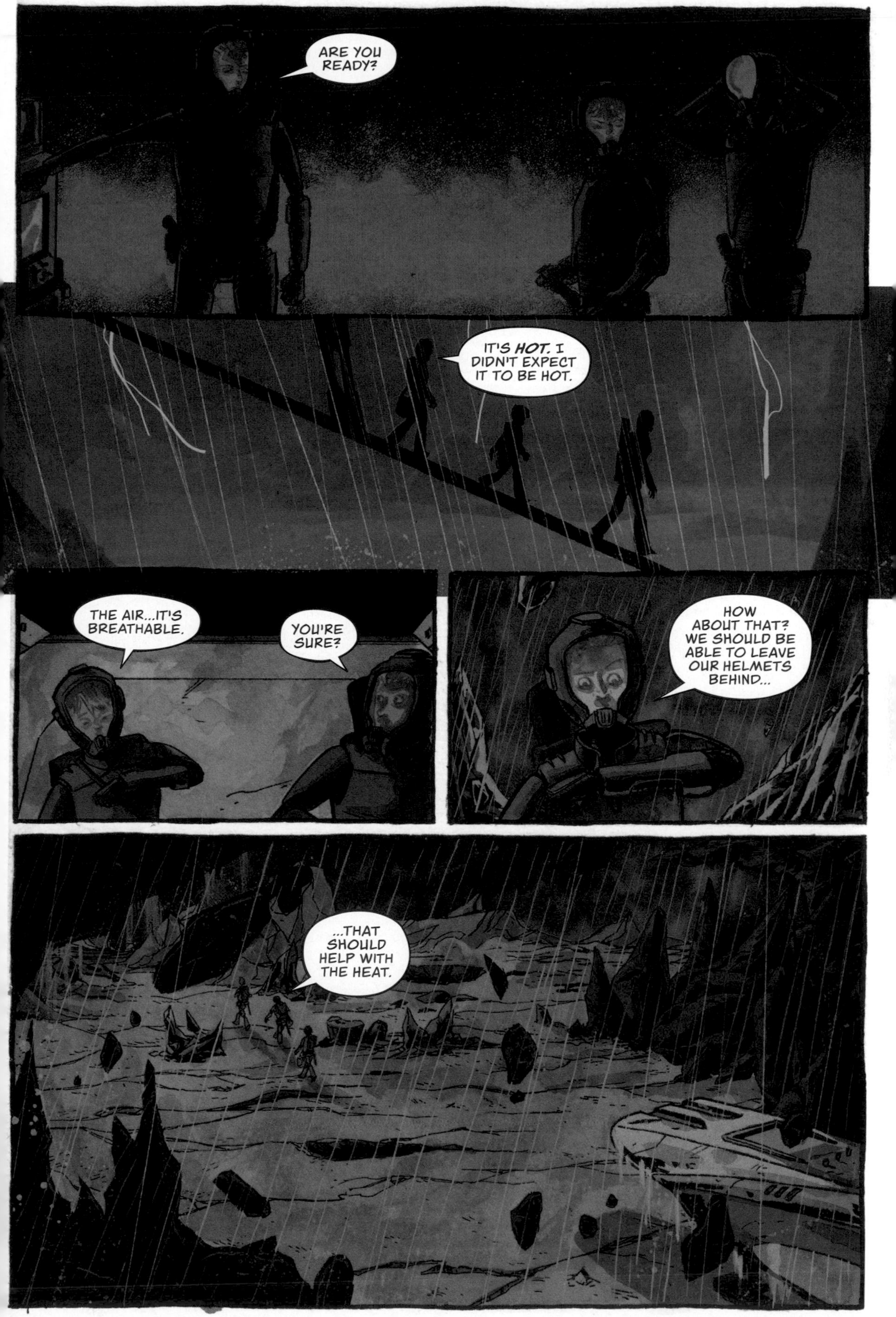
ARE YOU READY?
IT'S HOT. I DIDN'T EXPECT IT TO BE HOT.
THE AIR...IT'S BREATHABLE.
YOU'RE SURE?
HOW ABOUT THAT? WE SHOULD BE ABLE TO LEAVE OUR HELMETS BEHIND...
...THAT SHOULD HELP WITH THE HEAT.

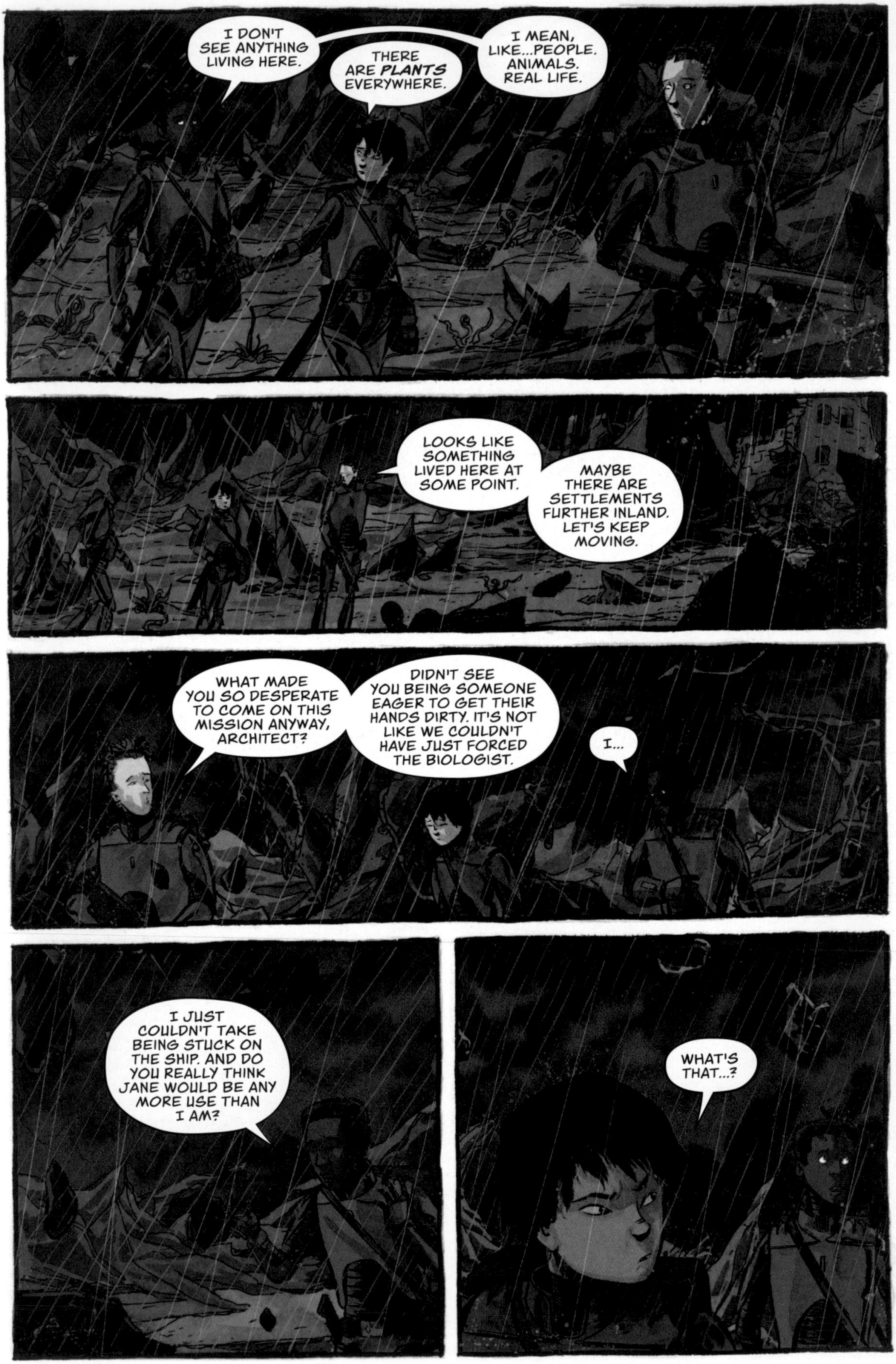
I DON'T SEE ANYTHING LIVING HERE.
THERE ARE **PLANTS** EVERYWHERE.
I MEAN, LIKE...PEOPLE. ANIMALS. REAL LIFE.
LOOKS LIKE SOMETHING LIVED HERE AT SOME POINT.
MAYBE THERE ARE SETTLEMENTS FURTHER INLAND. LET'S KEEP MOVING.
WHAT MADE YOU SO DESPERATE TO COME ON THIS MISSION ANYWAY, ARCHITECT?
DIDN'T SEE YOU BEING SOMEONE EAGER TO GET THEIR HANDS DIRTY. IT'S NOT LIKE WE COULDN'T HAVE JUST FORCED THE BIOLOGIST.
I...
I JUST COULDN'T TAKE BEING STUCK ON THE SHIP. AND DO YOU REALLY THINK JANE WOULD BE ANY MORE USE THAN I AM?
WHAT'S THAT...?

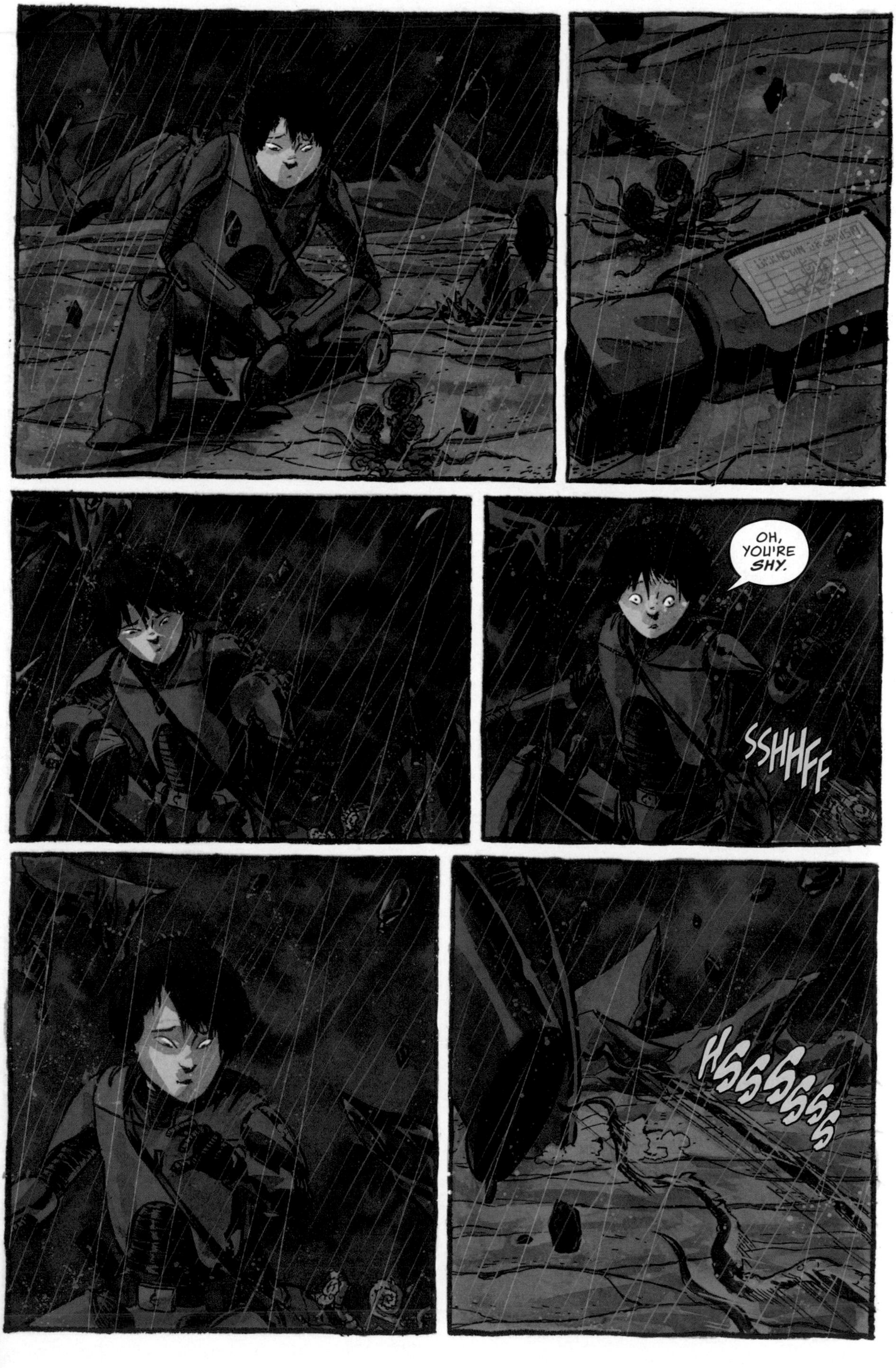
OH, YOU'RE SHY.
SSHHFF
HSSSSSS

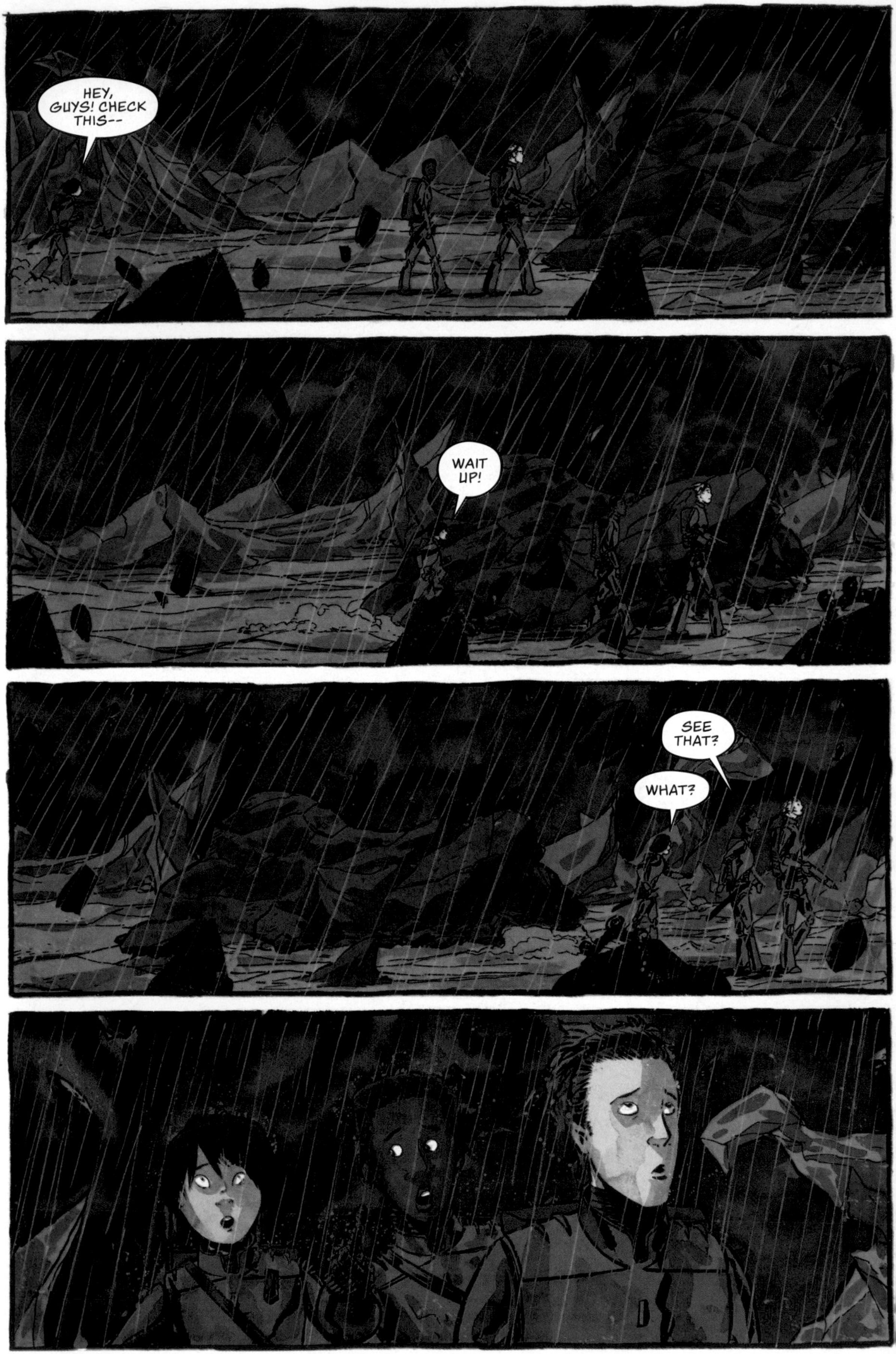
HEY, GUYS! CHECK THIS--
WAIT UP!
SEE THAT?
WHAT?

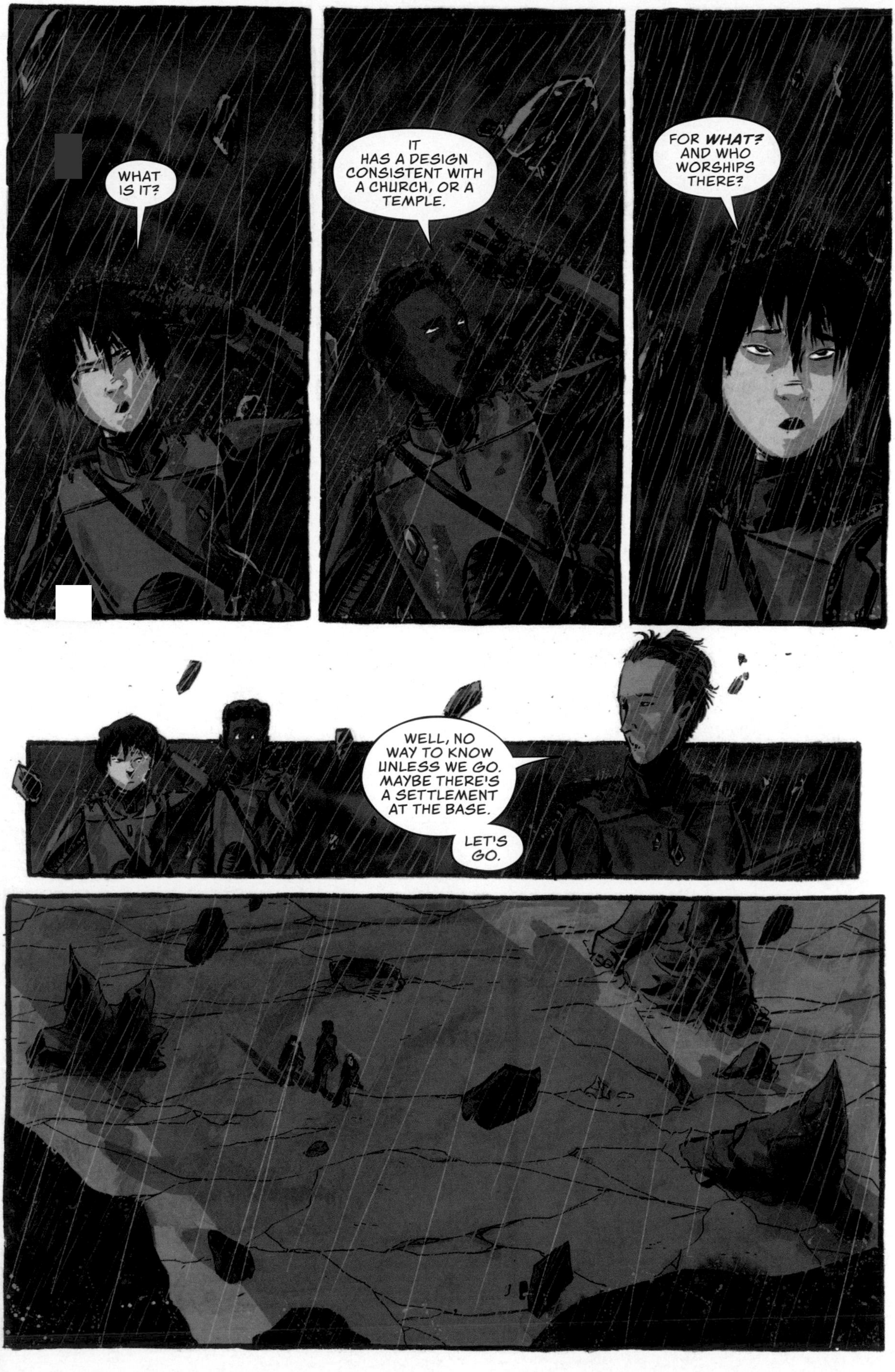
WHAT IS IT?
IT HAS A DESIGN CONSISTENT WITH A CHURCH, OR A TEMPLE.
FOR WHAT? AND WHO WORSHIPS THERE?
WELL, NO WAY TO KNOW UNLESS WE GO. MAYBE THERE'S A SETTLEMENT AT THE BASE.
LET'S GO.

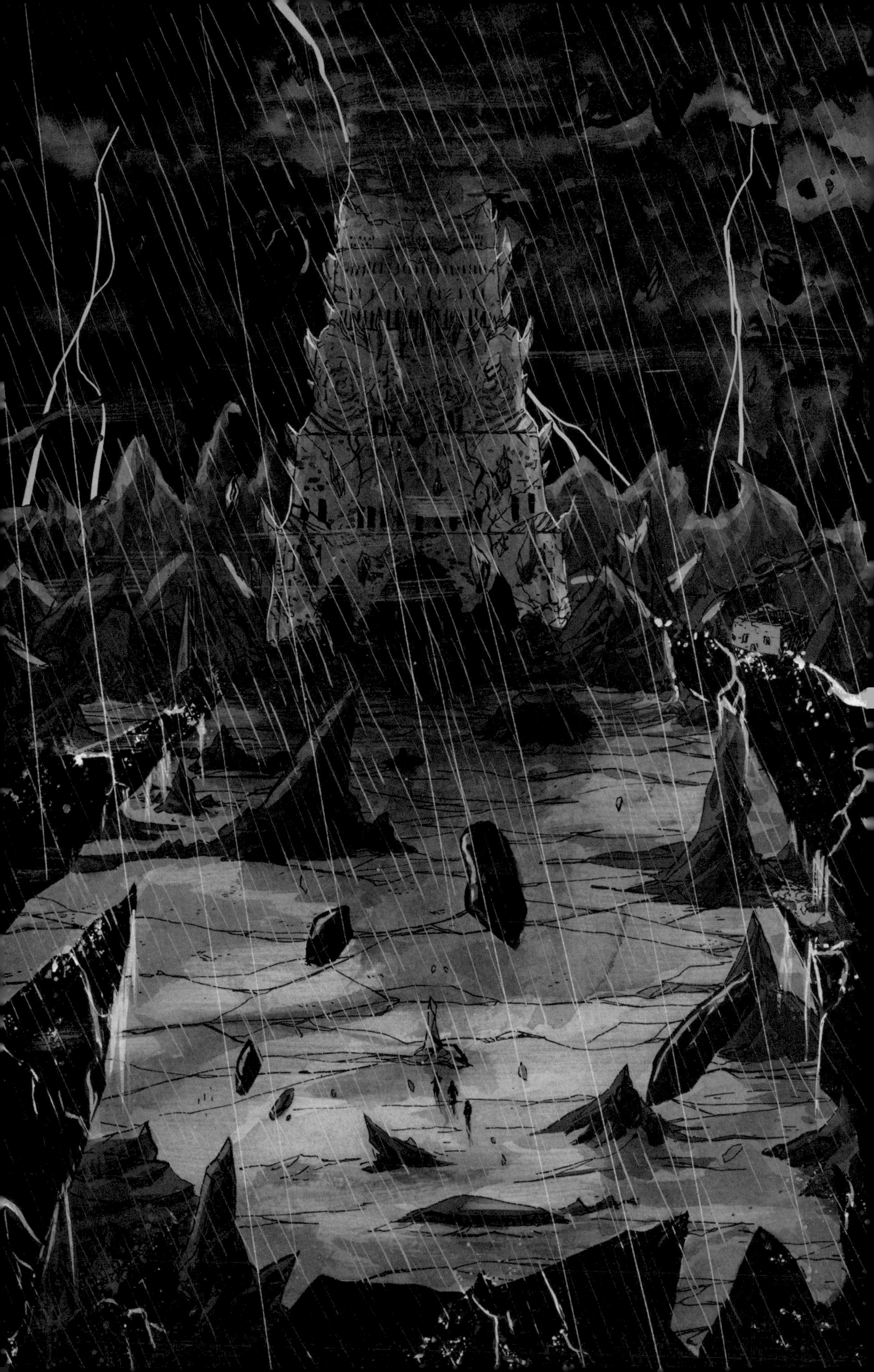

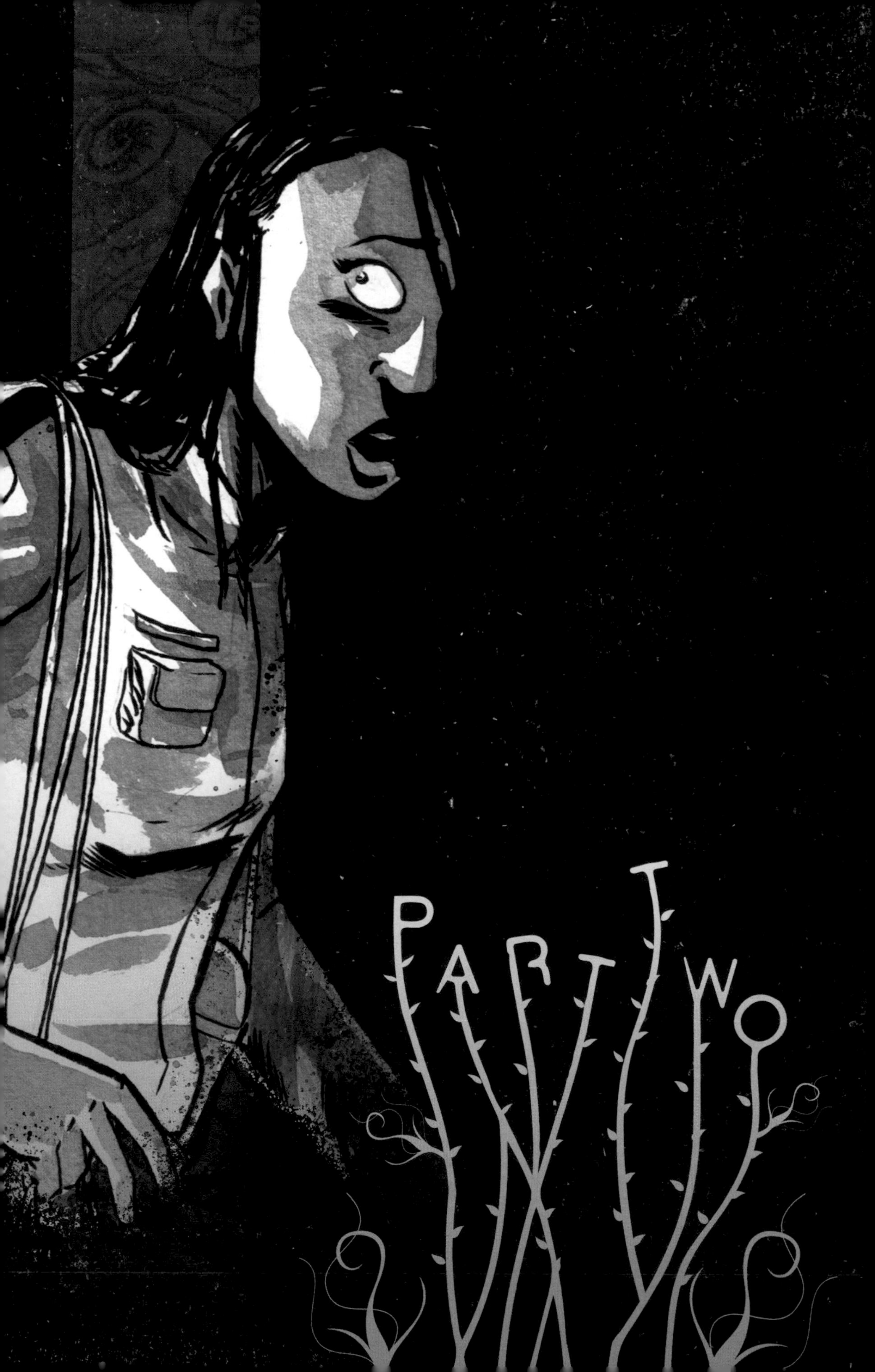
PART TWO

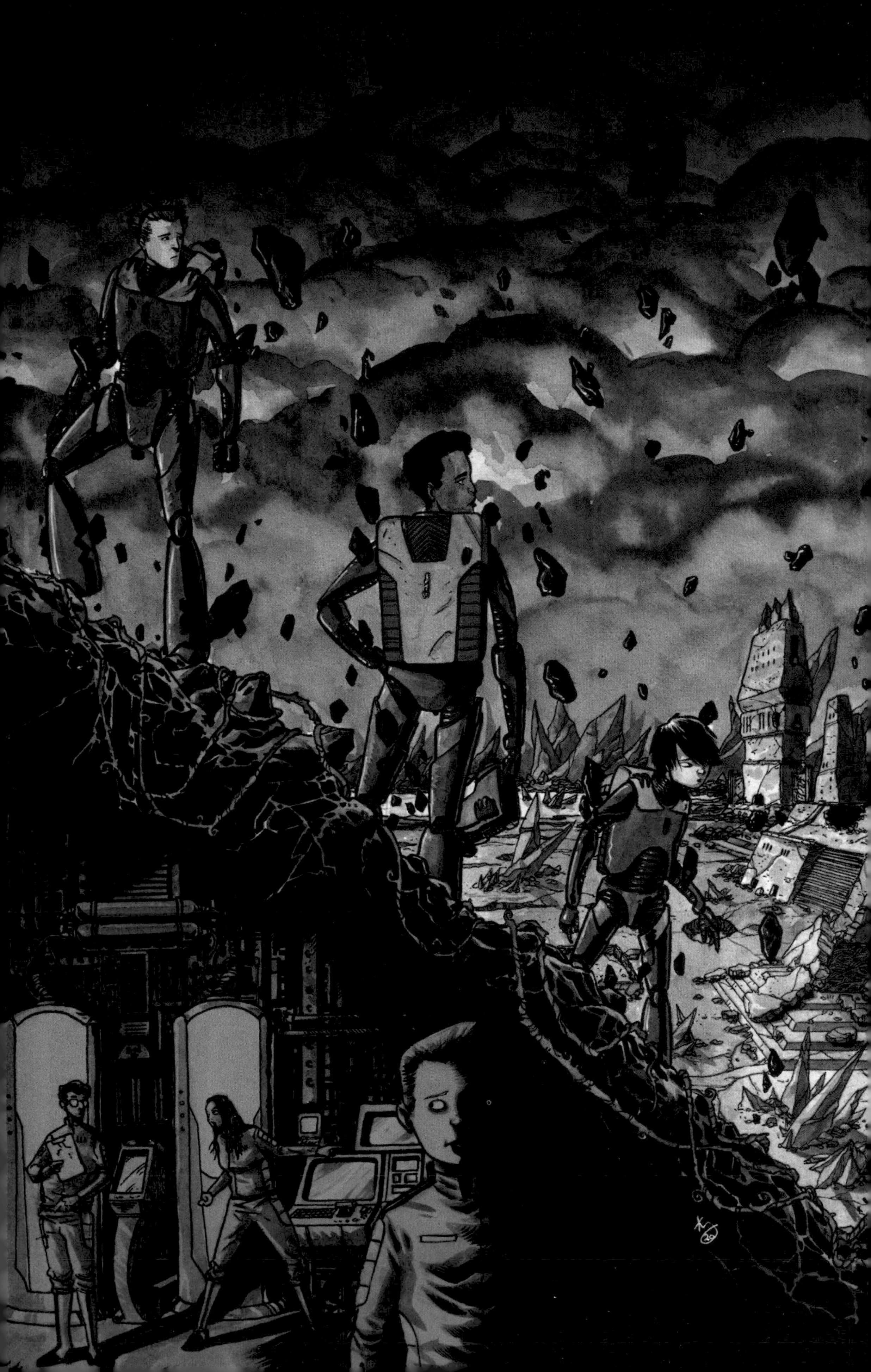

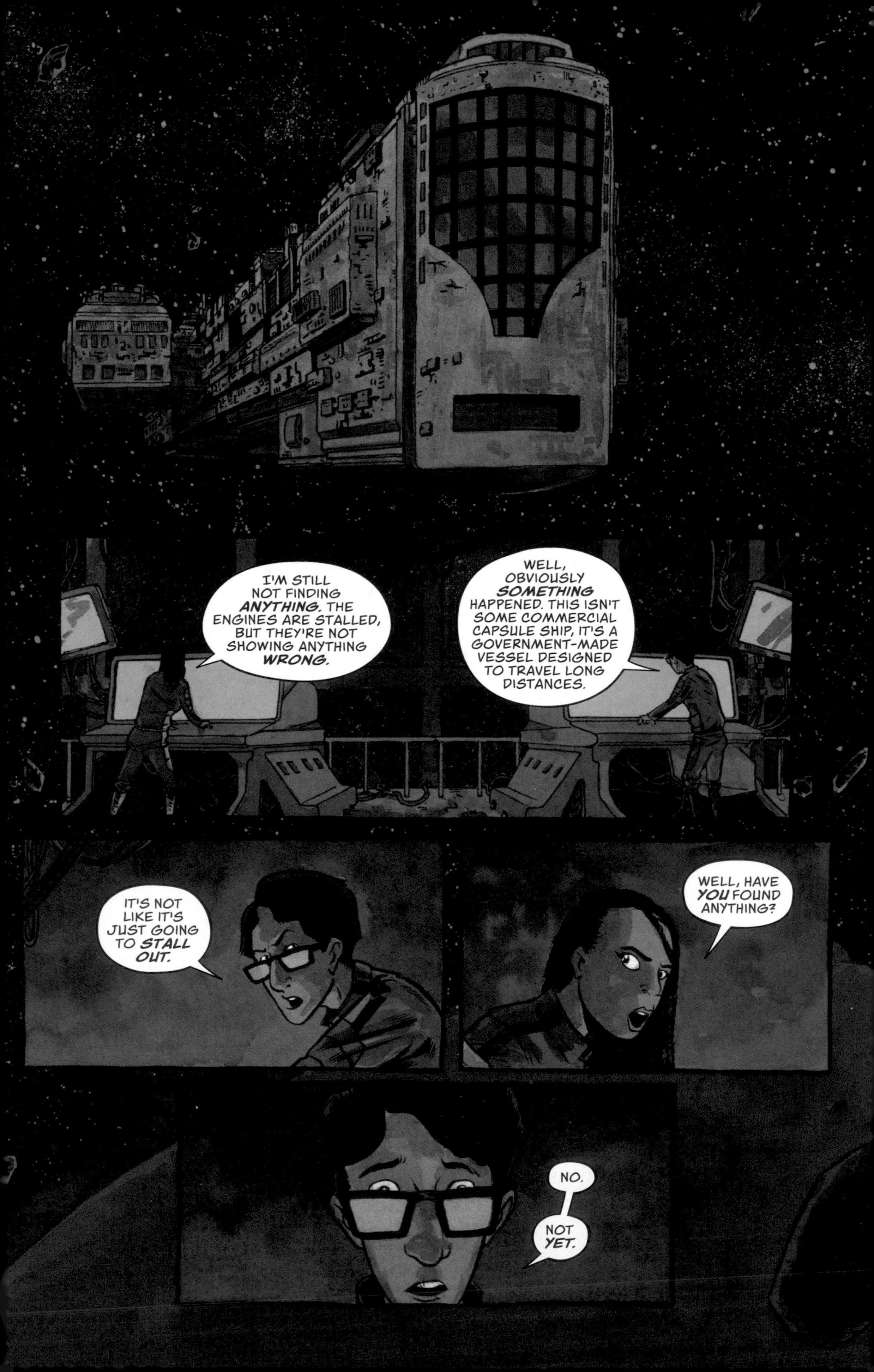
I'M STILL NOT FINDING ANYTHING. THE ENGINES ARE STALLED, BUT THEY'RE NOT SHOWING ANYTHING WRONG.
WELL, OBVIOUSLY SOMETHING HAPPENED. THIS ISN'T SOME COMMERCIAL CAPSULE SHIP, IT'S A GOVERNMENT-MADE VESSEL DESIGNED TO TRAVEL LONG DISTANCES.
IT'S NOT LIKE IT'S JUST GOING TO STALL OUT.
WELL, HAVE YOU FOUND ANYTHING?
NO.
NOT YET.

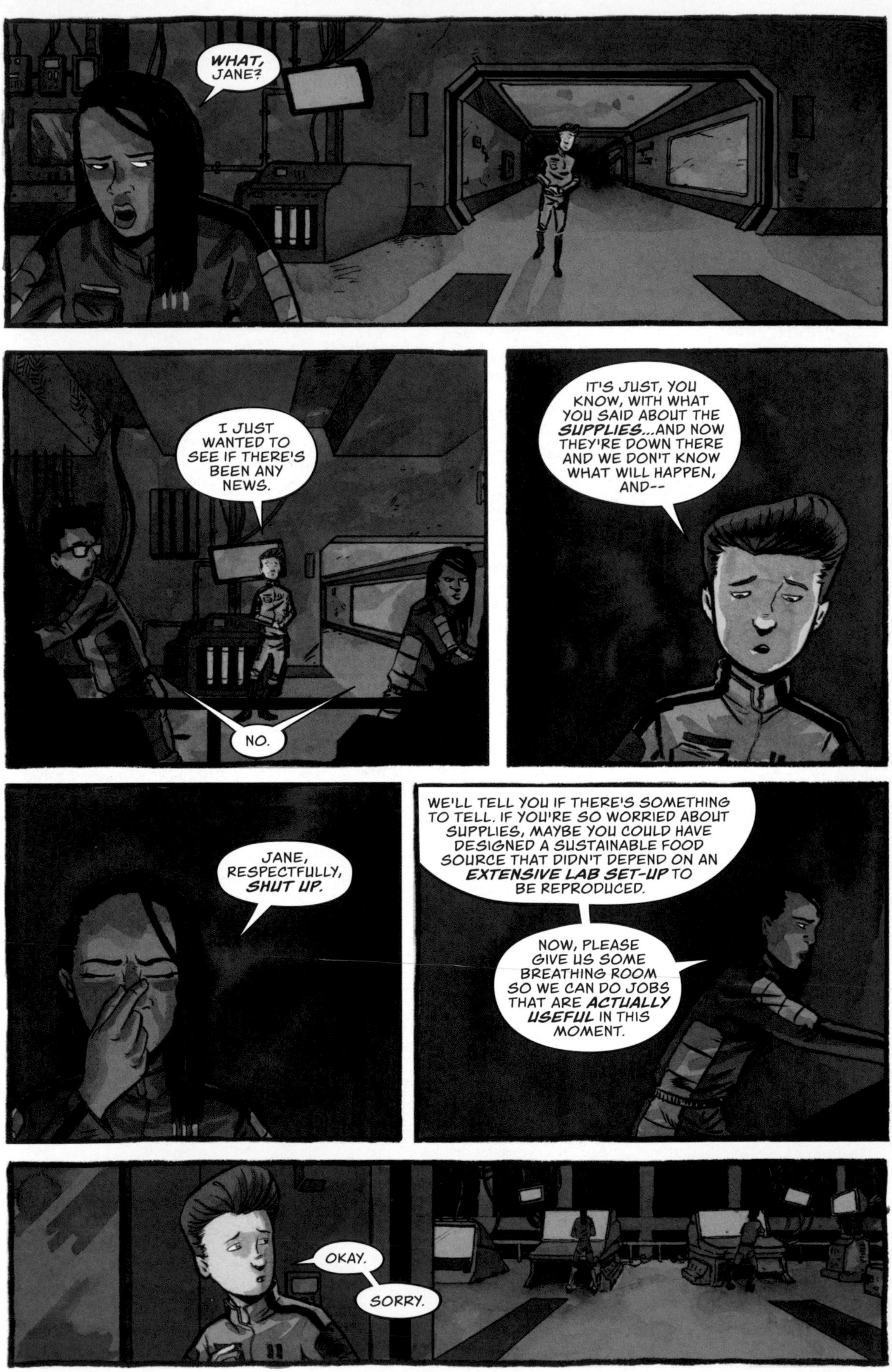
WHAT, JANE?
I JUST WANTED TO SEE IF THERE'S BEEN ANY NEWS.
NO.
IT'S JUST, YOU KNOW, WITH WHAT YOU SAID ABOUT THE SUPPLIES...AND NOW THEY'RE DOWN THERE AND WE DON'T KNOW WHAT WILL HAPPEN, AND--
JANE, RESPECTFULLY, SHUT UP.
WE'LL TELL YOU IF THERE'S SOMETHING TO TELL. IF YOU'RE SO WORRIED ABOUT SUPPLIES, MAYBE YOU COULD HAVE DESIGNED A SUSTAINABLE FOOD SOURCE THAT DIDN'T DEPEND ON AN EXTENSIVE LAB SET-UP TO BE REPRODUCED.
NOW, PLEASE GIVE US SOME BREATHING ROOM SO WE CAN DO JOBS THAT ARE ACTUALLY USEFUL IN THIS MOMENT.
OKAY.
SORRY.

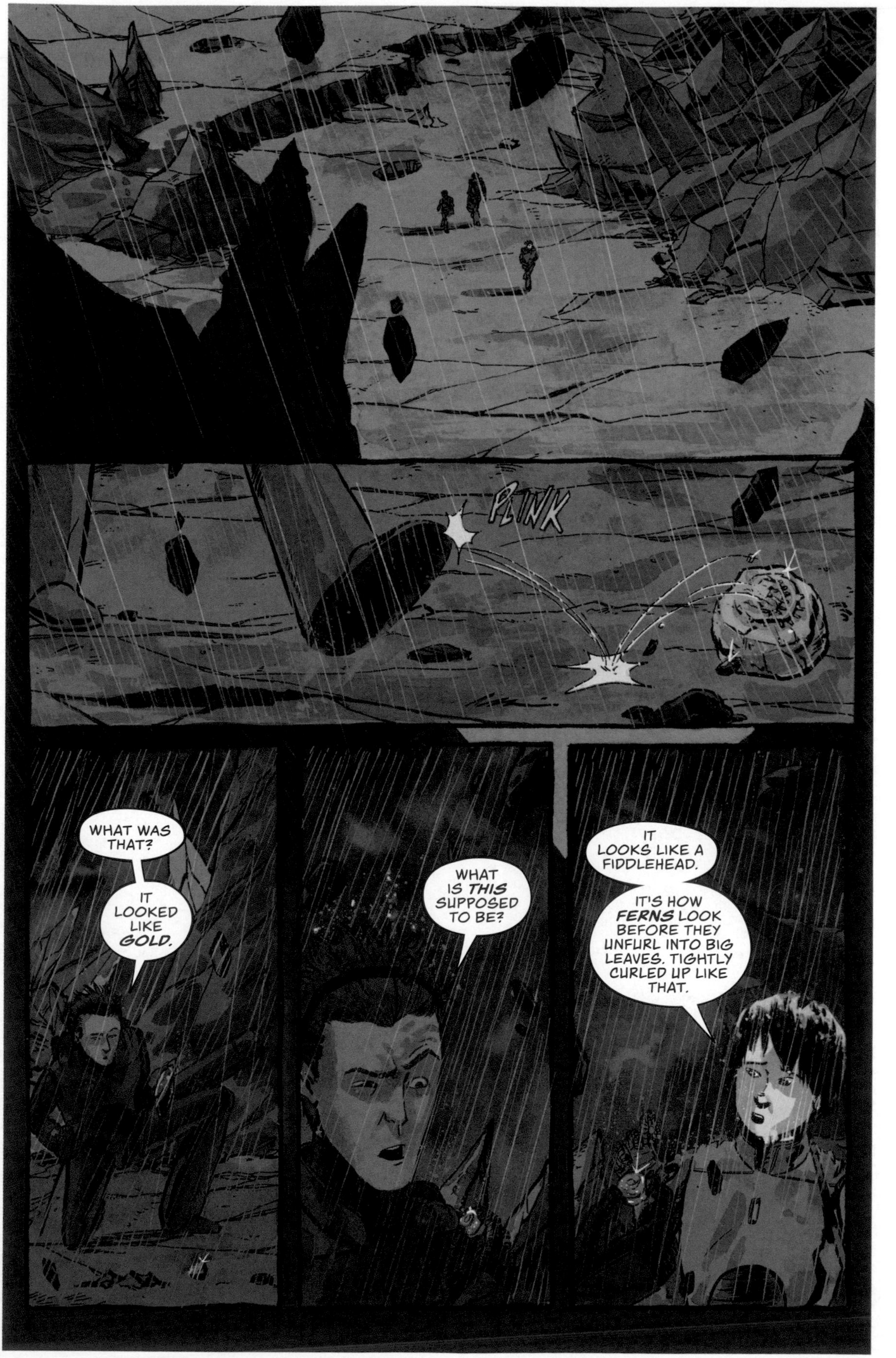
PLINK
WHAT WAS THAT?
IT LOOKED LIKE GOLD.
WHAT IS THIS SUPPOSED TO BE?
IT LOOKS LIKE A FIDDLEHEAD.
IT'S HOW FERNS LOOK BEFORE THEY UNFURL INTO BIG LEAVES. TIGHTLY CURLED UP LIKE THAT.

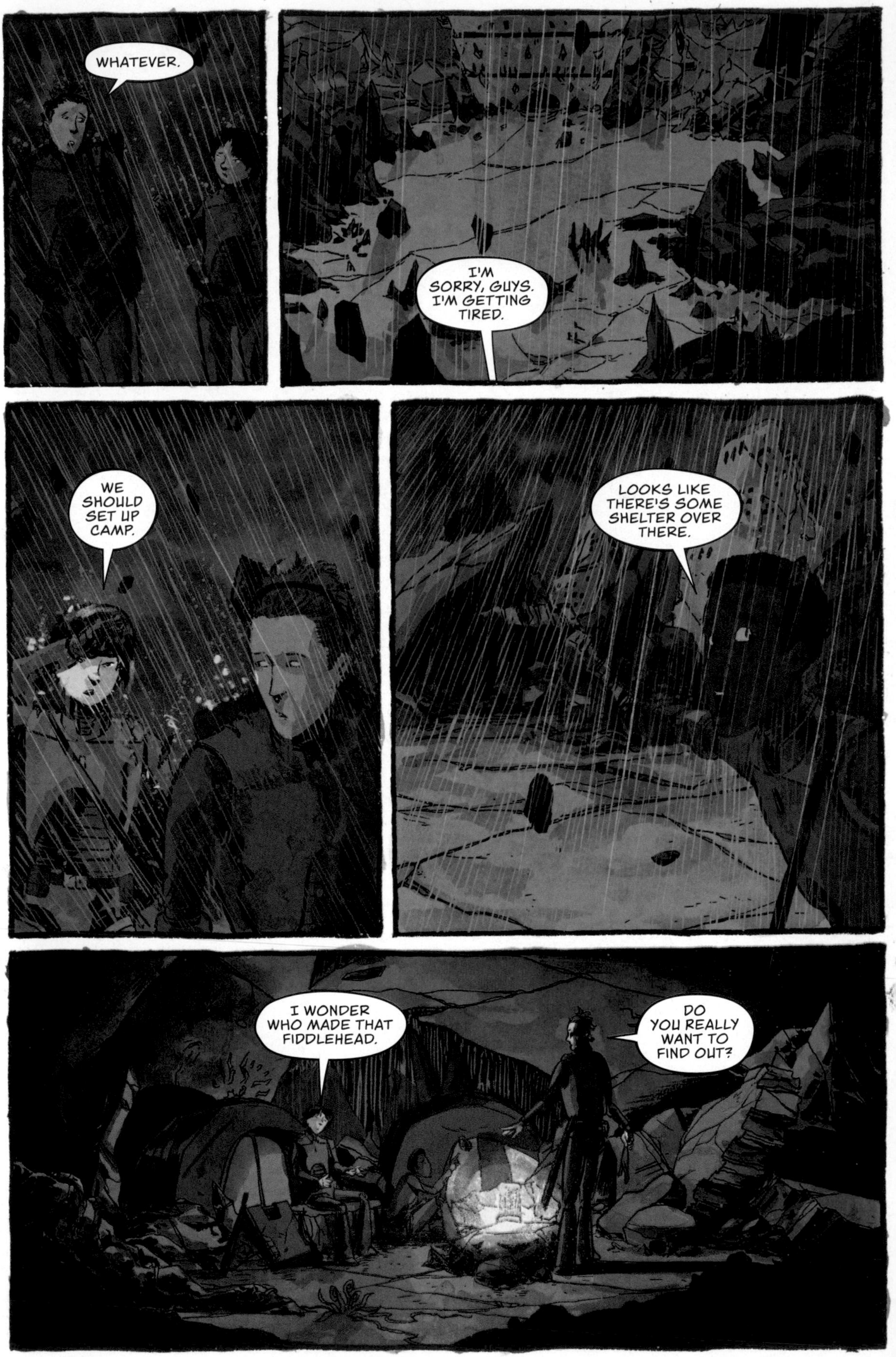
WHATEVER.
I'M SORRY, GUYS. I'M GETTING TIRED.
WE SHOULD SET UP CAMP.
LOOKS LIKE THERE'S SOME SHELTER OVER THERE.
I WONDER WHO MADE THAT FIDDLEHEAD.
DO YOU REALLY WANT TO FIND OUT?

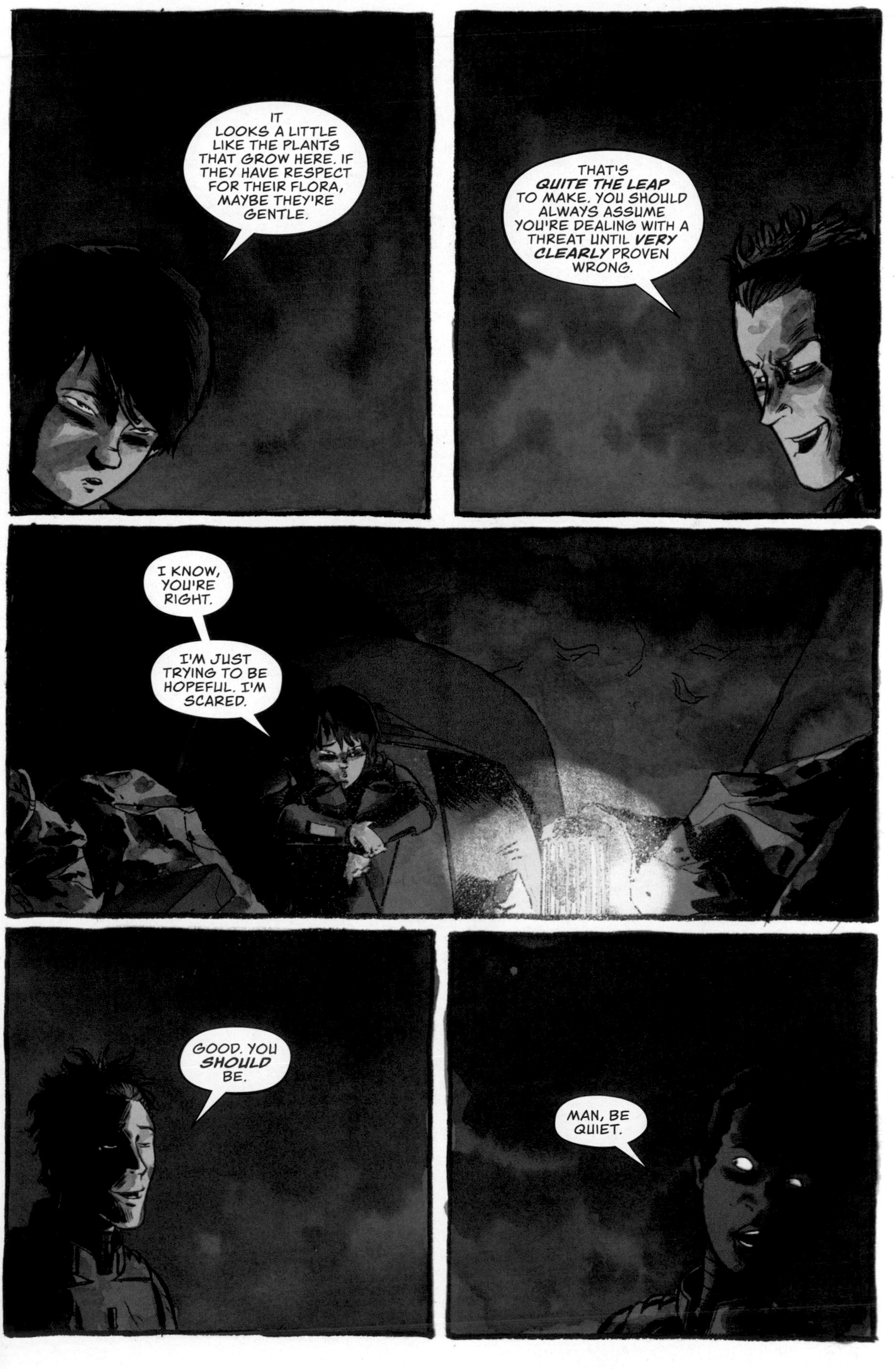
IT LOOKS A LITTLE LIKE THE PLANTS THAT GROW HERE. IF THEY HAVE RESPECT FOR THEIR FLORA, MAYBE THEY'RE GENTLE.
THAT'S ***QUITE THE LEAP*** TO MAKE. YOU SHOULD ALWAYS ASSUME YOU'RE DEALING WITH A THREAT UNTIL ***VERY CLEARLY*** PROVEN WRONG.
I KNOW, YOU'RE RIGHT.
I'M JUST TRYING TO BE HOPEFUL. I'M SCARED.
GOOD. YOU ***SHOULD*** BE.
MAN, BE QUIET.

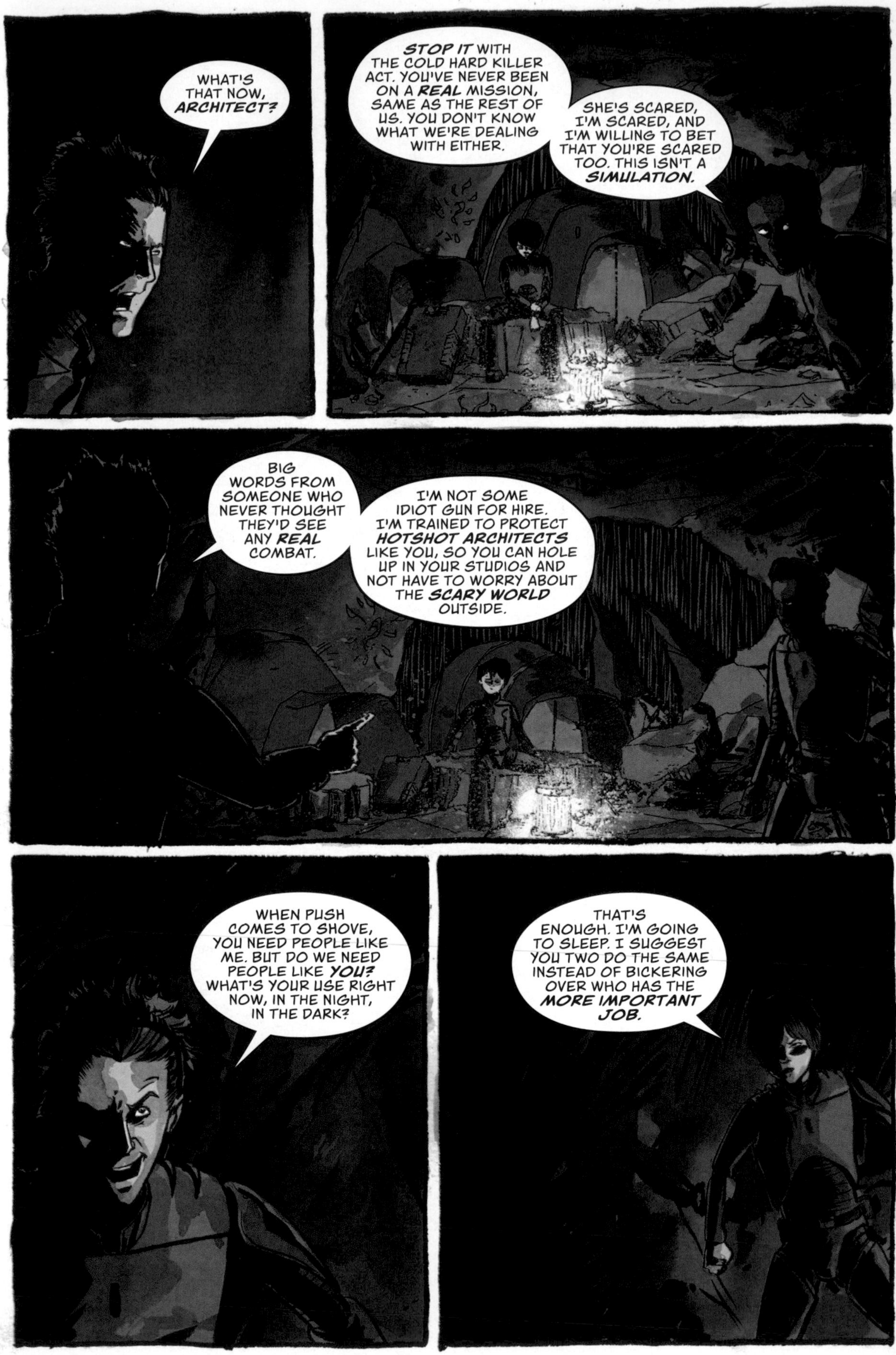

WHAT'S THAT NOW, ARCHITECT?
STOP IT WITH THE COLD HARD KILLER ACT. YOU'VE NEVER BEEN ON A REAL MISSION, SAME AS THE REST OF US. YOU DON'T KNOW WHAT WE'RE DEALING WITH EITHER.
SHE'S SCARED, I'M SCARED, AND I'M WILLING TO BET THAT YOU'RE SCARED TOO. THIS ISN'T A SIMULATION.
BIG WORDS FROM SOMEONE WHO NEVER THOUGHT THEY'D SEE ANY REAL COMBAT.
I'M NOT SOME IDIOT GUN FOR HIRE. I'M TRAINED TO PROTECT HOTSHOT ARCHITECTS LIKE YOU, SO YOU CAN HOLE UP IN YOUR STUDIOS AND NOT HAVE TO WORRY ABOUT THE SCARY WORLD OUTSIDE.
WHEN PUSH COMES TO SHOVE, YOU NEED PEOPLE LIKE ME. BUT DO WE NEED PEOPLE LIKE YOU? WHAT'S YOUR USE RIGHT NOW, IN THE NIGHT, IN THE DARK?
THAT'S ENOUGH. I'M GOING TO SLEEP. I SUGGEST YOU TWO DO THE SAME INSTEAD OF BICKERING OVER WHO HAS THE MORE IMPORTANT JOB.

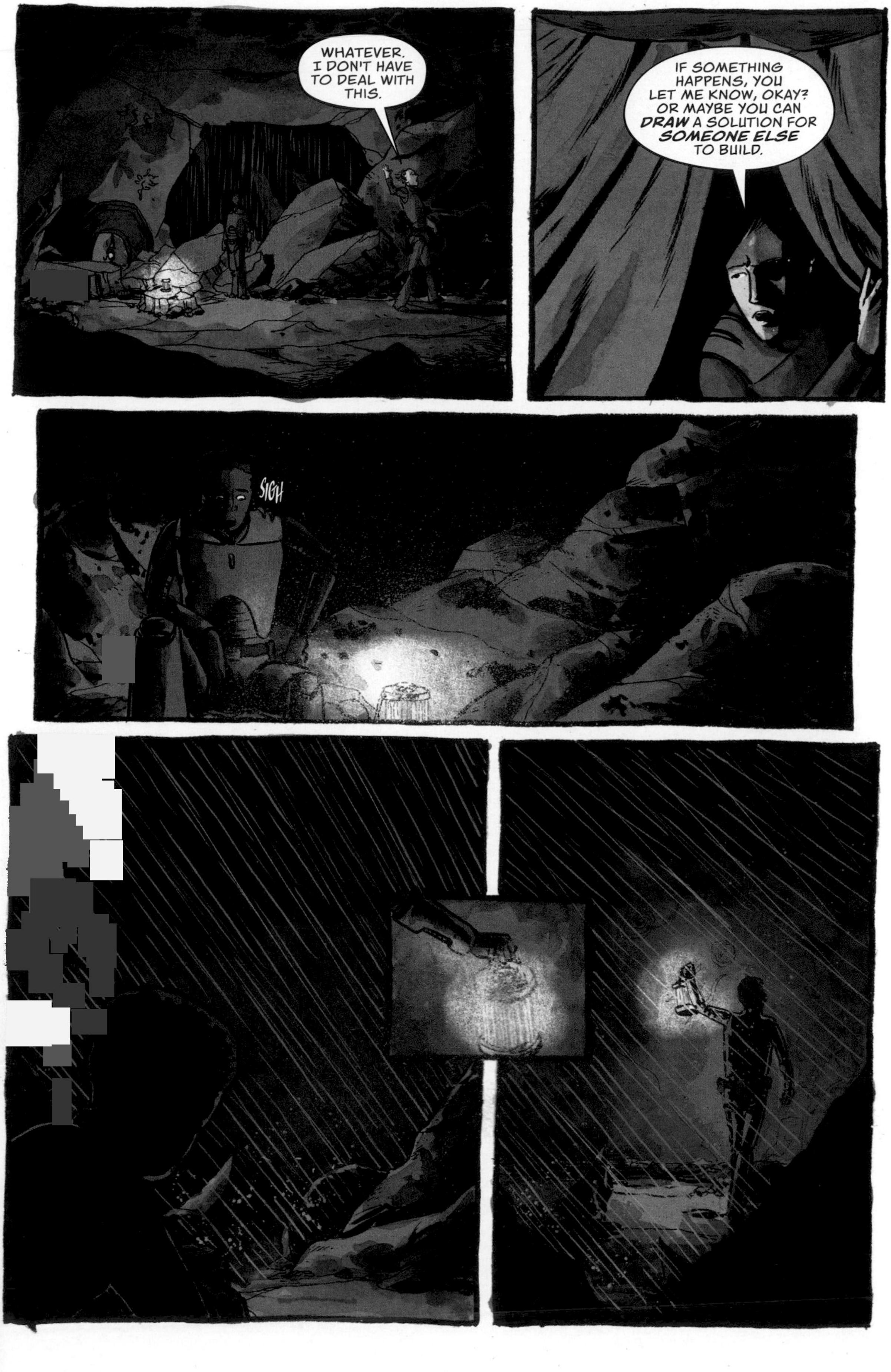
WHATEVER. I DON'T HAVE TO DEAL WITH THIS.
IF SOMETHING HAPPENS, YOU LET ME KNOW, OKAY? OR MAYBE YOU CAN DRAW A SOLUTION FOR SOMEONE ELSE TO BUILD.
SIGH

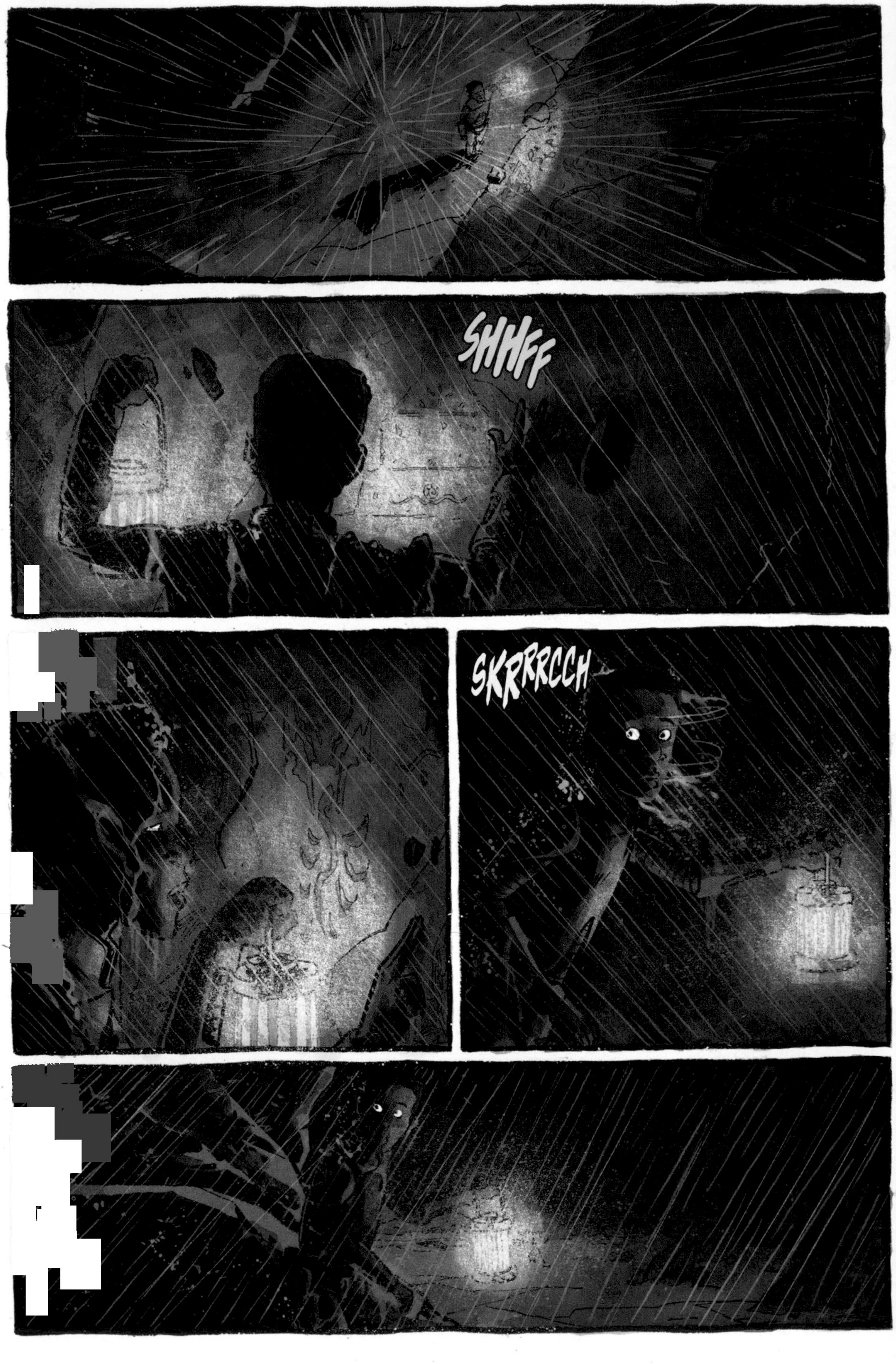
SHHFF
SKRRRCCH

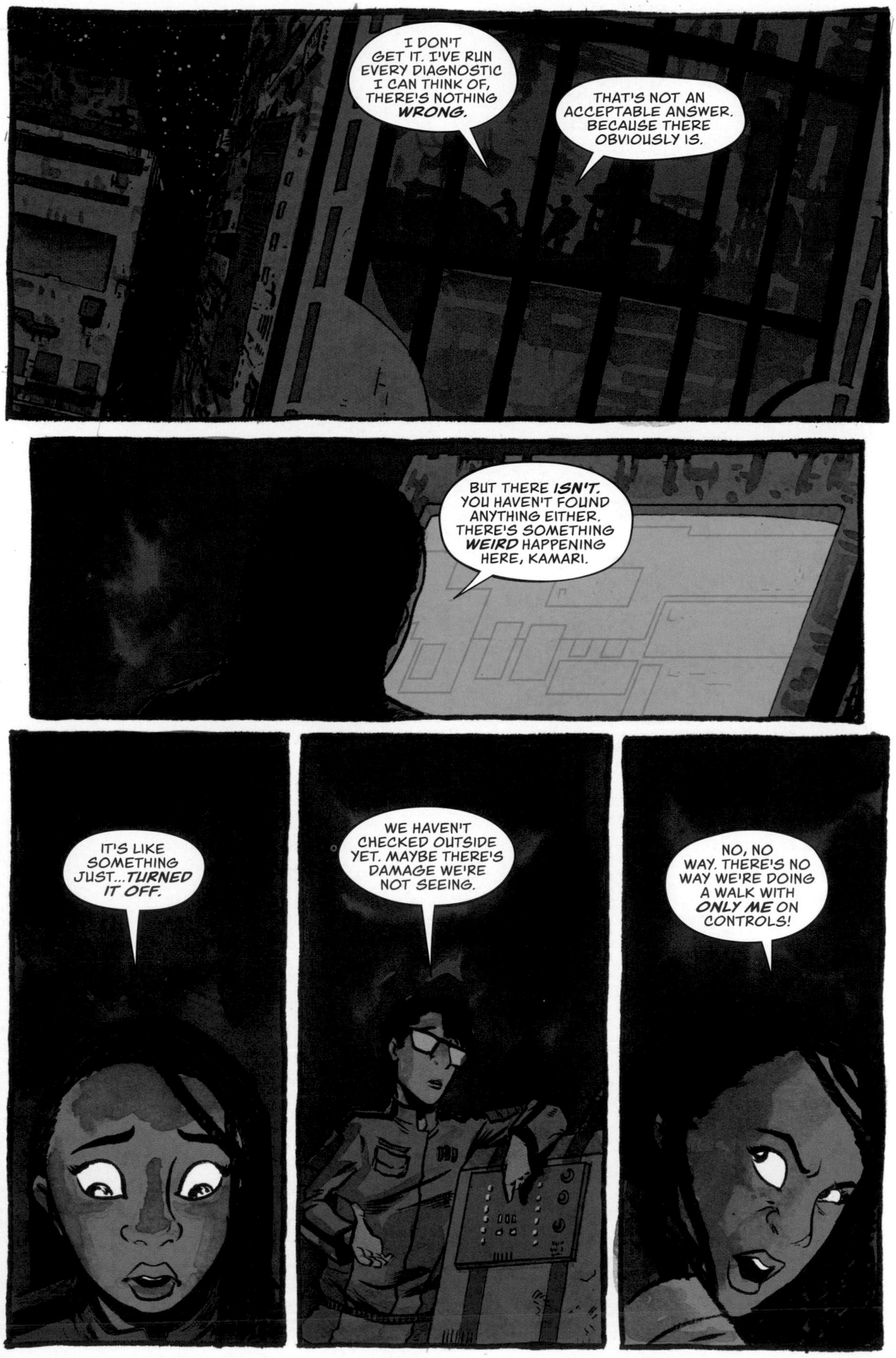
I DON'T GET IT. I'VE RUN EVERY DIAGNOSTIC I CAN THINK OF, THERE'S NOTHING *WRONG.*
THAT'S NOT AN ACCEPTABLE ANSWER. BECAUSE THERE OBVIOUSLY IS.
BUT THERE *ISN'T.* YOU HAVEN'T FOUND ANYTHING EITHER. THERE'S SOMETHING *WEIRD* HAPPENING HERE, KAMARI.
IT'S LIKE SOMETHING JUST...*TURNED IT OFF.*
WE HAVEN'T CHECKED OUTSIDE YET. MAYBE THERE'S DAMAGE WE'RE NOT SEEING.
NO, NO WAY. THERE'S NO WAY WE'RE DOING A WALK WITH *ONLY ME* ON CONTROLS!

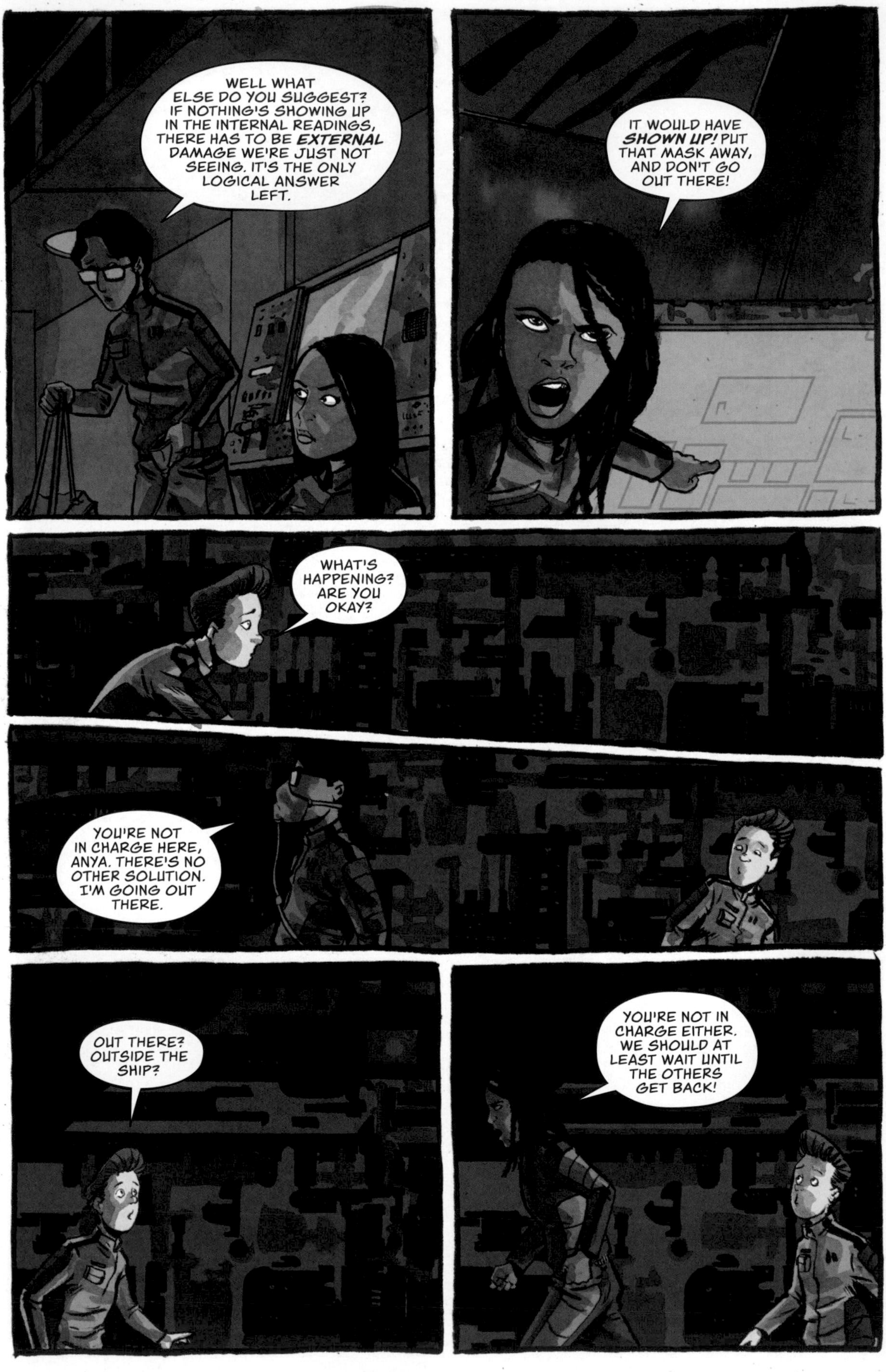
WELL WHAT ELSE DO YOU SUGGEST? IF NOTHING'S SHOWING UP IN THE INTERNAL READINGS, THERE HAS TO BE *EXTERNAL* DAMAGE WE'RE JUST NOT SEEING. IT'S THE ONLY LOGICAL ANSWER LEFT.
IT WOULD HAVE *SHOWN UP!* PUT THAT MASK AWAY, AND DON'T GO OUT THERE!
WHAT'S HAPPENING? ARE YOU OKAY?
YOU'RE NOT IN CHARGE HERE, ANYA. THERE'S NO OTHER SOLUTION. I'M GOING OUT THERE.
OUT THERE? OUTSIDE THE SHIP?
YOU'RE NOT IN CHARGE EITHER. WE SHOULD AT LEAST WAIT UNTIL THE OTHERS GET BACK!

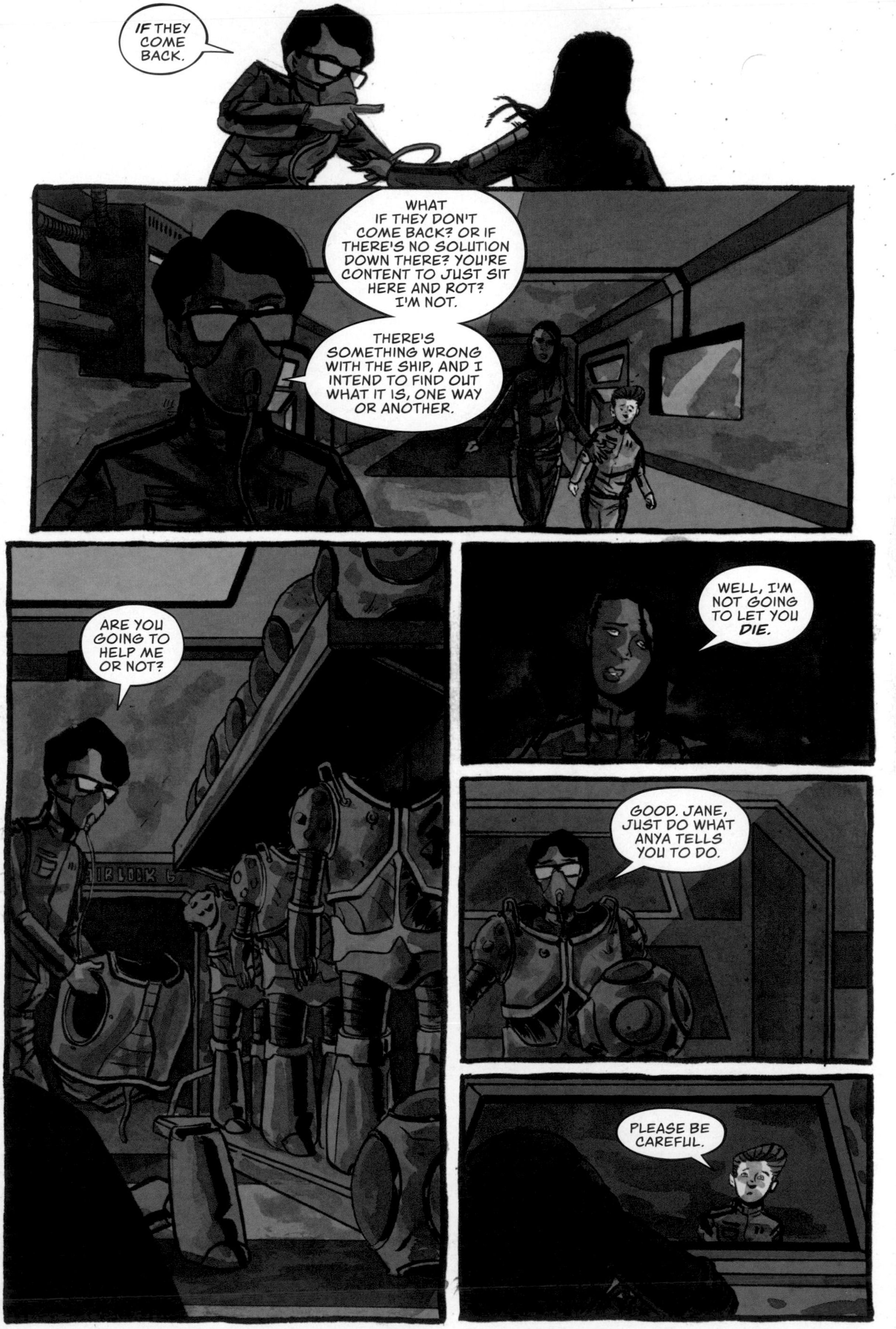
IF THEY COME BACK.
WHAT IF THEY DON'T COME BACK? OR IF THERE'S NO SOLUTION DOWN THERE? YOU'RE CONTENT TO JUST SIT HERE AND ROT? I'M NOT.
THERE'S SOMETHING WRONG WITH THE SHIP, AND I INTEND TO FIND OUT WHAT IT IS, ONE WAY OR ANOTHER.
ARE YOU GOING TO HELP ME OR NOT?
WELL, I'M NOT GOING TO LET YOU DIE.
GOOD. JANE, JUST DO WHAT ANYA TELLS YOU TO DO.
PLEASE BE CAREFUL.

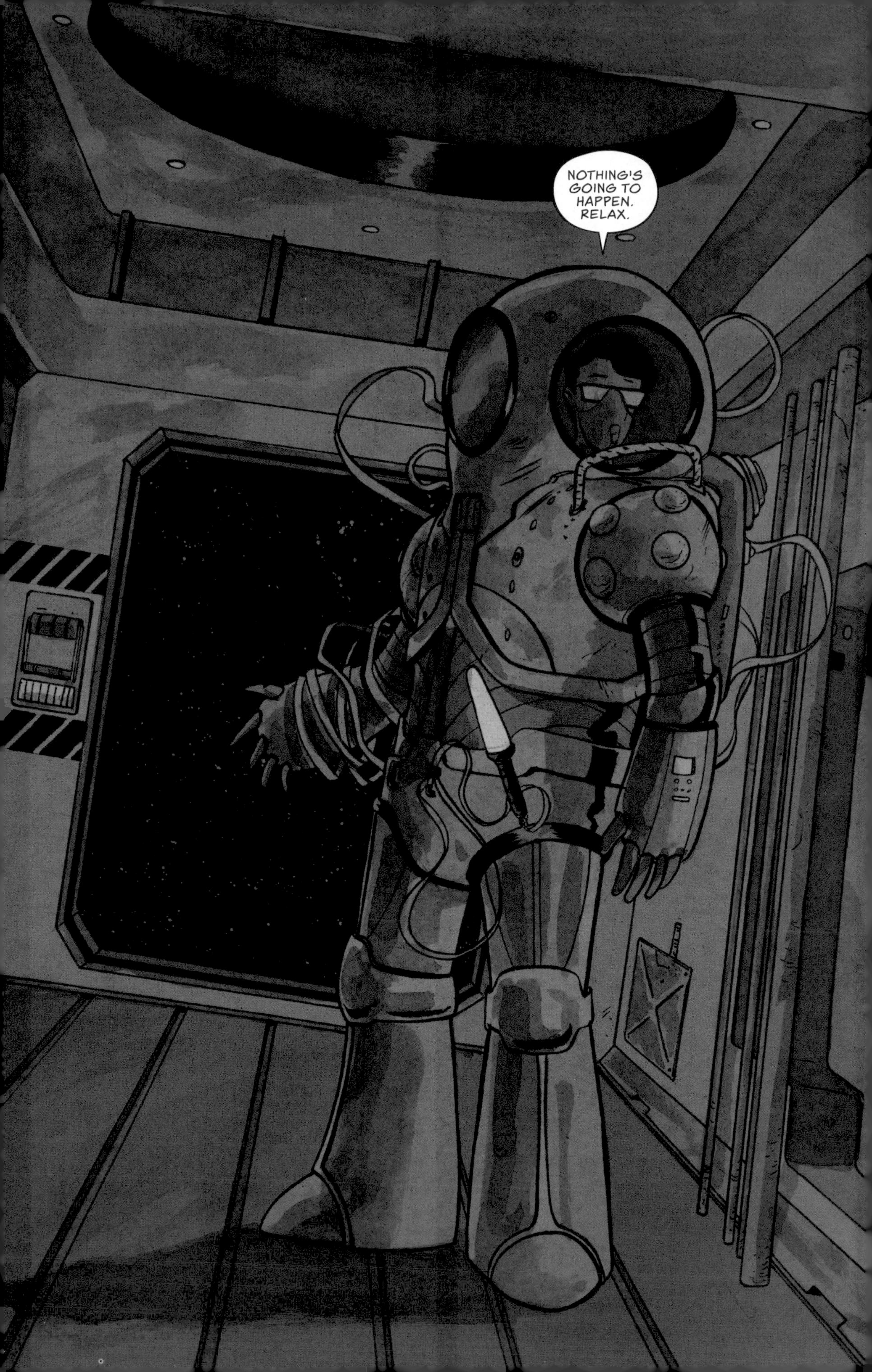
NOTHING'S GOING TO HAPPEN. RELAX.

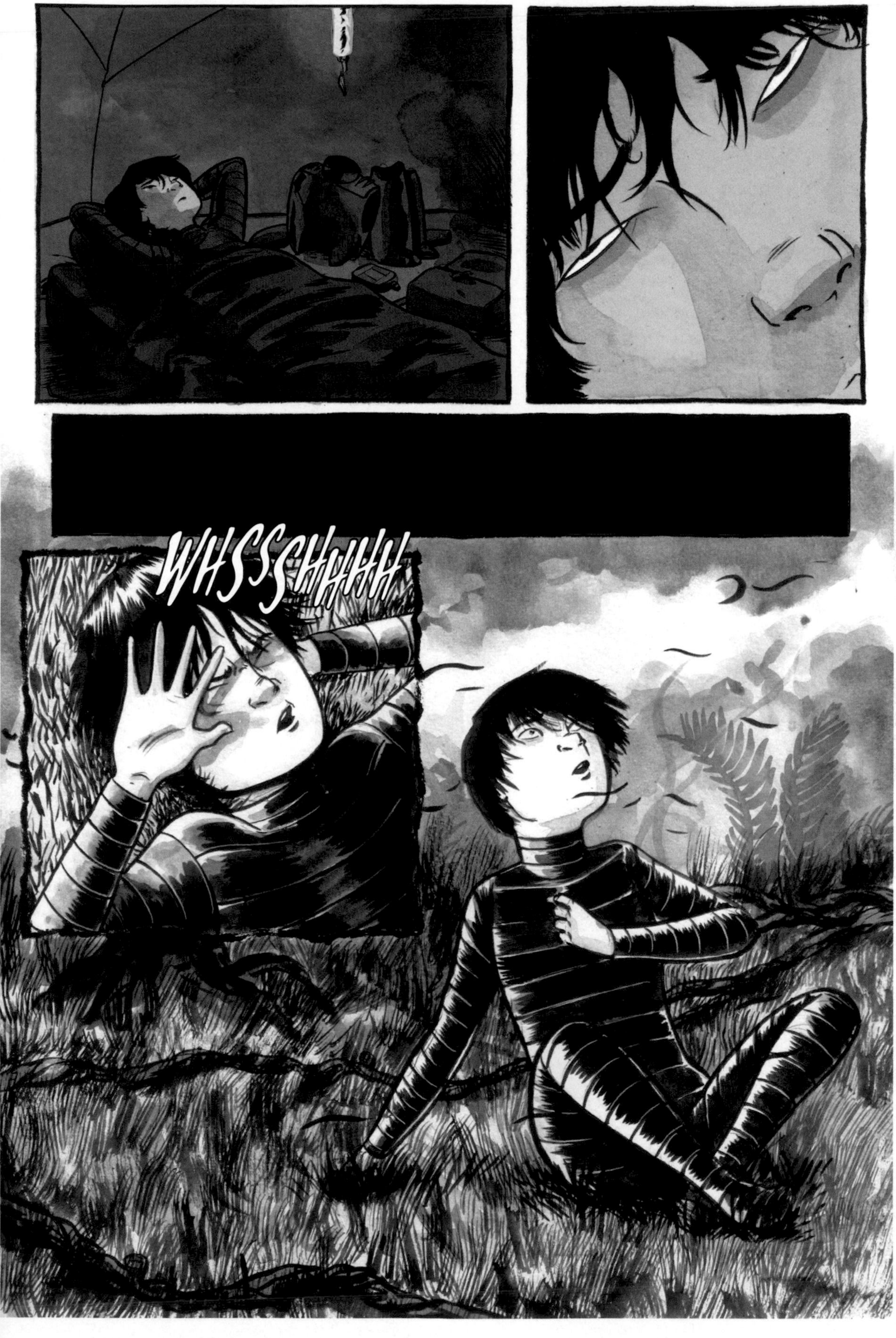
[redacted]
WHSSCHHHH

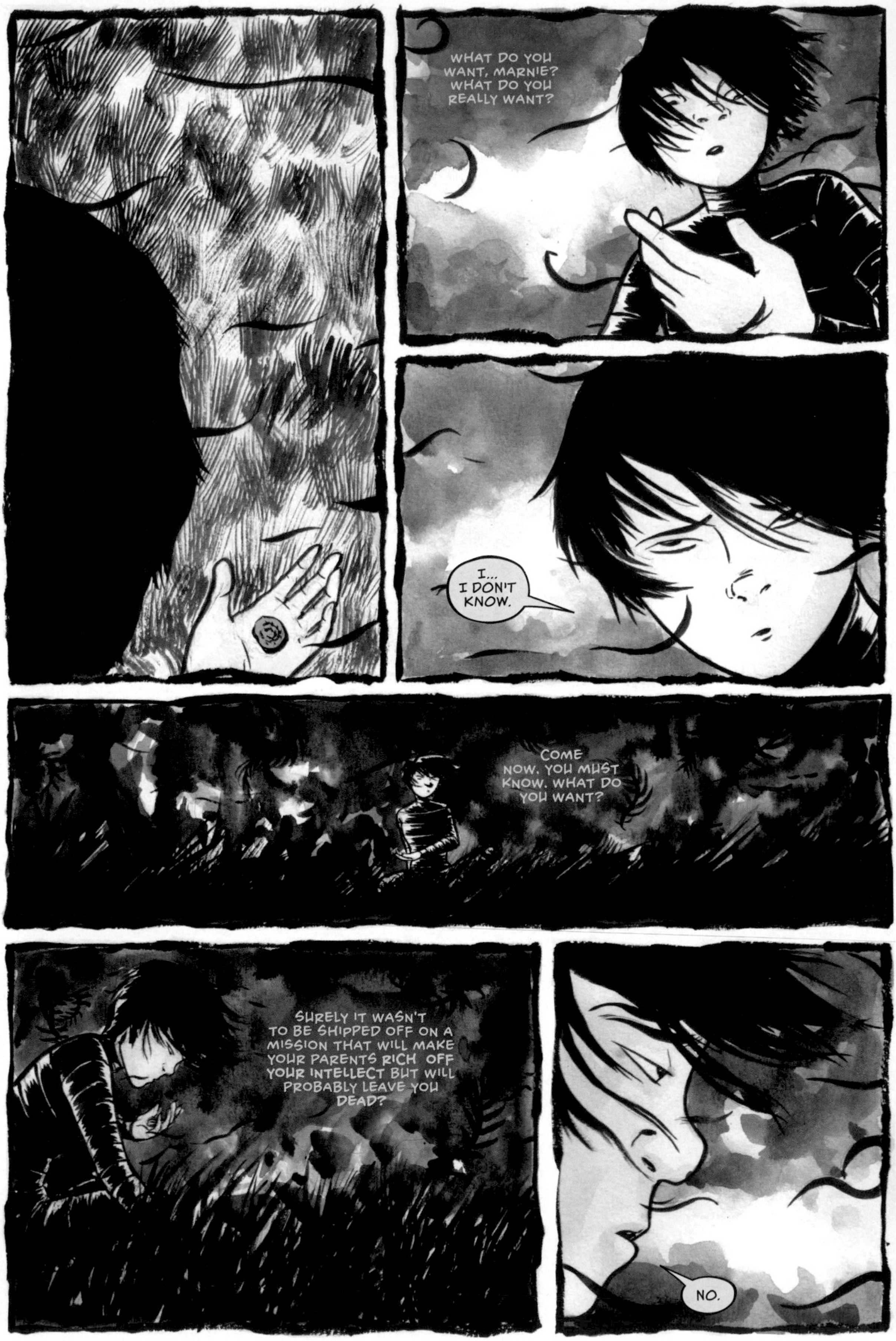
WHAT DO YOU WANT, MARNIE? WHAT DO YOU REALLY WANT?
I... I DON'T KNOW.
COME NOW. YOU MUST KNOW. WHAT DO YOU WANT?
SURELY IT WASN'T TO BE SHIPPED OFF ON A MISSION THAT WILL MAKE YOUR PARENTS RICH OFF YOUR INTELLECT BUT WILL PROBABLY LEAVE YOU DEAD?
NO.

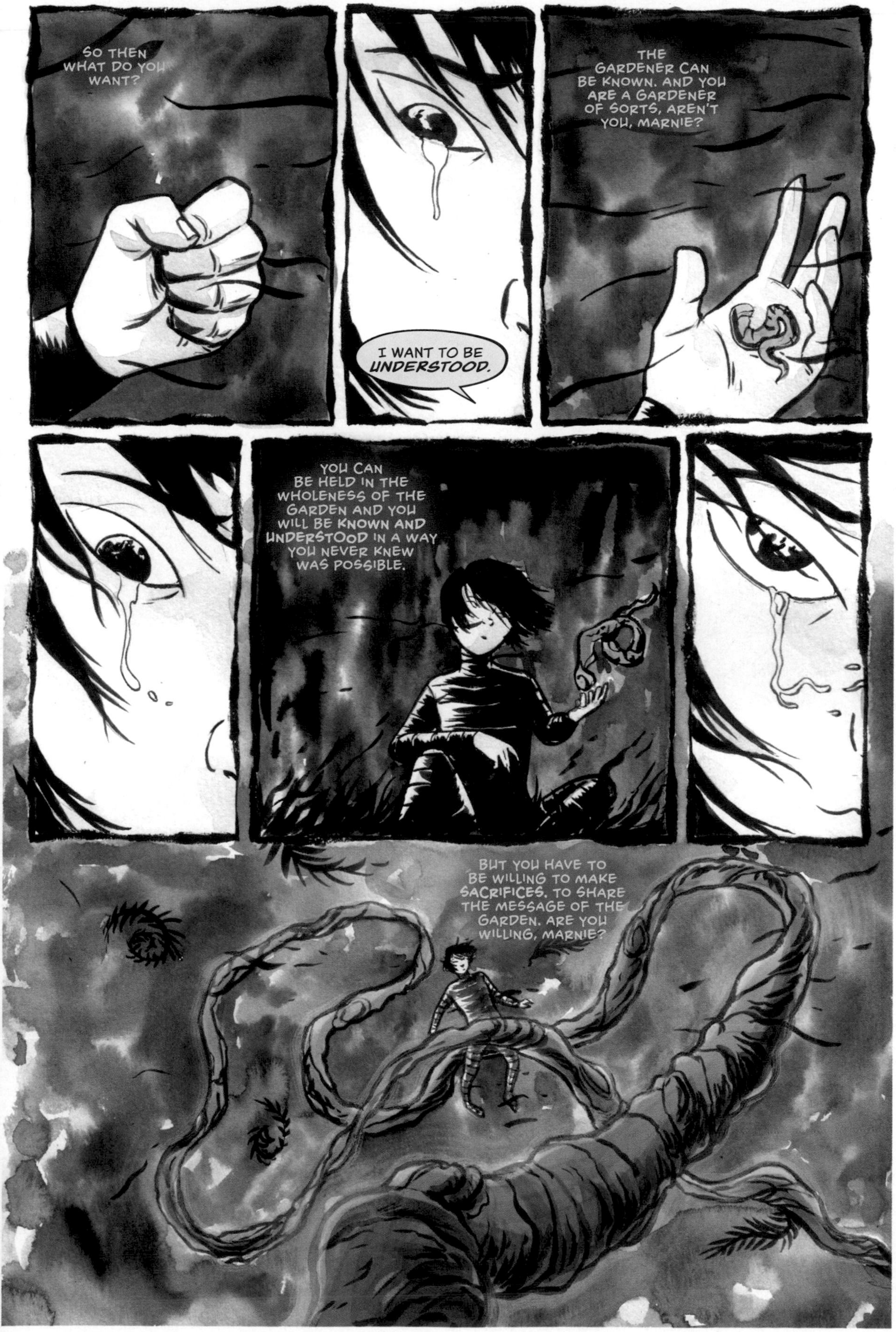
SO THEN WHAT DO YOU WANT?
I WANT TO BE UNDERSTOOD.
THE GARDENER CAN BE KNOWN. AND YOU ARE A GARDENER OF SORTS, AREN'T YOU, MARNIE?
YOU CAN BE HELD IN THE WHOLENESS OF THE GARDEN AND YOU WILL BE KNOWN AND UNDERSTOOD IN A WAY YOU NEVER KNEW WAS POSSIBLE.
BUT YOU HAVE TO BE WILLING TO MAKE SACRIFICES. TO SHARE THE MESSAGE OF THE GARDEN. ARE YOU WILLING, MARNIE?

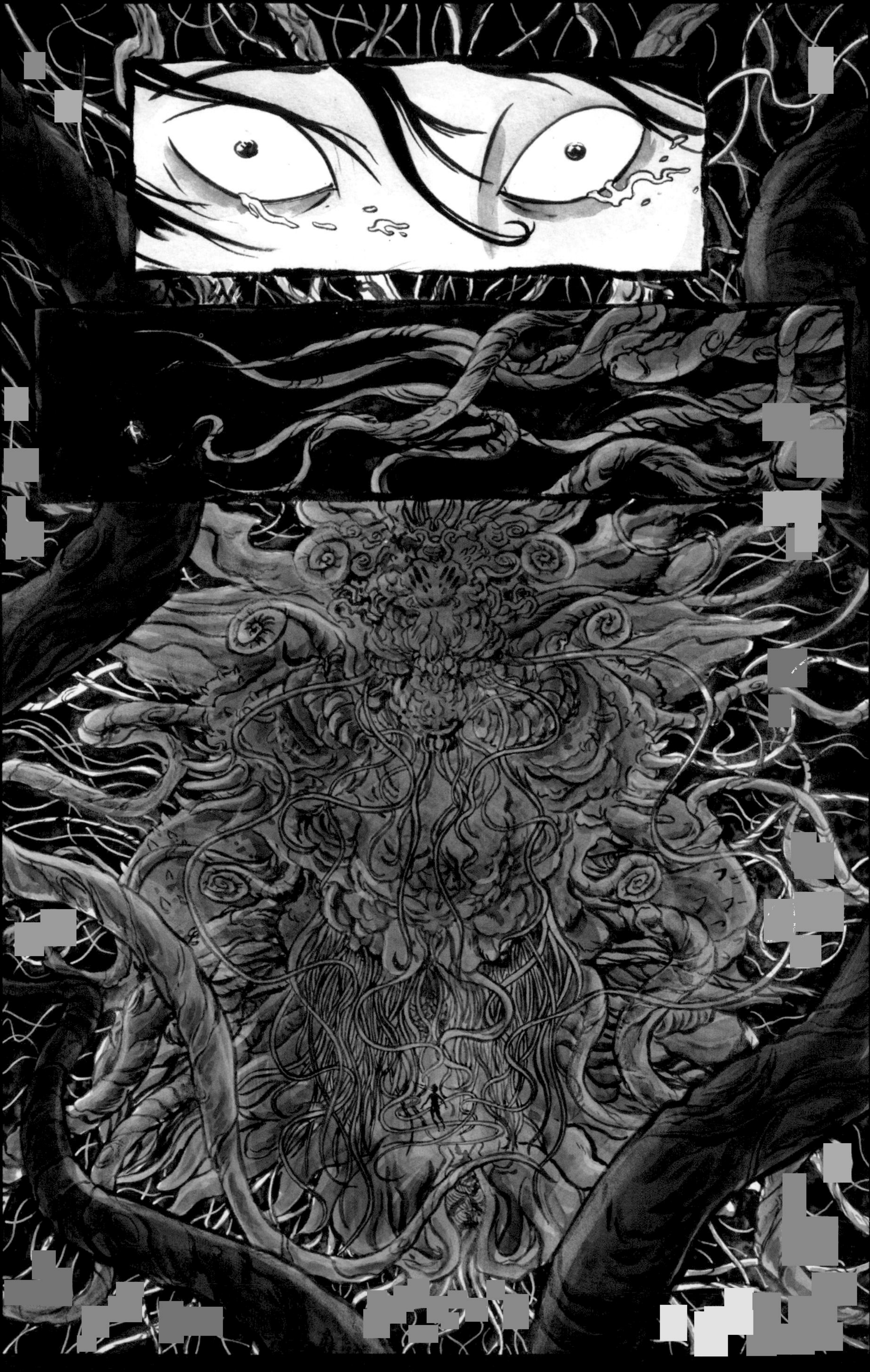

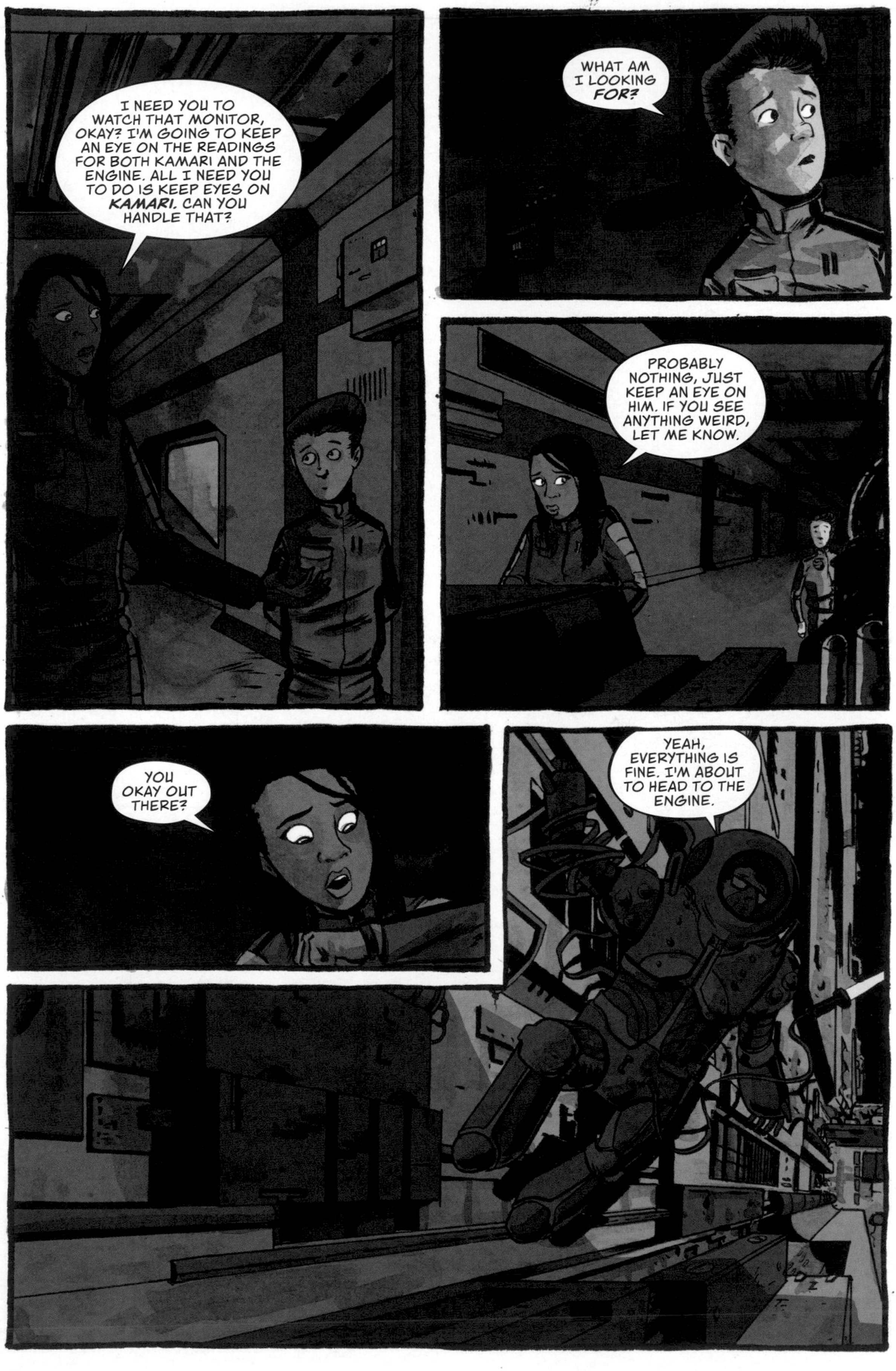
I NEED YOU TO WATCH THAT MONITOR, OKAY? I'M GOING TO KEEP AN EYE ON THE READINGS FOR BOTH KAMARI AND THE ENGINE. ALL I NEED YOU TO DO IS KEEP EYES ON KAMARI. CAN YOU HANDLE THAT?
WHAT AM I LOOKING FOR?
PROBABLY NOTHING, JUST KEEP AN EYE ON HIM. IF YOU SEE ANYTHING WEIRD, LET ME KNOW.
YOU OKAY OUT THERE?
YEAH, EVERYTHING IS FINE. I'M ABOUT TO HEAD TO THE ENGINE.

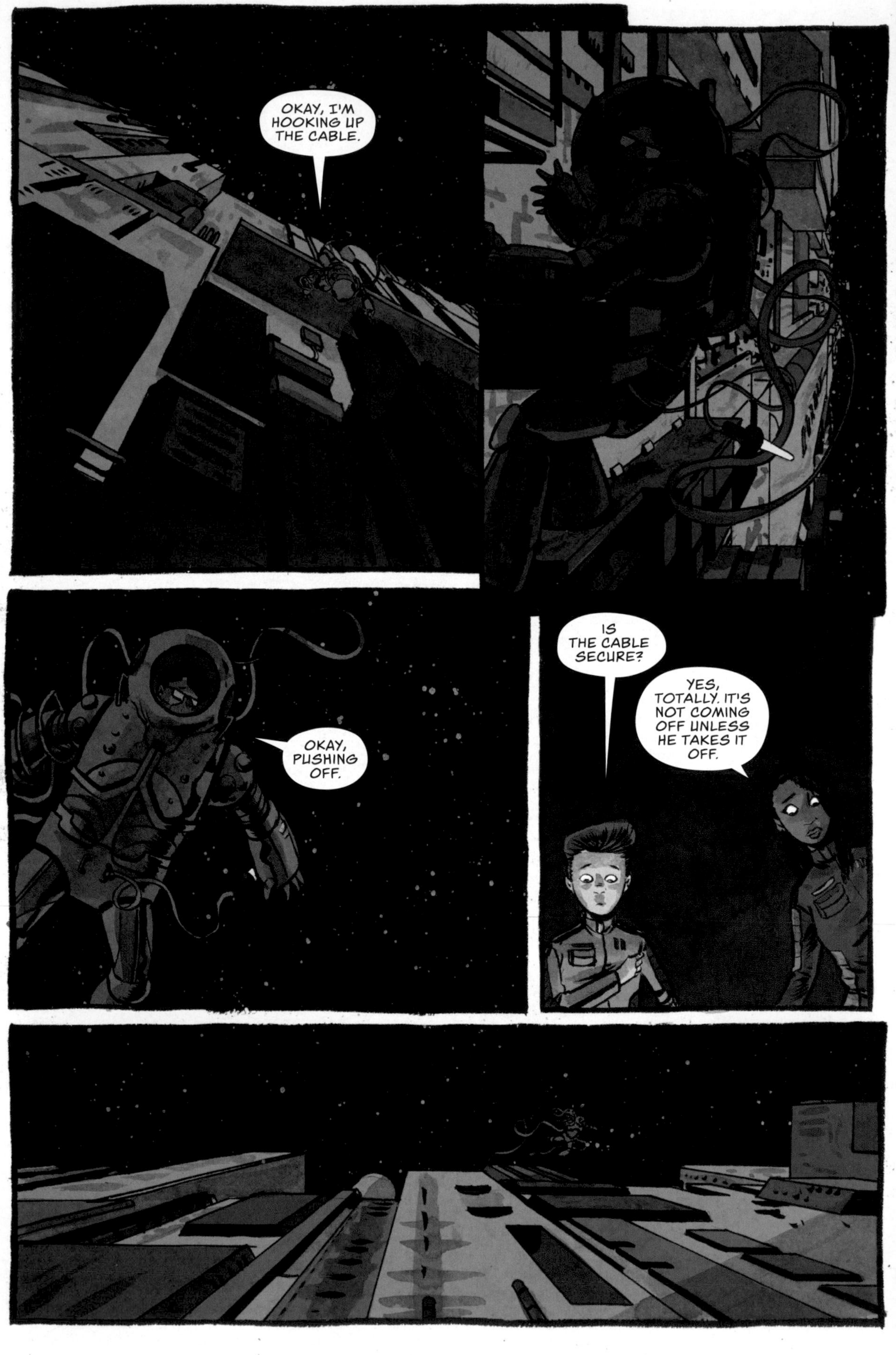
OKAY, I'M HOOKING UP THE CABLE.
OKAY, PUSHING OFF.
IS THE CABLE SECURE?
YES, TOTALLY. IT'S NOT COMING OFF UNLESS HE TAKES IT OFF.

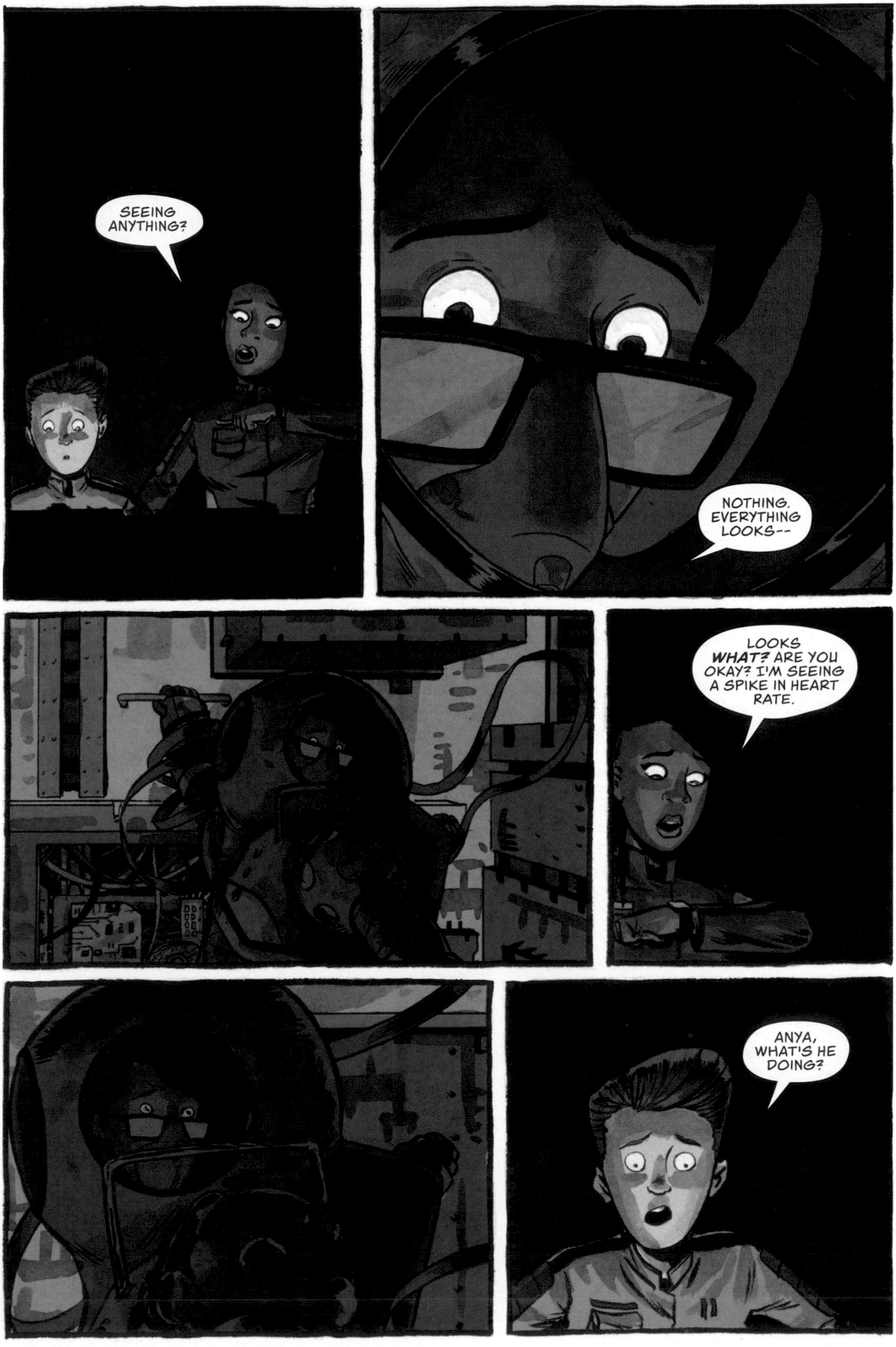
SEEING ANYTHING?
NOTHING. EVERYTHING LOOKS--
LOOKS ***WHAT?*** ARE YOU OKAY? I'M SEEING A SPIKE IN HEART RATE.
ANYA, WHAT'S HE DOING?

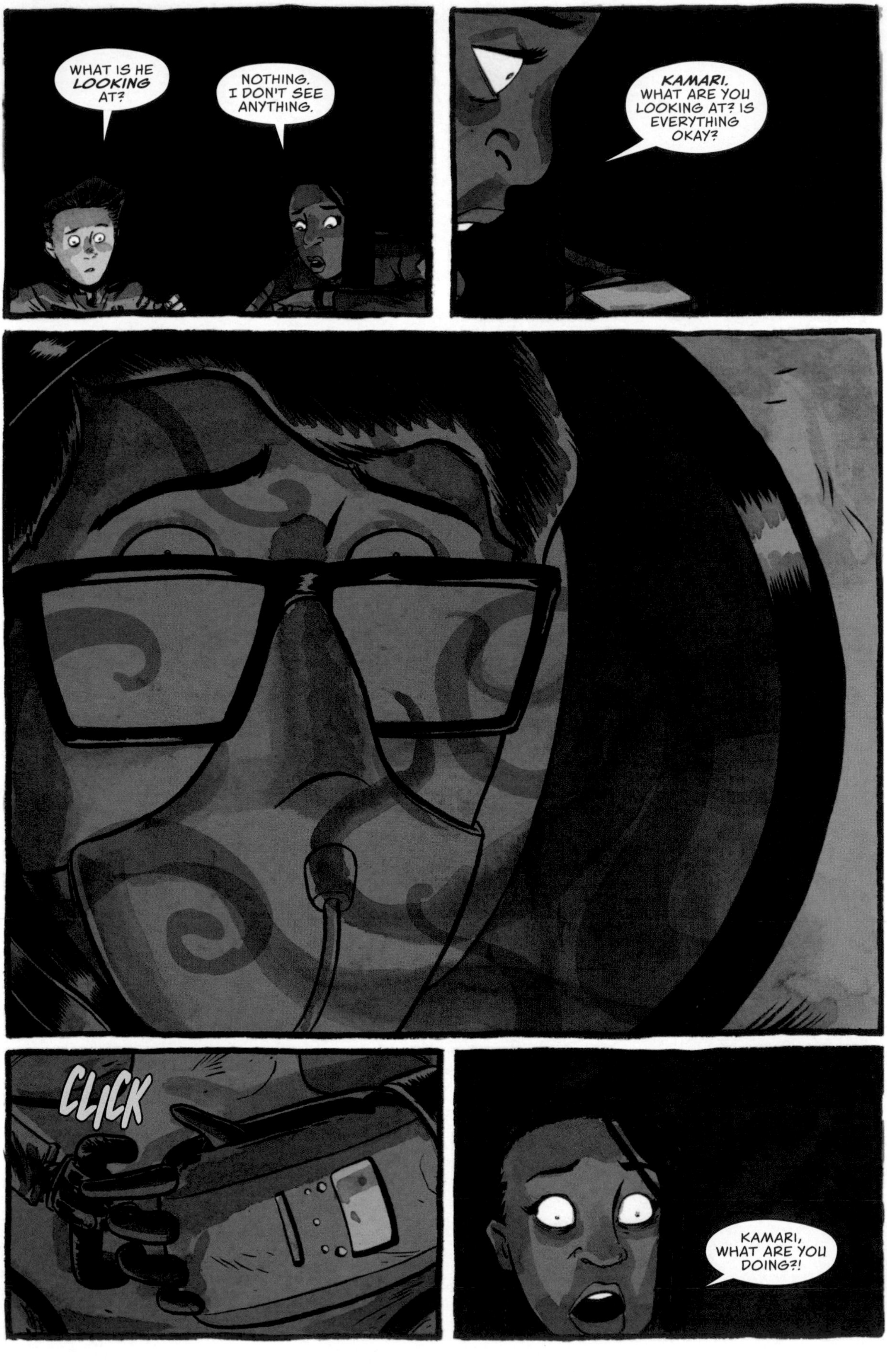
WHAT IS HE LOOKING AT?
NOTHING. I DON'T SEE ANYTHING.
KAMARI. WHAT ARE YOU LOOKING AT? IS EVERYTHING OKAY?
CLICK
KAMARI, WHAT ARE YOU DOING?!

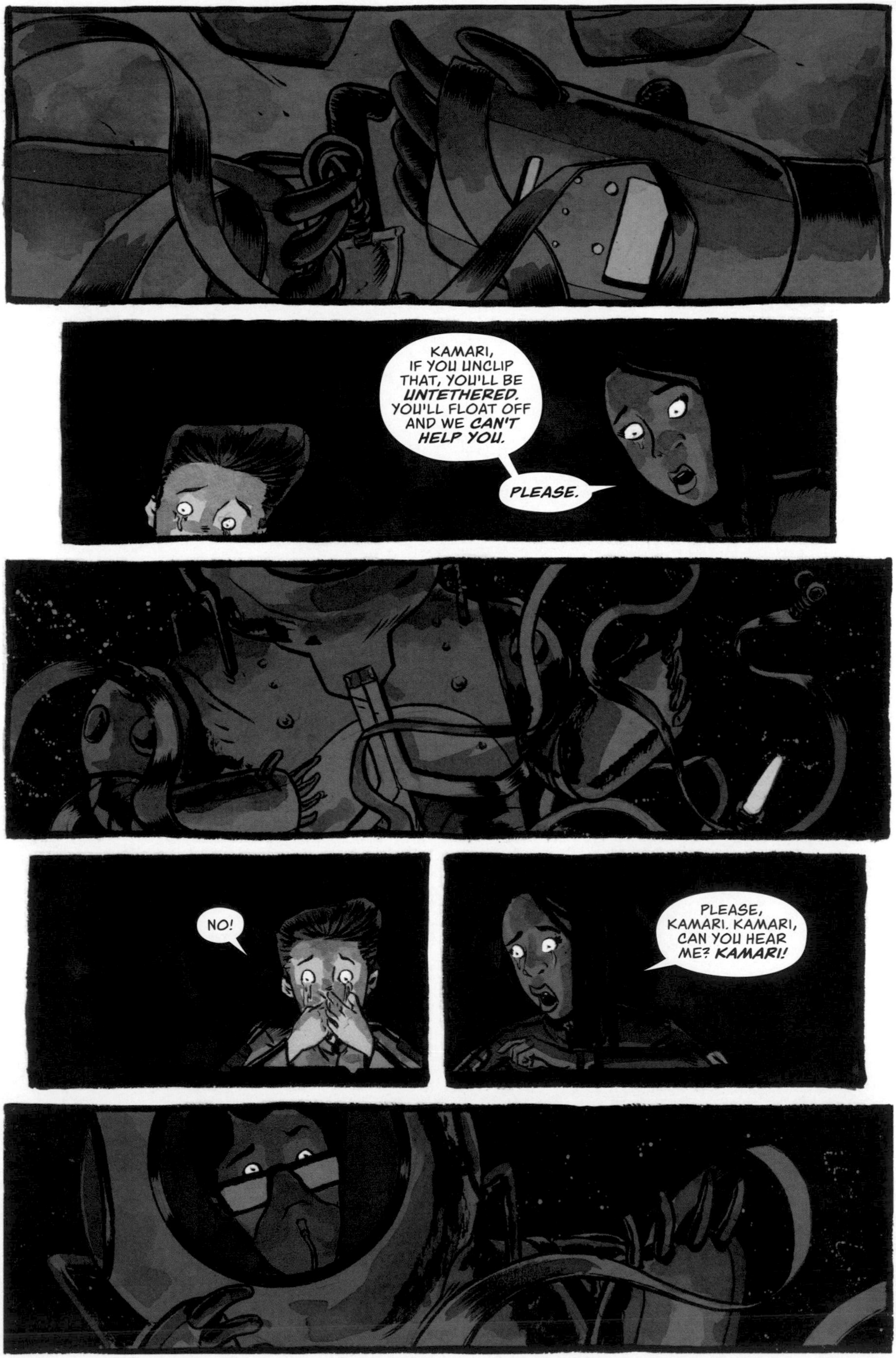
KAMARI, IF YOU UNCLIP THAT, YOU'LL BE ***UNTETHERED.*** YOU'LL FLOAT OFF AND WE ***CAN'T HELP YOU.***
PLEASE.
NO!
PLEASE, KAMARI. KAMARI, CAN YOU HEAR ME? ***KAMARI!***

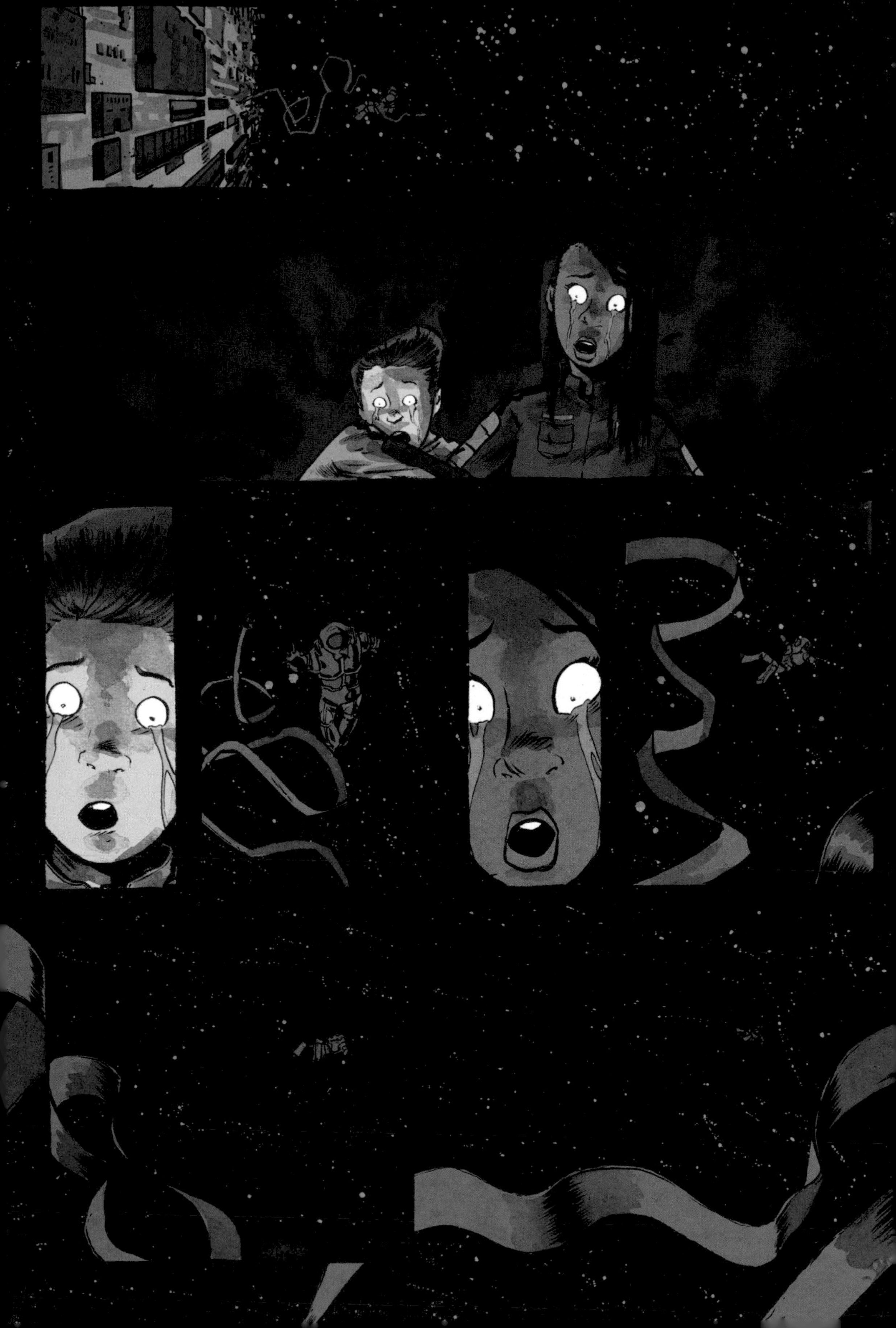

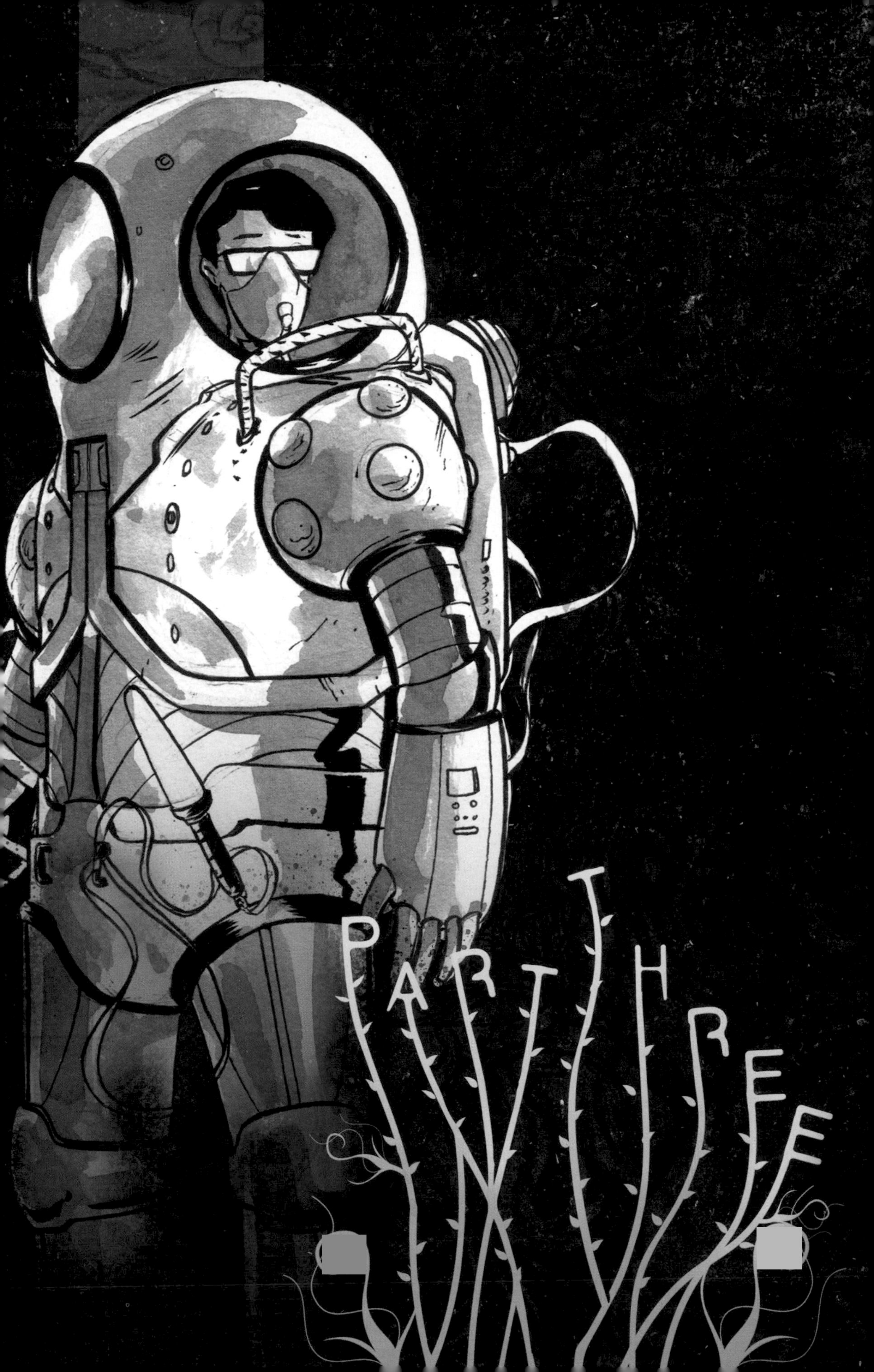
PART THREE

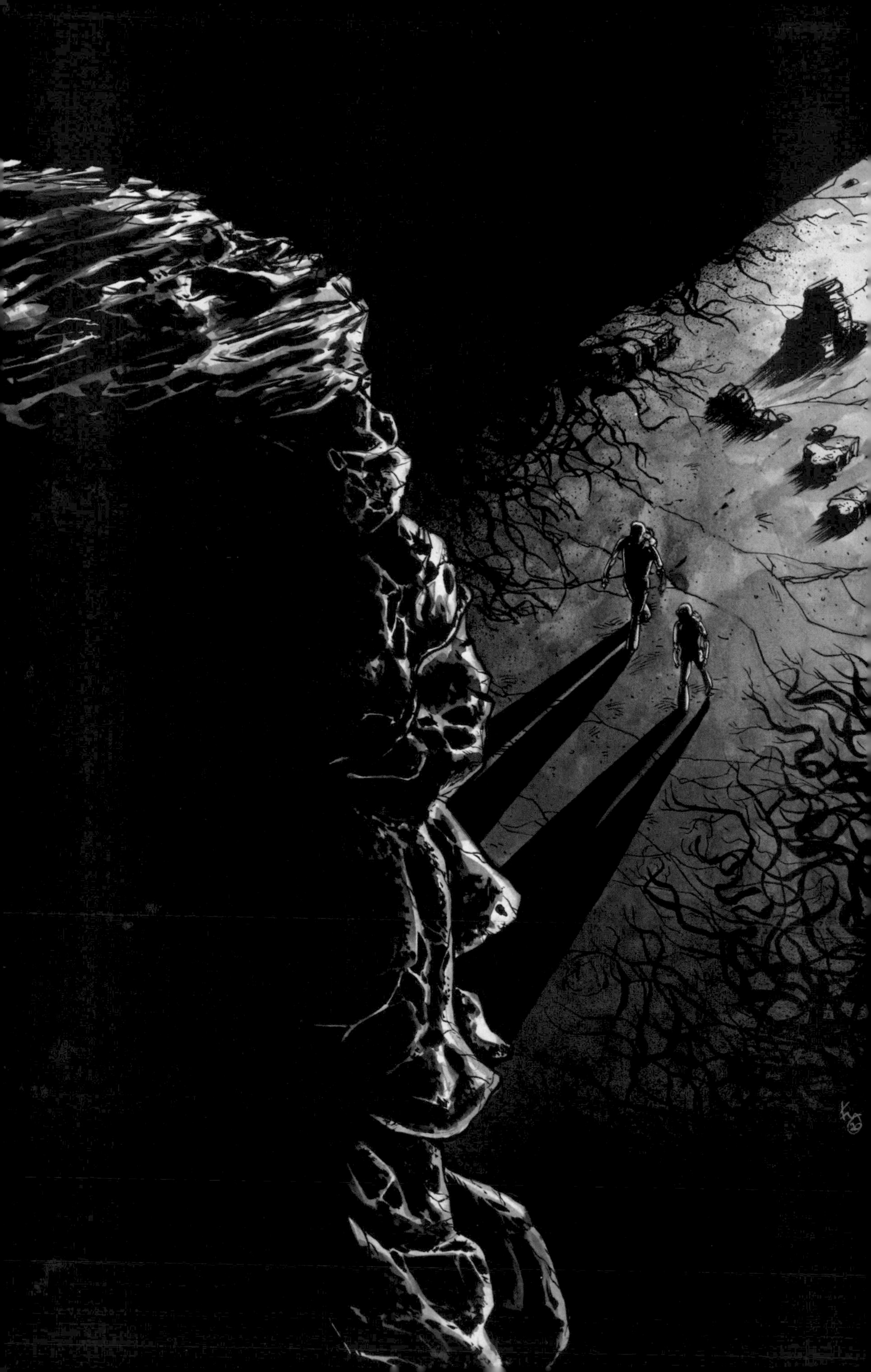

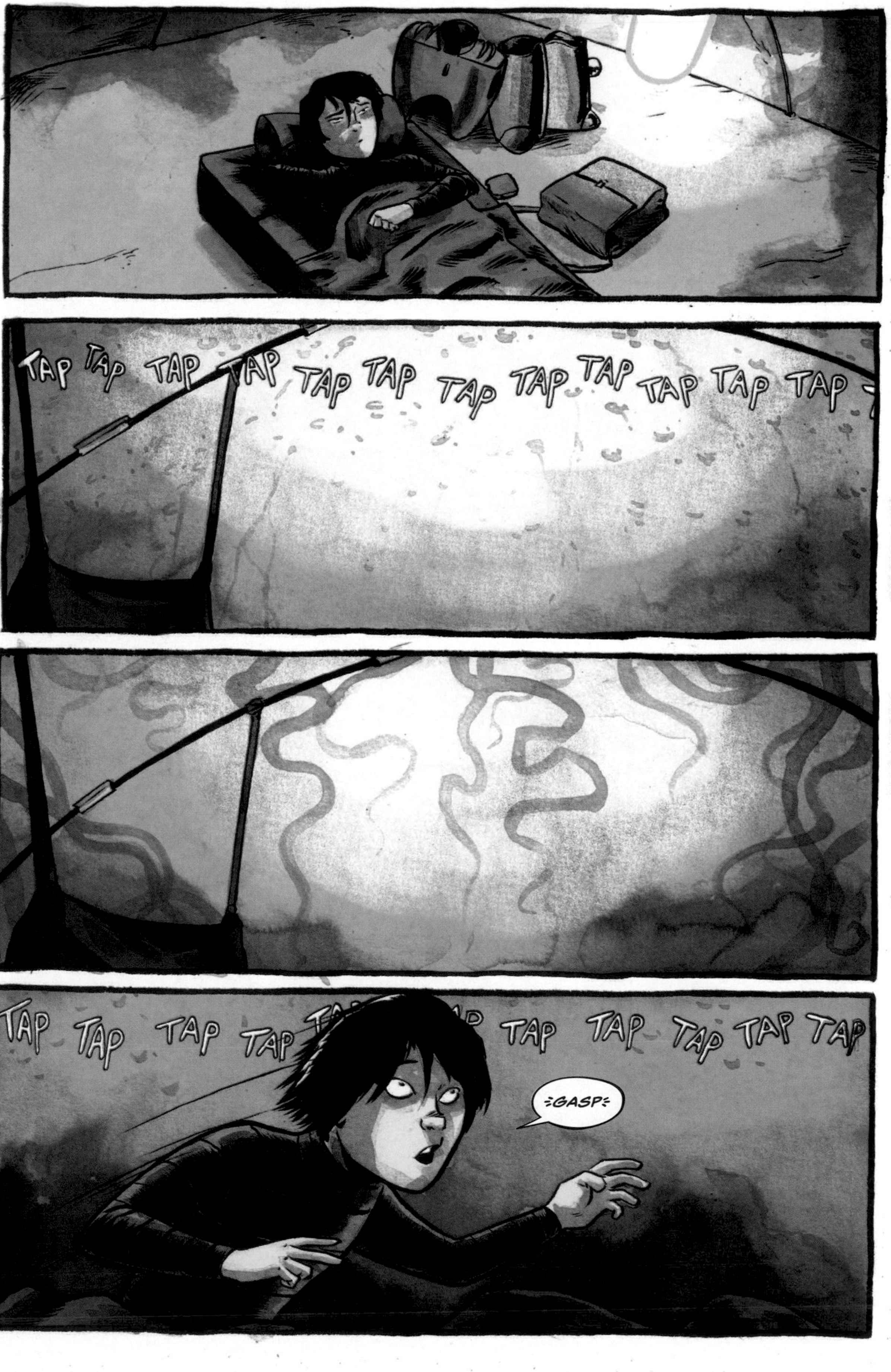
TAP TAP TAP TAP TAP TAP TAP TAP TAP TAP TAP TAP
TAP TAP TAP TAP TAP TAP TAP TAP TAP
GASP

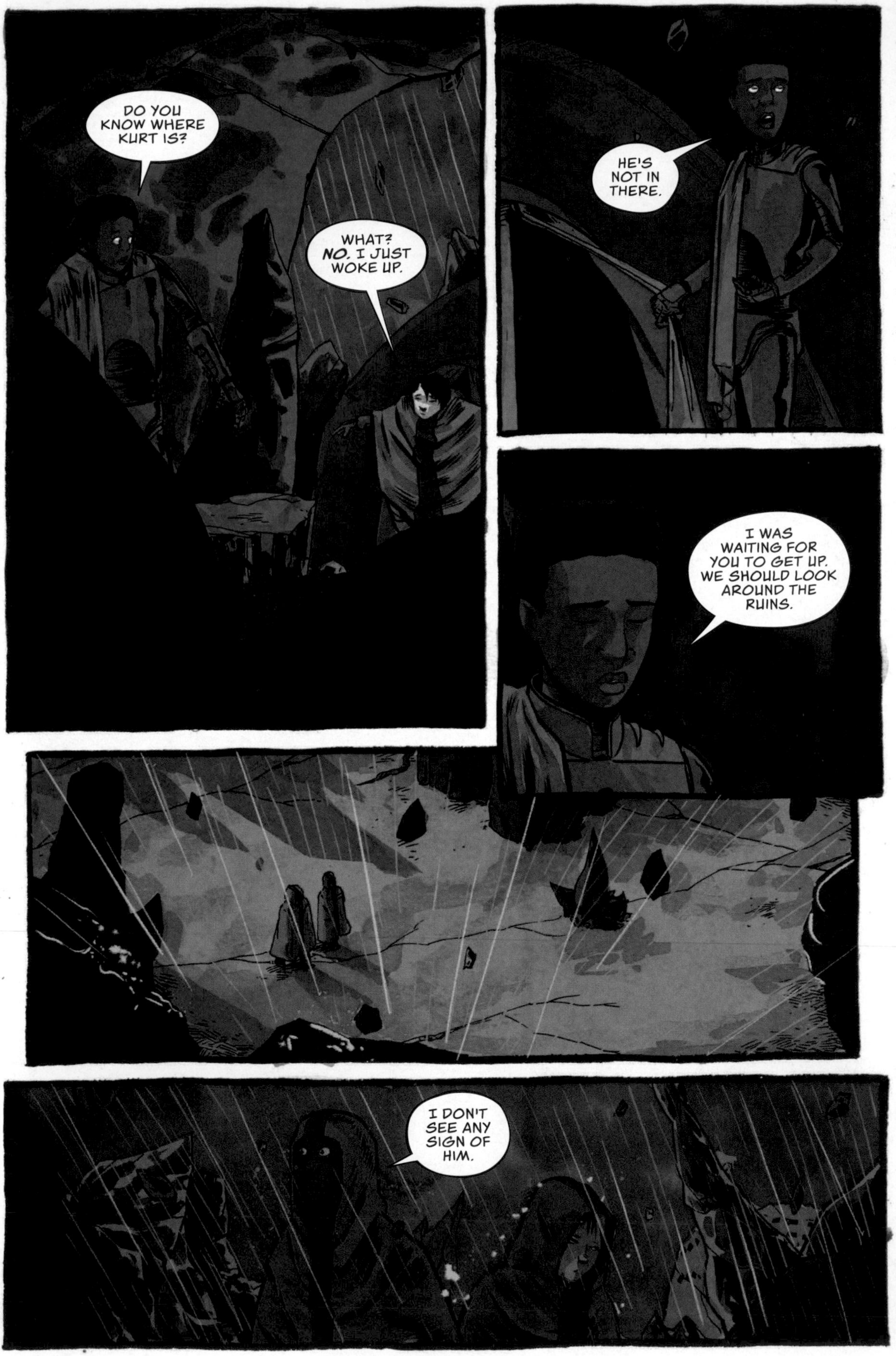
DO YOU KNOW WHERE KURT IS?
WHAT? NO. I JUST WOKE UP.
HE'S NOT IN THERE.
I WAS WAITING FOR YOU TO GET UP. WE SHOULD LOOK AROUND THE RUINS.
I DON'T SEE ANY SIGN OF HIM.

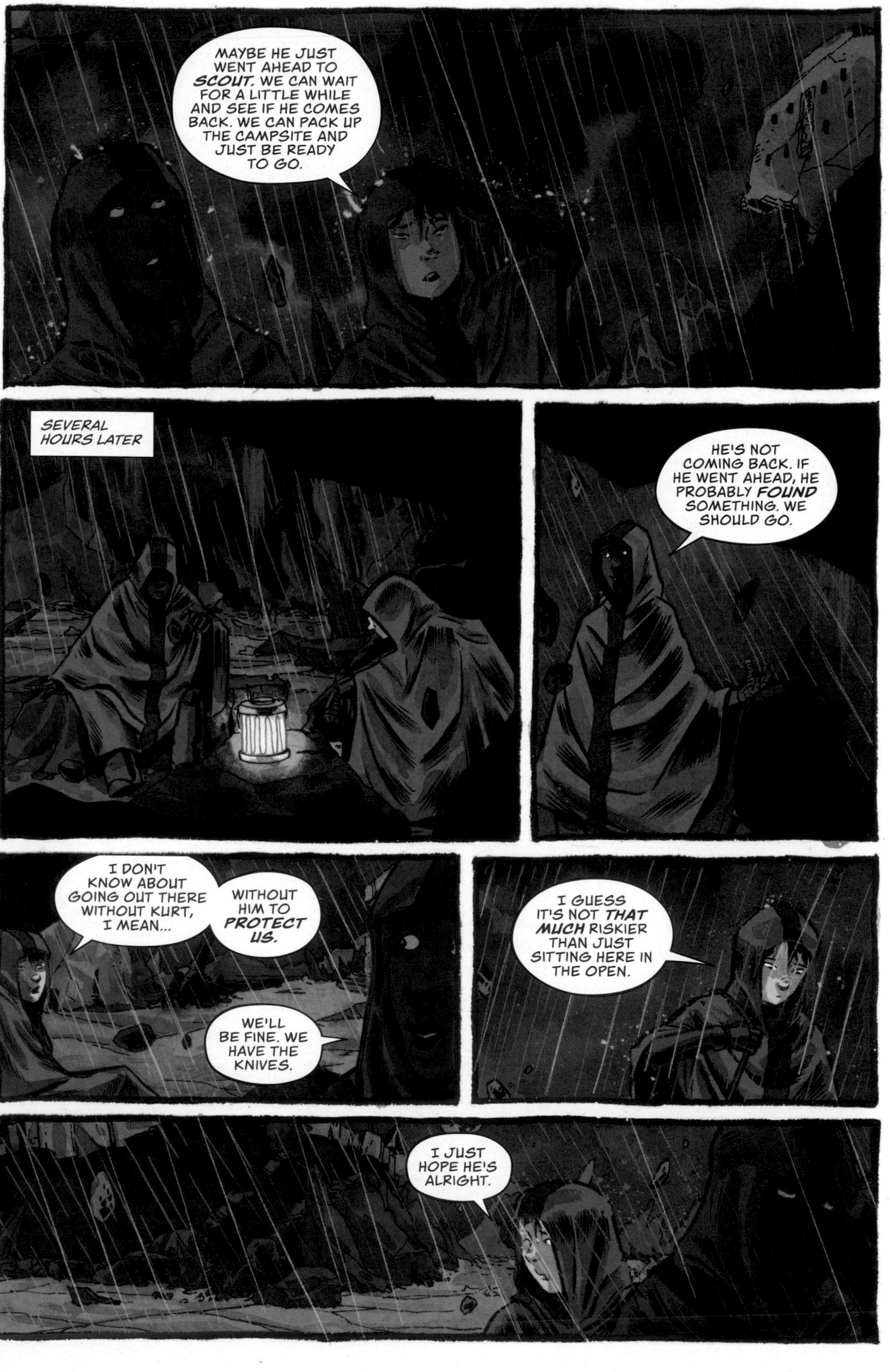
MAYBE HE JUST WENT AHEAD TO SCOUT. WE CAN WAIT FOR A LITTLE WHILE AND SEE IF HE COMES BACK. WE CAN PACK UP THE CAMPSITE AND JUST BE READY TO GO.
SEVERAL HOURS LATER
HE'S NOT COMING BACK. IF HE WENT AHEAD, HE PROBABLY FOUND SOMETHING. WE SHOULD GO.
I DON'T KNOW ABOUT GOING OUT THERE WITHOUT KURT, I MEAN...
WITHOUT HIM TO PROTECT US.
WE'LL BE FINE. WE HAVE THE KNIVES.
I GUESS IT'S NOT THAT MUCH RISKIER THAN JUST SITTING HERE IN THE OPEN.
I JUST HOPE HE'S ALRIGHT.

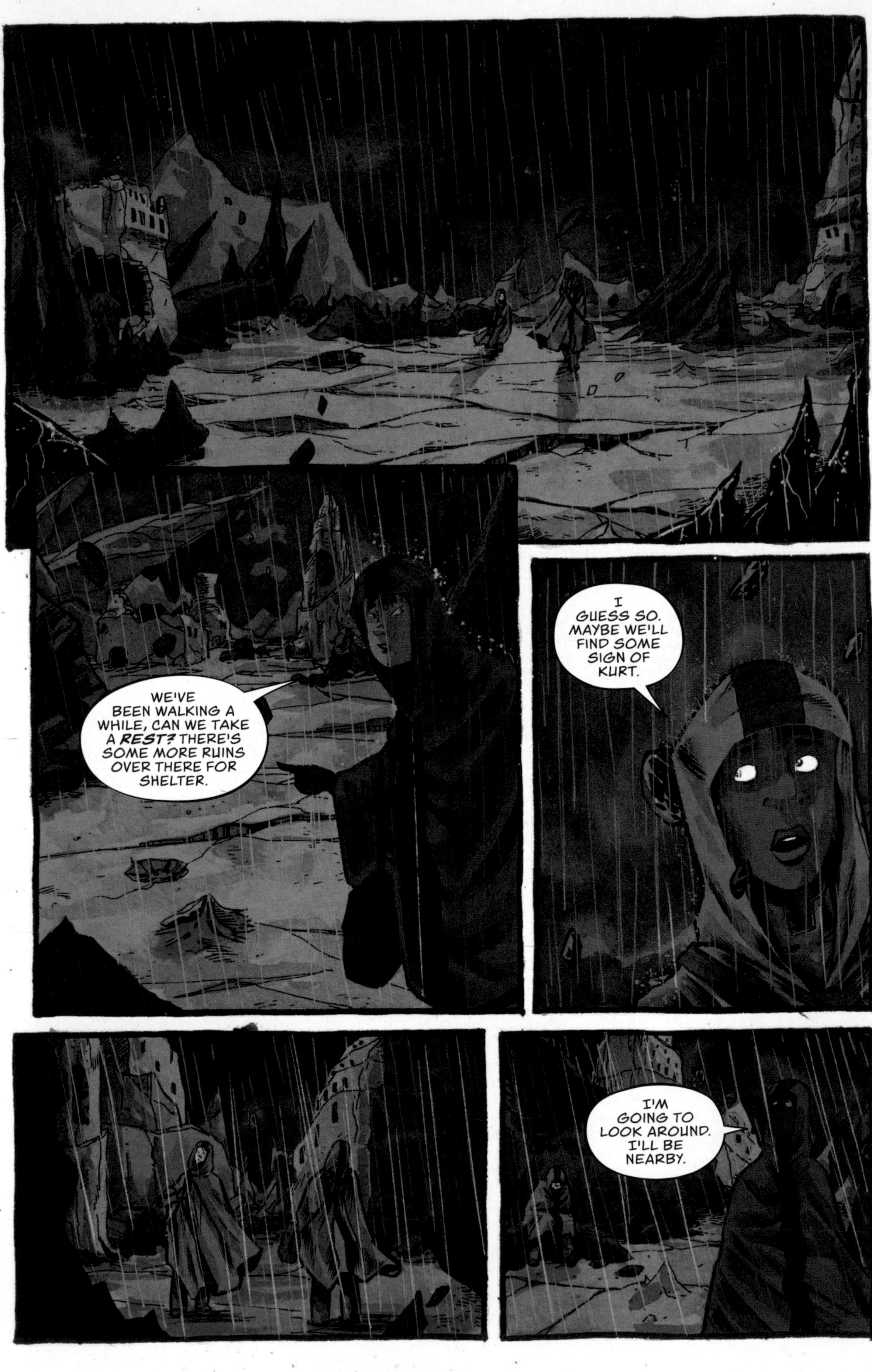
WE'VE BEEN WALKING A WHILE, CAN WE TAKE A ***REST?*** THERE'S SOME MORE RUINS OVER THERE FOR SHELTER.
I GUESS SO. MAYBE WE'LL FIND SOME SIGN OF KURT.
I'M GOING TO LOOK AROUND. I'LL BE NEARBY.

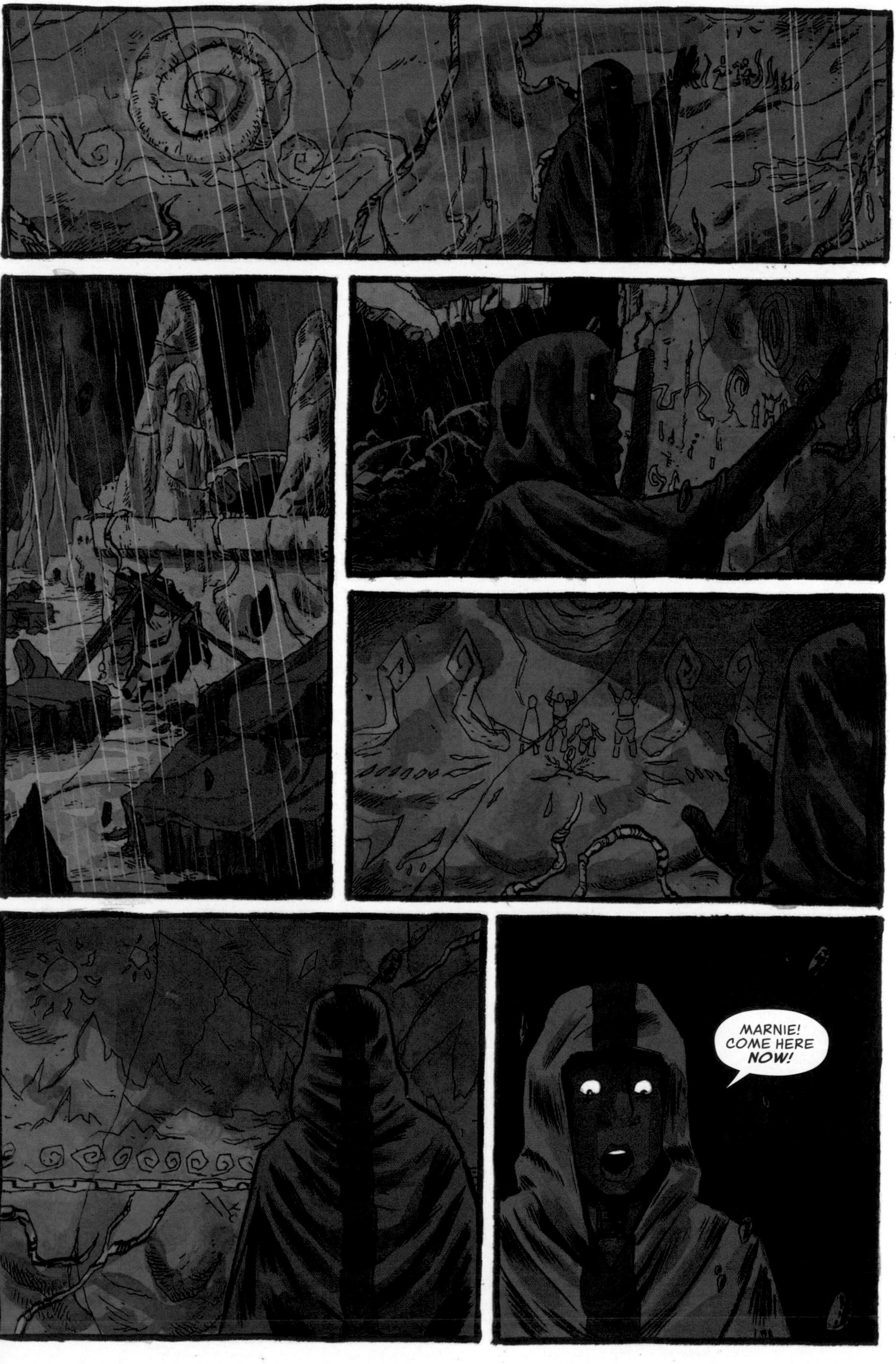
MARNIE! COME HERE NOW!

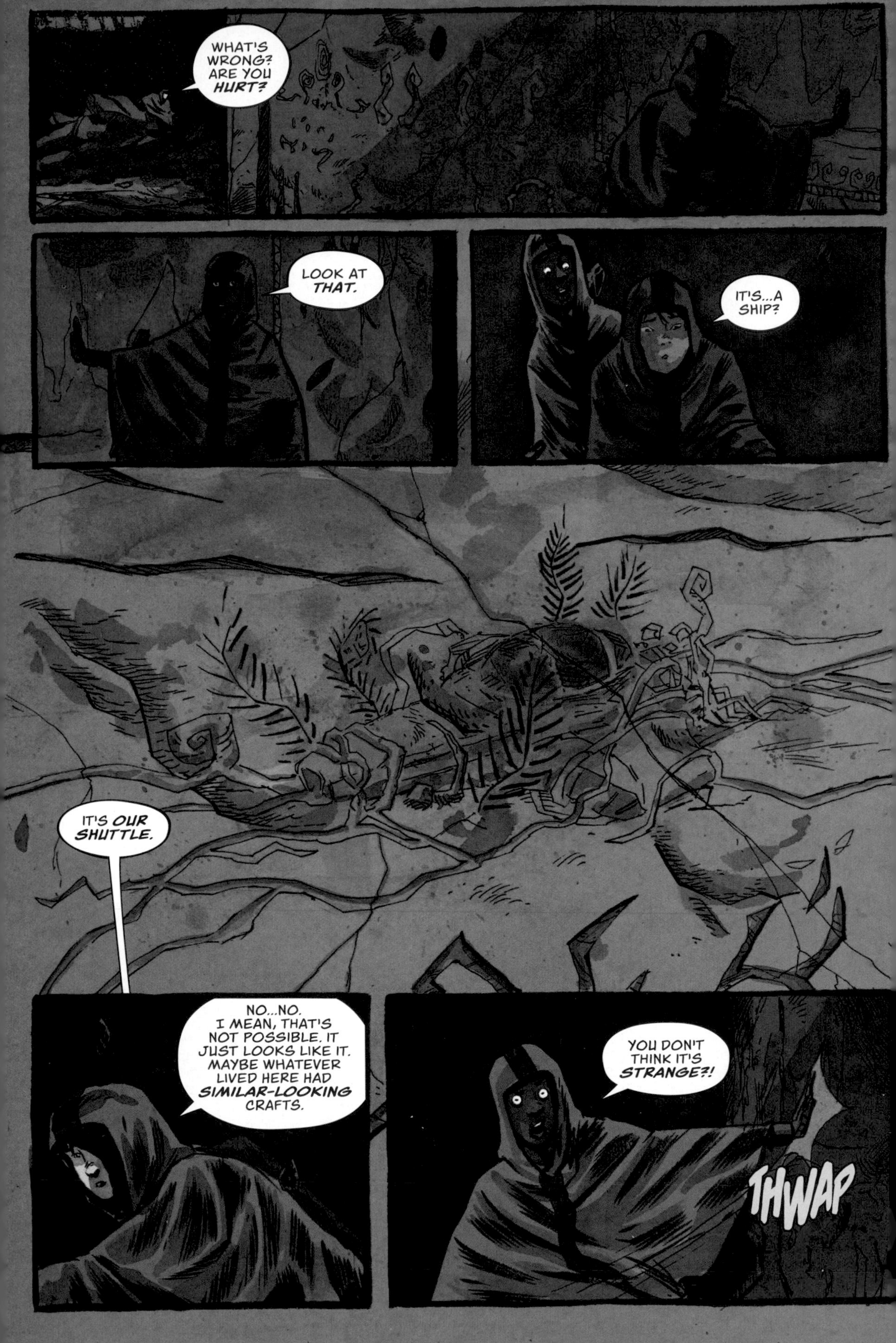
WHAT'S WRONG? ARE YOU HURT?
LOOK AT THAT.
IT'S...A SHIP?
IT'S OUR SHUTTLE.
NO...NO. I MEAN, THAT'S NOT POSSIBLE. IT JUST LOOKS LIKE IT. MAYBE WHATEVER LIVED HERE HAD SIMILAR-LOOKING CRAFTS.
YOU DON'T THINK IT'S STRANGE?!
THWAP

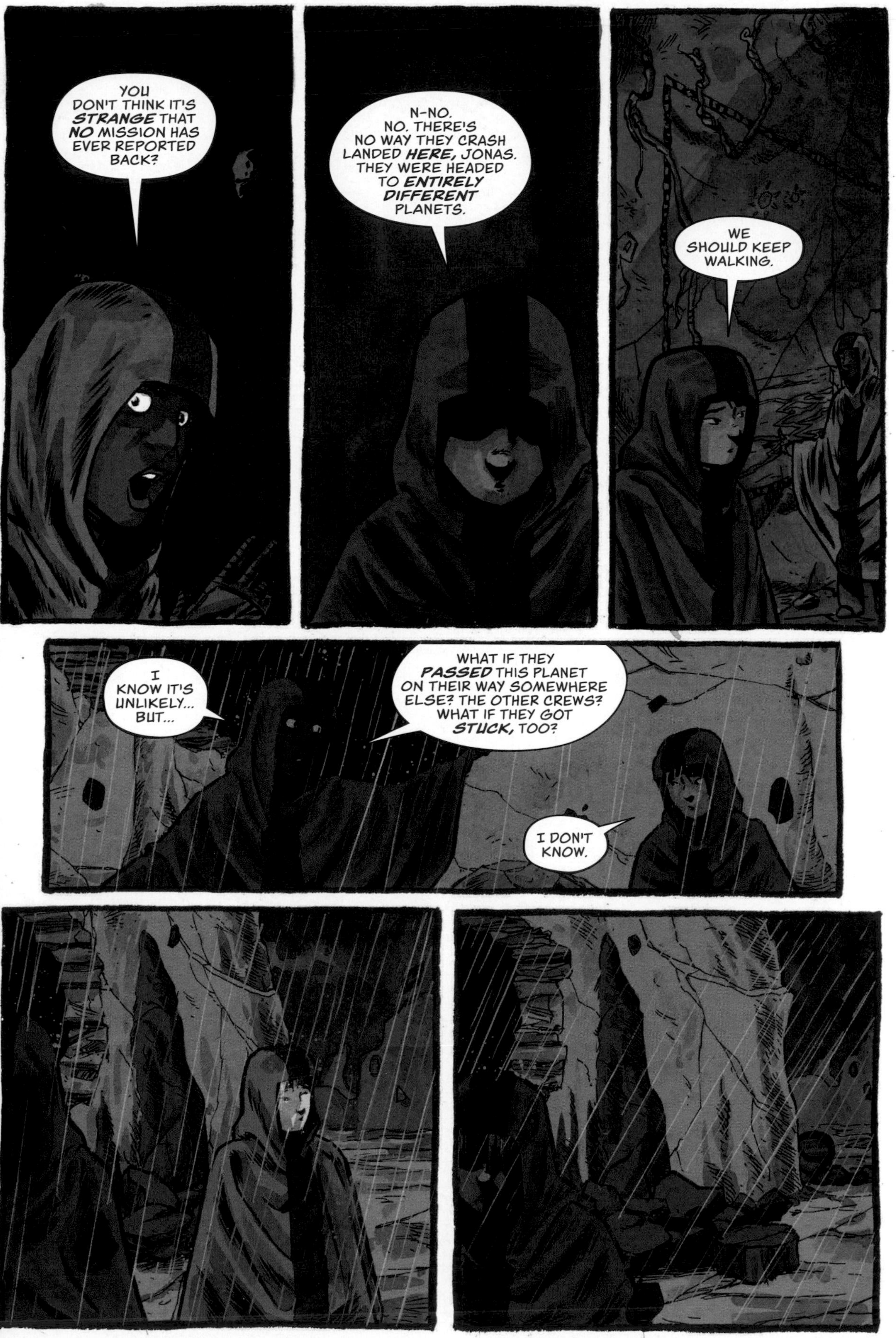
YOU DON'T THINK IT'S STRANGE THAT NO MISSION HAS EVER REPORTED BACK?
N-NO. NO. THERE'S NO WAY THEY CRASH LANDED HERE, JONAS. THEY WERE HEADED TO ENTIRELY DIFFERENT PLANETS.
WE SHOULD KEEP WALKING.
I KNOW IT'S UNLIKELY... BUT...
WHAT IF THEY PASSED THIS PLANET ON THEIR WAY SOMEWHERE ELSE? THE OTHER CREWS? WHAT IF THEY GOT STUCK, TOO?
I DON'T KNOW.

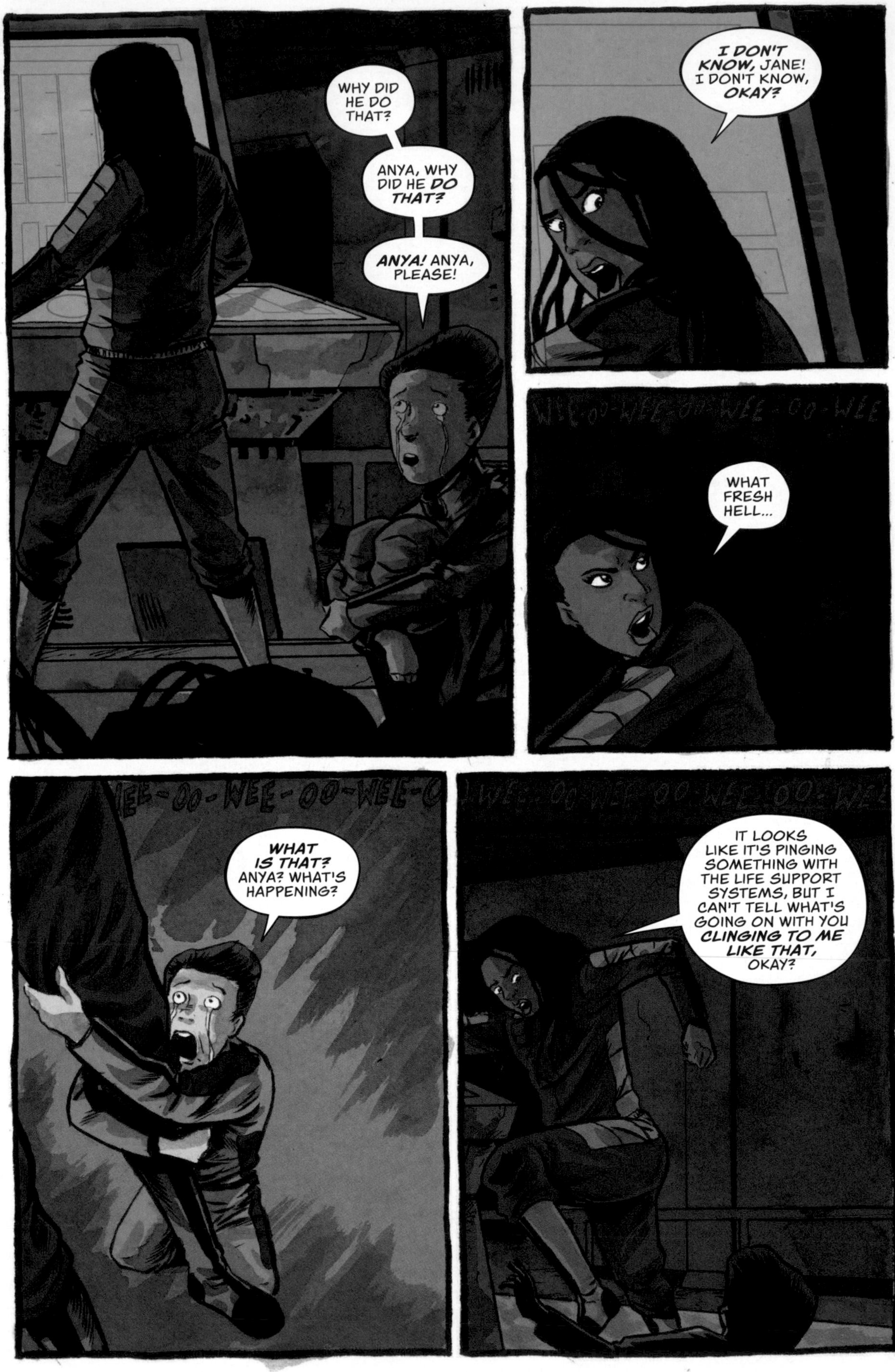
WHY DID HE DO THAT?
ANYA, WHY DID HE *DO THAT?*
ANYA! ANYA, PLEASE!
I DON'T KNOW, JANE! I DON'T KNOW, ***OKAY?***
WEE-OO-WEE-OO-WEE-OO-WEE
WHAT FRESH HELL...
WEE-OO-WEE-OO-WEE-
WHAT IS THAT? ANYA? WHAT'S HAPPENING?
WEE-OO-WEE-OO-WEE-OO-WEE
IT LOOKS LIKE IT'S PINGING SOMETHING WITH THE LIFE SUPPORT SYSTEMS, BUT I CAN'T TELL WHAT'S GOING ON WITH YOU ***CLINGING TO ME LIKE THAT,*** OKAY?

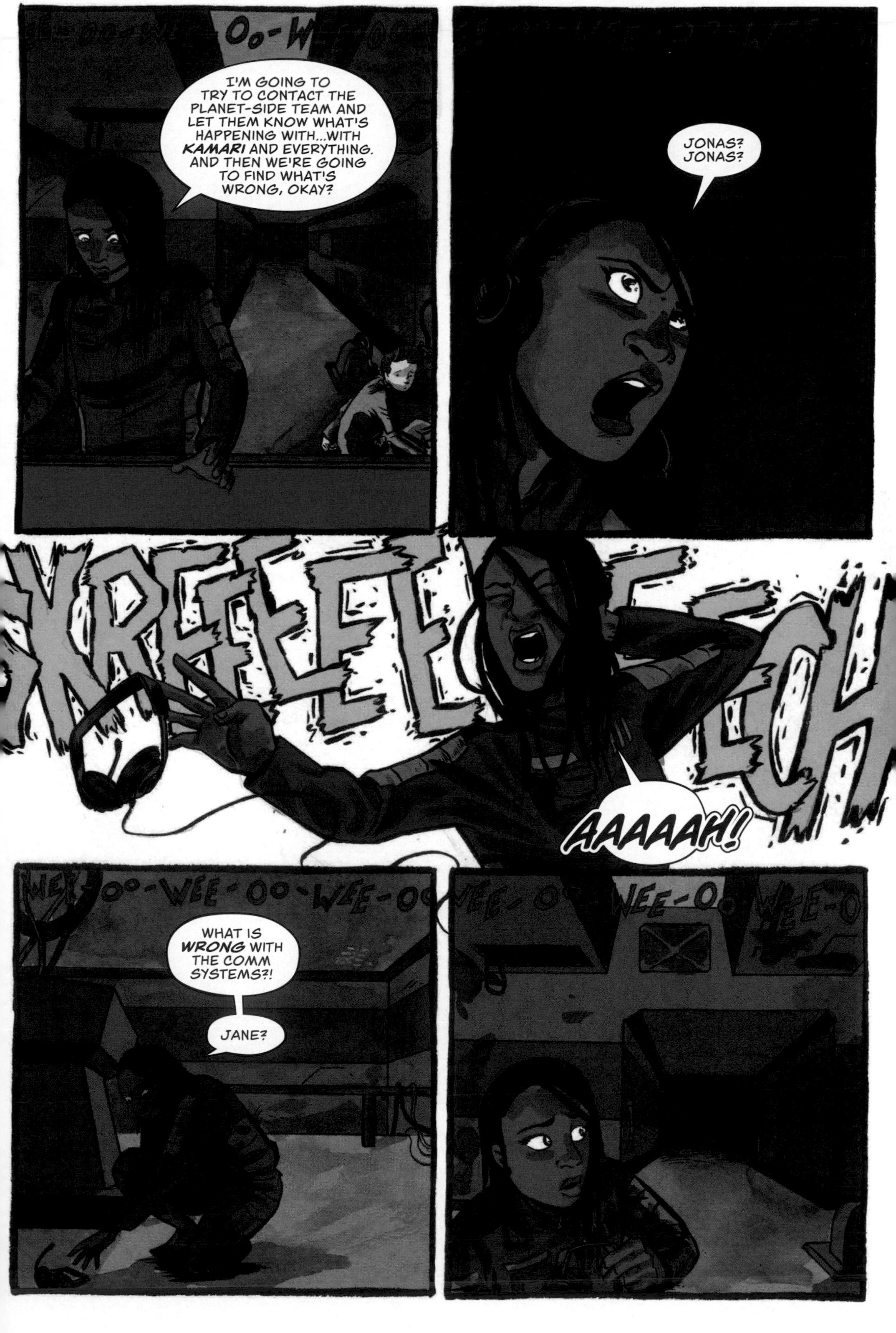

OO-WEE
I'M GOING TO TRY TO CONTACT THE PLANET-SIDE TEAM AND LET THEM KNOW WHAT'S HAPPENING WITH...WITH KAMARI AND EVERYTHING. AND THEN WE'RE GOING TO FIND WHAT'S WRONG, OKAY?
JONAS? JONAS?
KREEEEEECH
AAAAAH!
WEE-OO-WEE-OO-WEE-OO
WHAT IS WRONG WITH THE COMM SYSTEMS?!
JANE?
WEE-O-WEE-O-WEE-O

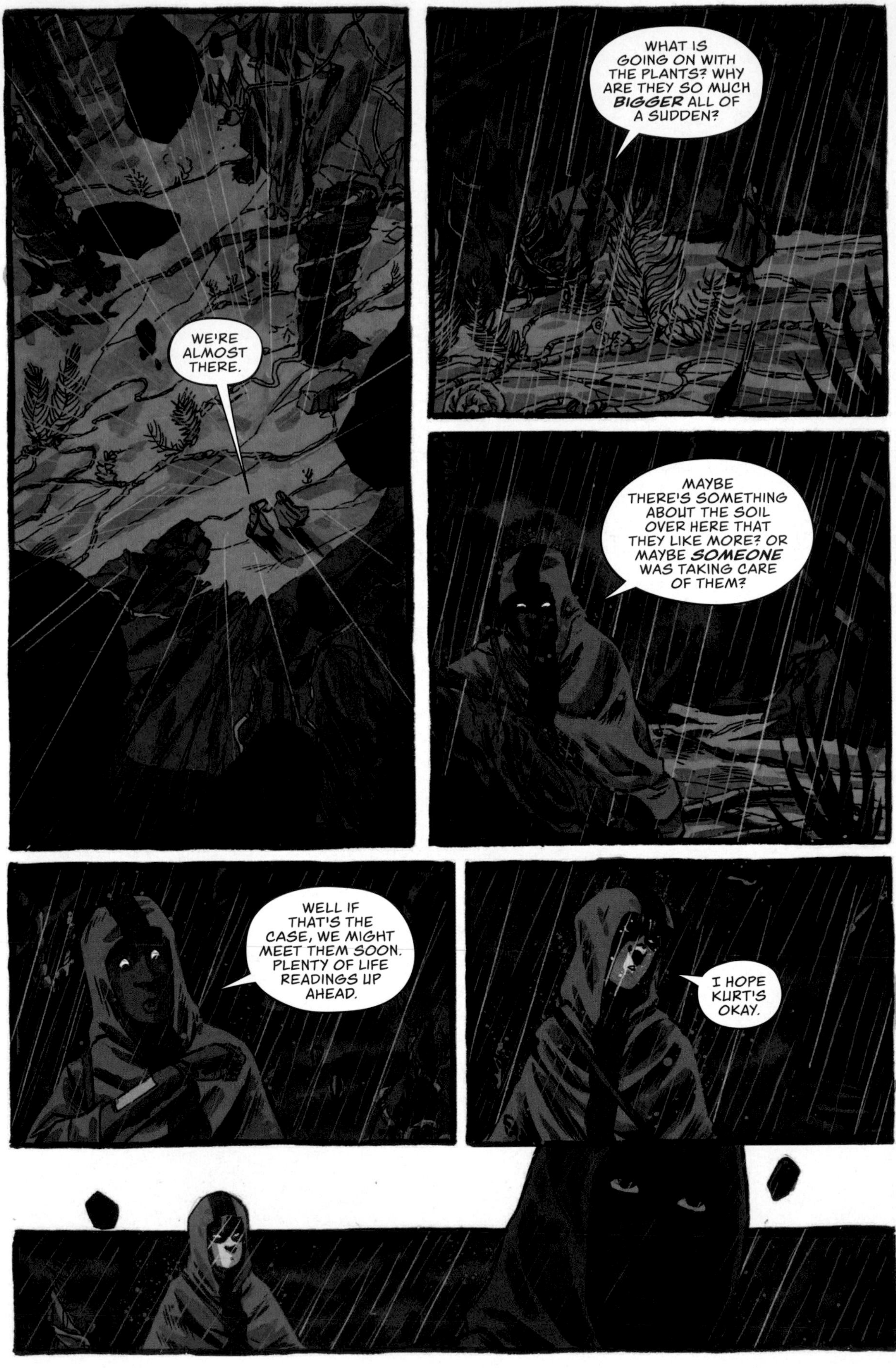
WE'RE ALMOST THERE.
WHAT IS GOING ON WITH THE PLANTS? WHY ARE THEY SO MUCH BIGGER ALL OF A SUDDEN?
MAYBE THERE'S SOMETHING ABOUT THE SOIL OVER HERE THAT THEY LIKE MORE? OR MAYBE SOMEONE WAS TAKING CARE OF THEM?
WELL IF THAT'S THE CASE, WE MIGHT MEET THEM SOON. PLENTY OF LIFE READINGS UP AHEAD.
I HOPE KURT'S OKAY.

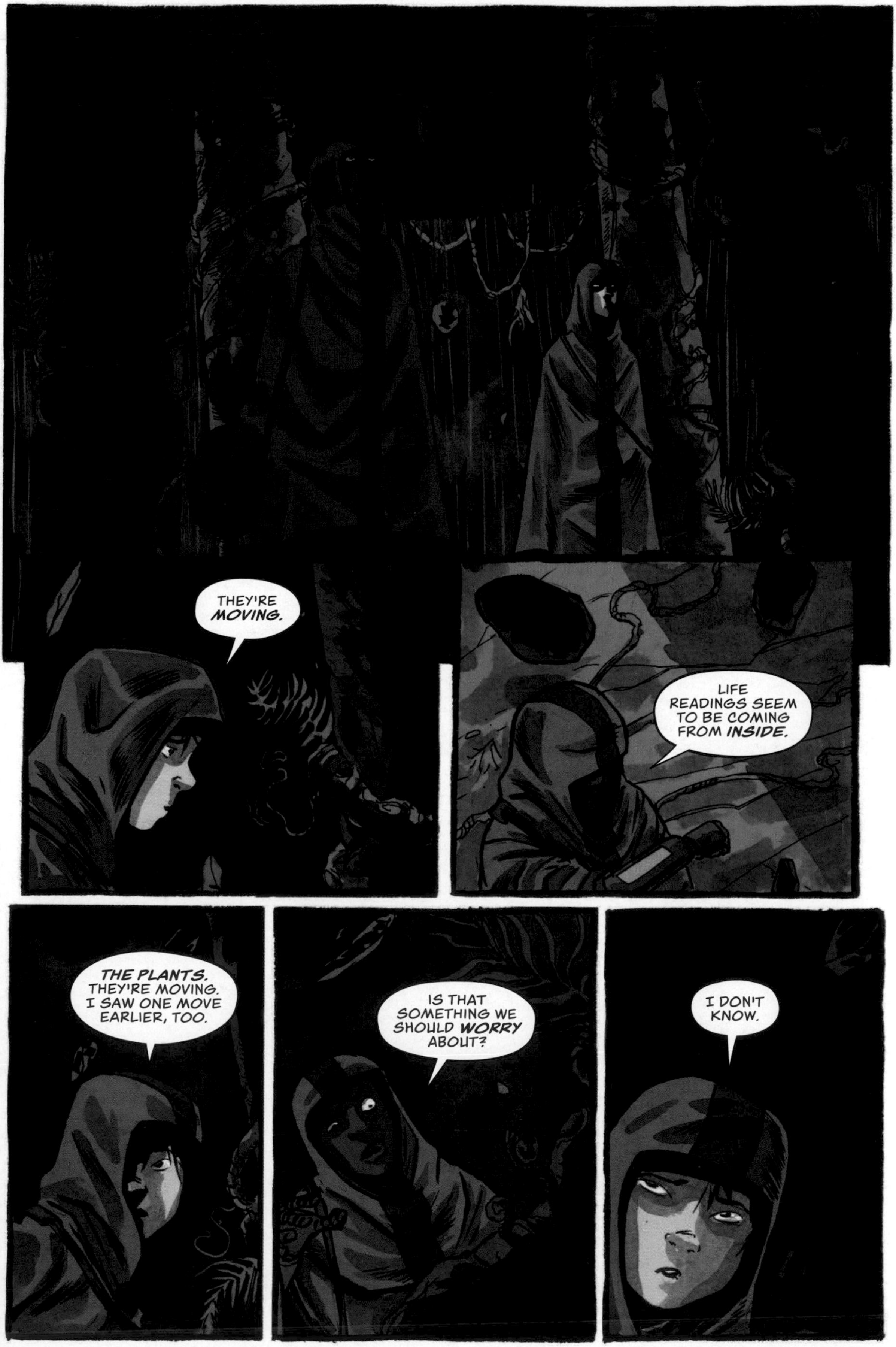
THEY'RE MOVING.
LIFE READINGS SEEM TO BE COMING FROM INSIDE.
THE PLANTS. THEY'RE MOVING. I SAW ONE MOVE EARLIER, TOO.
IS THAT SOMETHING WE SHOULD WORRY ABOUT?
I DON'T KNOW.

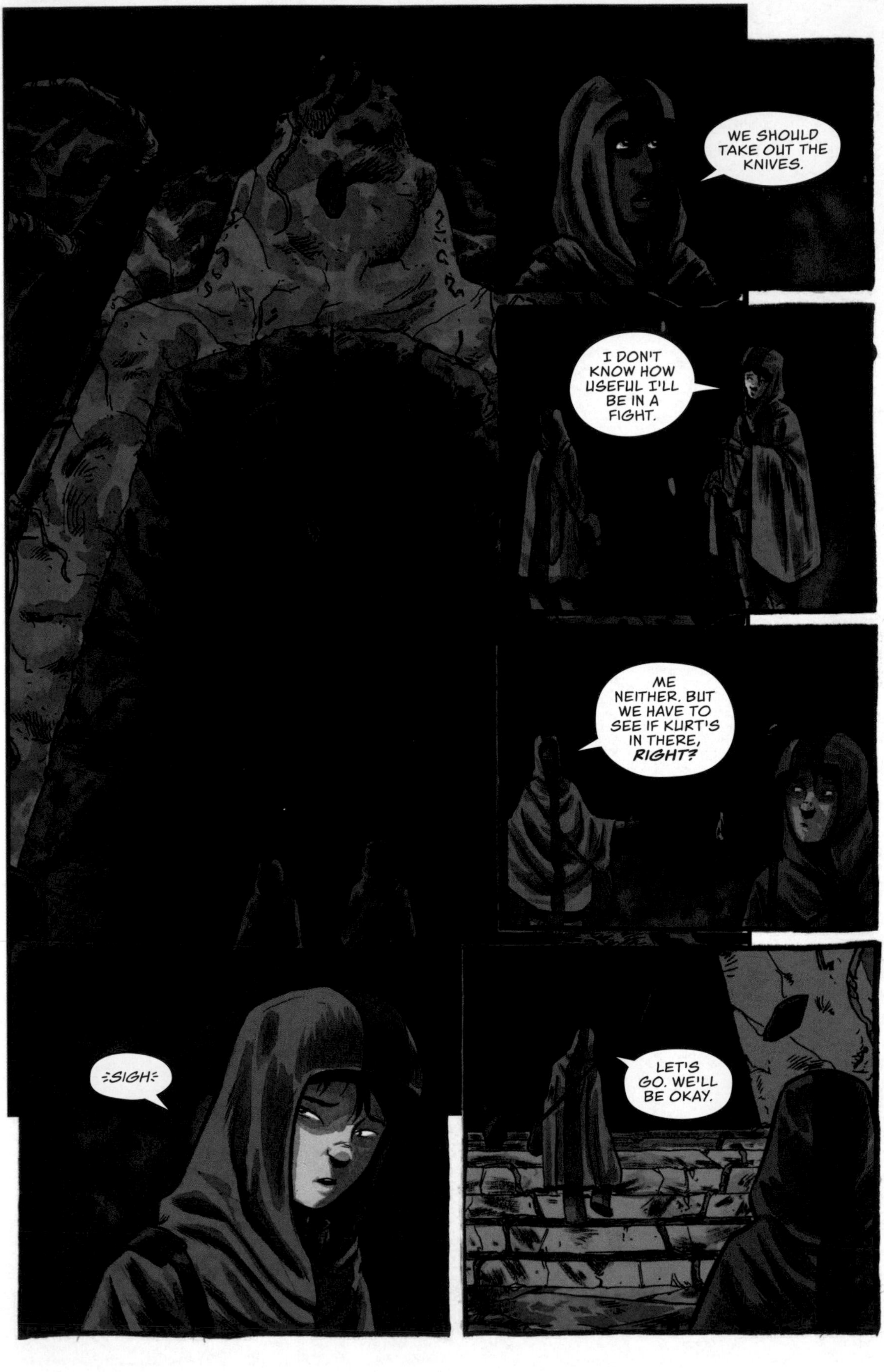
WE SHOULD TAKE OUT THE KNIVES.
I DON'T KNOW HOW USEFUL I'LL BE IN A FIGHT.
ME NEITHER. BUT WE HAVE TO SEE IF KURT'S IN THERE, RIGHT?
=SIGH=
LET'S GO. WE'LL BE OKAY.

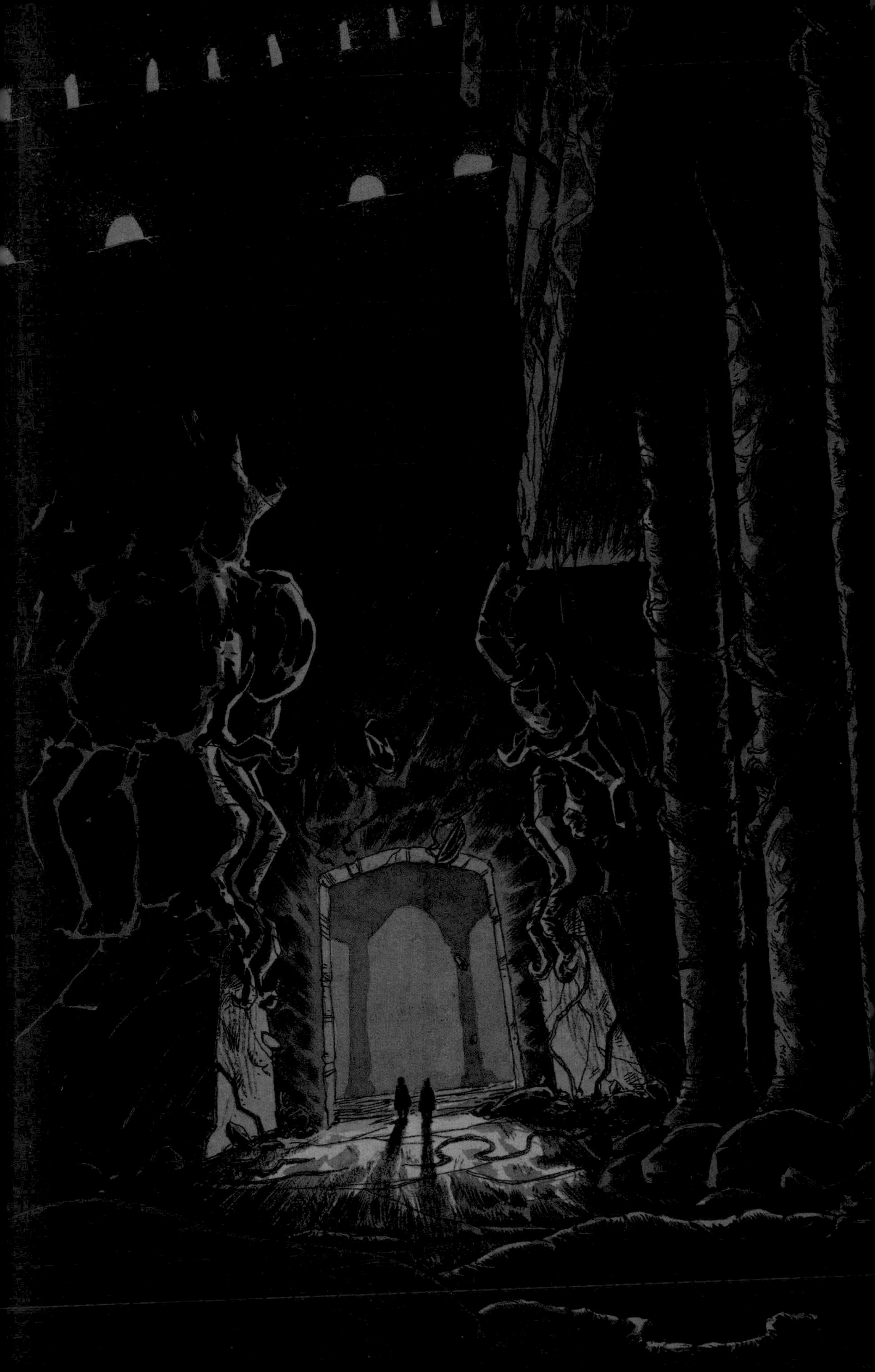

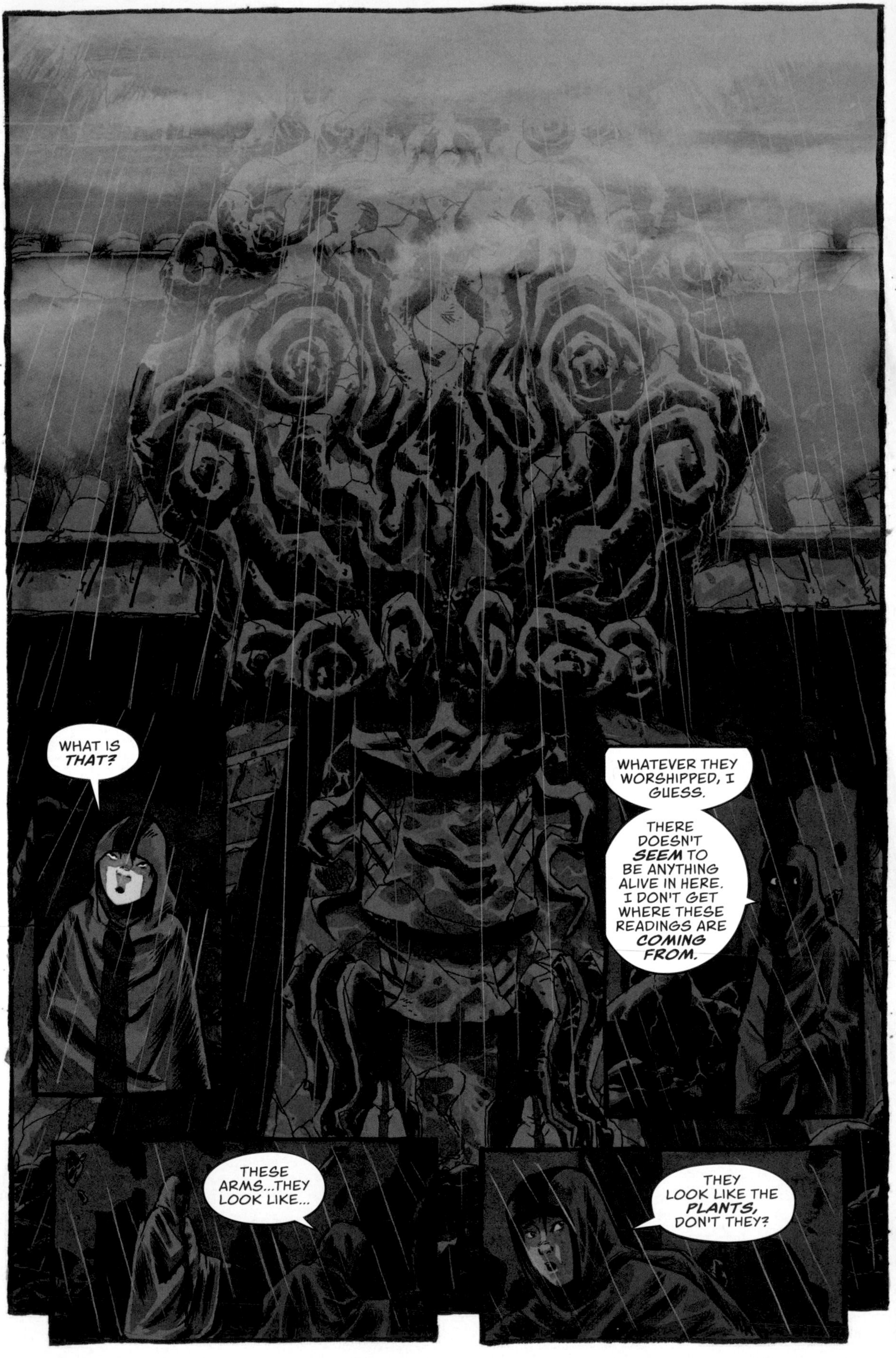
WHAT IS THAT?
WHATEVER THEY WORSHIPPED, I GUESS.
THERE DOESN'T SEEM TO BE ANYTHING ALIVE IN HERE. I DON'T GET WHERE THESE READINGS ARE COMING FROM.
THESE ARMS...THEY LOOK LIKE...
THEY LOOK LIKE THE PLANTS, DON'T THEY?

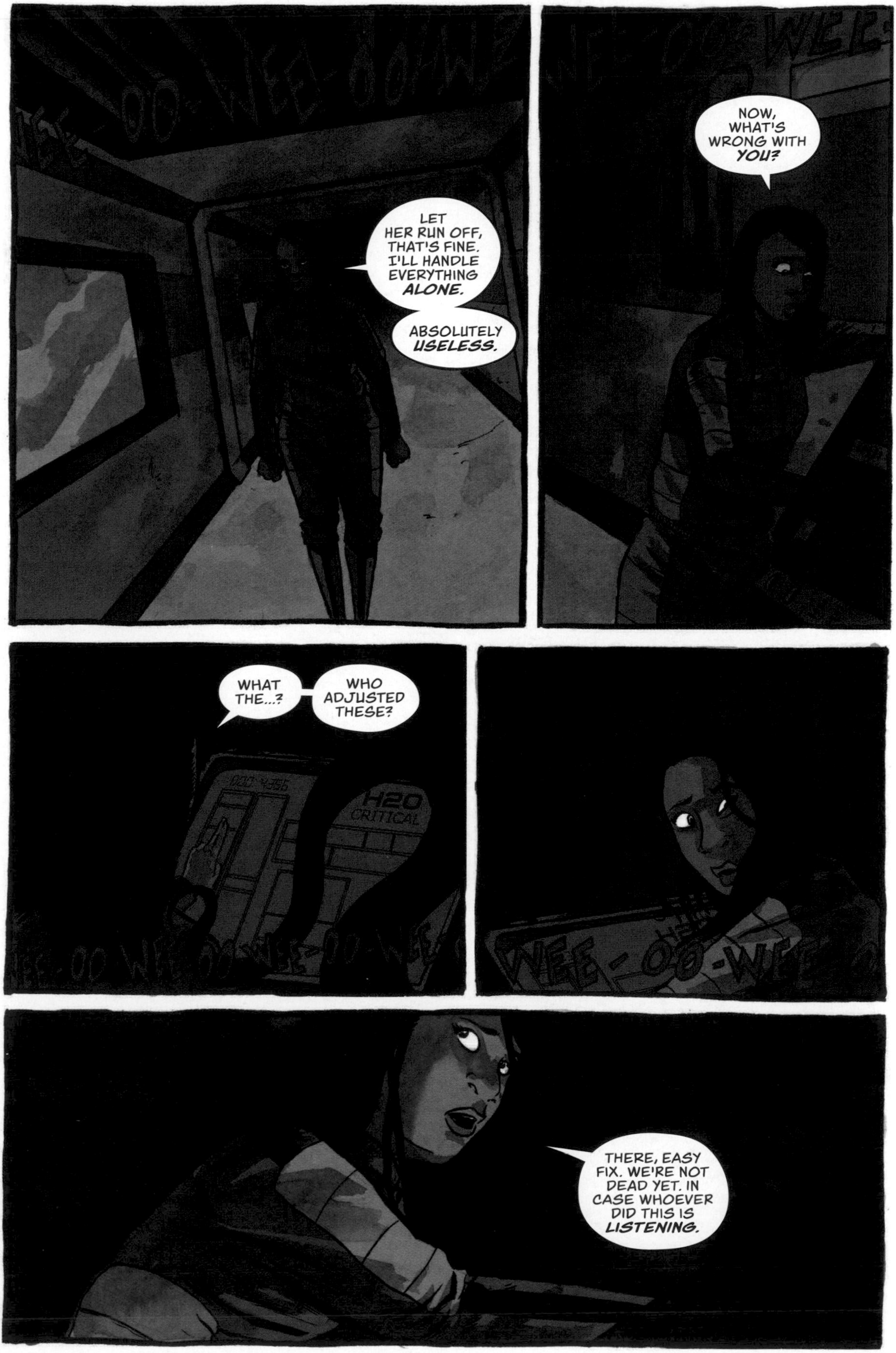

LET HER RUN OFF, THAT'S FINE. I'LL HANDLE EVERYTHING ALONE.
ABSOLUTELY USELESS.
NOW, WHAT'S WRONG WITH YOU?
WHAT THE...?
WHO ADJUSTED THESE?
H2O CRITICAL
THERE, EASY FIX. WE'RE NOT DEAD YET. IN CASE WHOEVER DID THIS IS LISTENING.

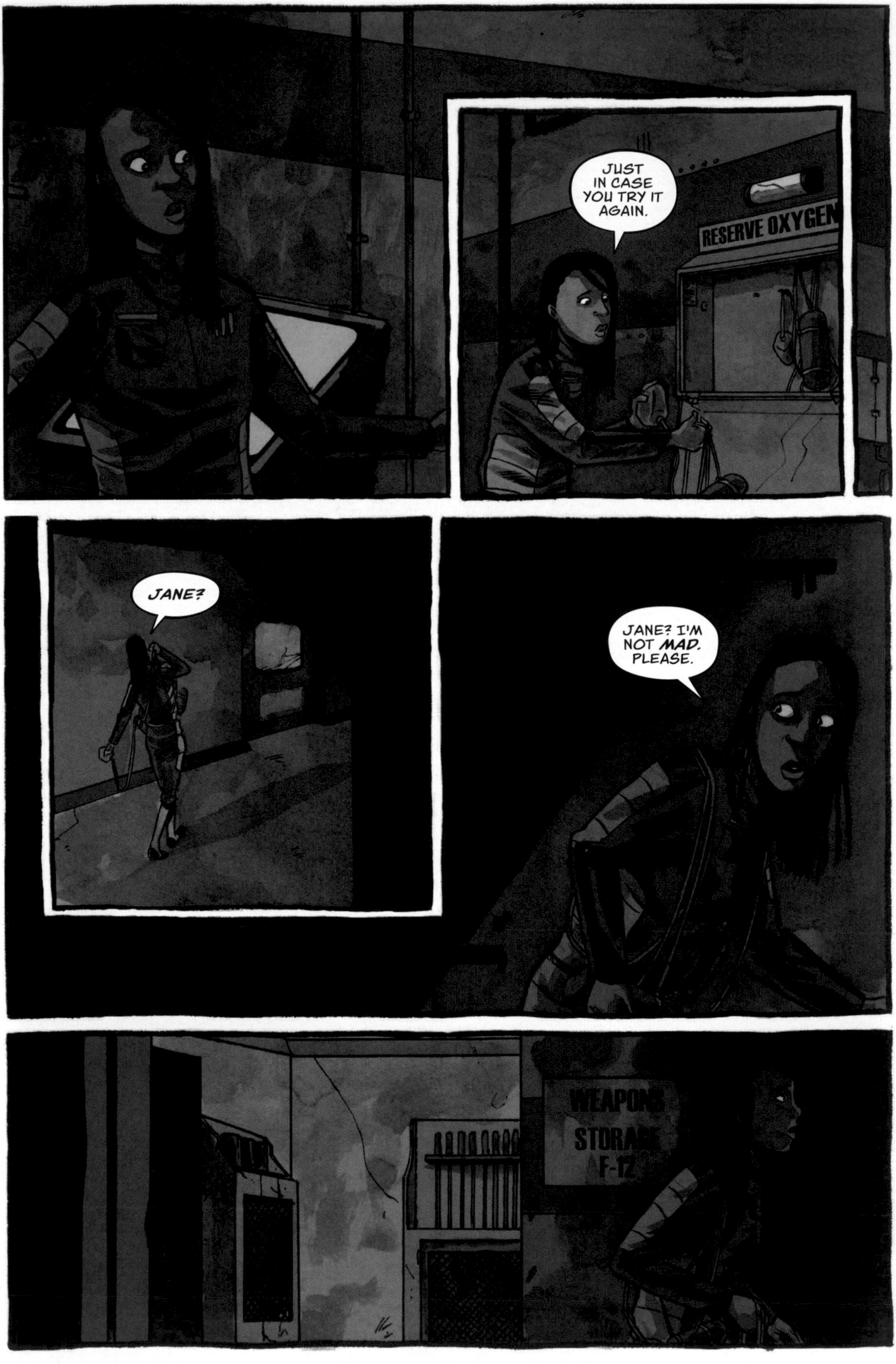
JUST IN CASE YOU TRY IT AGAIN.
RESERVE OXYGEN
JANE?
JANE? I'M NOT MAD. PLEASE.
WEAPONS STORAGE F-12

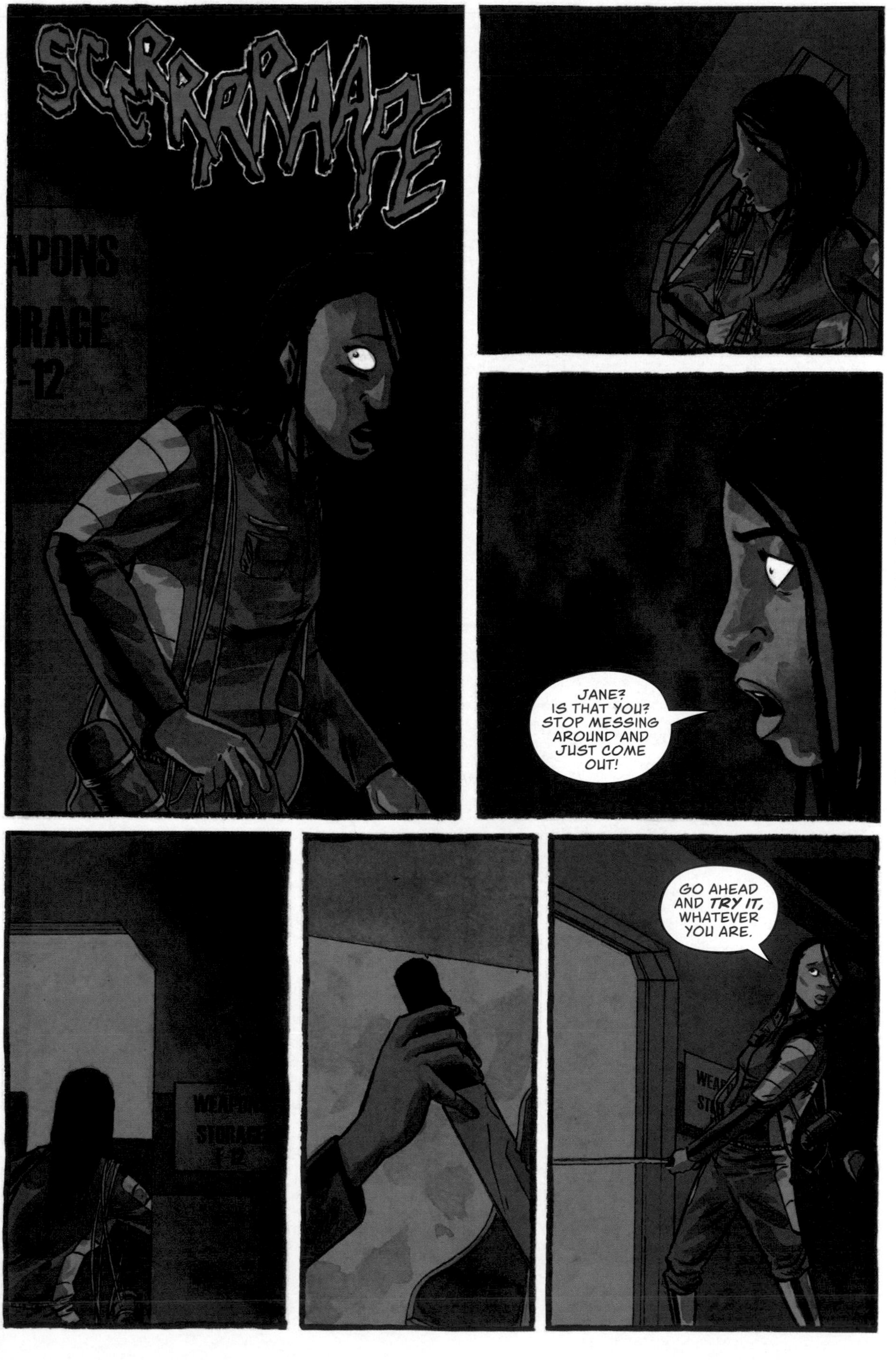
SCCRRRAAPE
JANE? IS THAT YOU? STOP MESSING AROUND AND JUST COME OUT!
GO AHEAD AND *TRY IT,* WHATEVER YOU ARE.

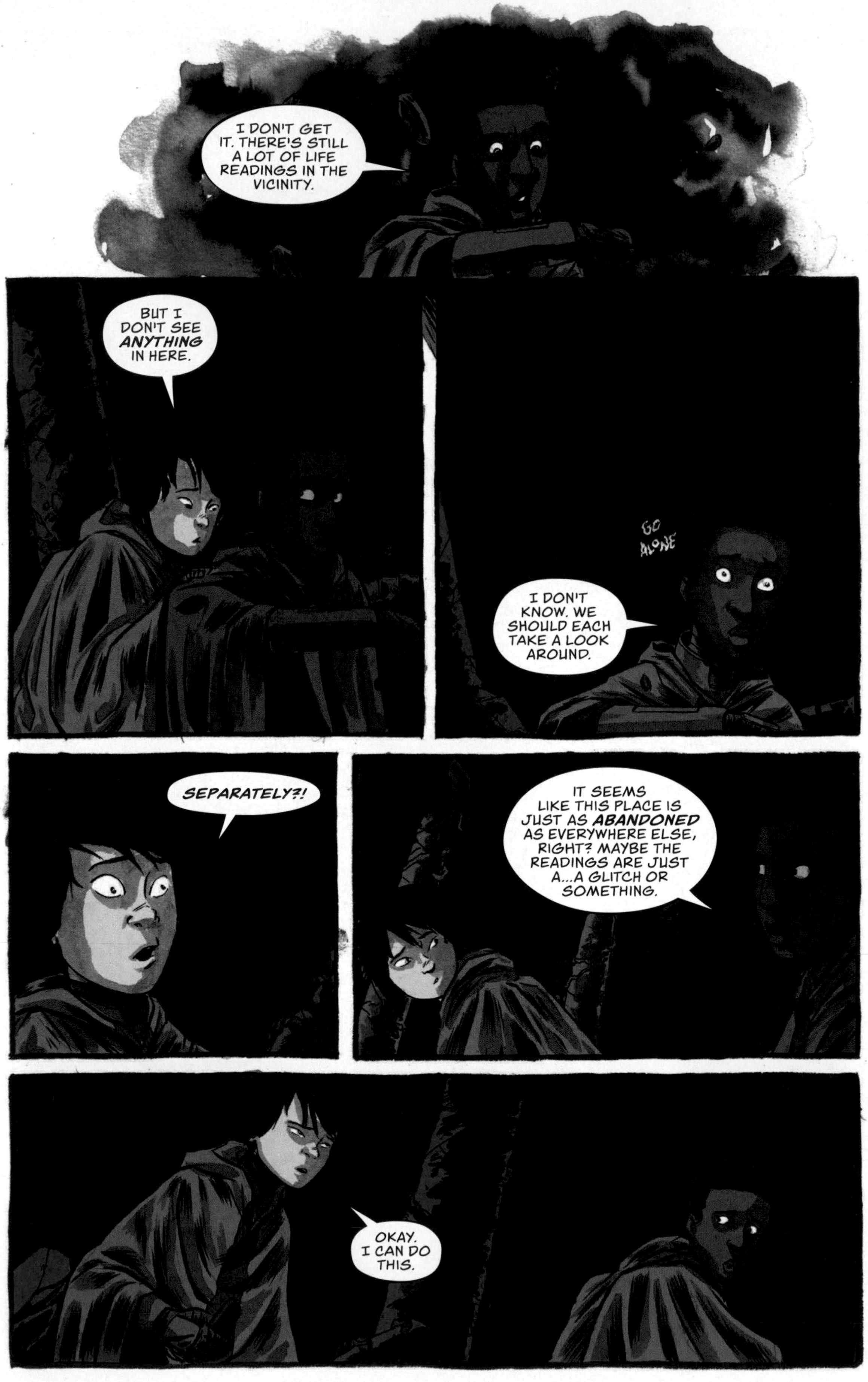
I DON'T GET IT. THERE'S STILL A LOT OF LIFE READINGS IN THE VICINITY.
BUT I DON'T SEE *ANYTHING* IN HERE.
GO ALONE
I DON'T KNOW. WE SHOULD EACH TAKE A LOOK AROUND.
SEPARATELY?!
IT SEEMS LIKE THIS PLACE IS JUST AS *ABANDONED* AS EVERYWHERE ELSE, RIGHT? MAYBE THE READINGS ARE JUST A...A GLITCH OR SOMETHING.
OKAY. I CAN DO THIS.

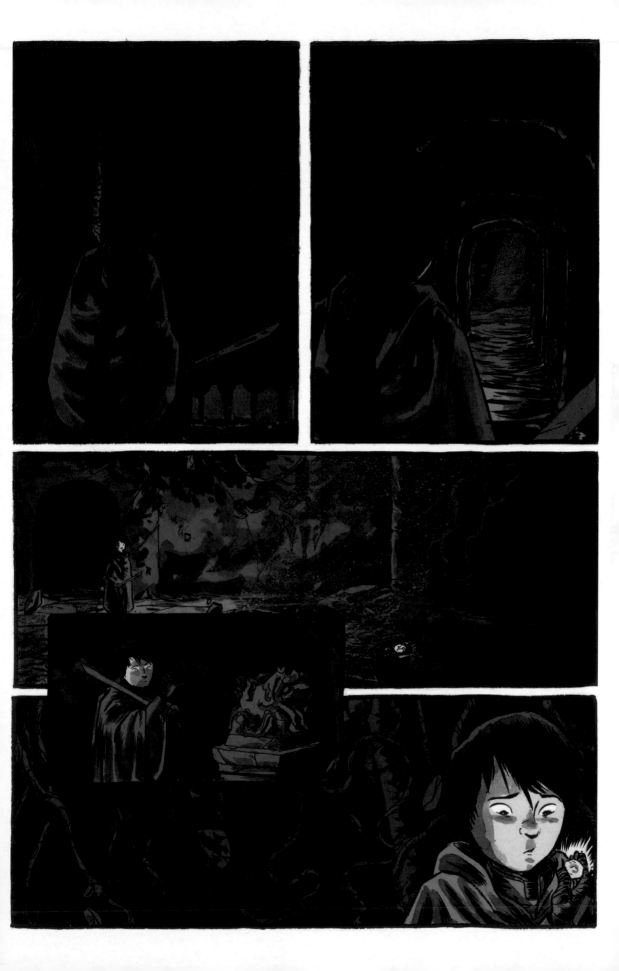

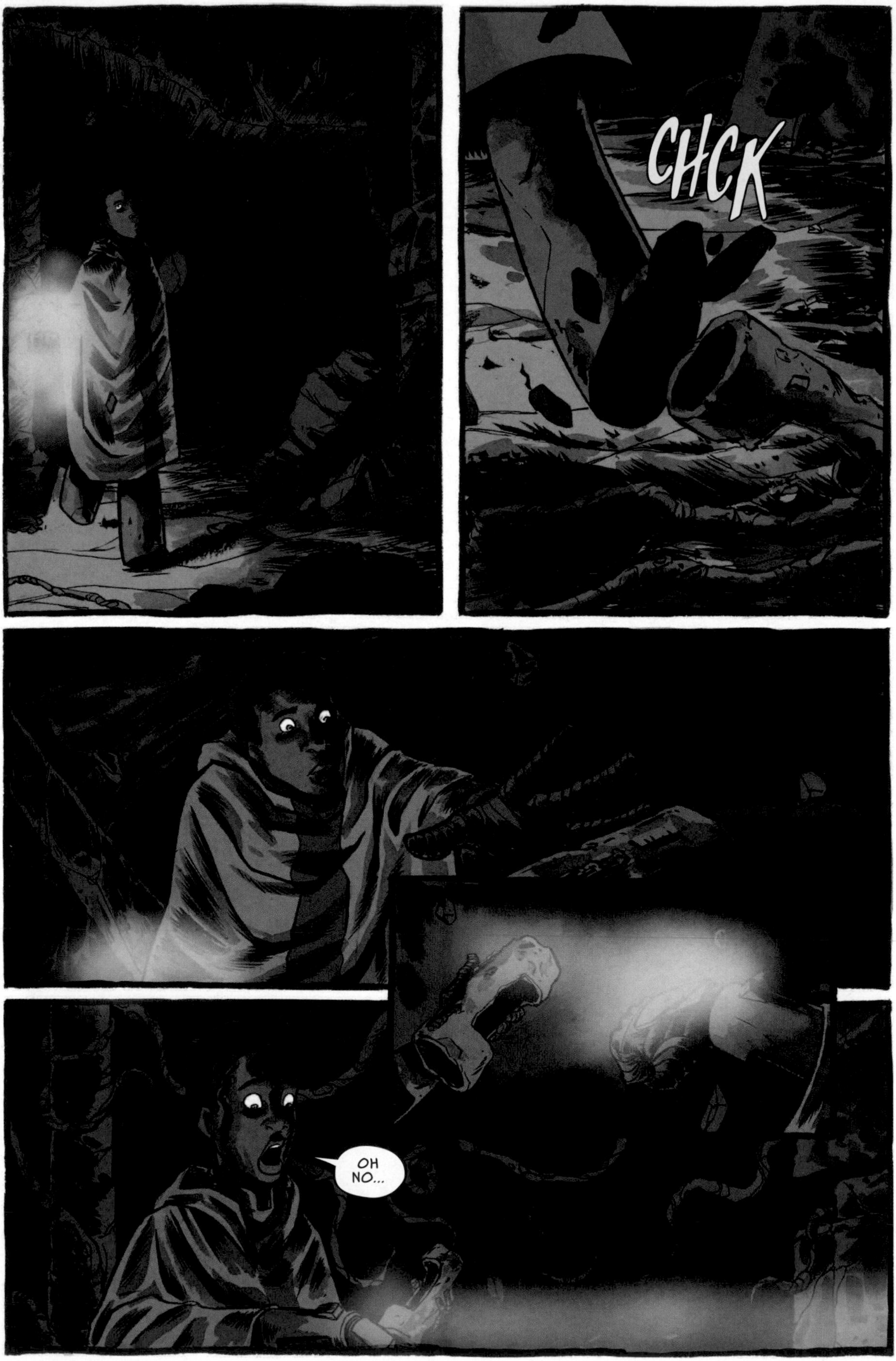
CHCK
OH NO...

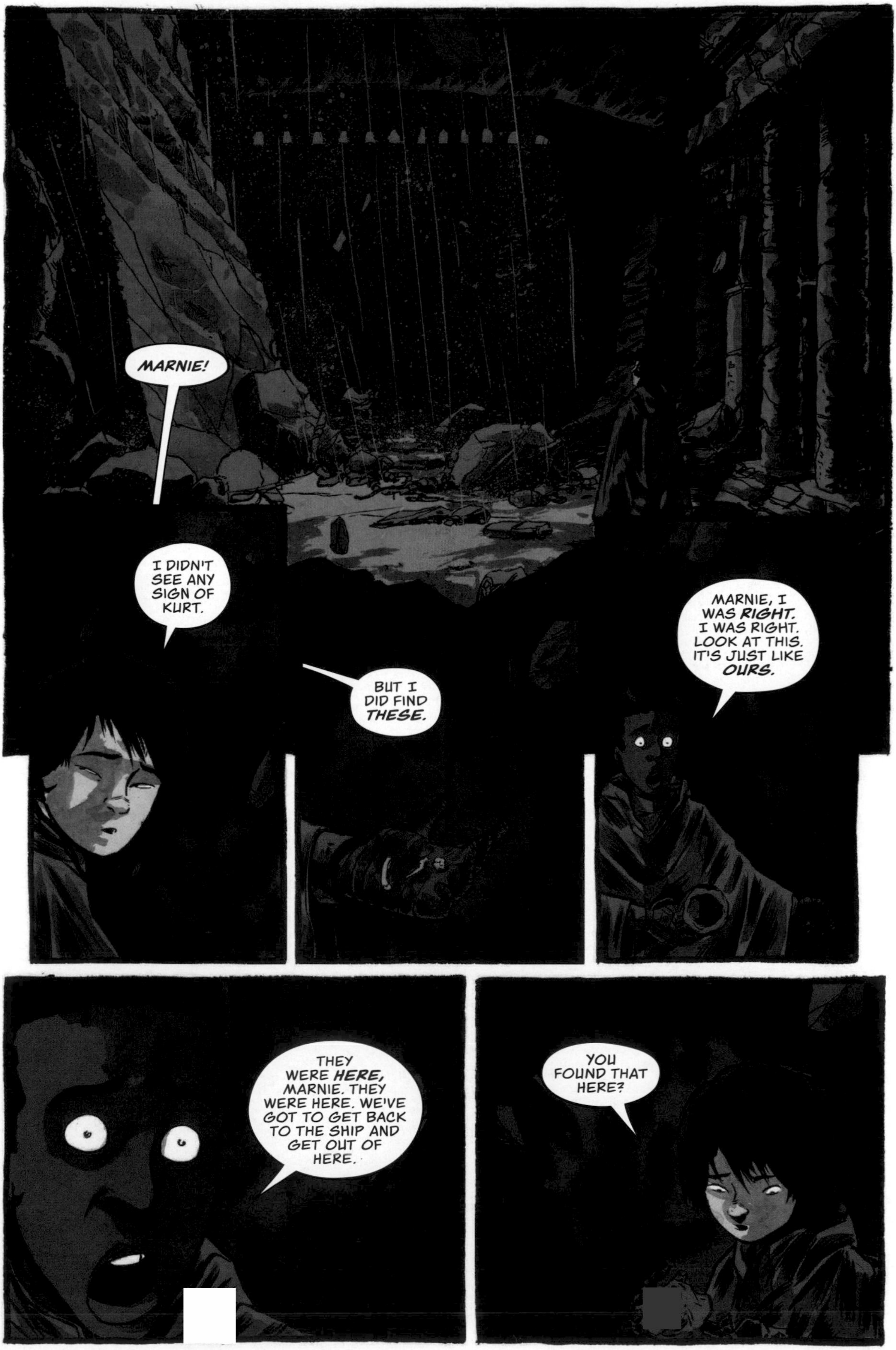
MARNIE!
I DIDN'T SEE ANY SIGN OF KURT.
BUT I DID FIND THESE.
MARNIE, I WAS RIGHT. I WAS RIGHT. LOOK AT THIS. IT'S JUST LIKE OURS.
THEY WERE HERE, MARNIE. THEY WERE HERE. WE'VE GOT TO GET BACK TO THE SHIP AND GET OUT OF HERE.
YOU FOUND THAT HERE?

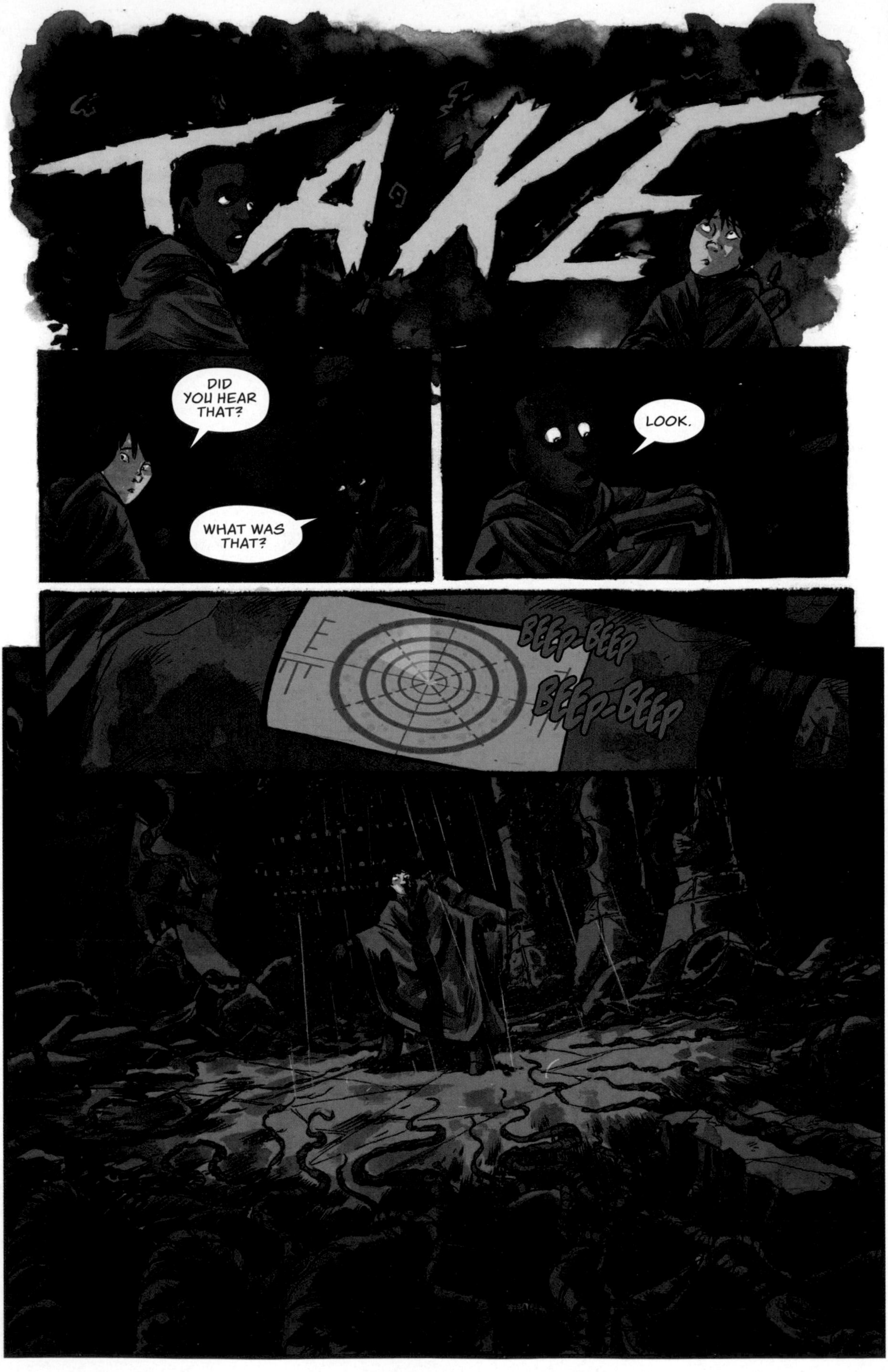
TAKE
DID YOU HEAR THAT?
WHAT WAS THAT?
LOOK.
BEEP-BEEP
BEEP-BEEP

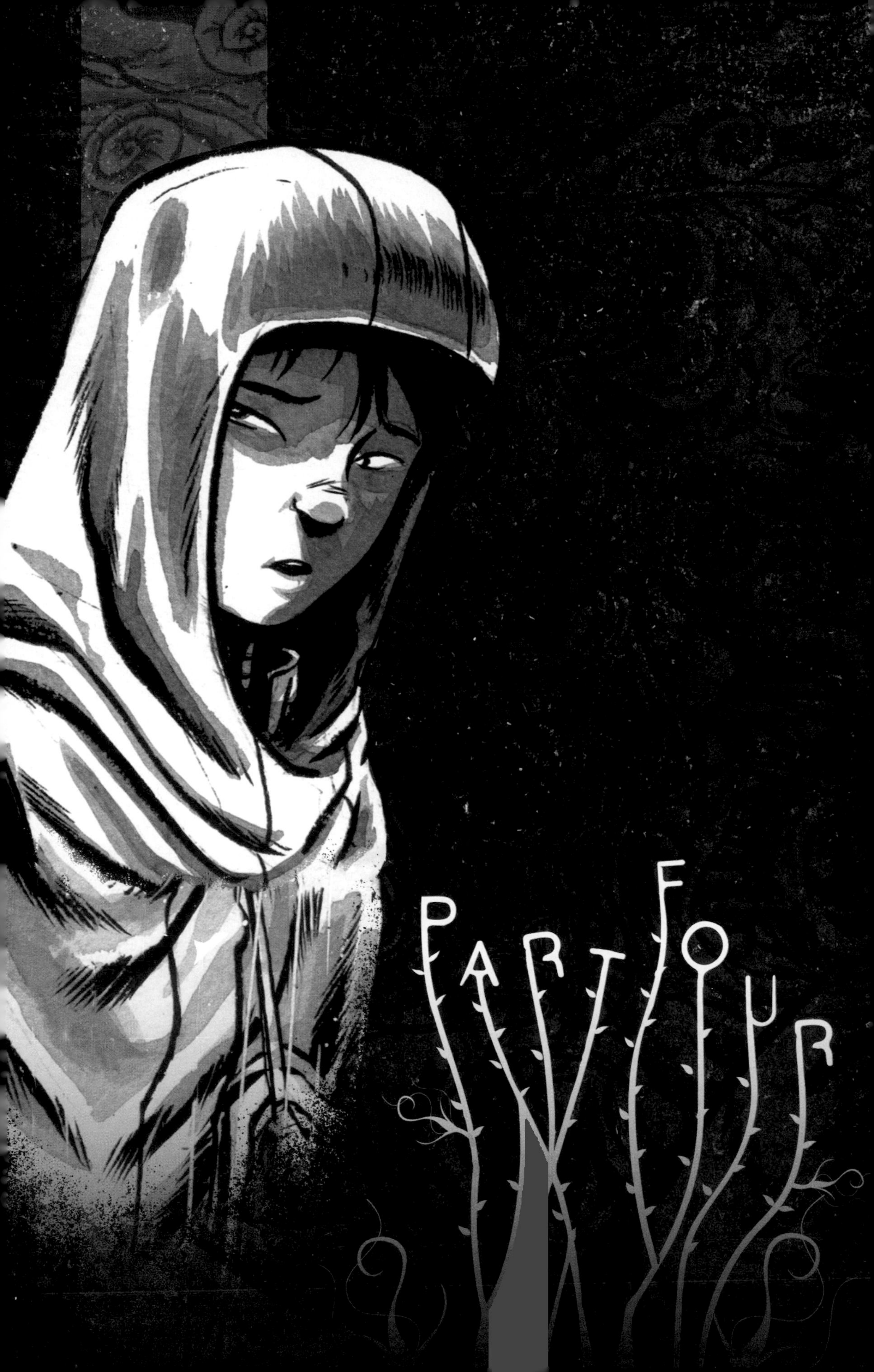
PART FOUR

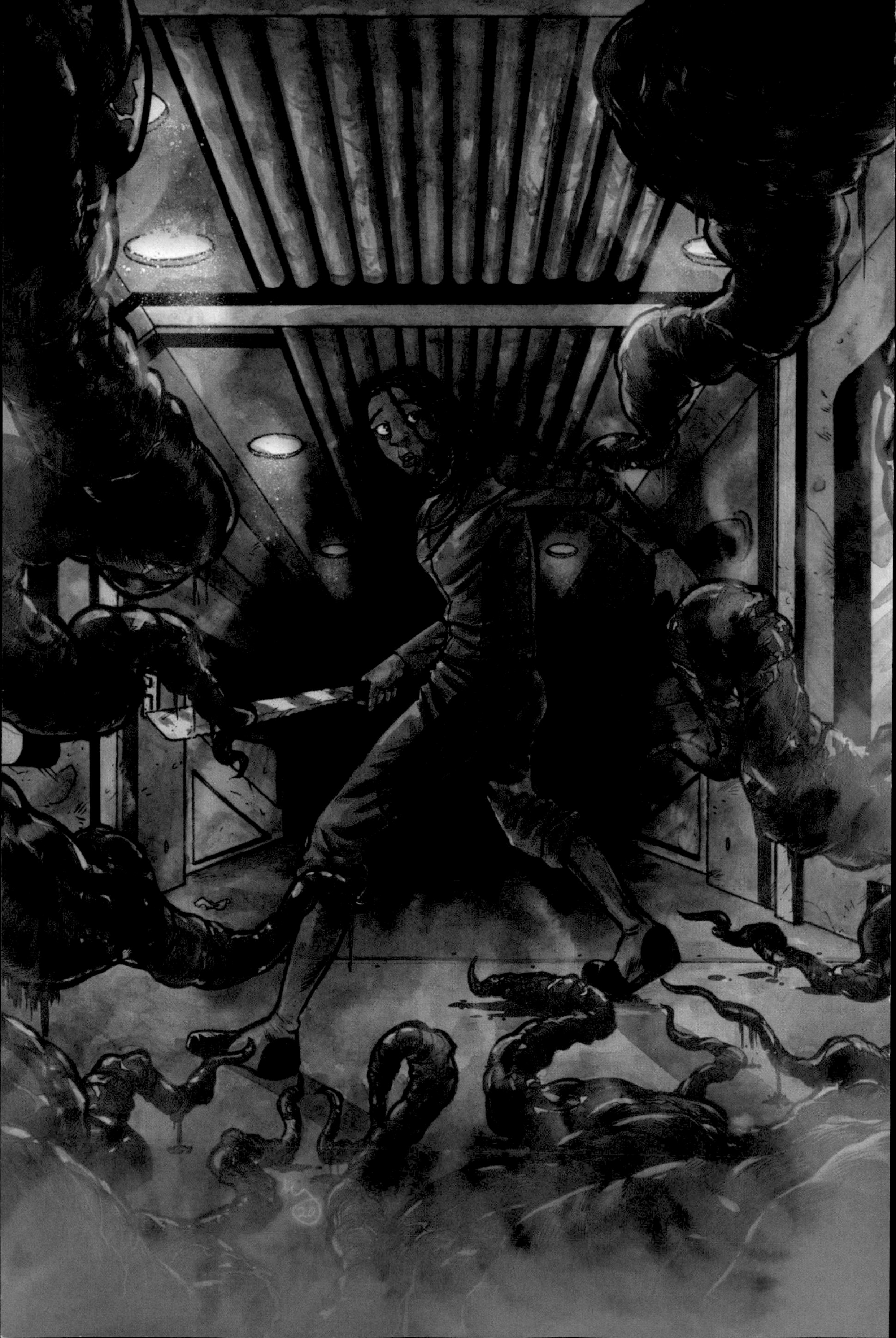

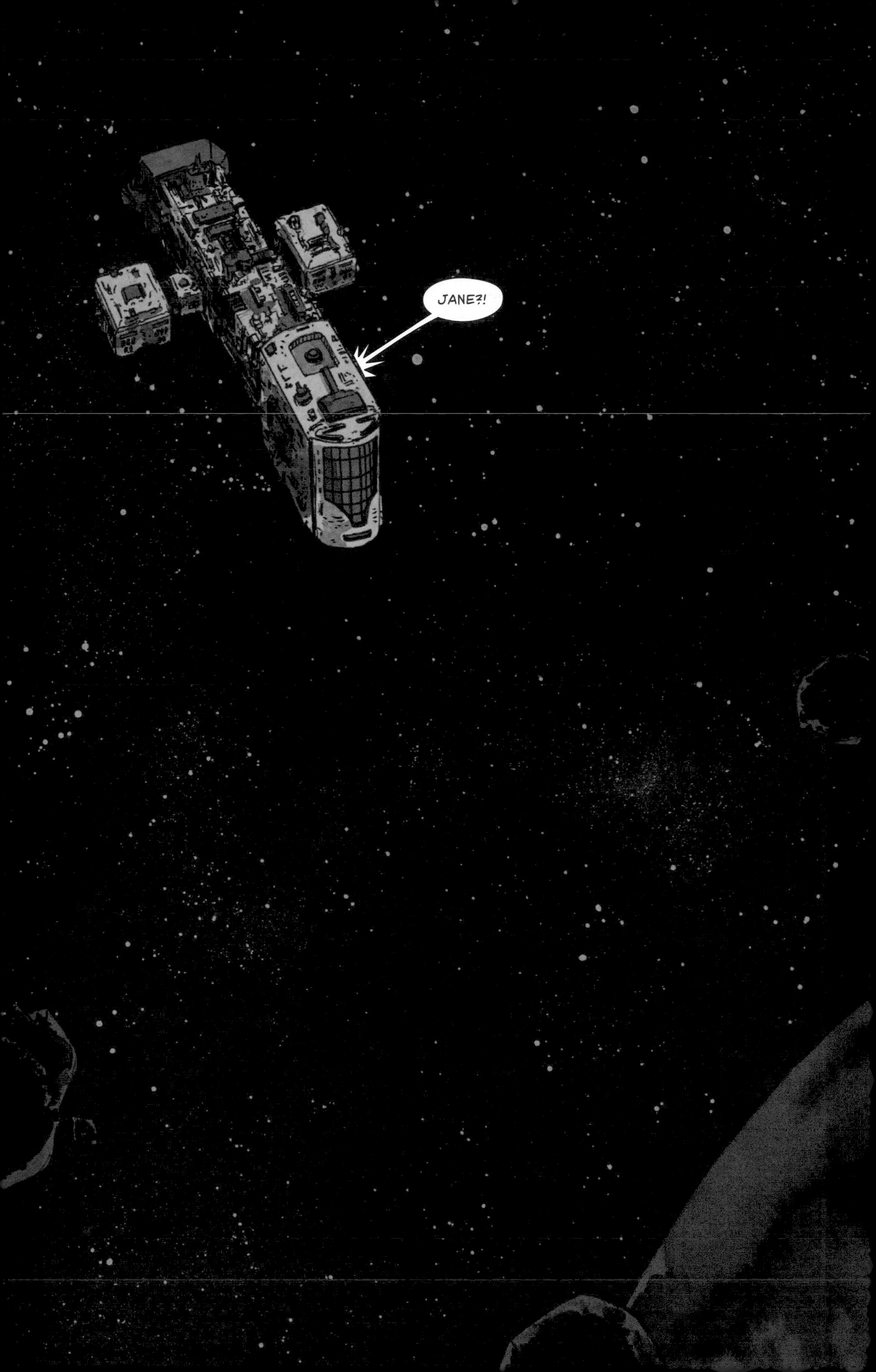
JANE?!

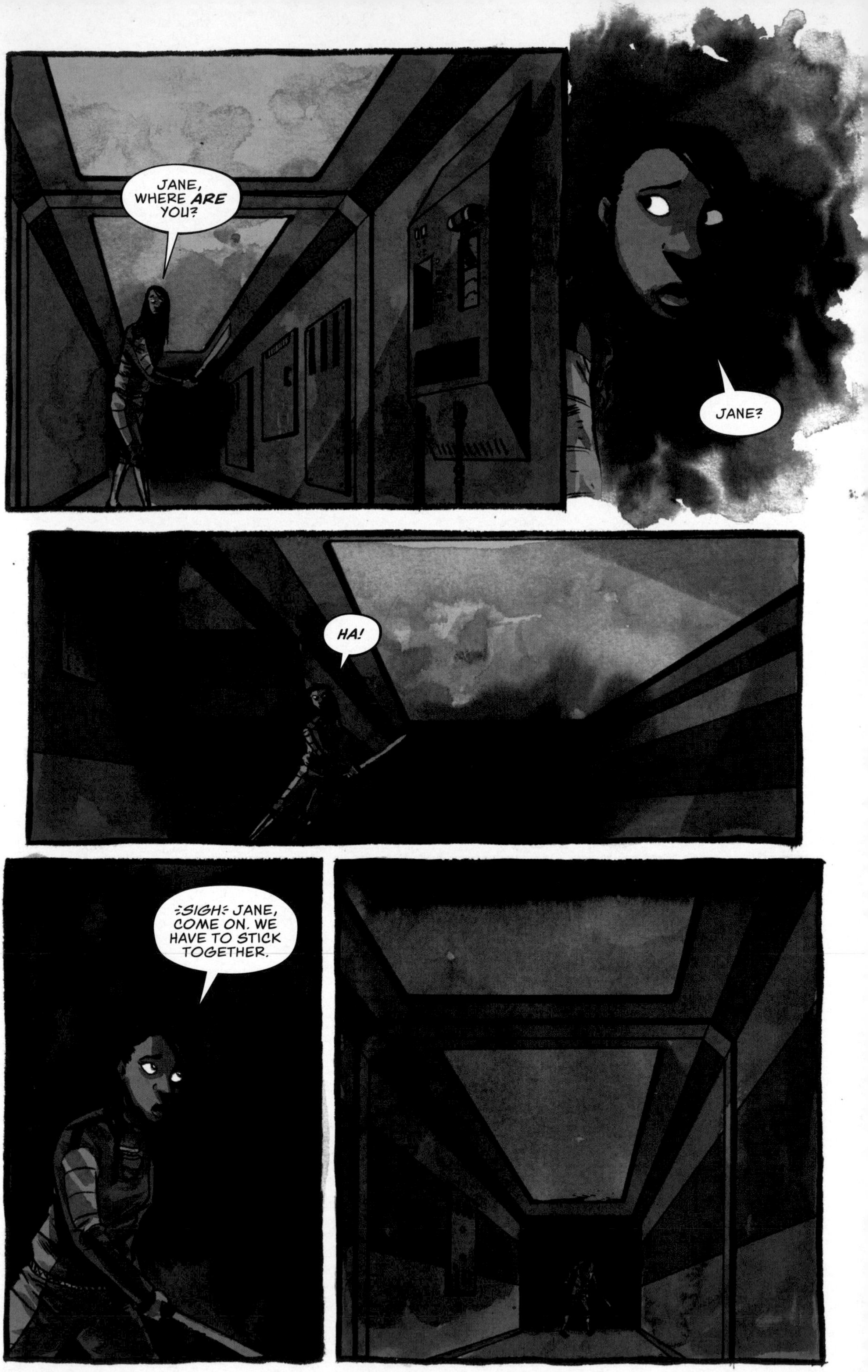
JANE, WHERE ARE YOU?
JANE?
HA!
=SIGH= JANE, COME ON. WE HAVE TO STICK TOGETHER.

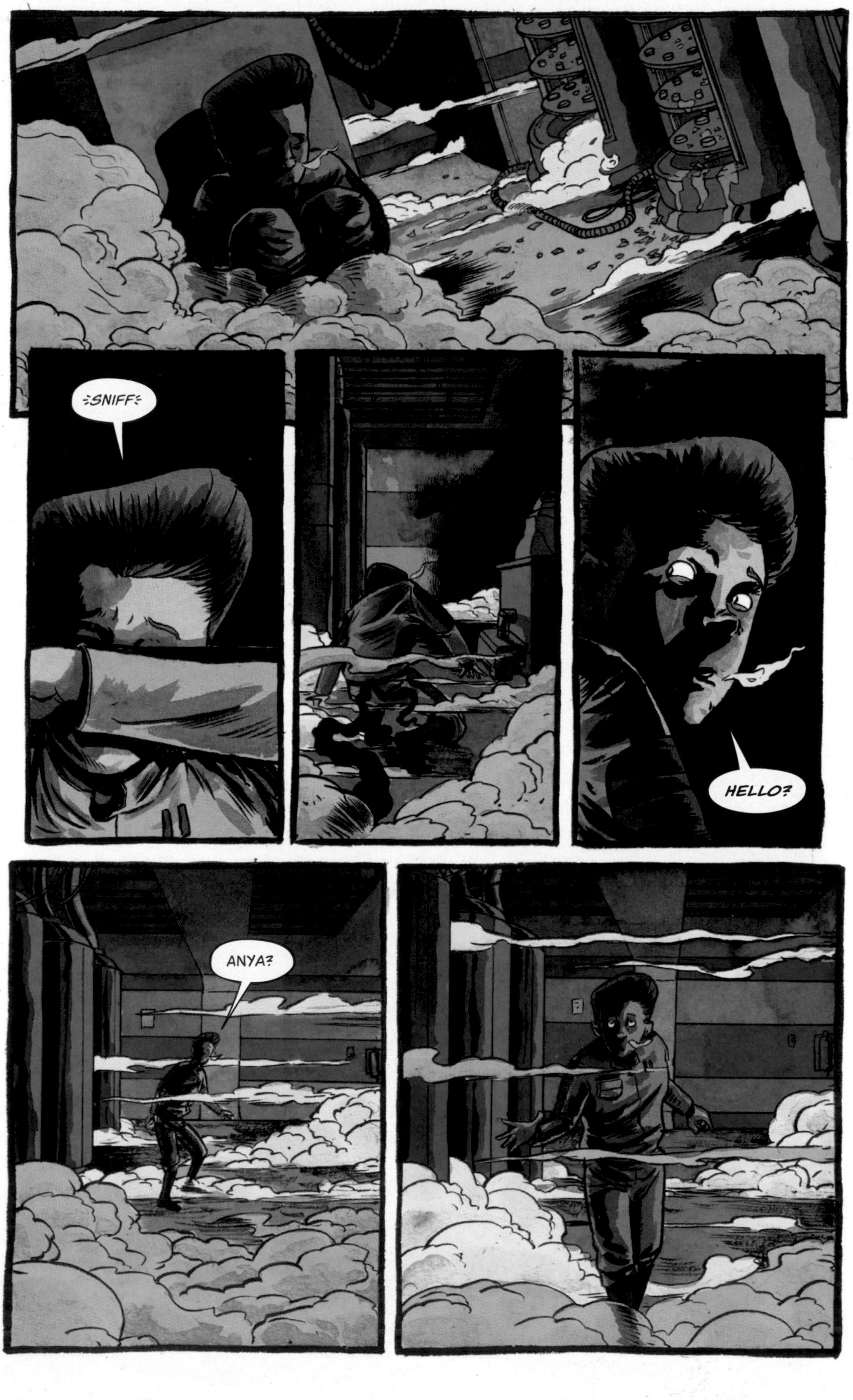
SNIFF
HELLO?
ANYA?

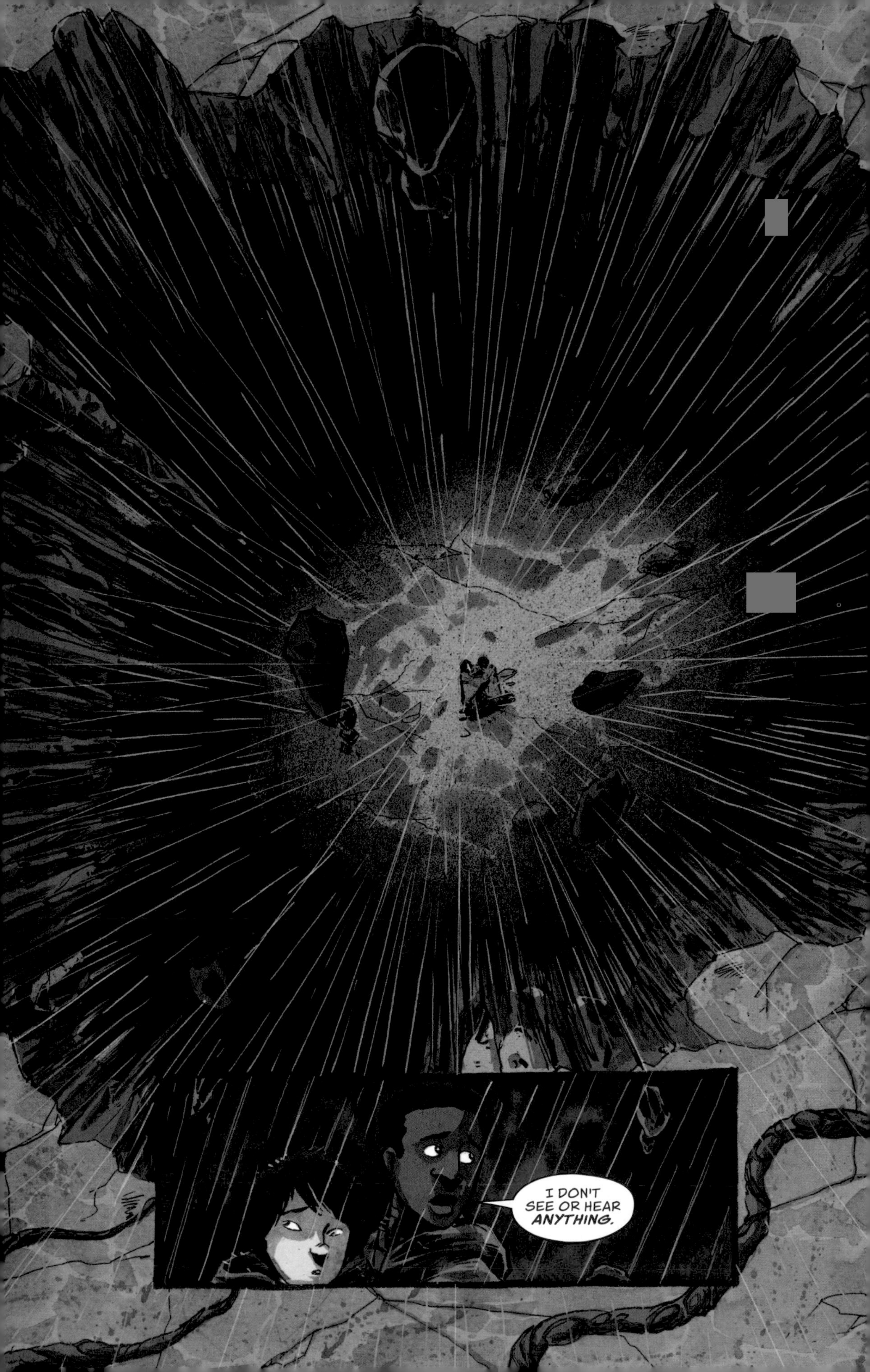
I DON'T SEE OR HEAR *ANYTHING.*

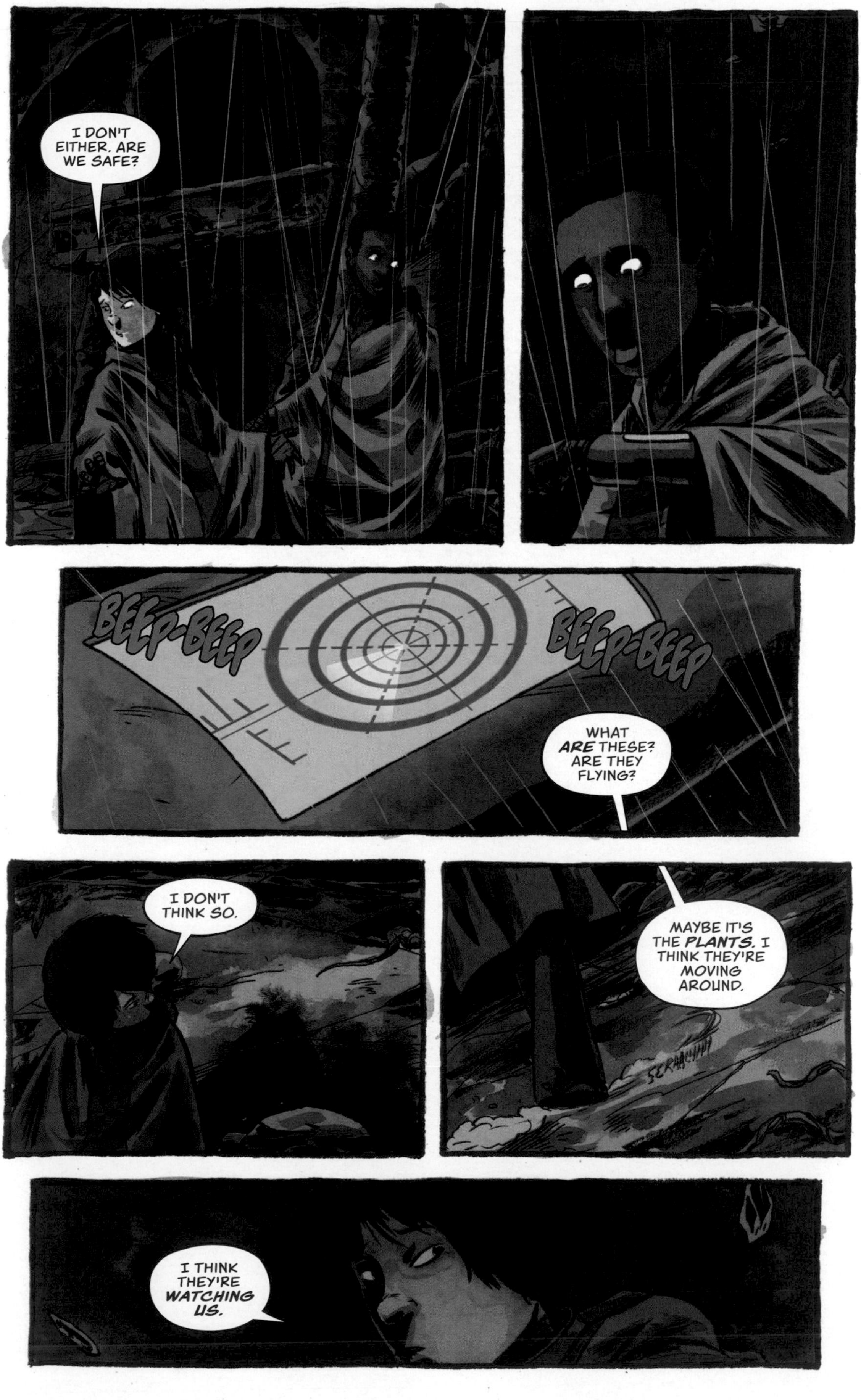
I DON'T EITHER. ARE WE SAFE?
BEEP-BEEP
BEEP-BEEP
WHAT **ARE** THESE? ARE THEY FLYING?
I DON'T THINK SO.
MAYBE IT'S THE **PLANTS.** I THINK THEY'RE MOVING AROUND.
I THINK THEY'RE **WATCHING US.**

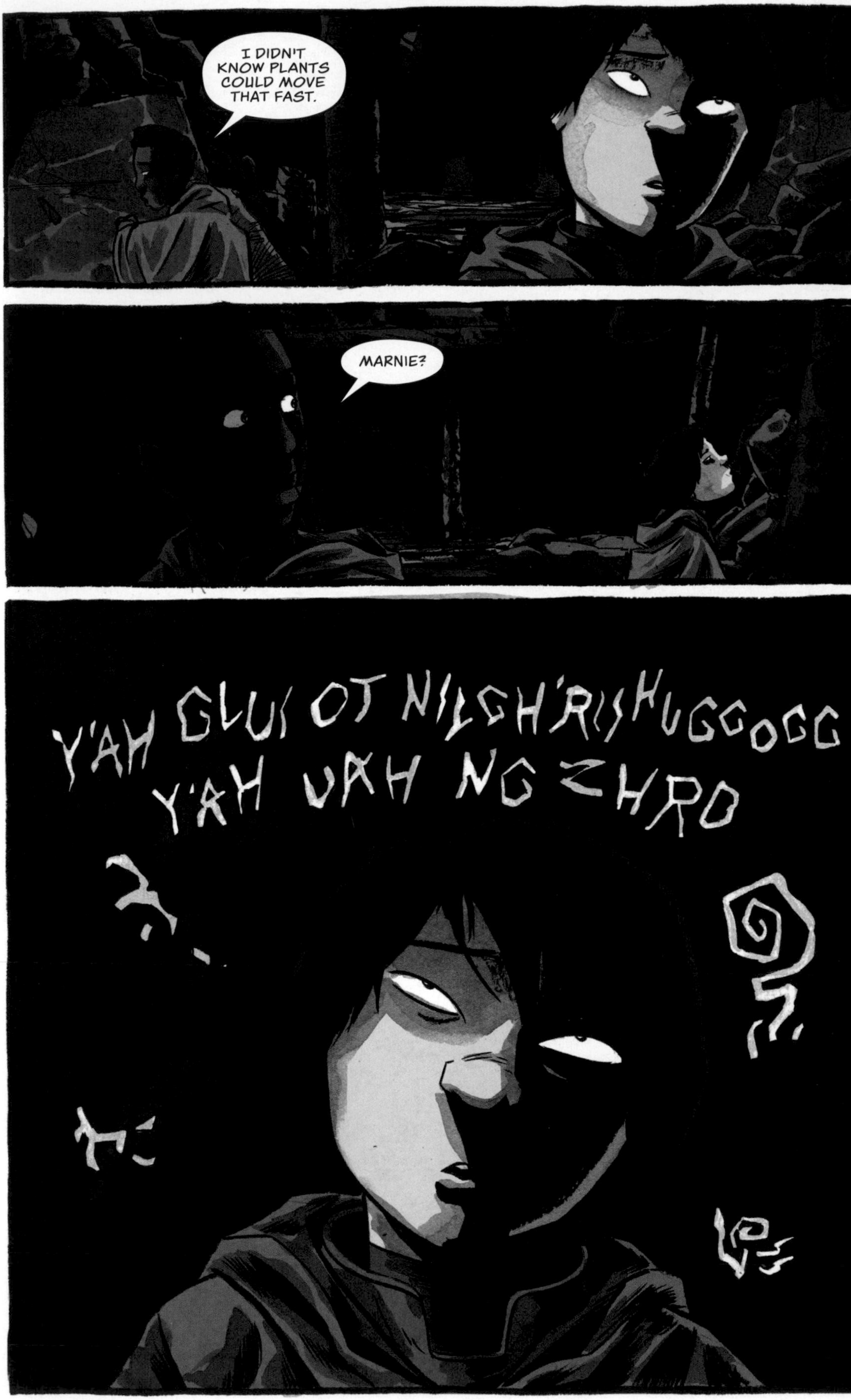
I DIDN'T KNOW PLANTS COULD MOVE THAT FAST.
MARNIE?
Y'AH GLUI OT NILGH'RISHUGGOGG
Y'AH UAH NG ZHRO

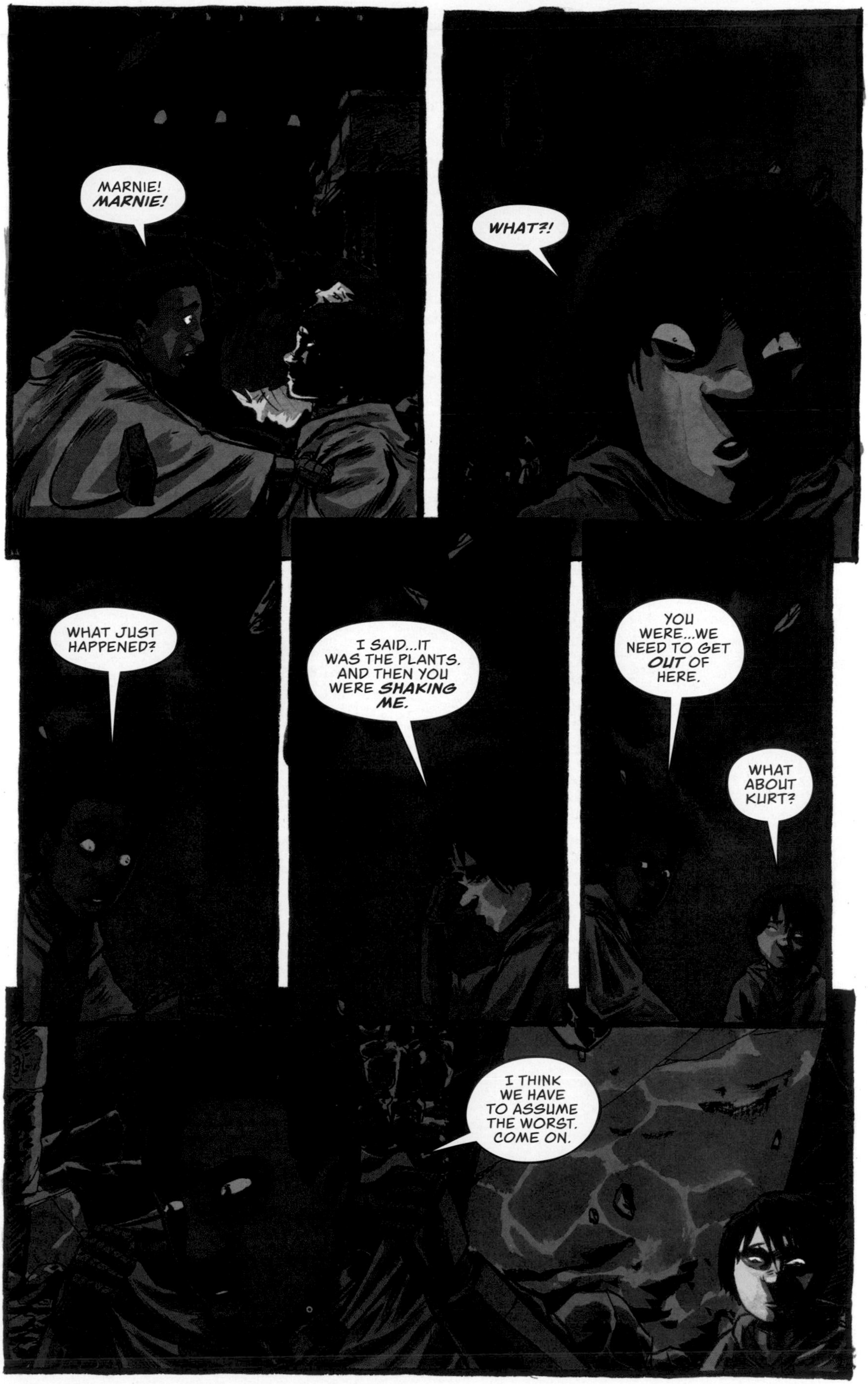
MARNIE! MARNIE!
WHAT?!
WHAT JUST HAPPENED?
I SAID...IT WAS THE PLANTS. AND THEN YOU WERE SHAKING ME.
YOU WERE...WE NEED TO GET OUT OF HERE.
WHAT ABOUT KURT?
I THINK WE HAVE TO ASSUME THE WORST. COME ON.

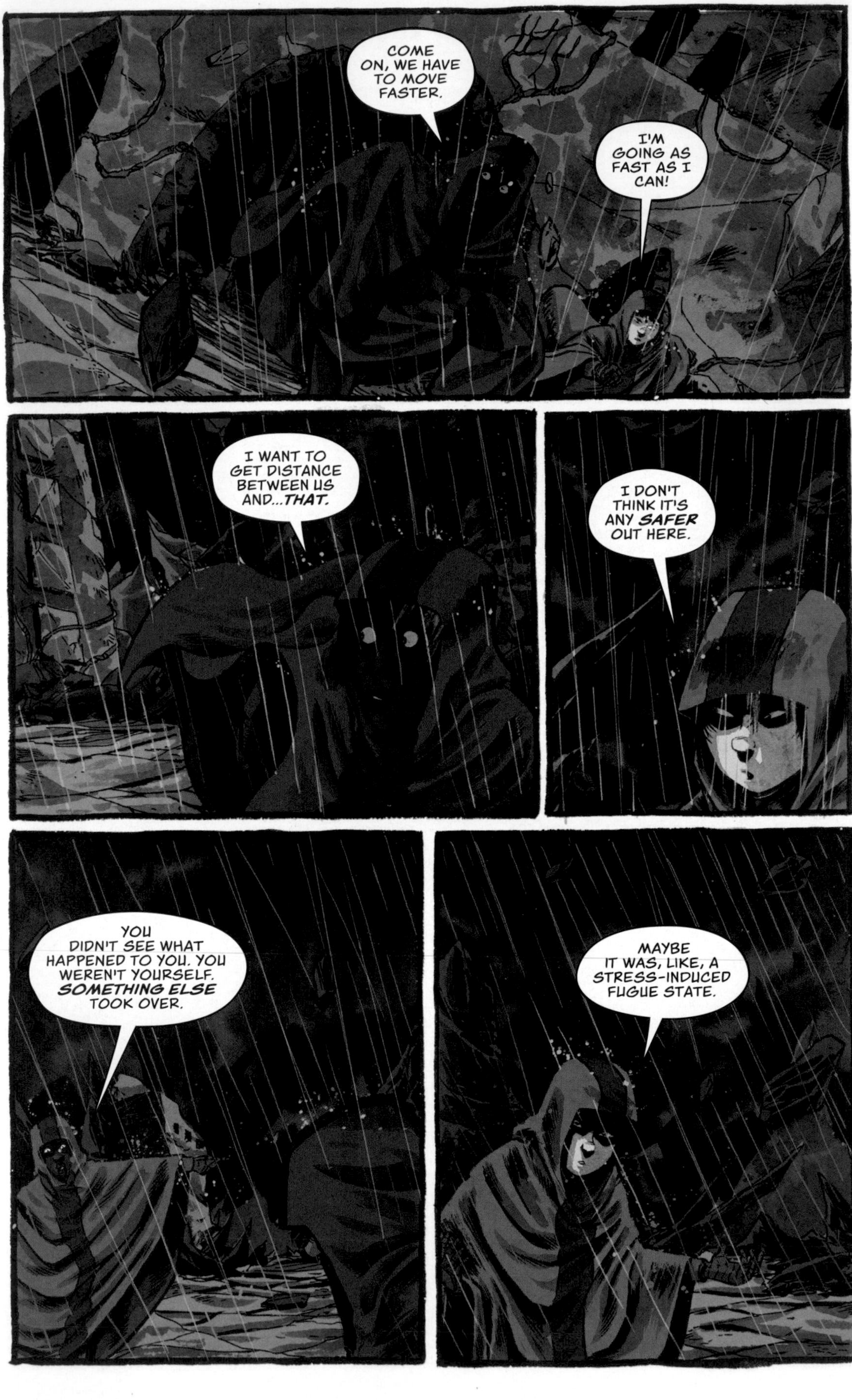
COME ON, WE HAVE TO MOVE FASTER.
I'M GOING AS FAST AS I CAN!
I WANT TO GET DISTANCE BETWEEN US AND...THAT.
I DON'T THINK IT'S ANY SAFER OUT HERE.
YOU DIDN'T SEE WHAT HAPPENED TO YOU. YOU WEREN'T YOURSELF. SOMETHING ELSE TOOK OVER.
MAYBE IT WAS, LIKE, A STRESS-INDUCED FUGUE STATE.

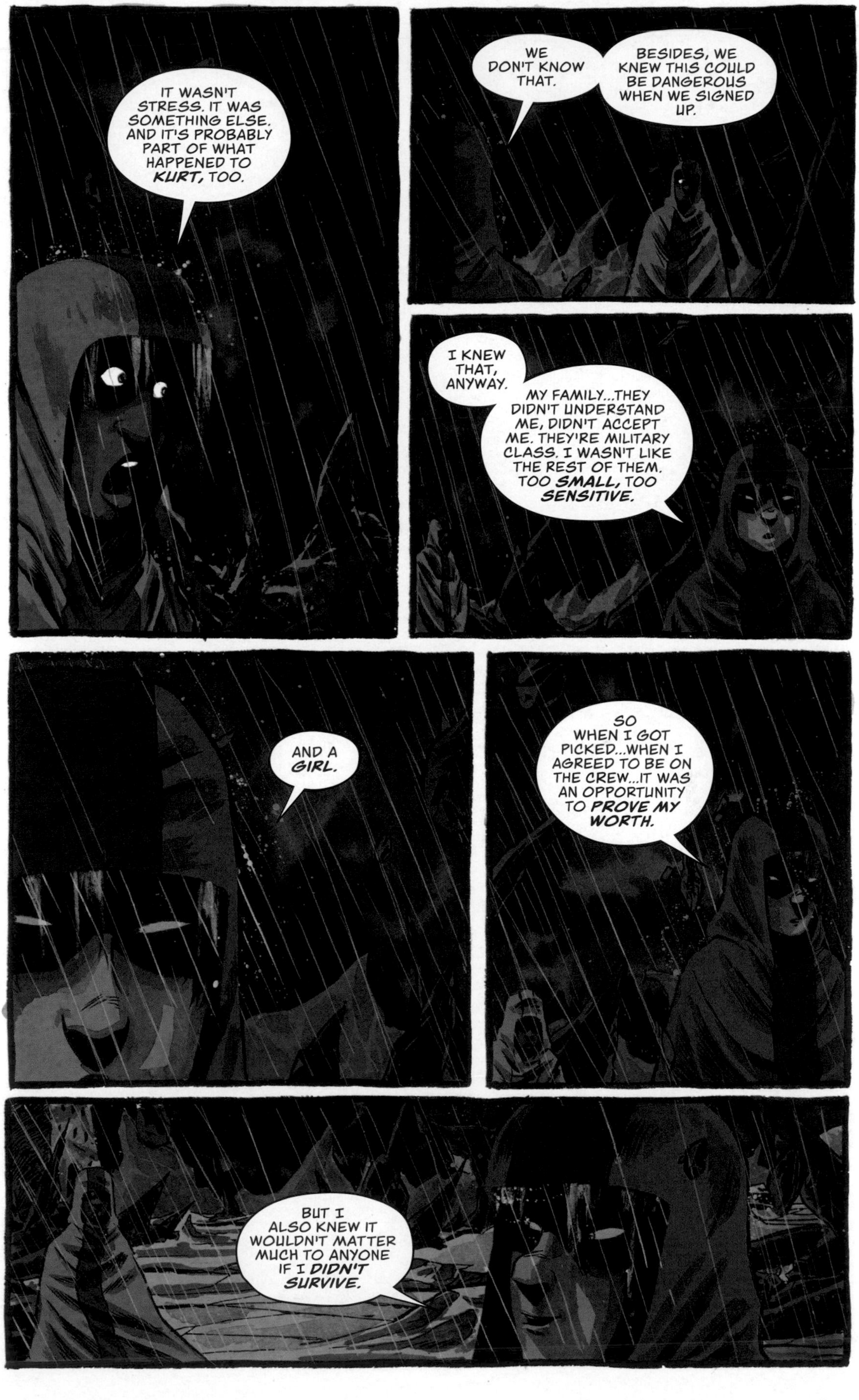
IT WASN'T STRESS. IT WAS SOMETHING ELSE. AND IT'S PROBABLY PART OF WHAT HAPPENED TO *KURT,* TOO.
WE DON'T KNOW THAT.
BESIDES, WE KNEW THIS COULD BE DANGEROUS WHEN WE SIGNED UP.
I KNEW THAT, ANYWAY.
MY FAMILY...THEY DIDN'T UNDERSTAND ME, DIDN'T ACCEPT ME. THEY'RE MILITARY CLASS. I WASN'T LIKE THE REST OF THEM. TOO *SMALL,* TOO *SENSITIVE.*
AND A *GIRL.*
SO WHEN I GOT PICKED...WHEN I AGREED TO BE ON THE CREW...IT WAS AN OPPORTUNITY TO *PROVE MY WORTH.*
BUT I ALSO KNEW IT WOULDN'T MATTER MUCH TO ANYONE IF I *DIDN'T SURVIVE.*

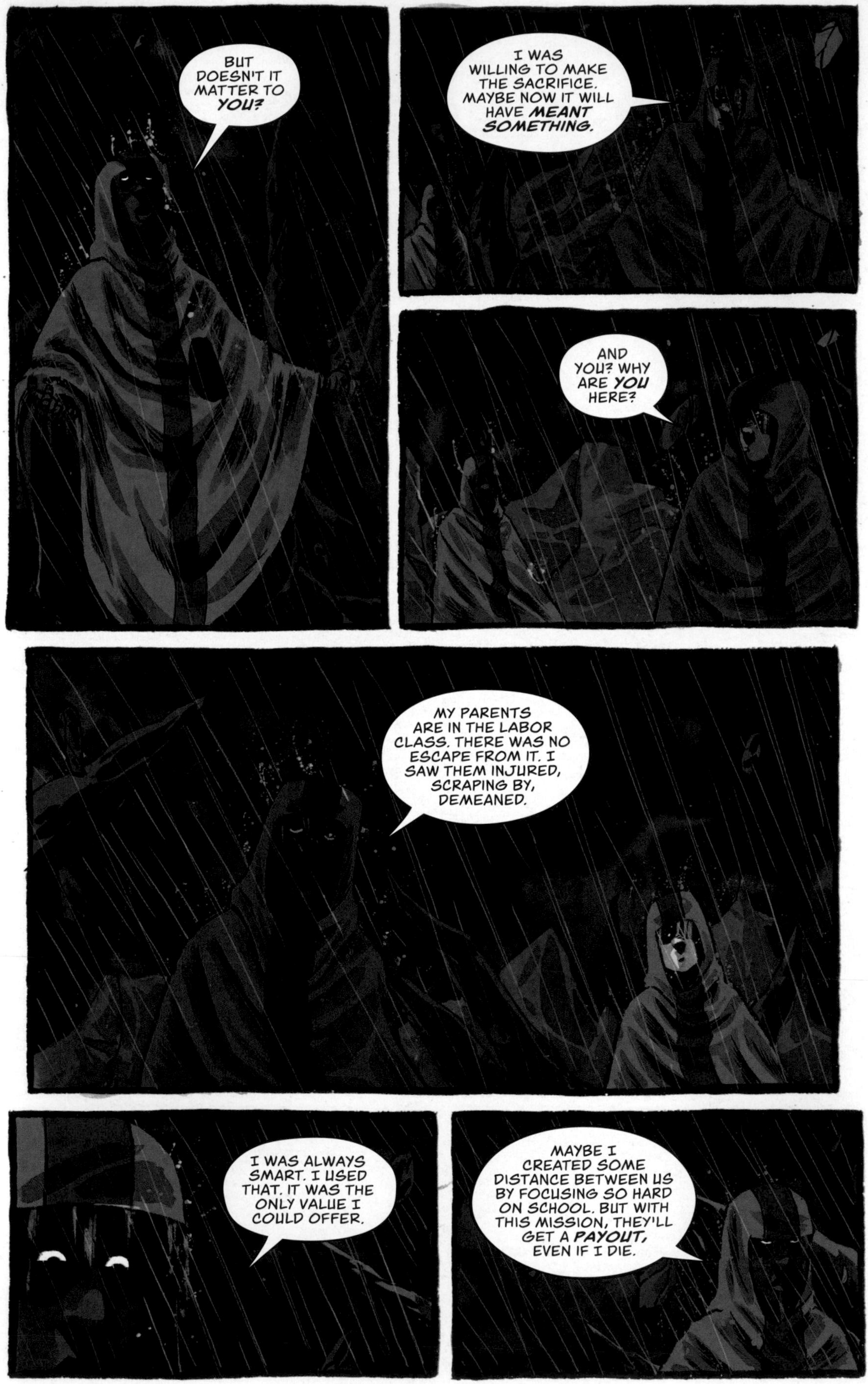
BUT DOESN'T IT MATTER TO *YOU?*
I WAS WILLING TO MAKE THE SACRIFICE. MAYBE NOW IT WILL HAVE *MEANT SOMETHING.*
AND YOU? WHY ARE *YOU* HERE?
MY PARENTS ARE IN THE LABOR CLASS. THERE WAS NO ESCAPE FROM IT. I SAW THEM INJURED, SCRAPING BY, DEMEANED.
I WAS ALWAYS SMART. I USED THAT. IT WAS THE ONLY VALUE I COULD OFFER.
MAYBE I CREATED SOME DISTANCE BETWEEN US BY FOCUSING SO HARD ON SCHOOL. BUT WITH THIS MISSION, THEY'LL GET A *PAYOUT,* EVEN IF I DIE.

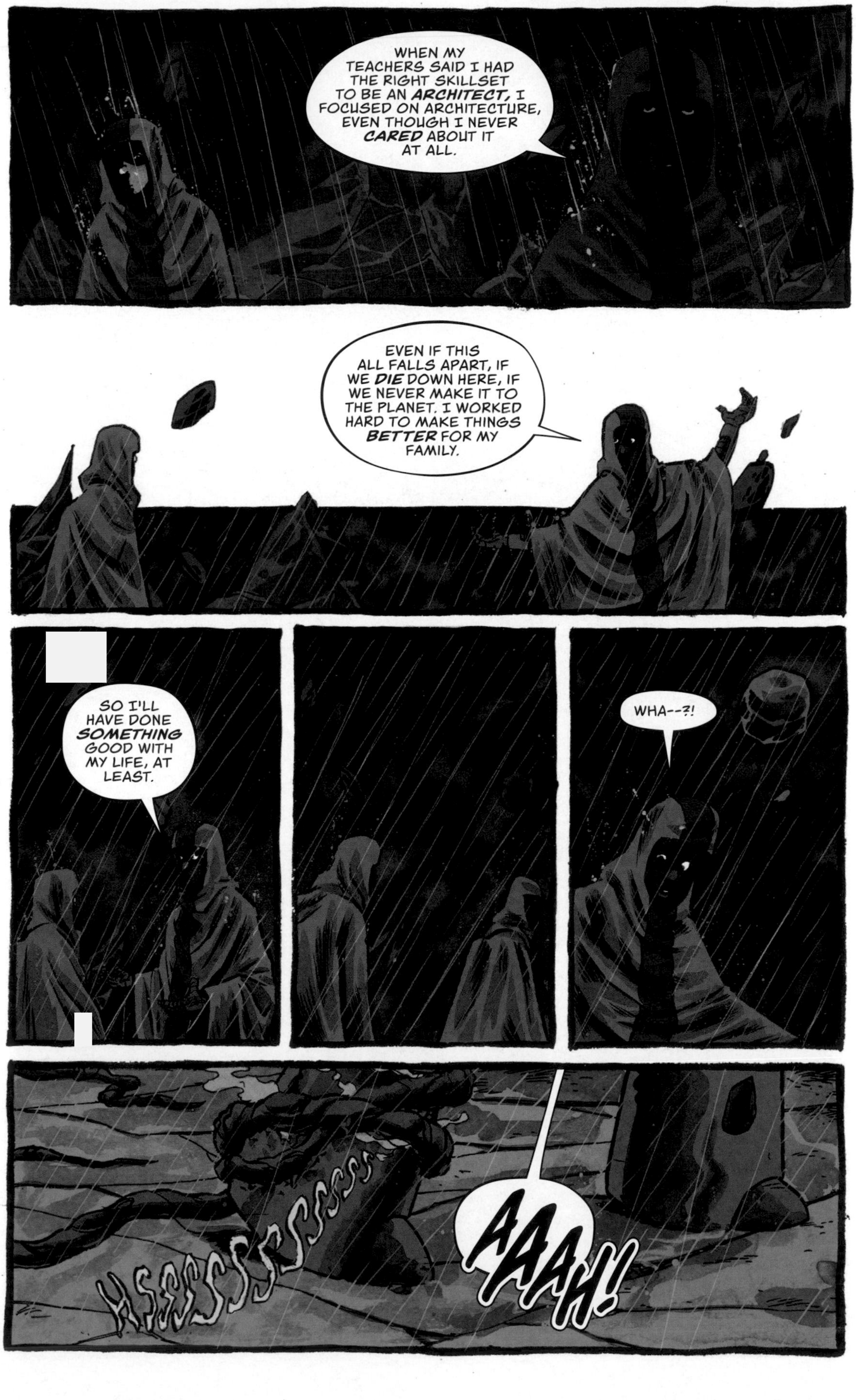
WHEN MY TEACHERS SAID I HAD THE RIGHT SKILLSET TO BE AN ARCHITECT, I FOCUSED ON ARCHITECTURE, EVEN THOUGH I NEVER CARED ABOUT IT AT ALL.
EVEN IF THIS ALL FALLS APART, IF WE DIE DOWN HERE, IF WE NEVER MAKE IT TO THE PLANET. I WORKED HARD TO MAKE THINGS BETTER FOR MY FAMILY.
SO I'LL HAVE DONE SOMETHING GOOD WITH MY LIFE, AT LEAST.
WHA--?!
HSSSSSSSSSSSSS
AAAH!

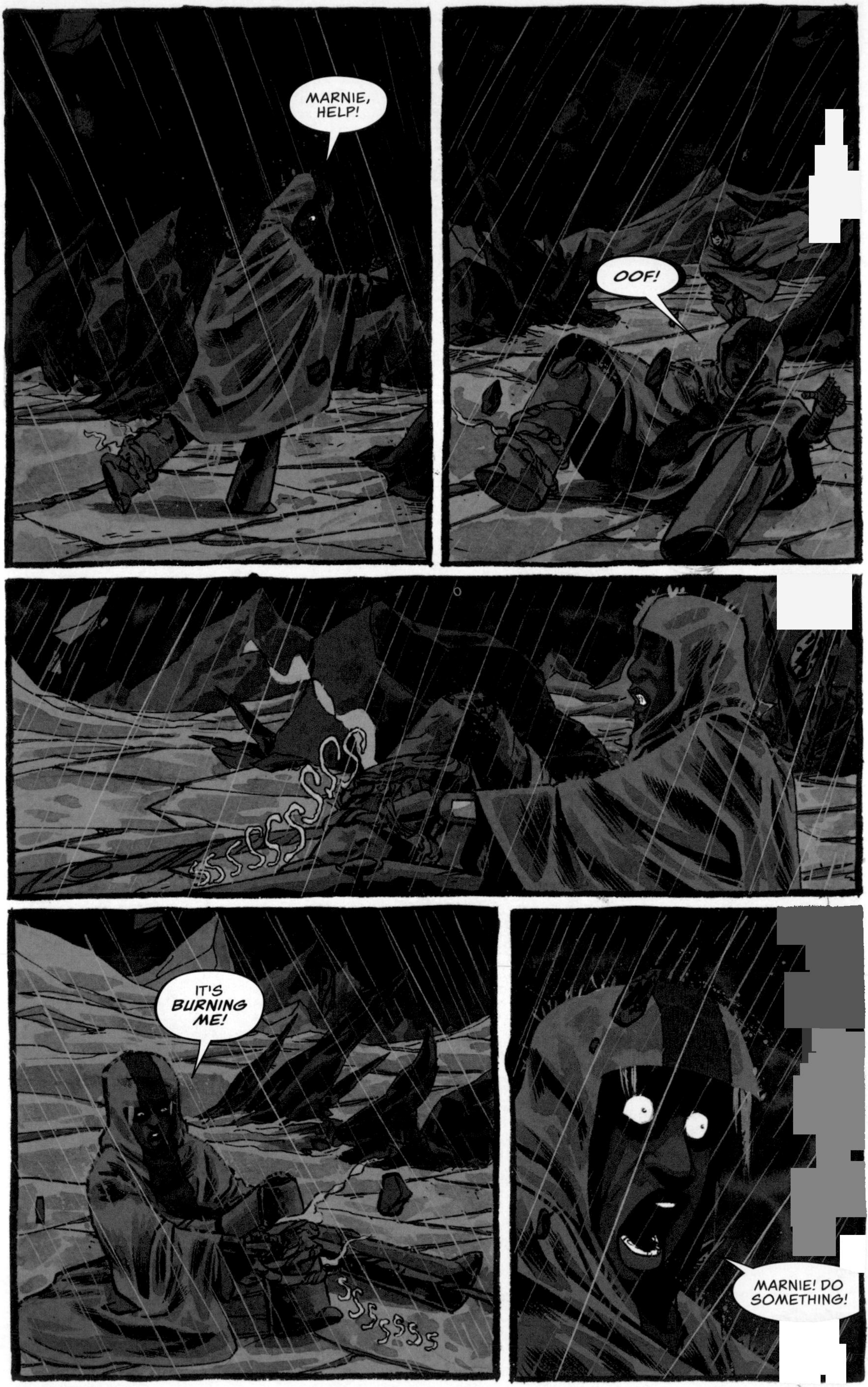
MARNIE, HELP!
OOF!
SSSSSSSSSS
IT'S BURNING ME!
SSSSSS
MARNIE! DO SOMETHING!

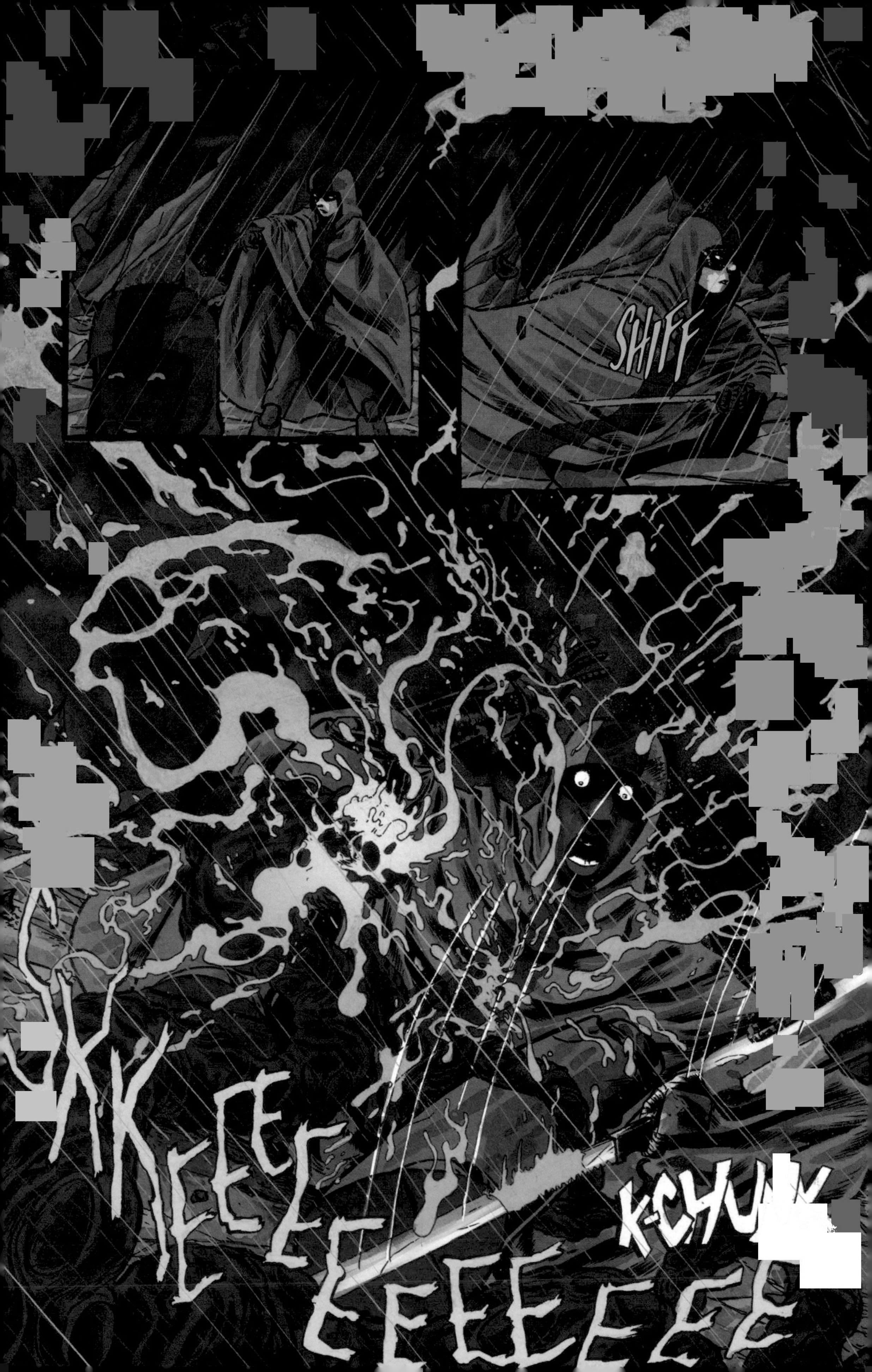
SHIFF
K-CHUNK

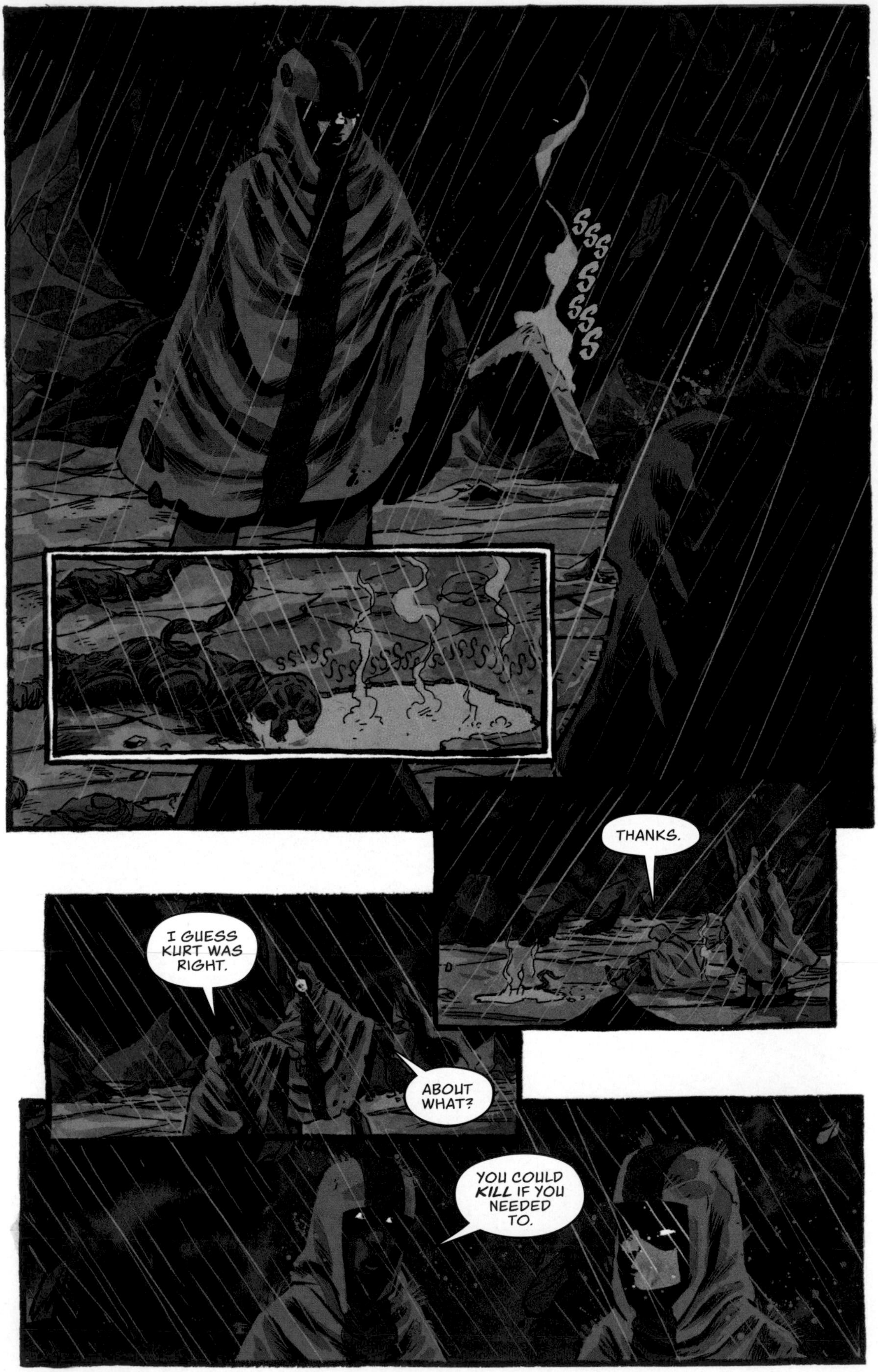
SSSSSSS
SSSSSSSSSSSSSSSSSSSSSSSSSSSS
THANKS.
I GUESS KURT WAS RIGHT.
ABOUT WHAT?
YOU COULD **KILL** IF YOU NEEDED TO.

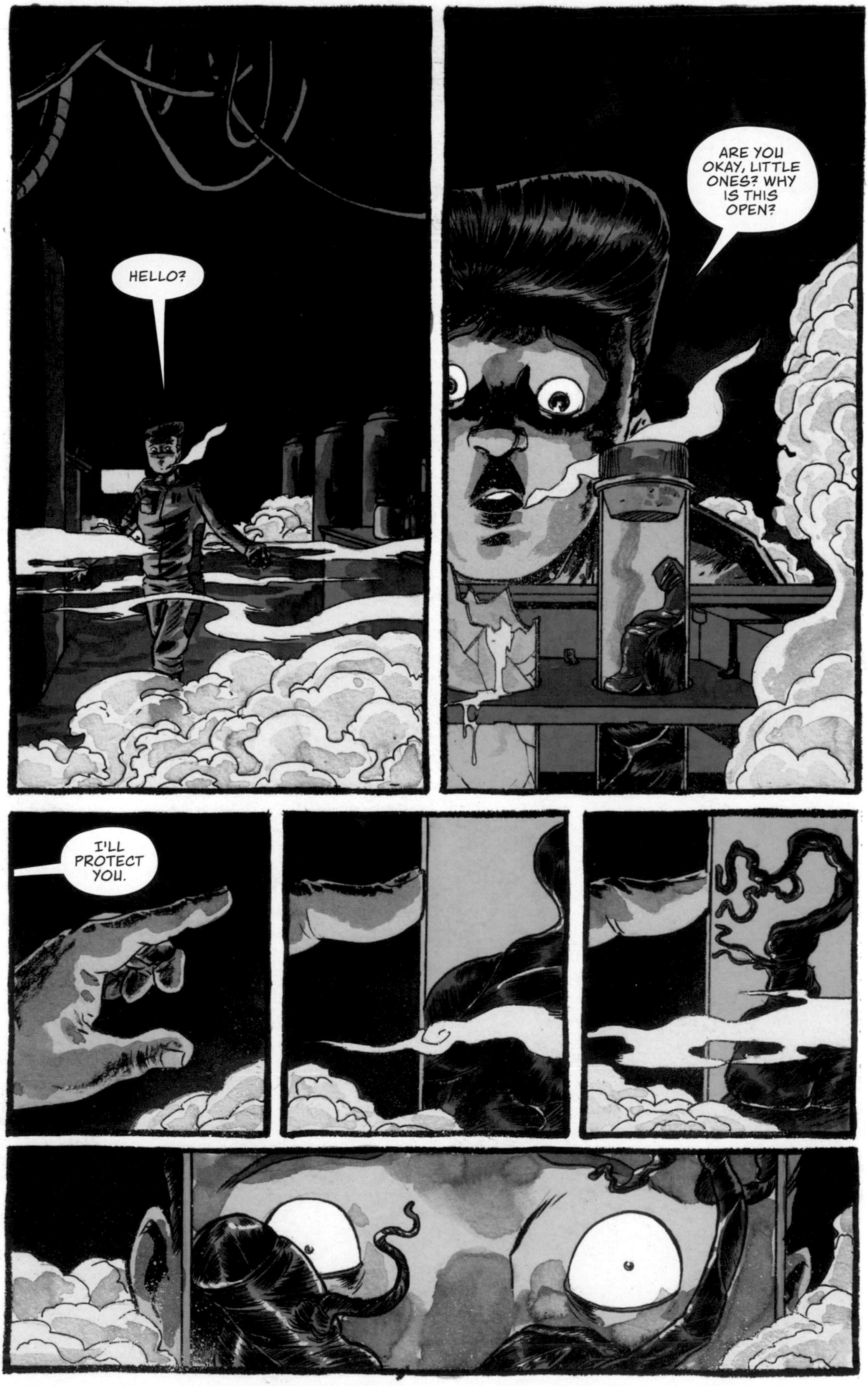
HELLO?
ARE YOU OKAY, LITTLE ONES? WHY IS THIS OPEN?
I'LL PROTECT YOU.

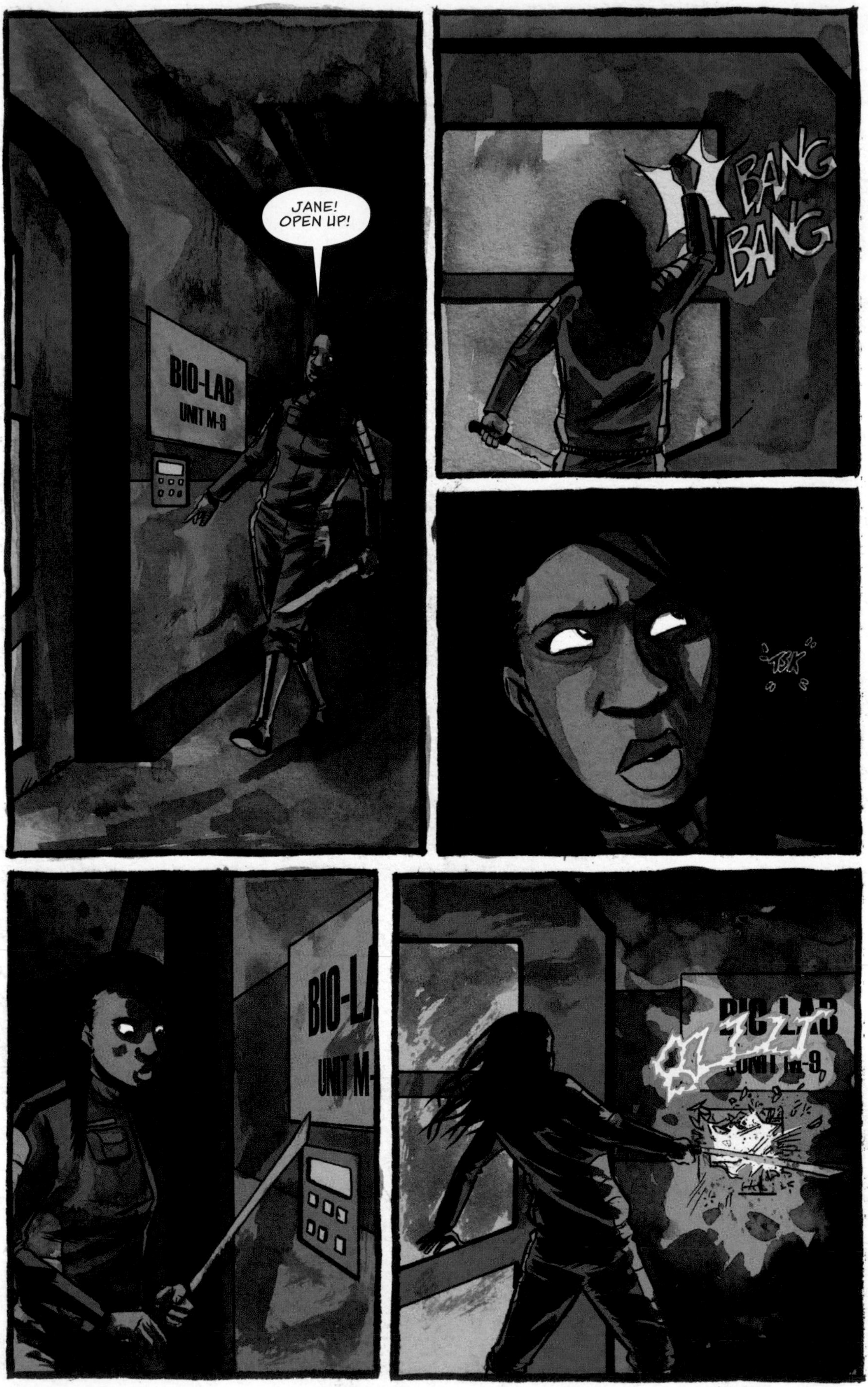
JANE! OPEN UP!
BIO-LAB
UNIT M-9
BANG
BANG
TSK
BIO-LAB
UNIT M-
BIO-LAB
UNIT M-9

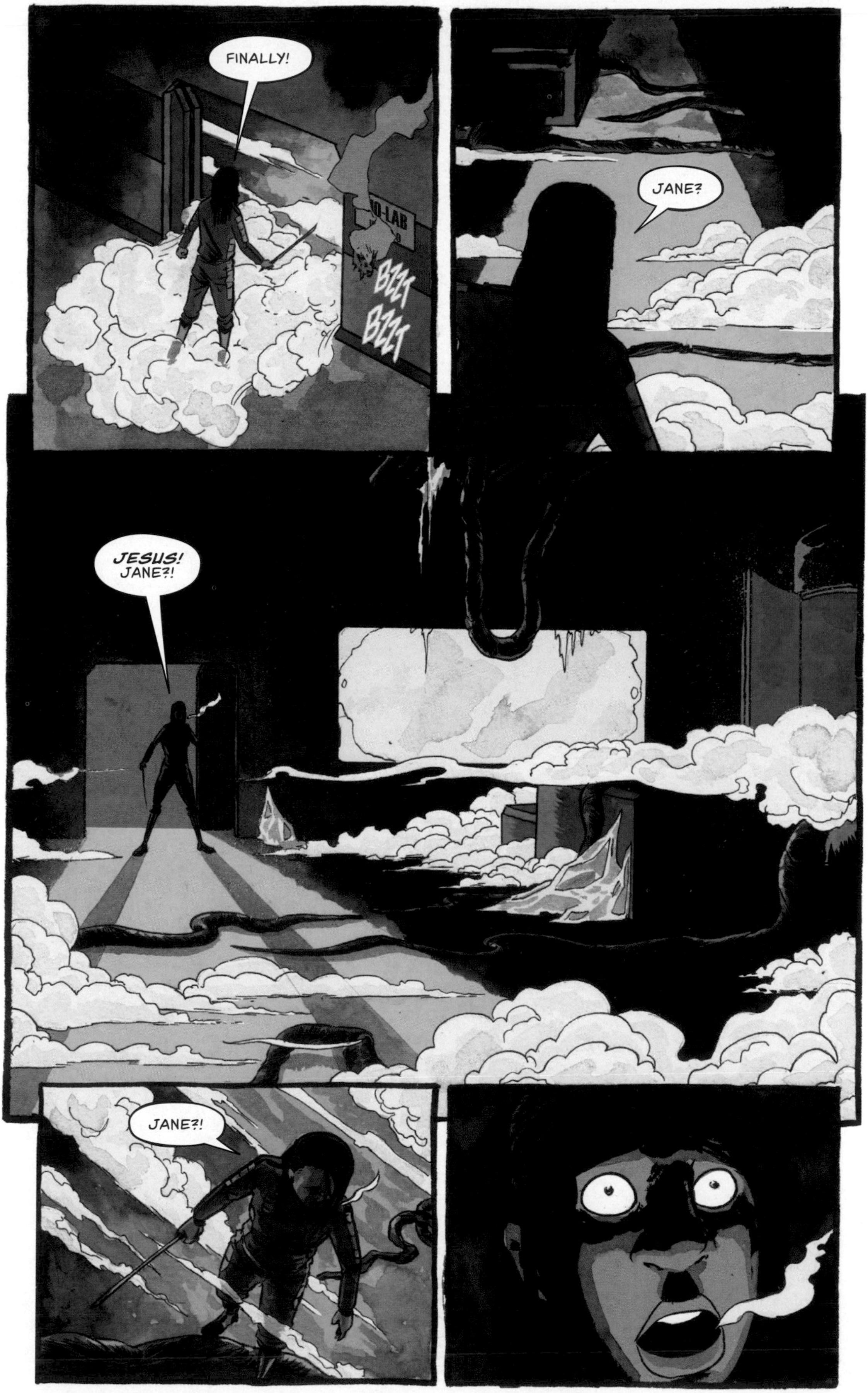
FINALLY!
BZZT
BZZT
JANE?
JESUS! JANE?!
JANE?!

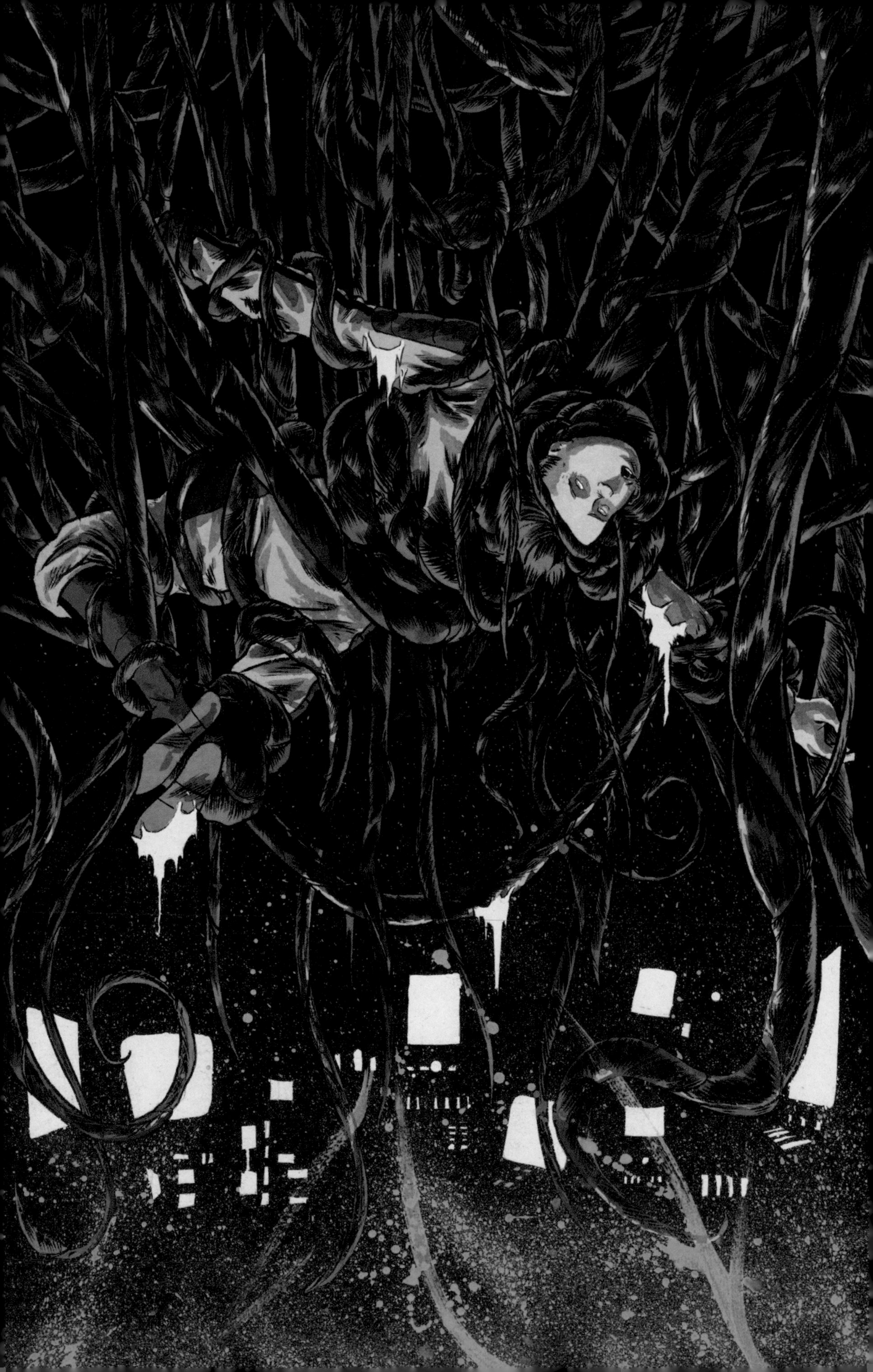

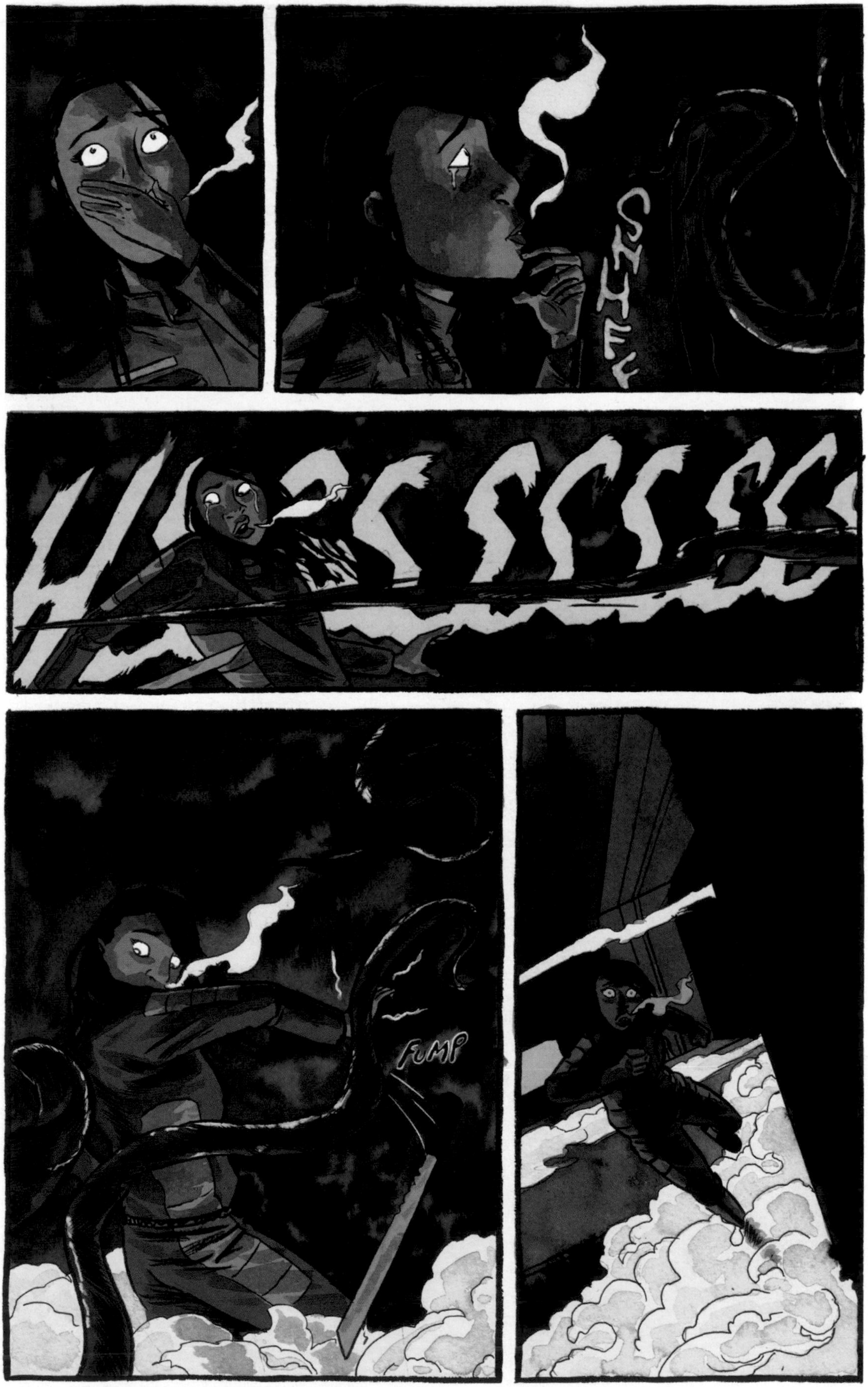
SNHFF
HSSSSSS
FUMP

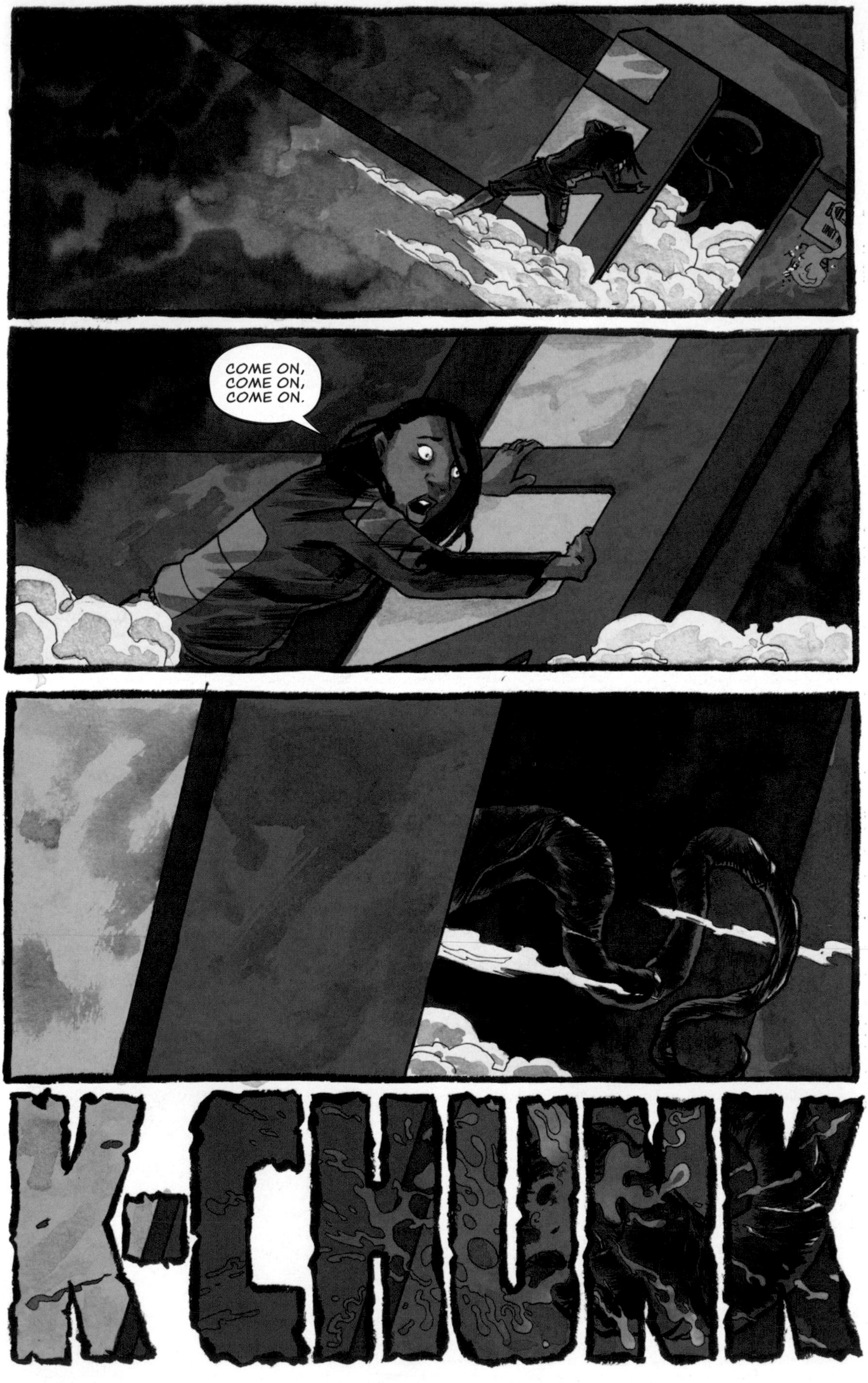
COME ON, COME ON, COME ON.
K-CHUNK

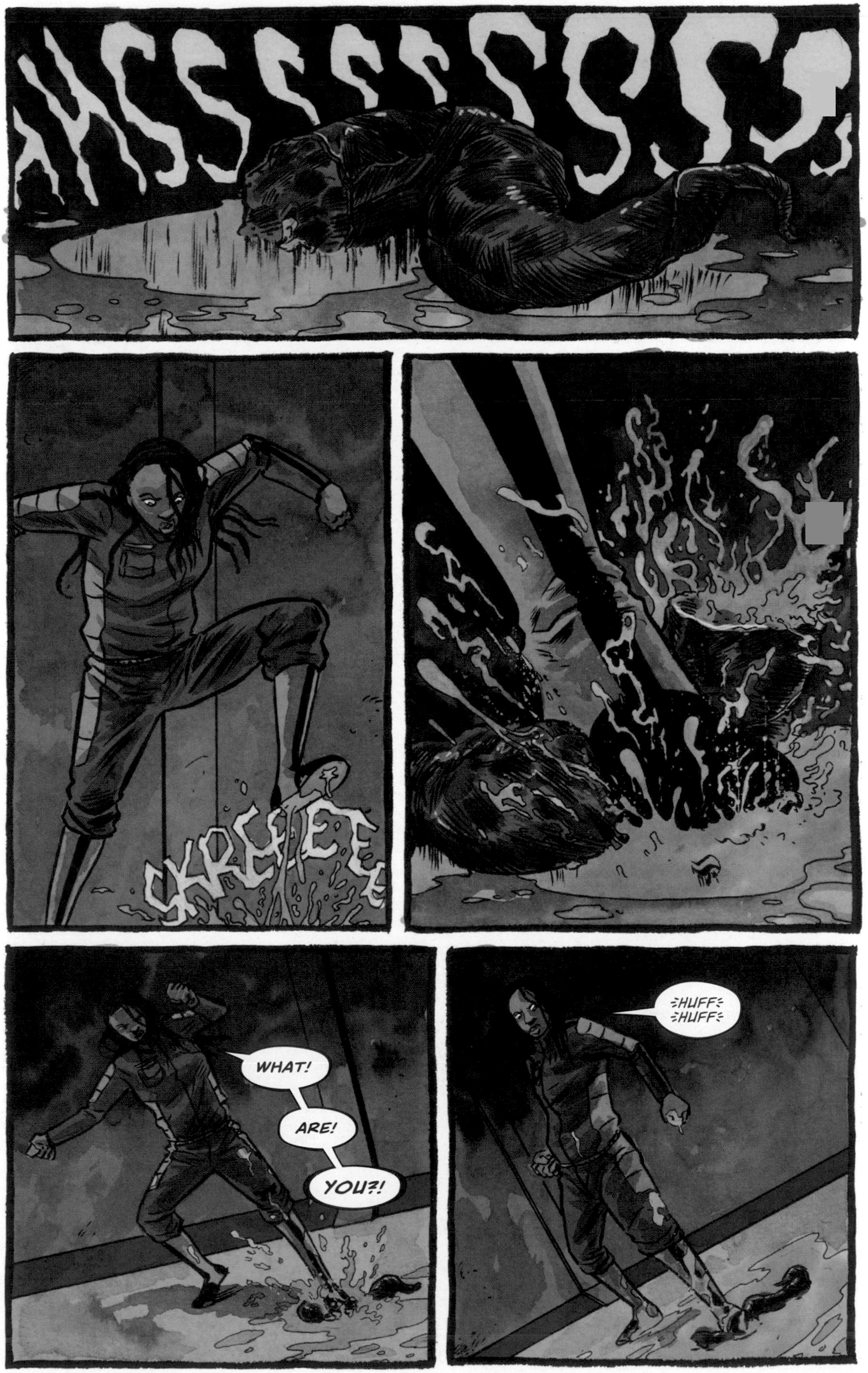
WHAT!
ARE!
YOU?!
HUFF HUFF

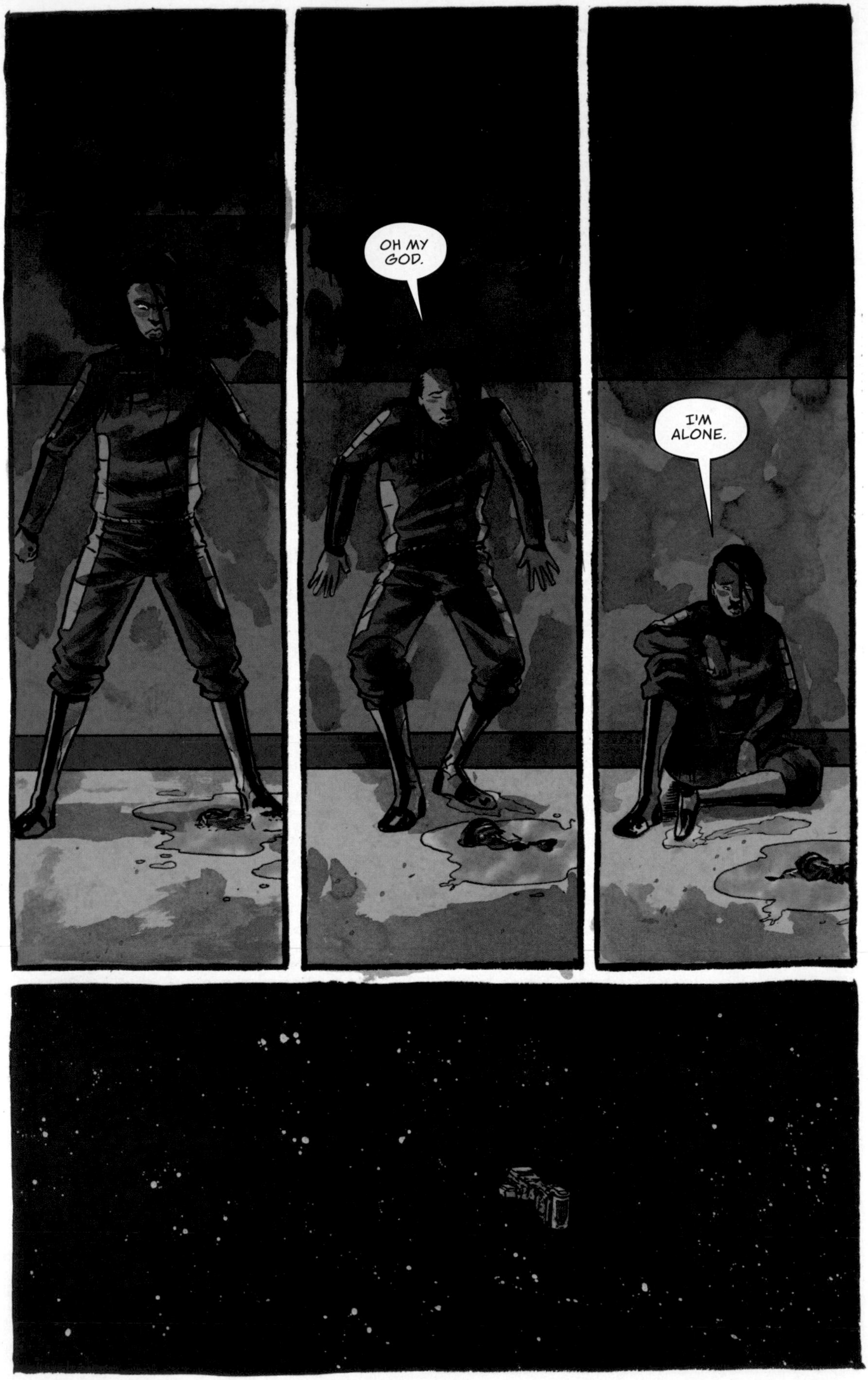
OH MY GOD.
I'M ALONE.

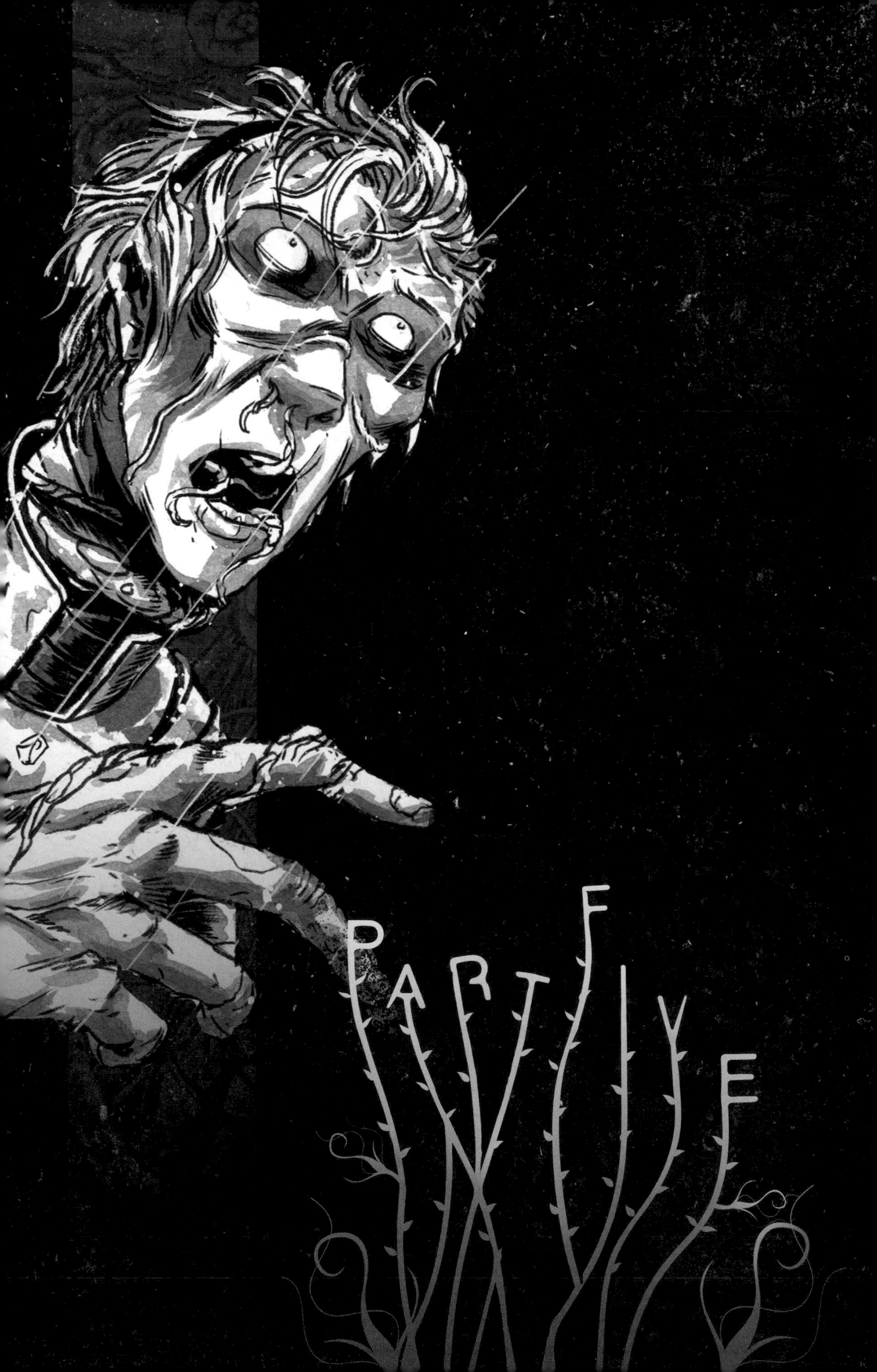
PART FIVE

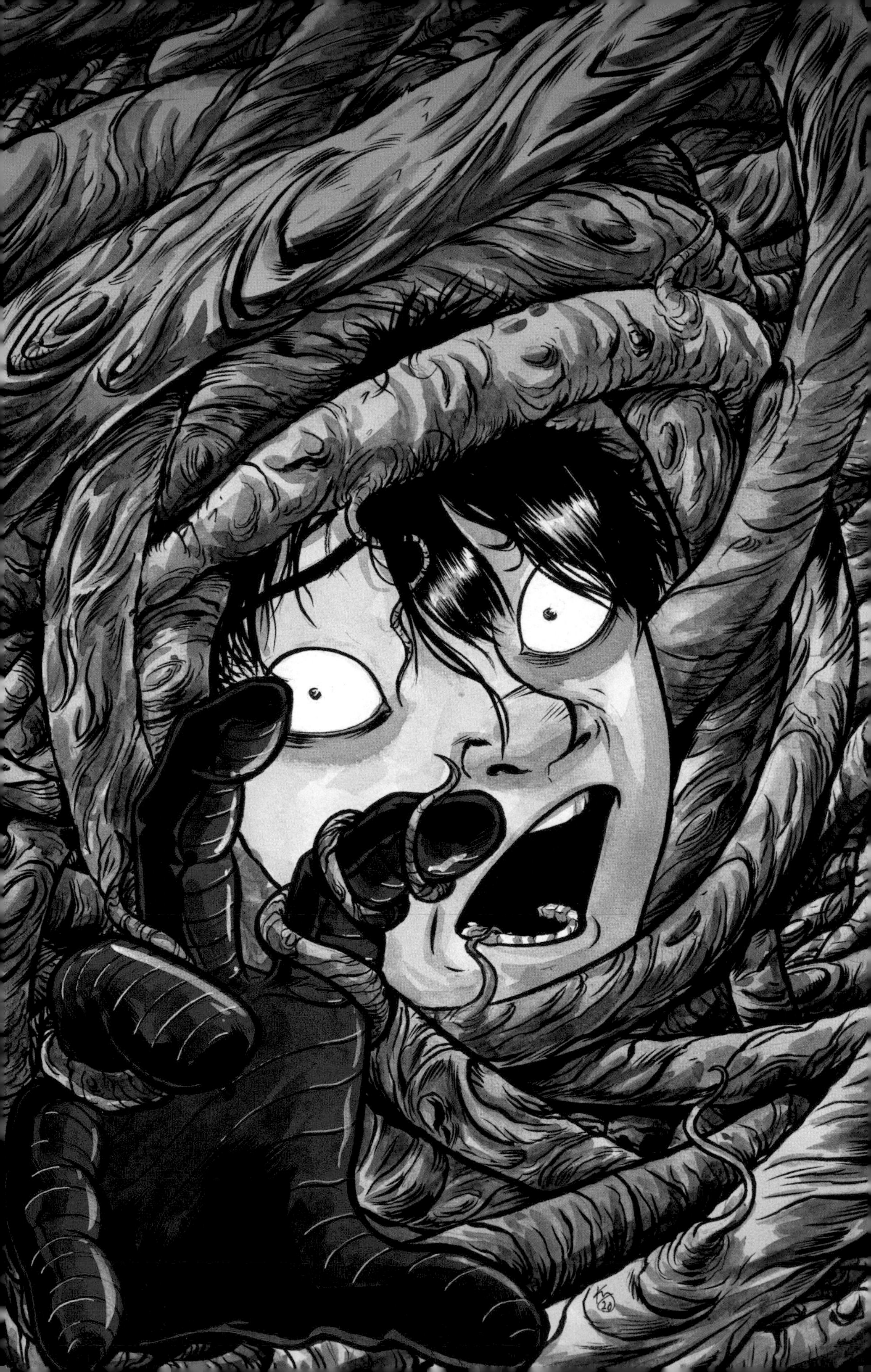

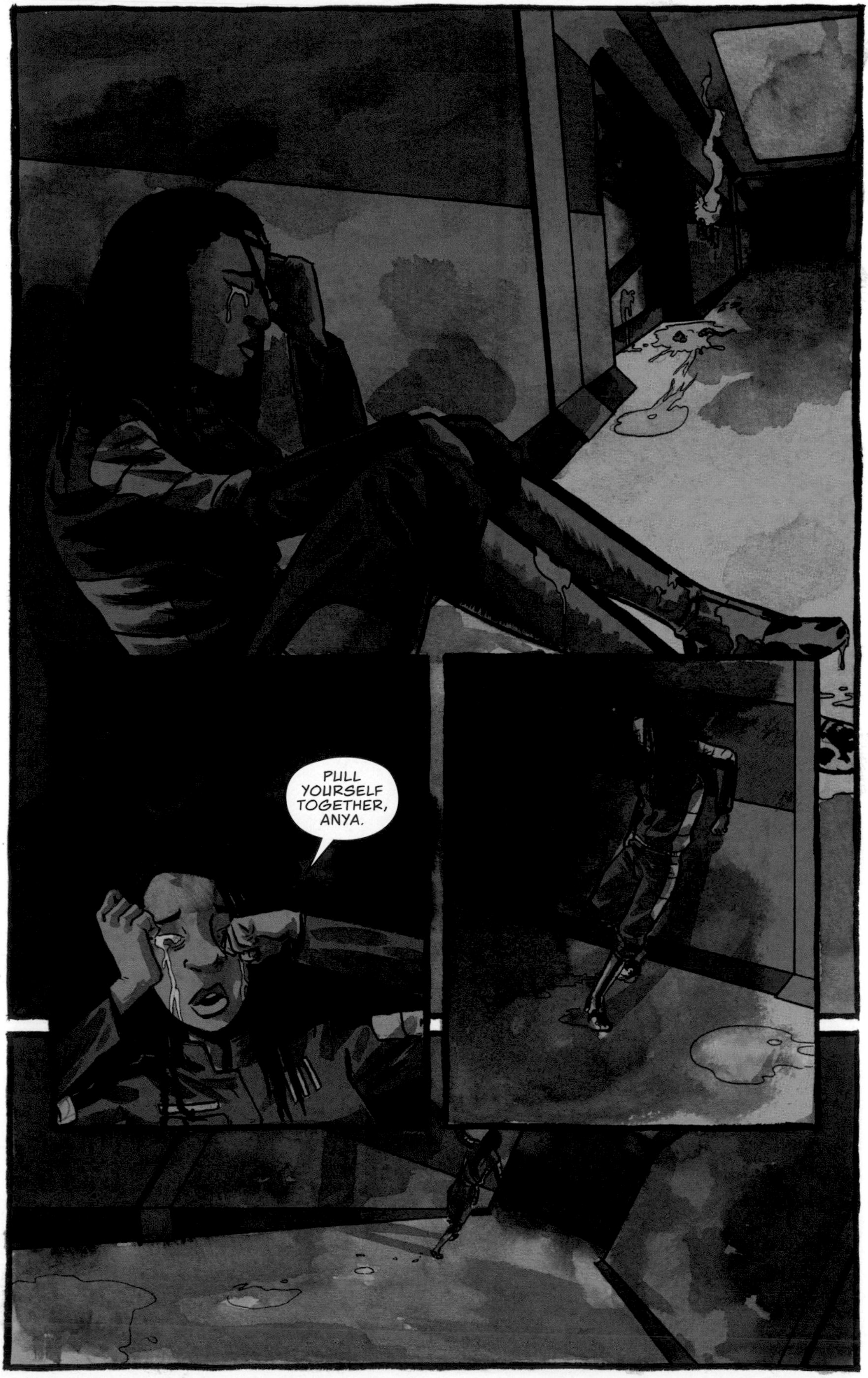
PULL YOURSELF TOGETHER, ANYA.

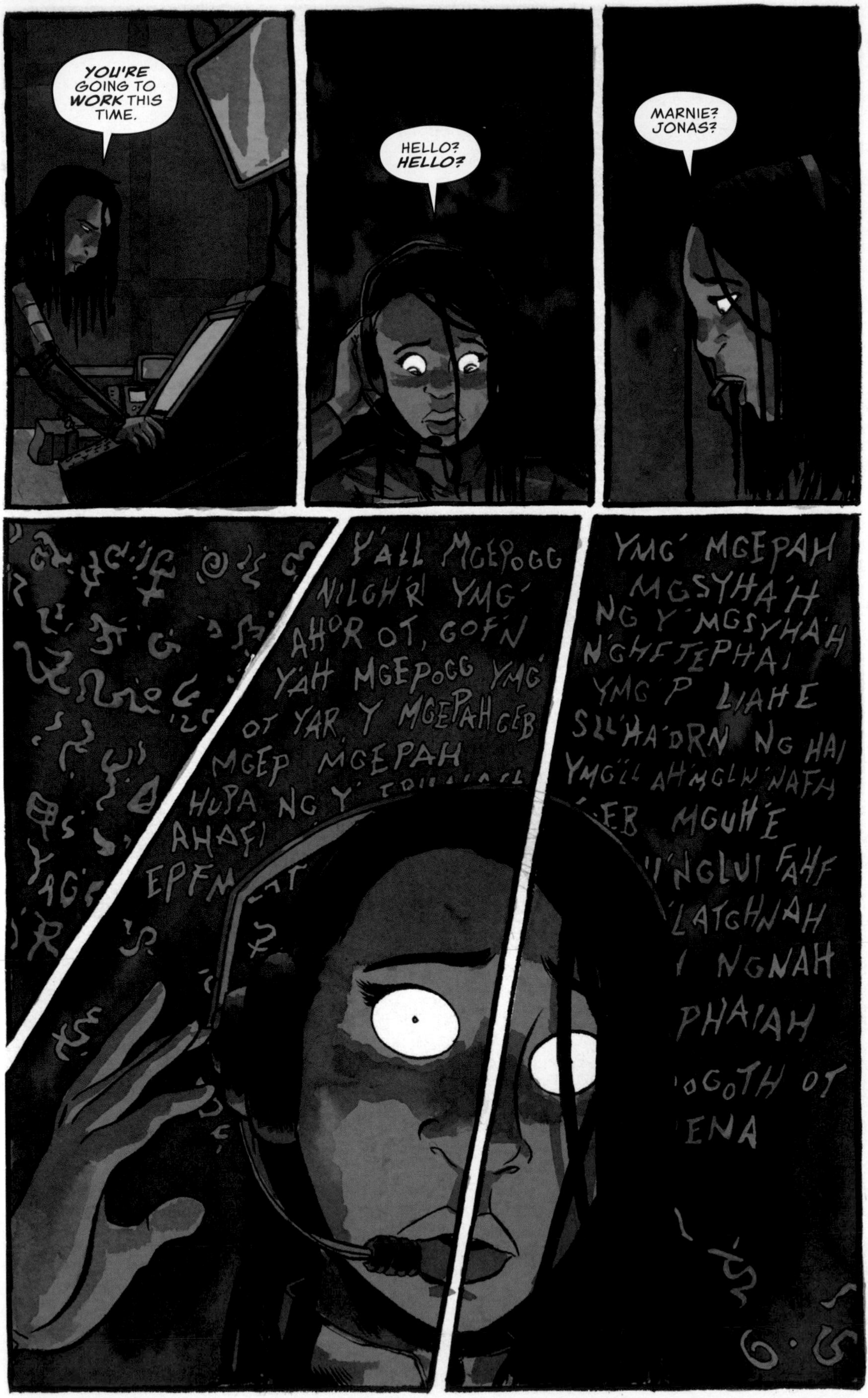
YOU'RE GOING TO WORK THIS TIME.
HELLO? HELLO?
MARNIE? JONAS?

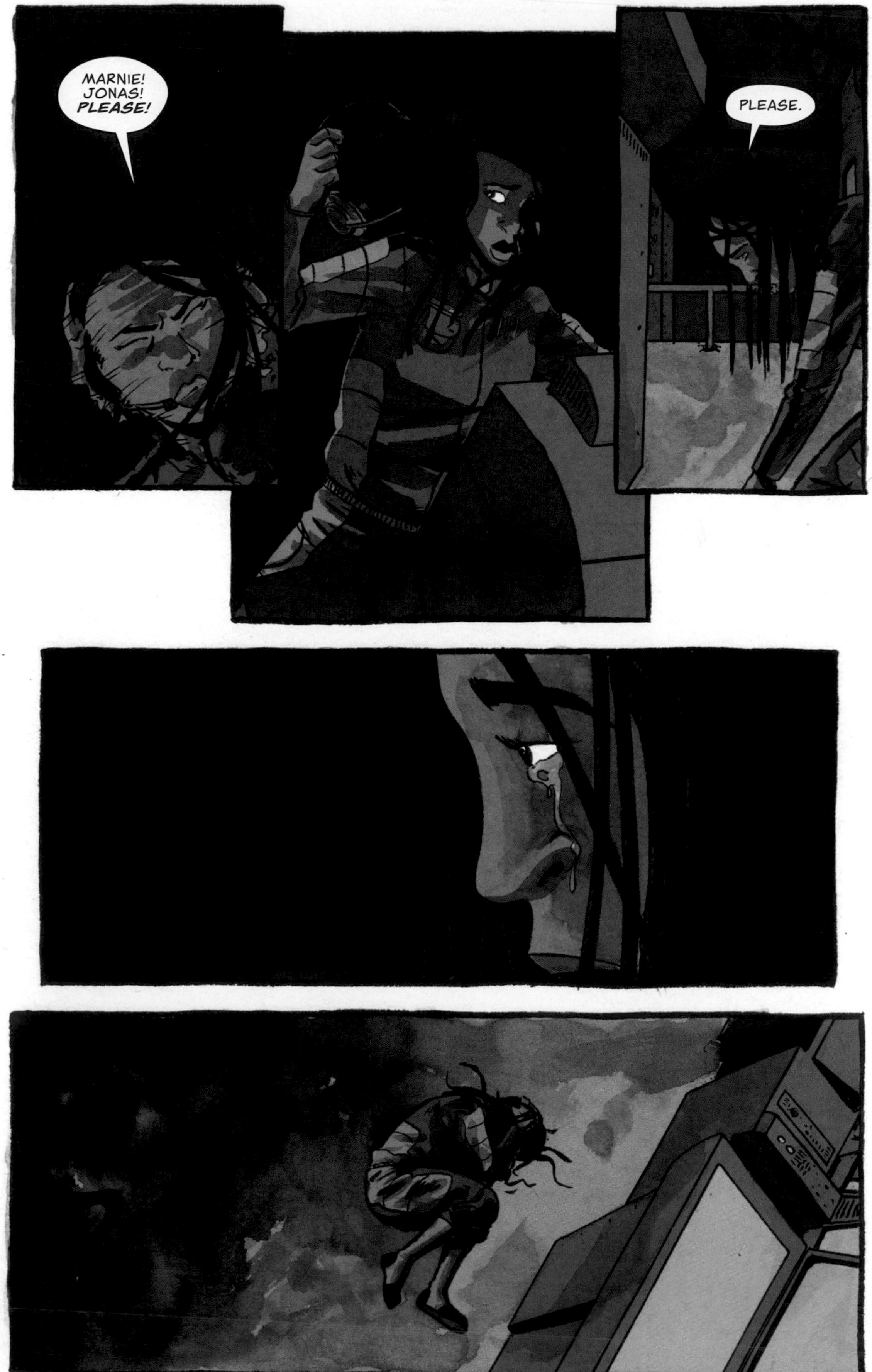
MARNIE! JONAS! *PLEASE!*
PLEASE.

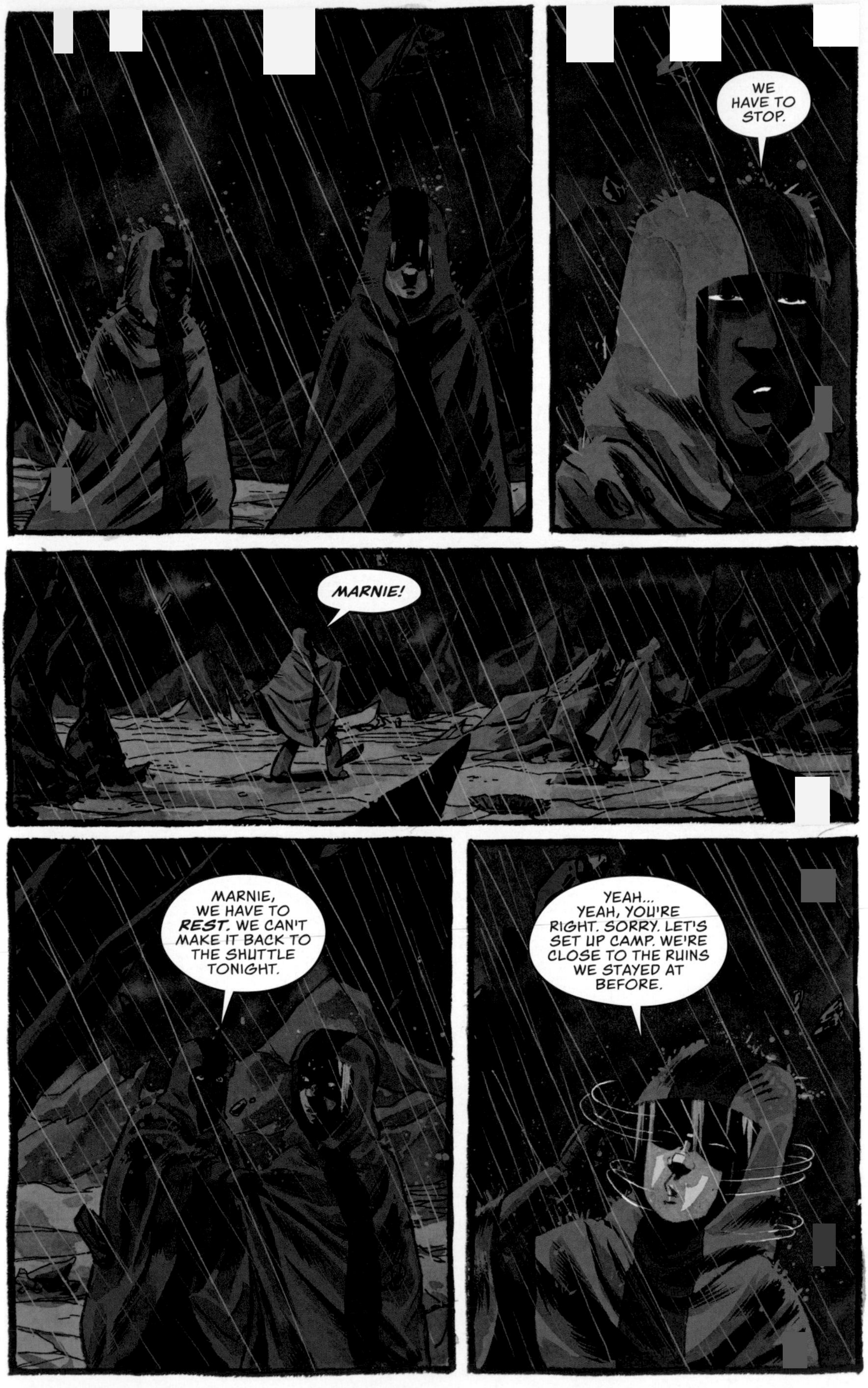
WE HAVE TO STOP.
MARNIE!
MARNIE, WE HAVE TO REST. WE CAN'T MAKE IT BACK TO THE SHUTTLE TONIGHT.
YEAH... YEAH, YOU'RE RIGHT. SORRY. LET'S SET UP CAMP. WE'RE CLOSE TO THE RUINS WE STAYED AT BEFORE.

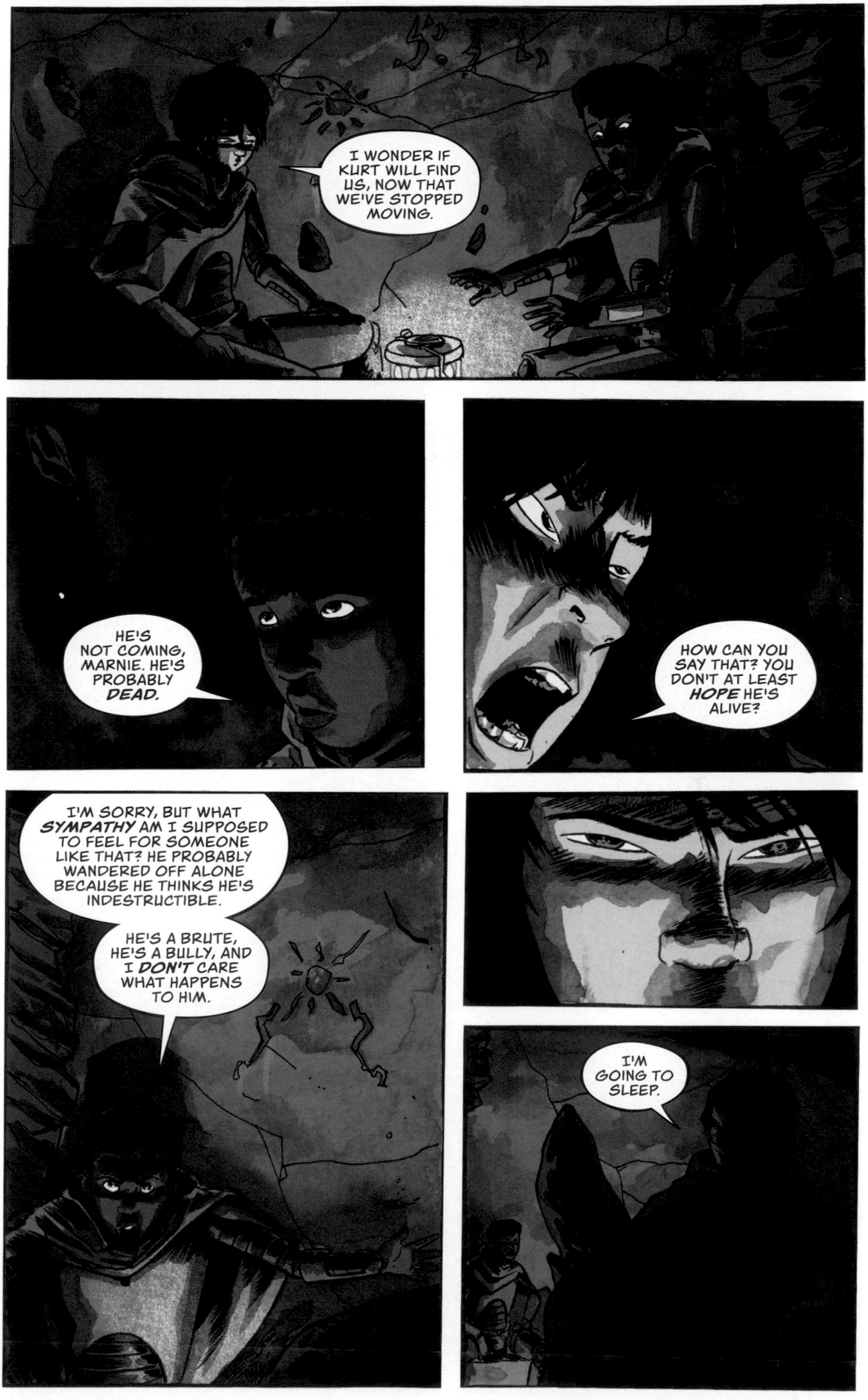
I WONDER IF KURT WILL FIND US, NOW THAT WE'VE STOPPED MOVING.
HE'S NOT COMING, MARNIE. HE'S PROBABLY **DEAD.**
HOW CAN YOU SAY THAT? YOU DON'T AT LEAST **HOPE** HE'S ALIVE?
I'M SORRY, BUT WHAT **SYMPATHY** AM I SUPPOSED TO FEEL FOR SOMEONE LIKE THAT? HE PROBABLY WANDERED OFF ALONE BECAUSE HE THINKS HE'S INDESTRUCTIBLE.
HE'S A BRUTE, HE'S A BULLY, AND I **DON'T** CARE WHAT HAPPENS TO HIM.
I'M GOING TO SLEEP.

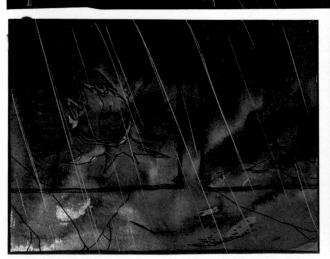

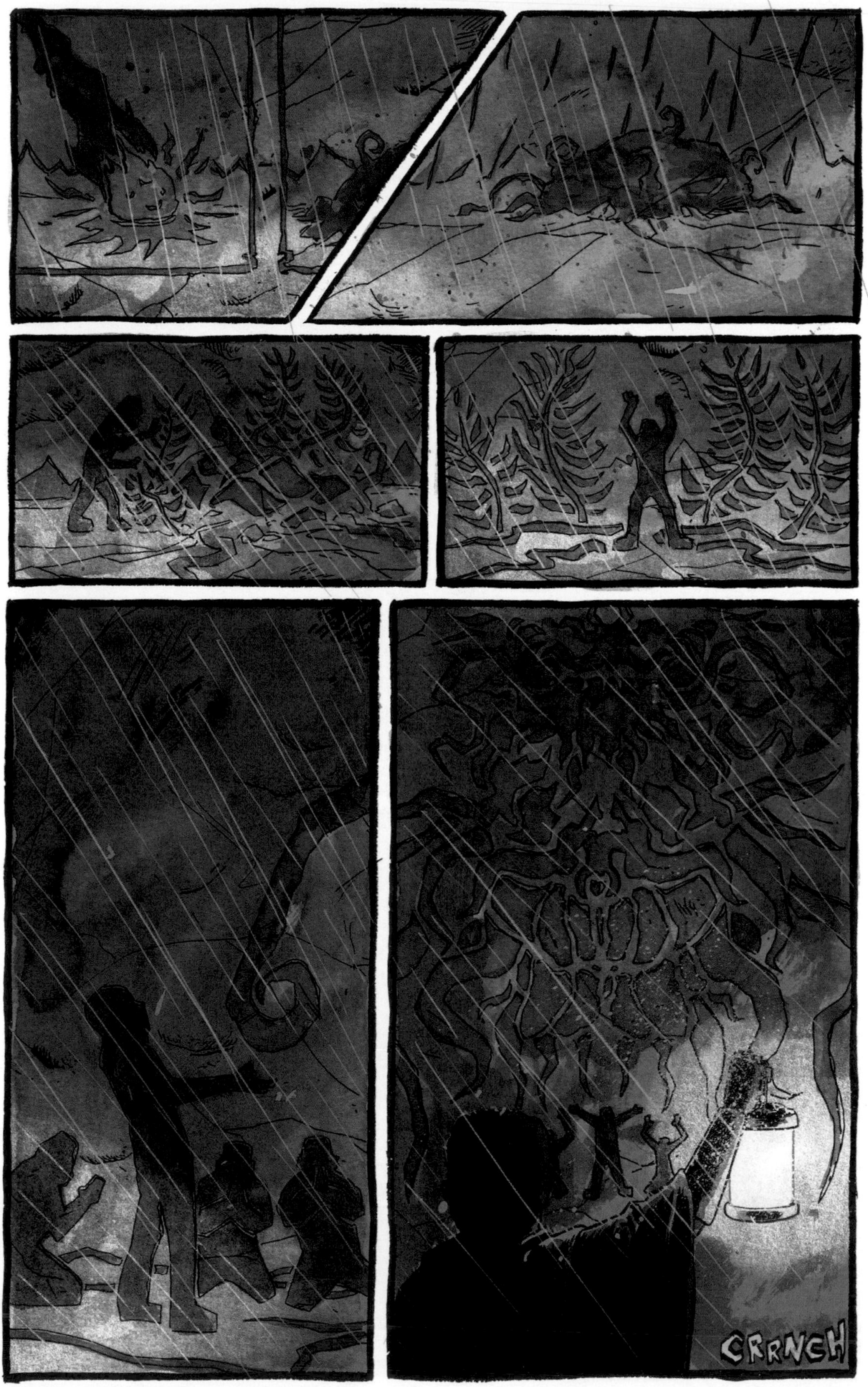
CRRNCH

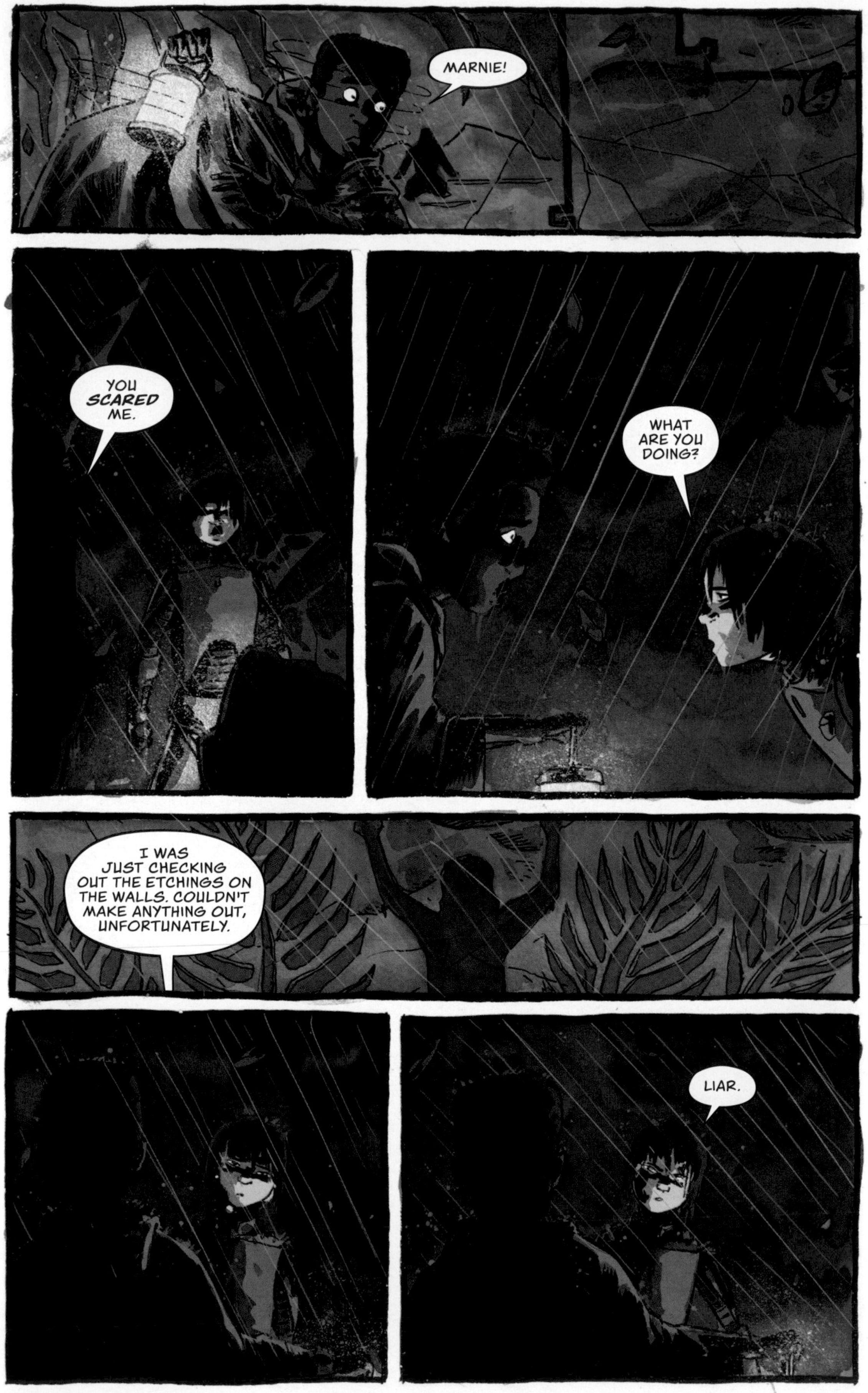
MARNIE!
YOU SCARED ME.
WHAT ARE YOU DOING?
I WAS JUST CHECKING OUT THE ETCHINGS ON THE WALLS. COULDN'T MAKE ANYTHING OUT, UNFORTUNATELY.
LIAR.

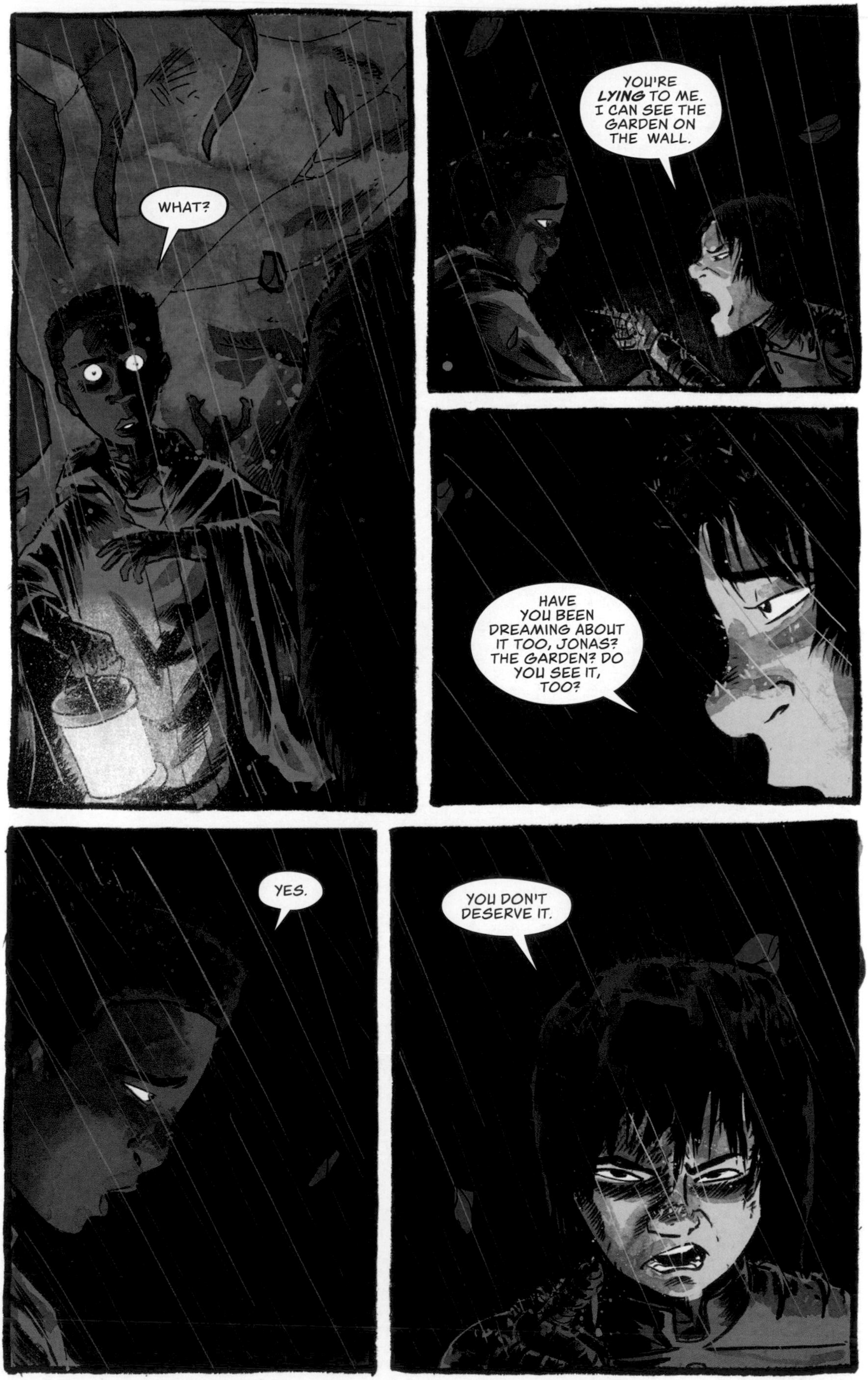
WHAT?
YOU'RE *LYING* TO ME. I CAN SEE THE GARDEN ON THE WALL.
HAVE YOU BEEN DREAMING ABOUT IT TOO, JONAS? THE GARDEN? DO YOU SEE IT, TOO?
YES.
YOU DON'T DESERVE IT.

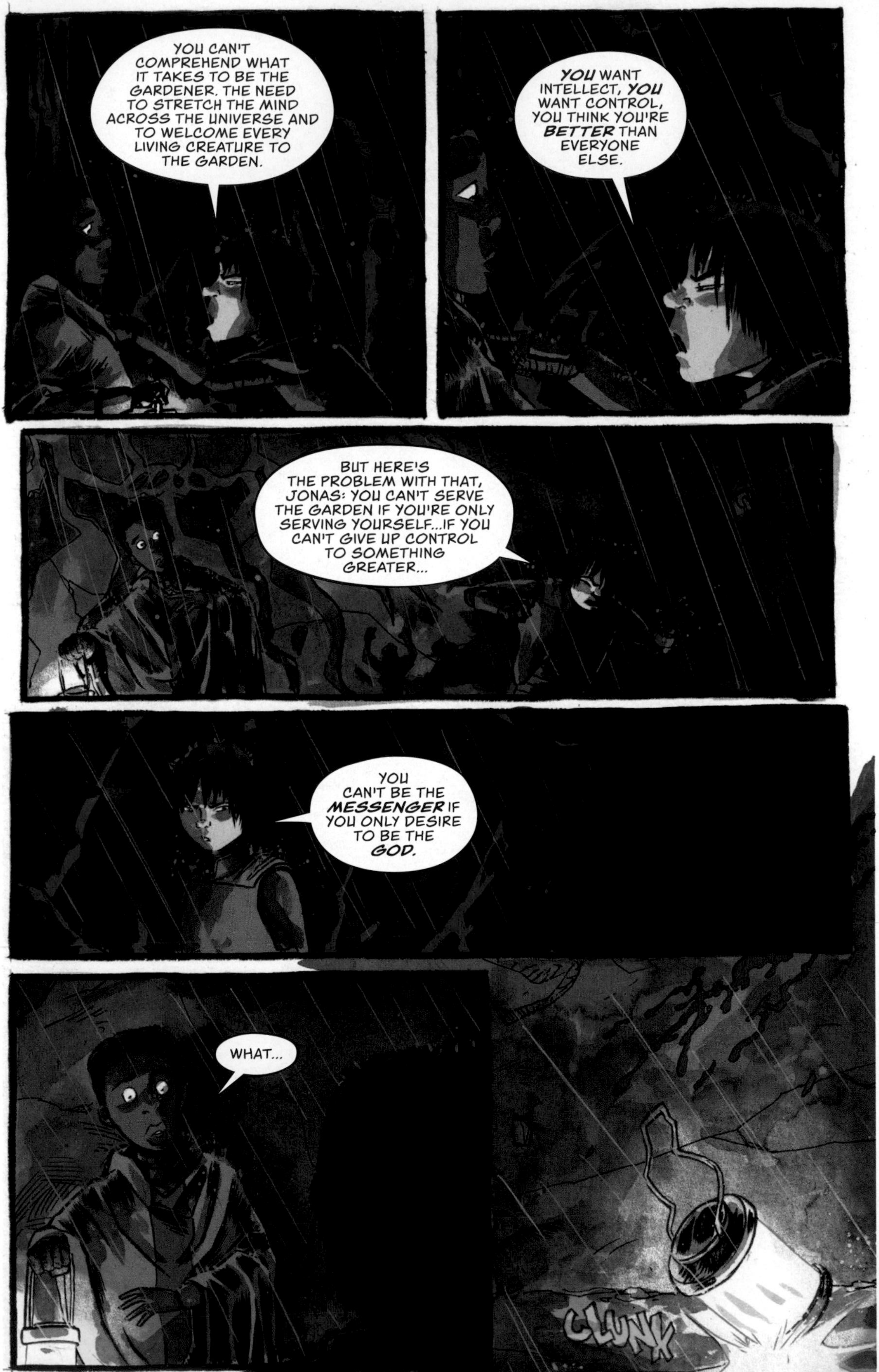
YOU CAN'T COMPREHEND WHAT IT TAKES TO BE THE GARDENER. THE NEED TO STRETCH THE MIND ACROSS THE UNIVERSE AND TO WELCOME EVERY LIVING CREATURE TO THE GARDEN.
YOU WANT INTELLECT, YOU WANT CONTROL, YOU THINK YOU'RE BETTER THAN EVERYONE ELSE.
BUT HERE'S THE PROBLEM WITH THAT, JONAS: YOU CAN'T SERVE THE GARDEN IF YOU'RE ONLY SERVING YOURSELF...IF YOU CAN'T GIVE UP CONTROL TO SOMETHING GREATER...
YOU CAN'T BE THE MESSENGER IF YOU ONLY DESIRE TO BE THE GOD.
WHAT...
CLUNK

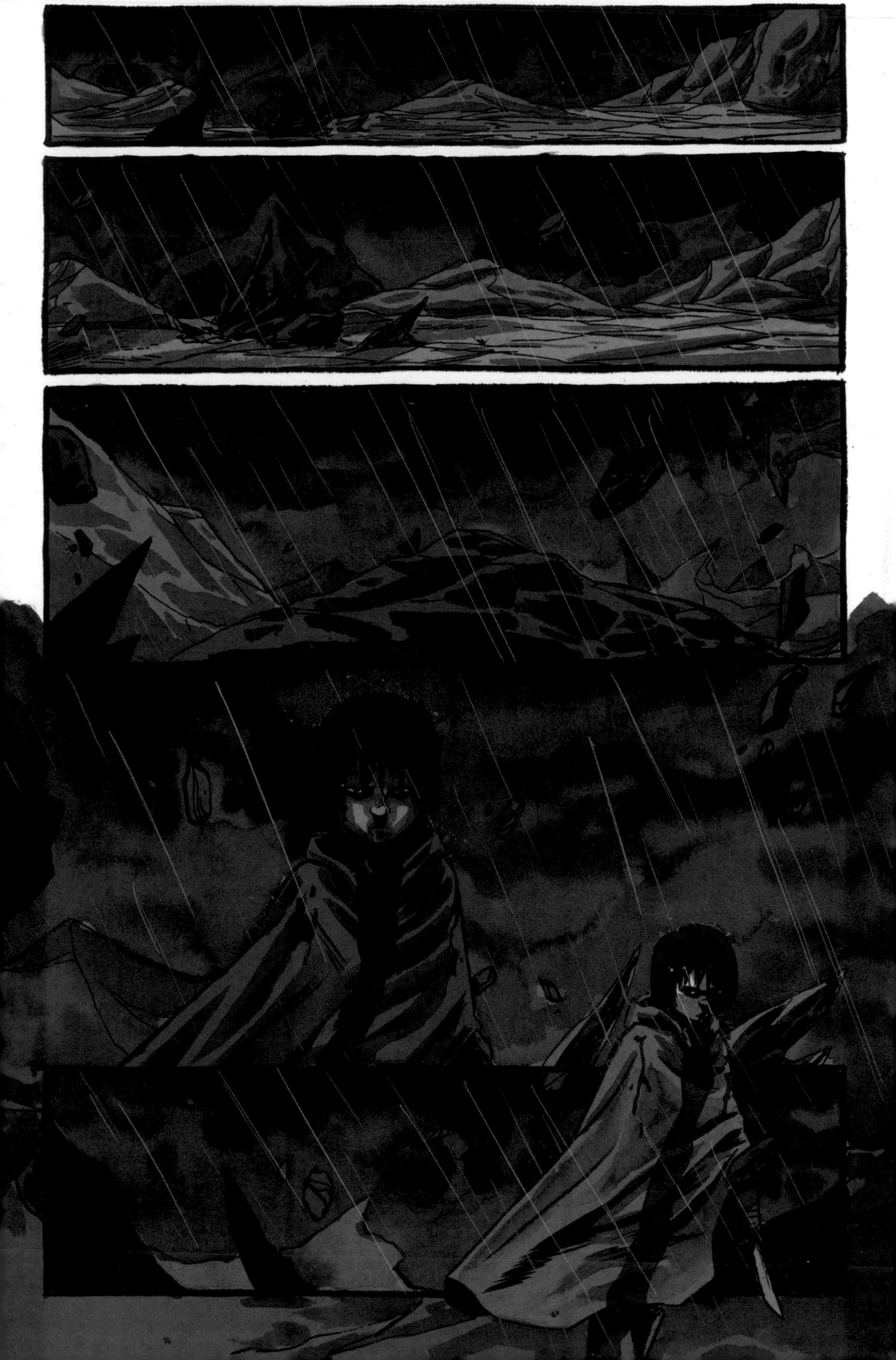

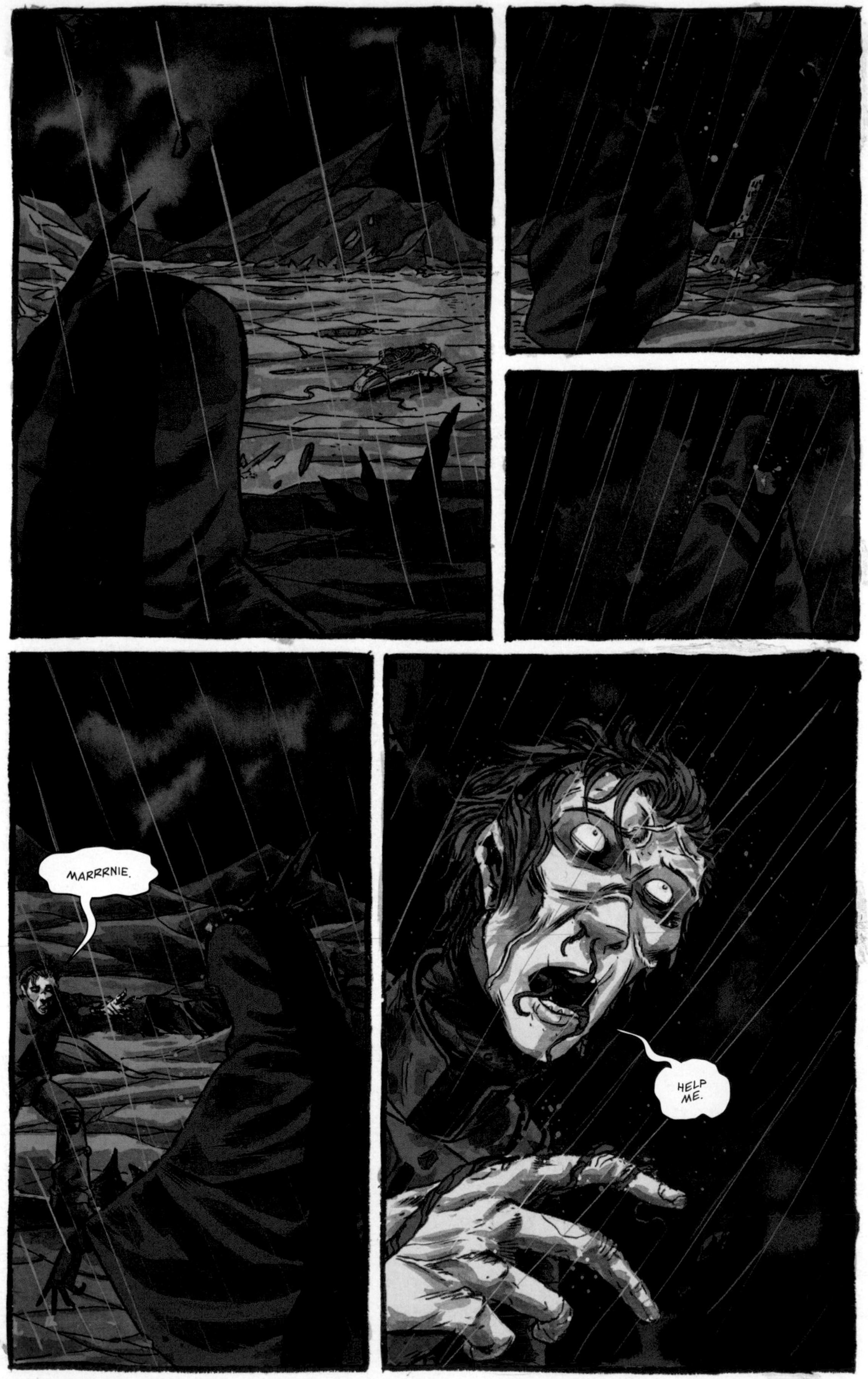
MARRRNIE.
HELP ME.

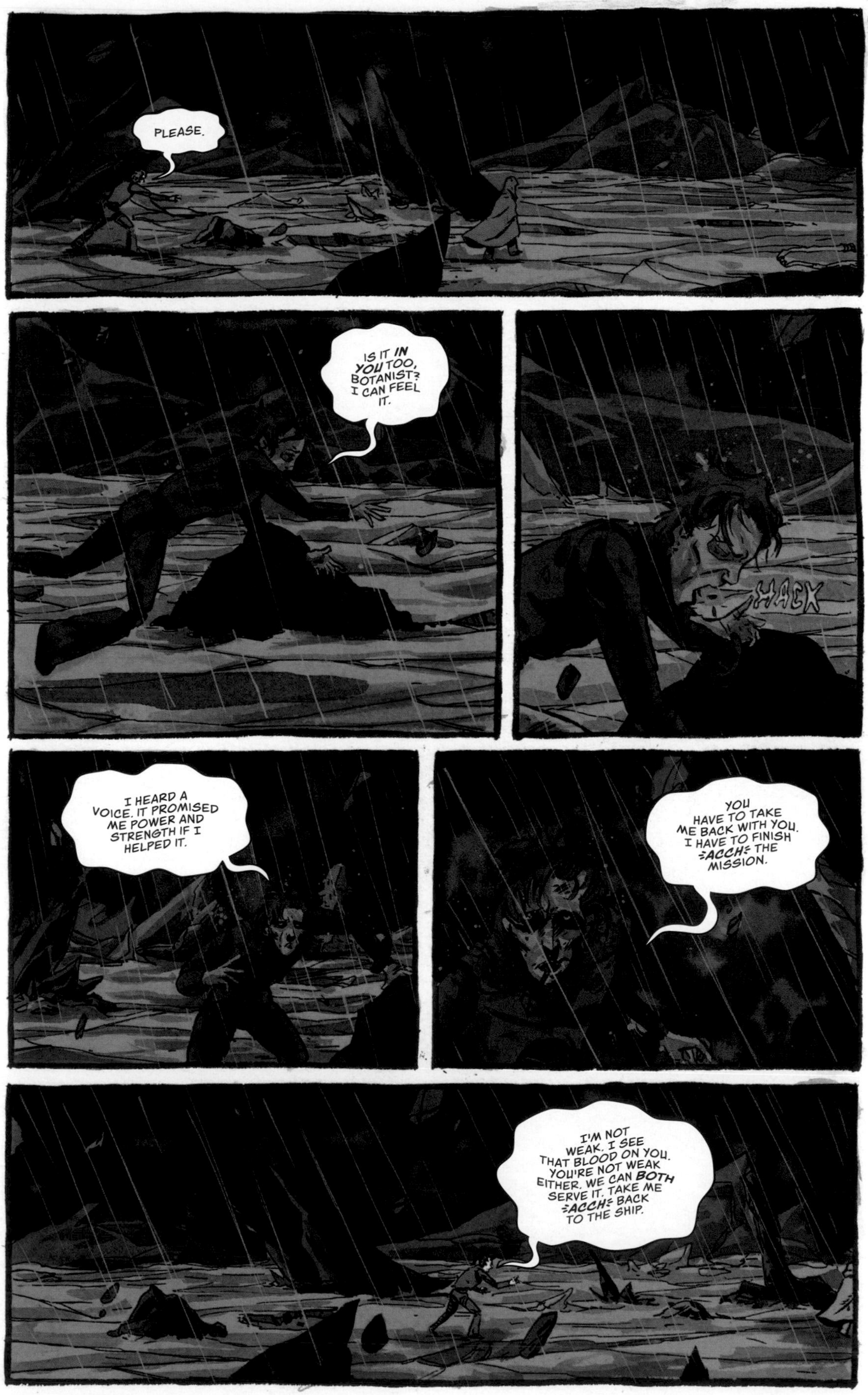
PLEASE.
IS IT IN YOU TOO, BOTANIST? I CAN FEEL IT.
HACK
I HEARD A VOICE. IT PROMISED ME POWER AND STRENGTH IF I HELPED IT.
YOU HAVE TO TAKE ME BACK WITH YOU. I HAVE TO FINISH =ACCH= THE MISSION.
I'M NOT WEAK. I SEE THAT BLOOD ON YOU. YOU'RE NOT WEAK EITHER. WE CAN BOTH SERVE IT. TAKE ME =ACCH= BACK TO THE SHIP.

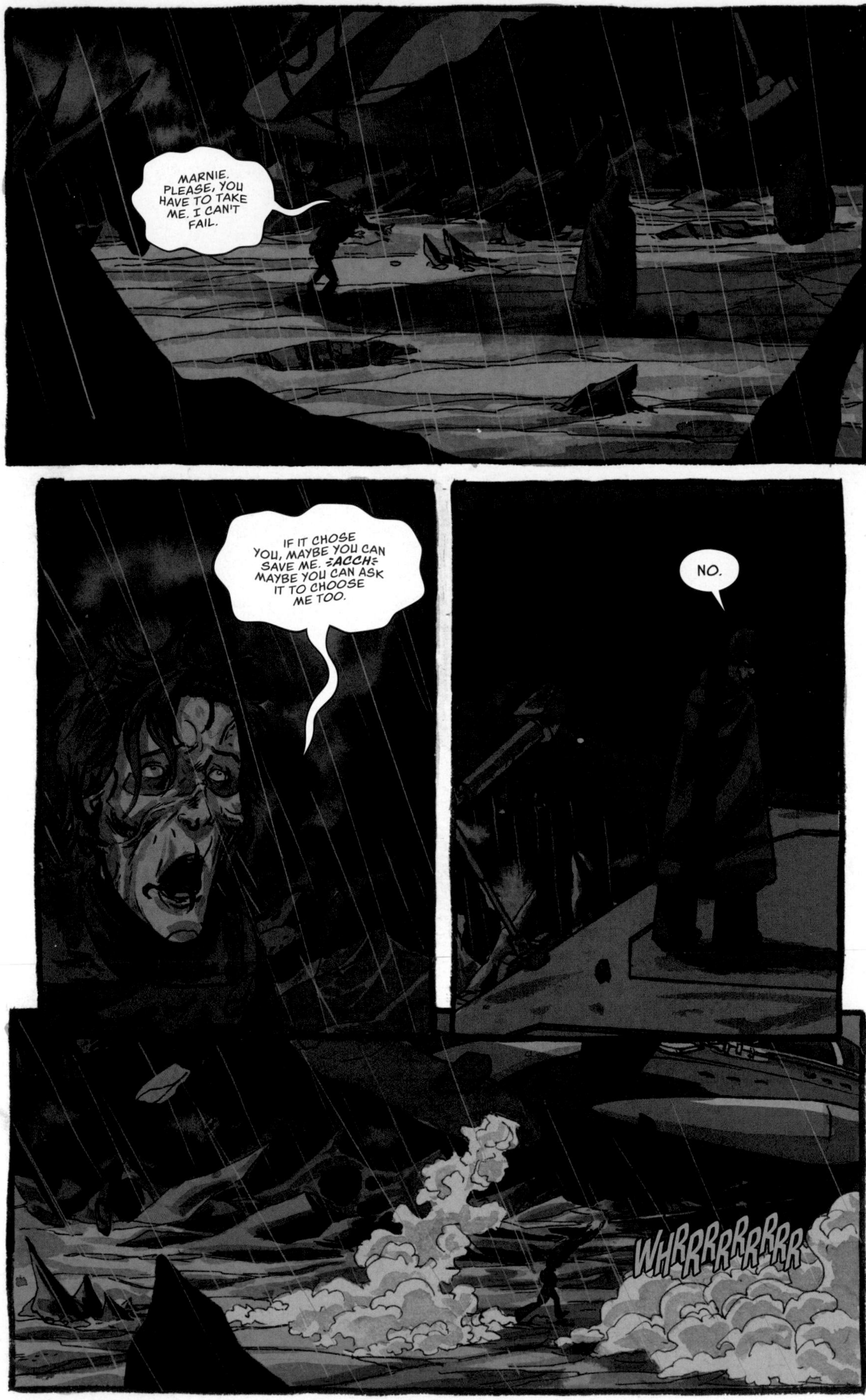
MARNIE. PLEASE, YOU HAVE TO TAKE ME. I CAN'T FAIL.
IF IT CHOSE YOU, MAYBE YOU CAN SAVE ME. ACCH MAYBE YOU CAN ASK IT TO CHOOSE ME TOO.
NO.
WHRRRRRRRR

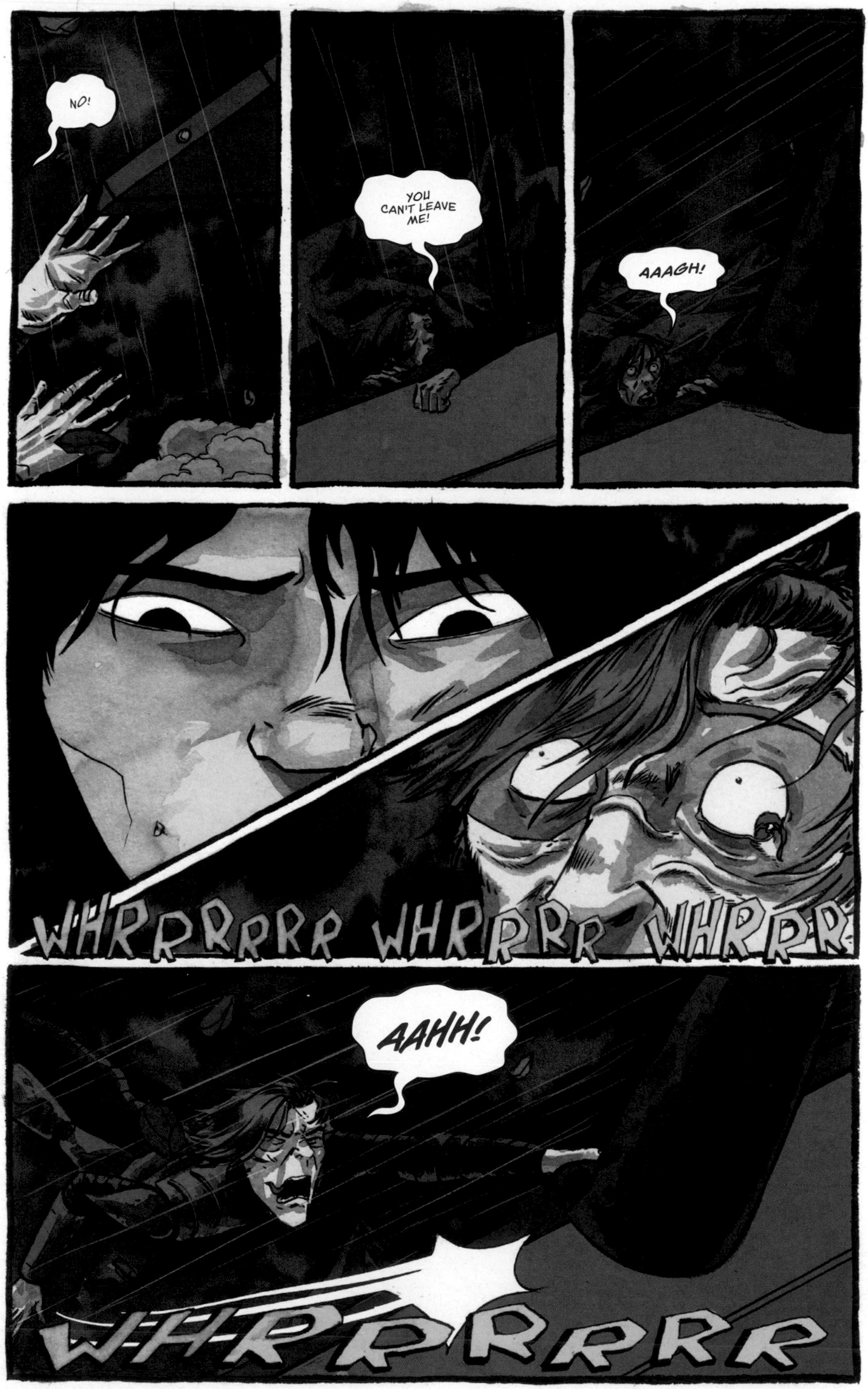
NO!
YOU CAN'T LEAVE ME!
AAAGH!
WHRRRRR WHRRRR WHRRR
AAHH!
WHRRRRRR

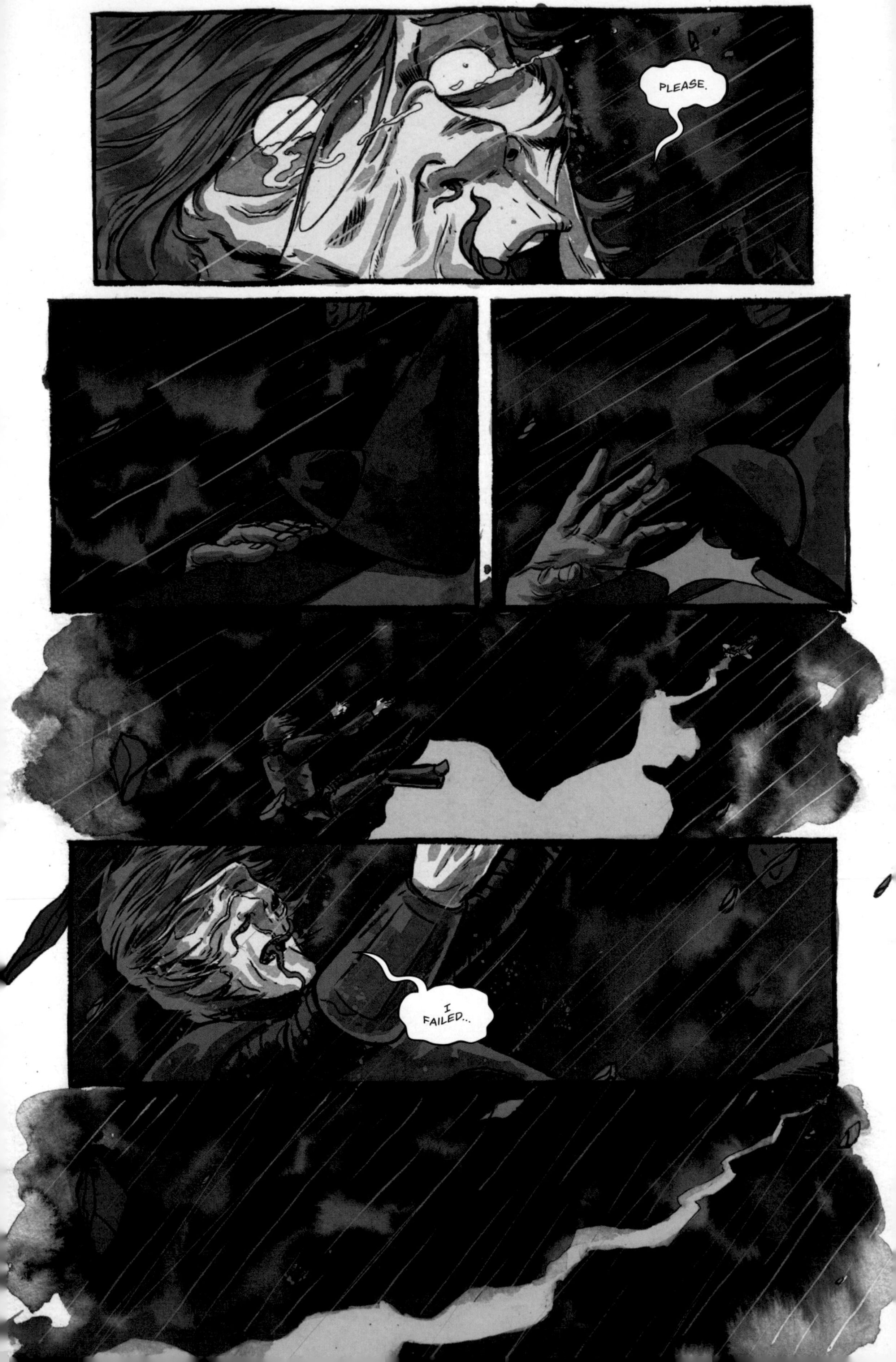
PLEASE.
I FAILED...

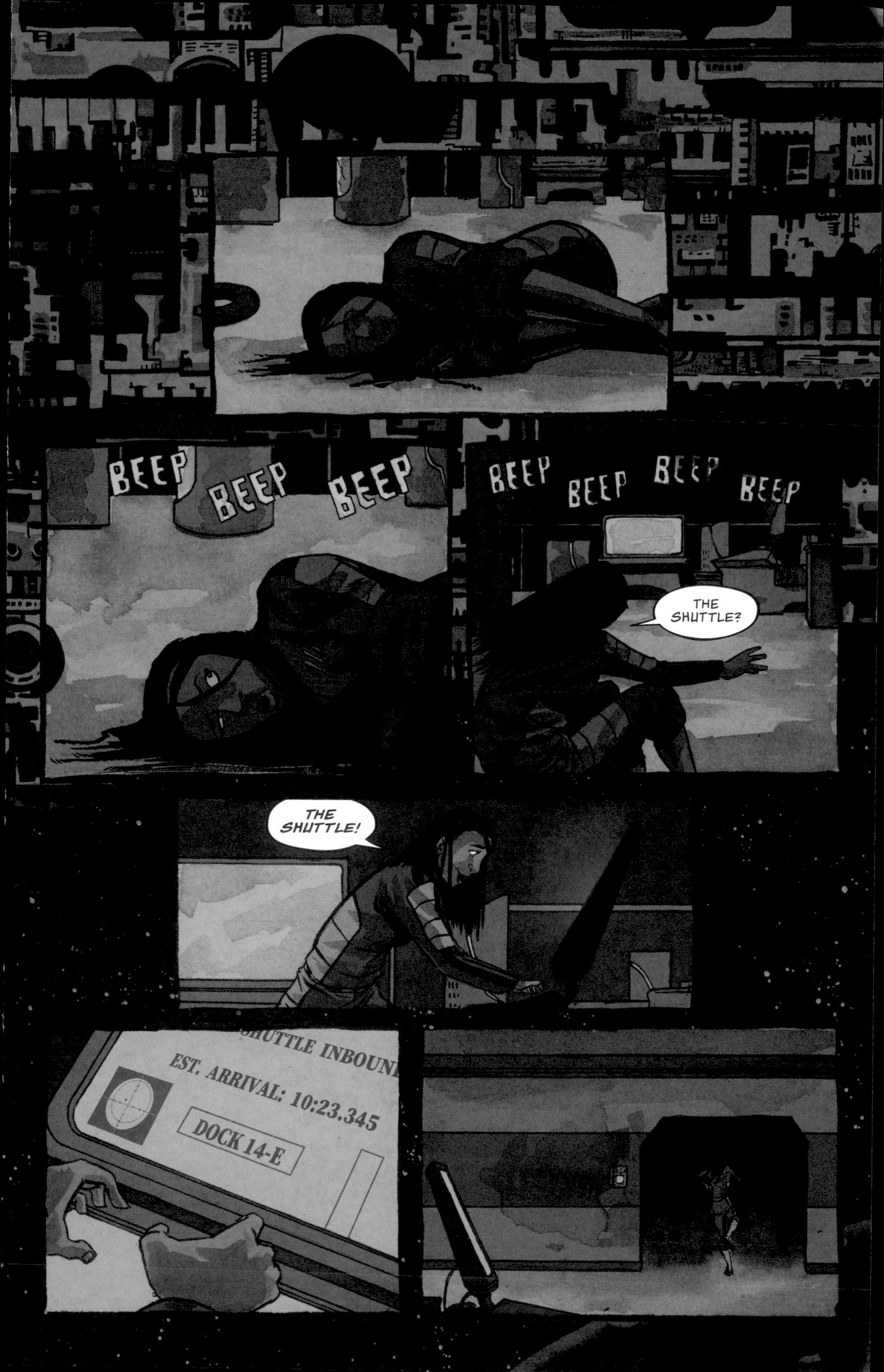
BEEP
BEEP
BEEP
BEEP
BEEP
BEEP
BEEP
THE SHUTTLE?
THE SHUTTLE!
SHUTTLE INBOUN
EST. ARRIVAL: 10:23.345
DOCK 14-E

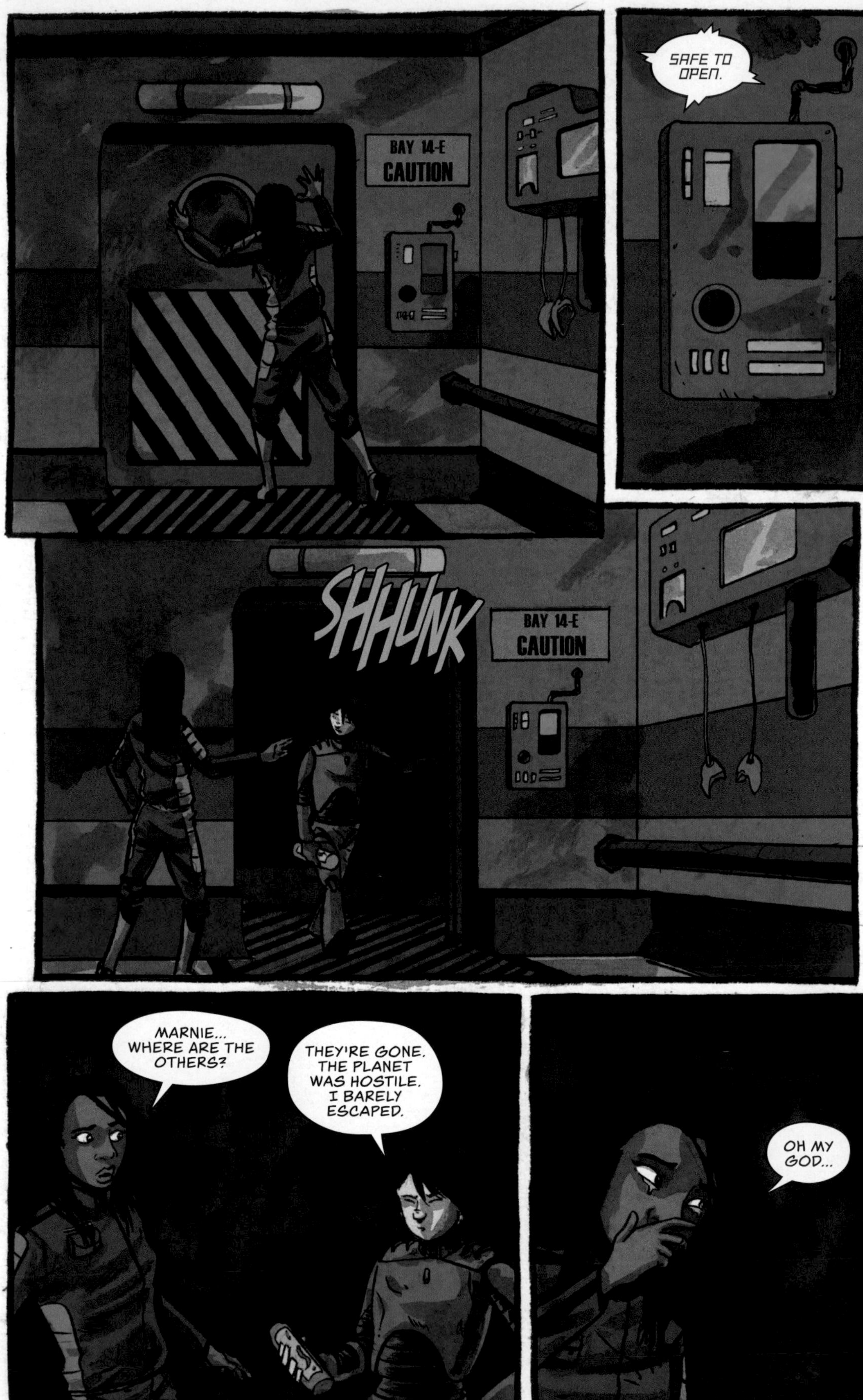
BAY 14-E
CAUTION
SAFE TO OPEN.
SHHUNK
BAY 14-E
CAUTION
MARNIE... WHERE ARE THE OTHERS?
THEY'RE GONE. THE PLANET WAS HOSTILE. I BARELY ESCAPED.
OH MY GOD...

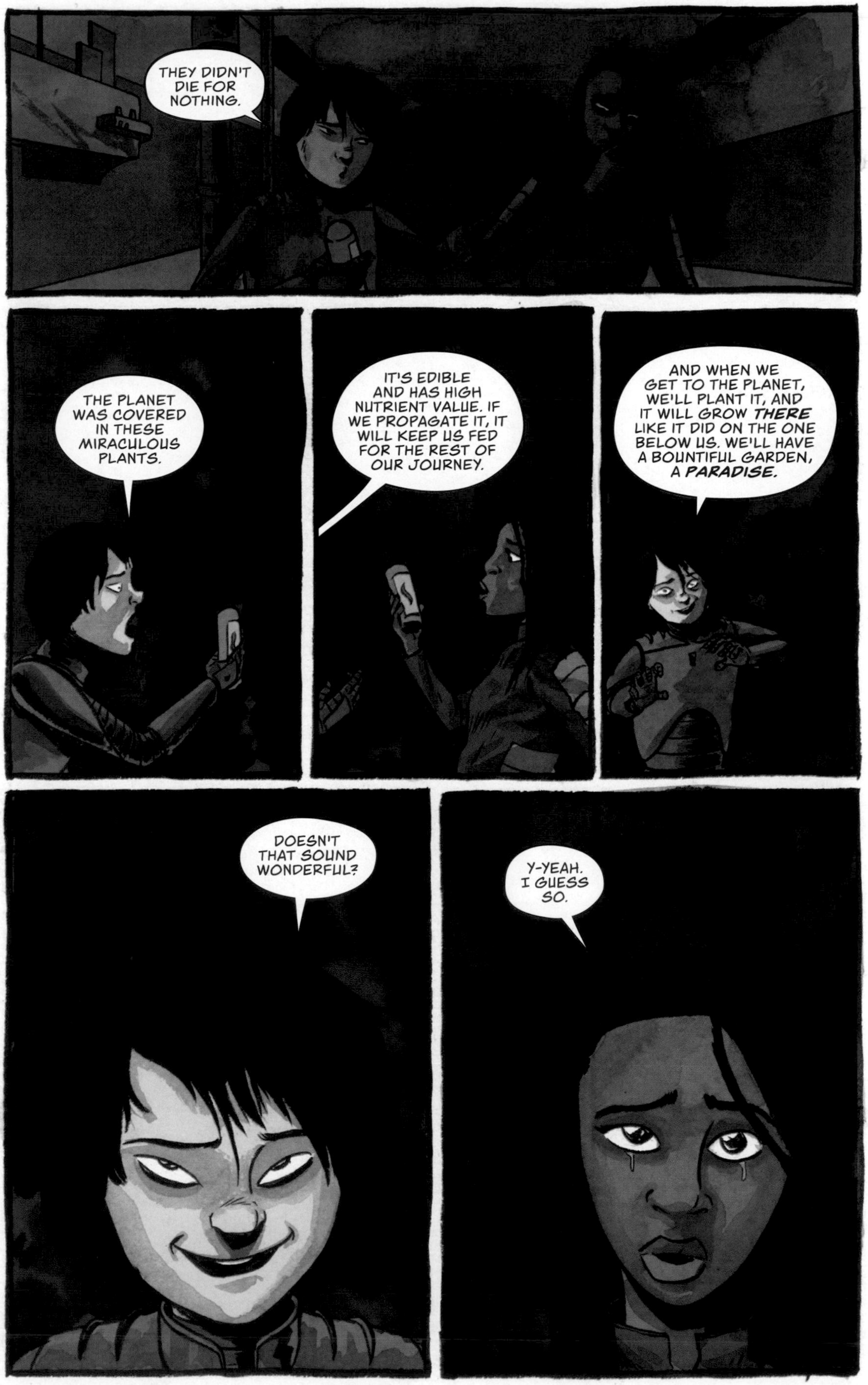
THEY DIDN'T DIE FOR NOTHING.
THE PLANET WAS COVERED IN THESE MIRACULOUS PLANTS.
IT'S EDIBLE AND HAS HIGH NUTRIENT VALUE. IF WE PROPAGATE IT, IT WILL KEEP US FED FOR THE REST OF OUR JOURNEY.
AND WHEN WE GET TO THE PLANET, WE'LL PLANT IT, AND IT WILL GROW ***THERE*** LIKE IT DID ON THE ONE BELOW US. WE'LL HAVE A BOUNTIFUL GARDEN, A ***PARADISE.***
DOESN'T THAT SOUND WONDERFUL?
Y-YEAH. I GUESS SO.

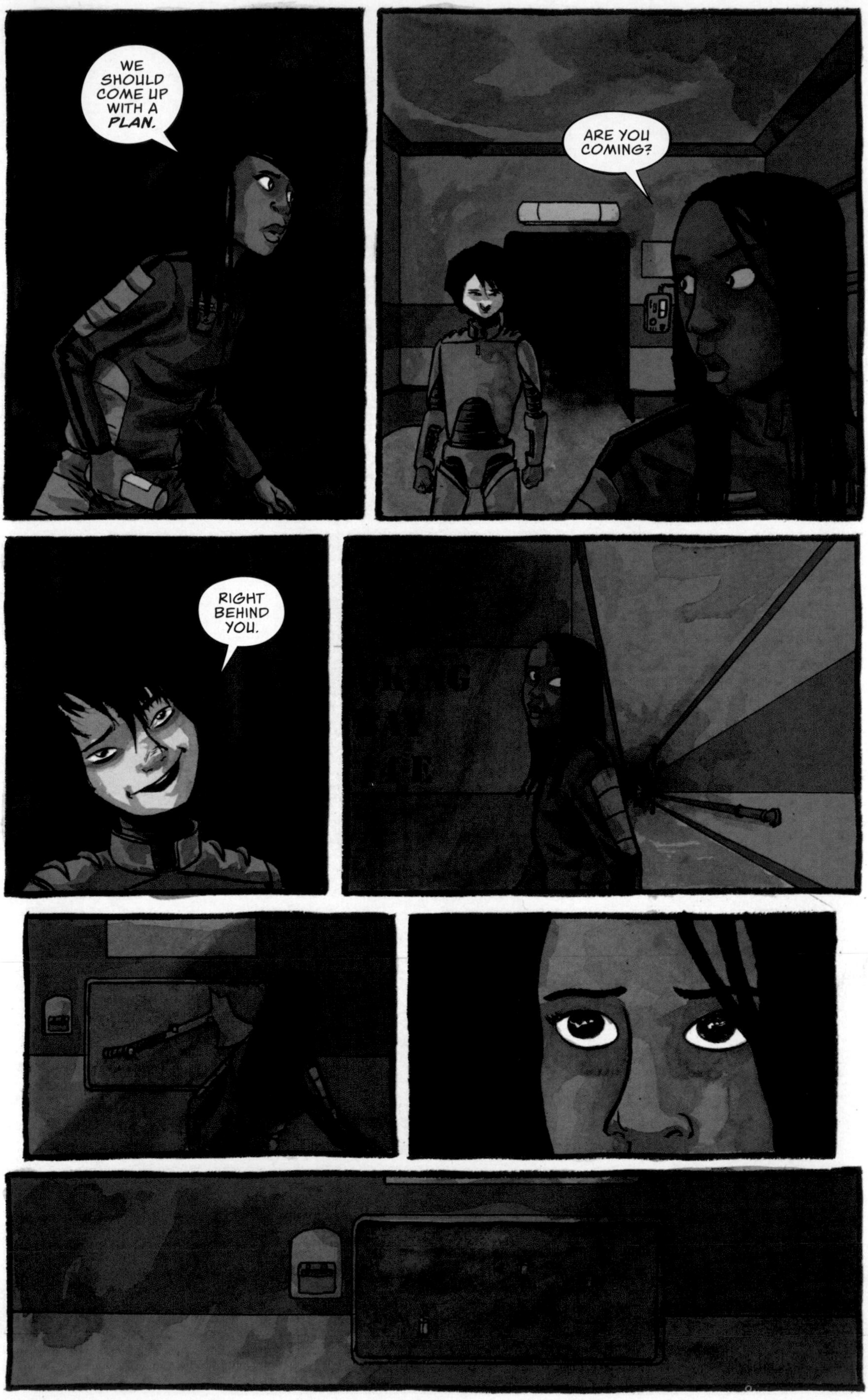
WE SHOULD COME UP WITH A *PLAN.*
ARE YOU COMING?
RIGHT BEHIND YOU.

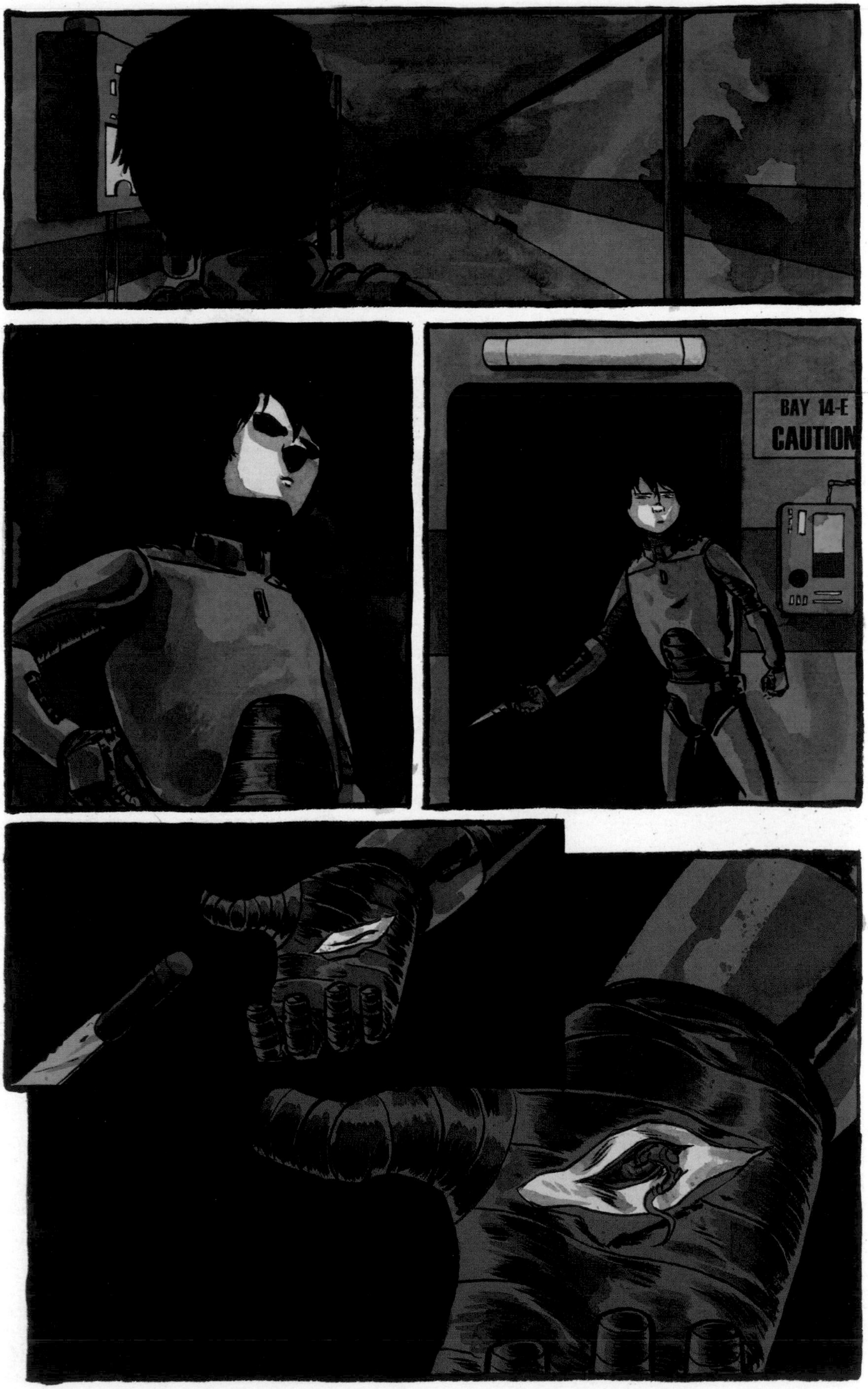
BAY 14-E
CAUTION

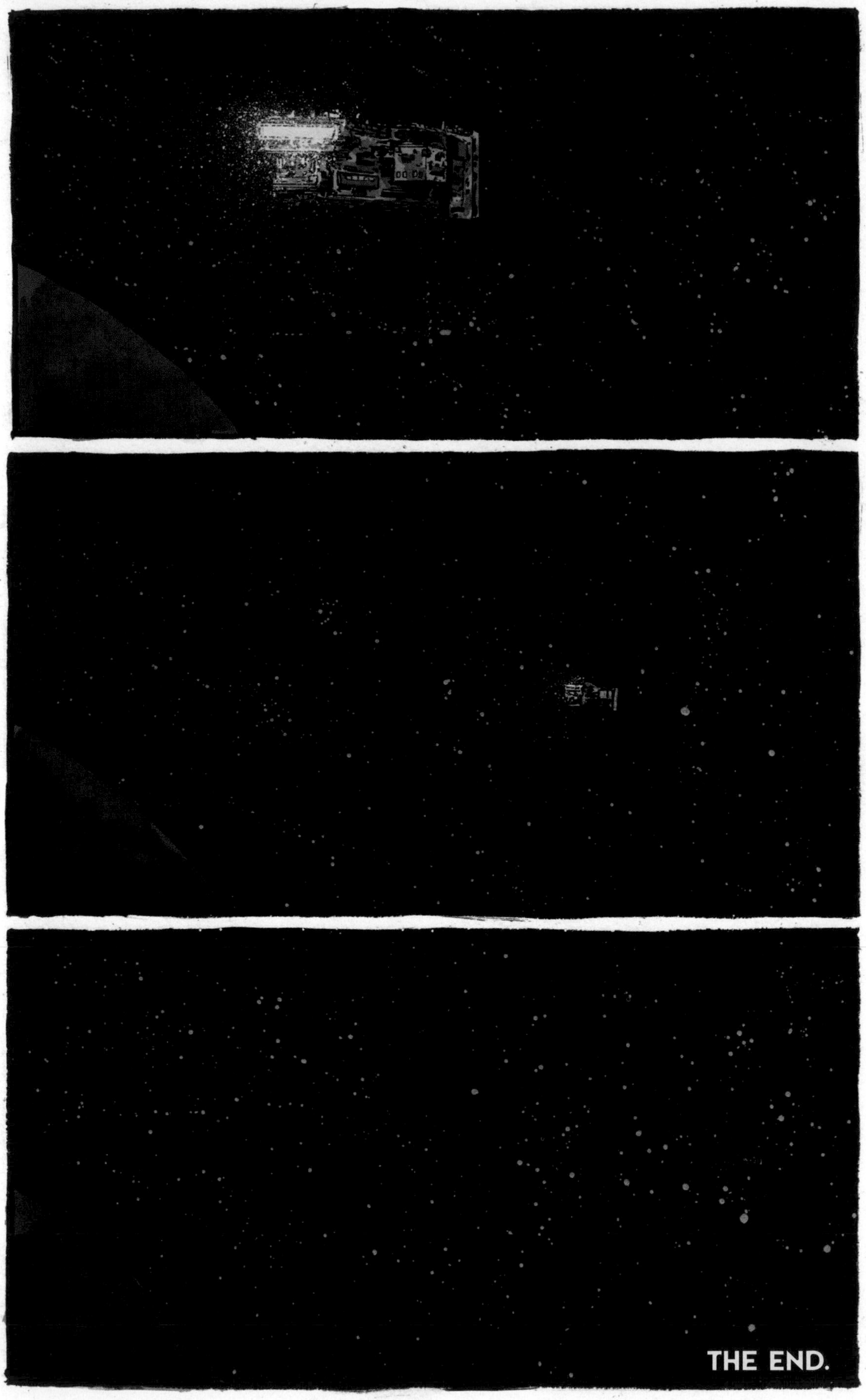

THE END.

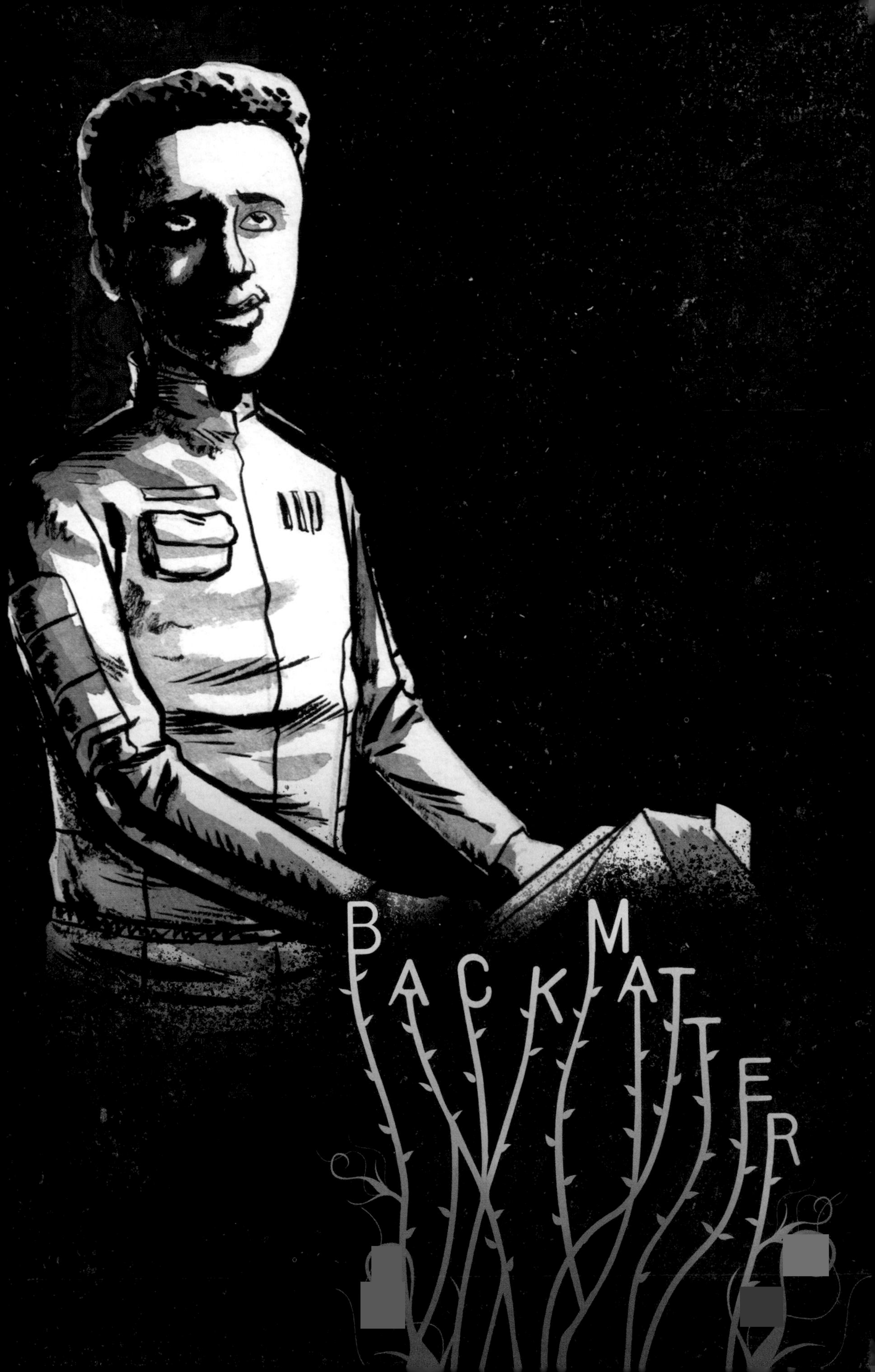
BACK MATTER

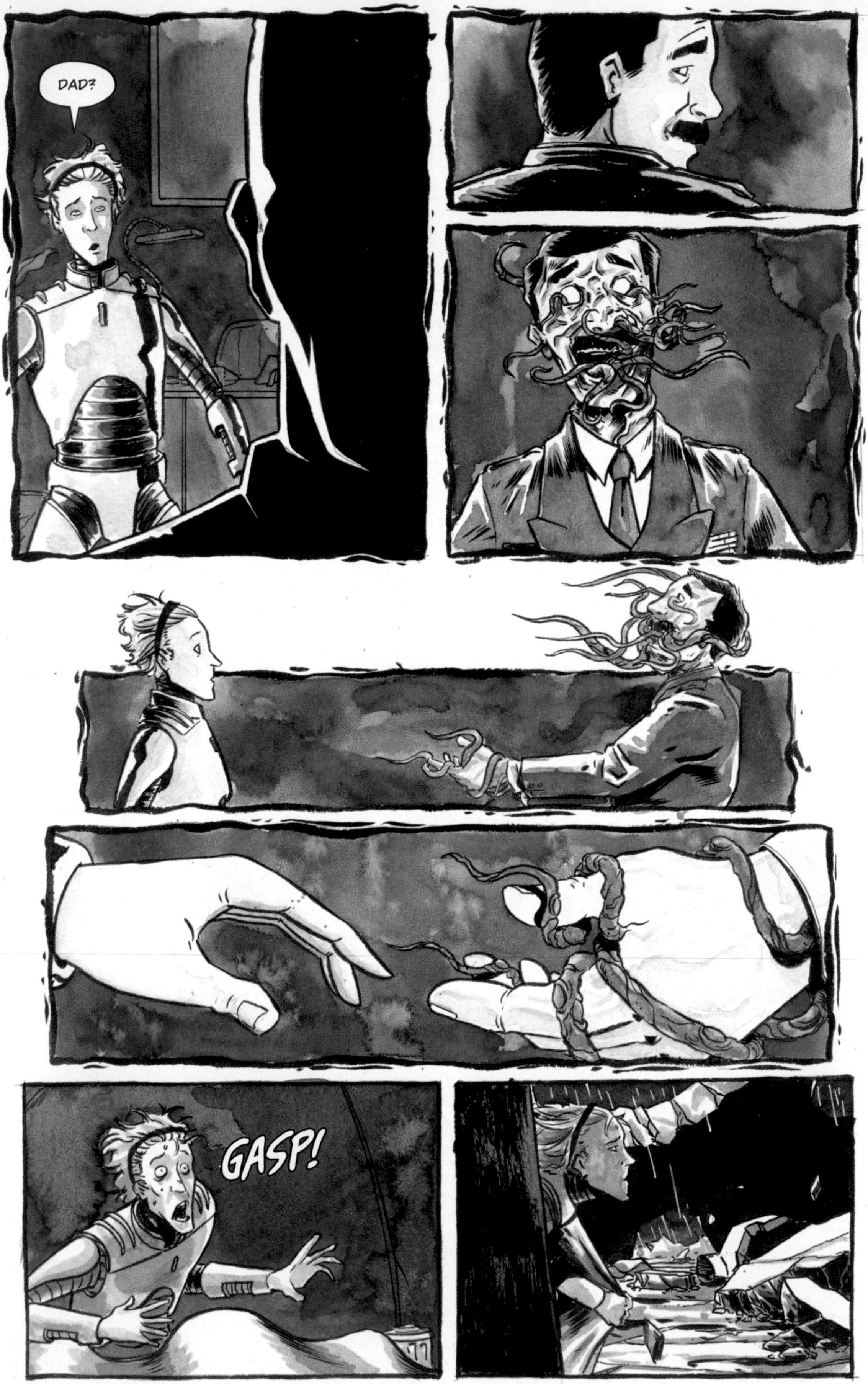
DAD?
GASP!

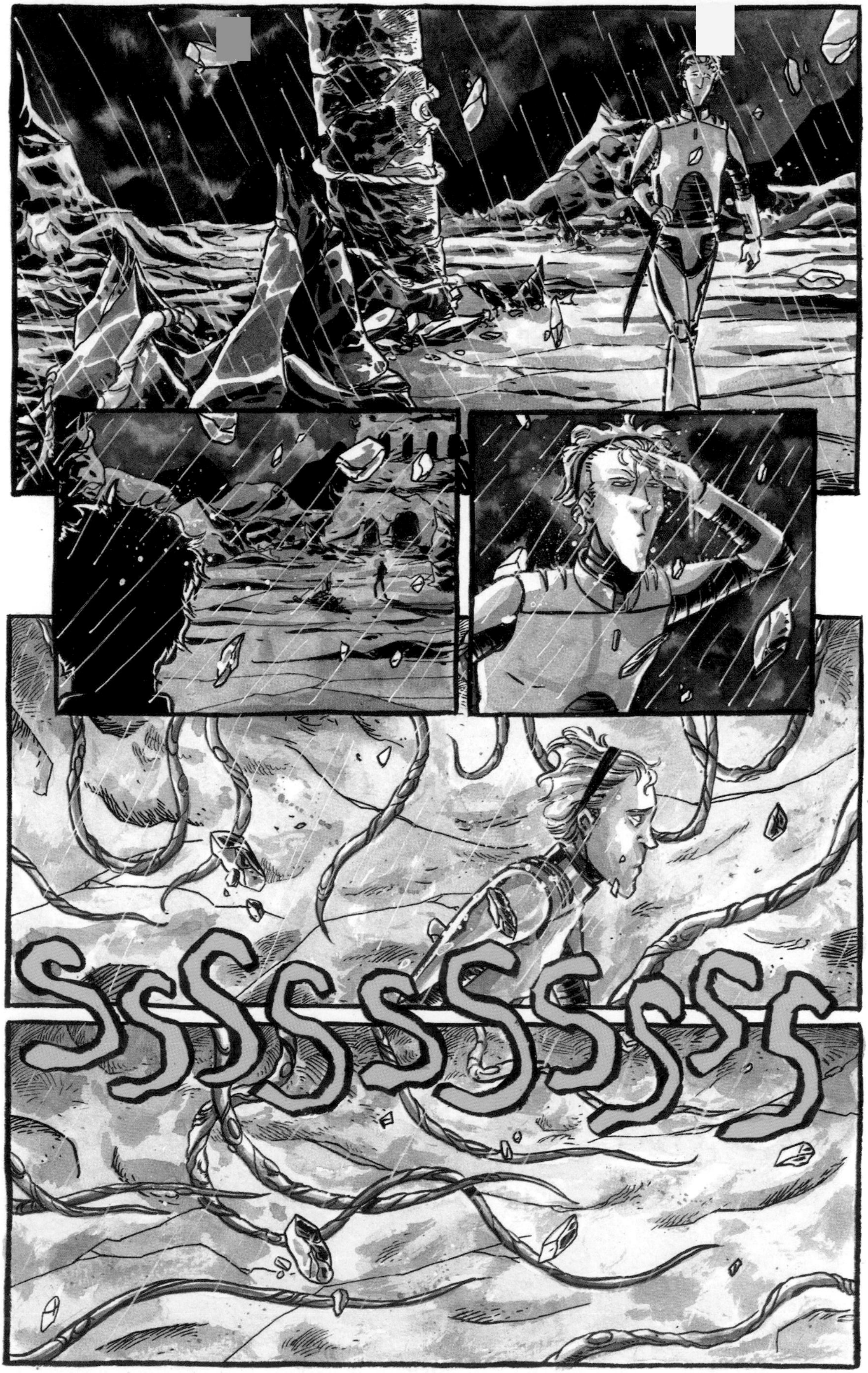
SSSSSSSSS

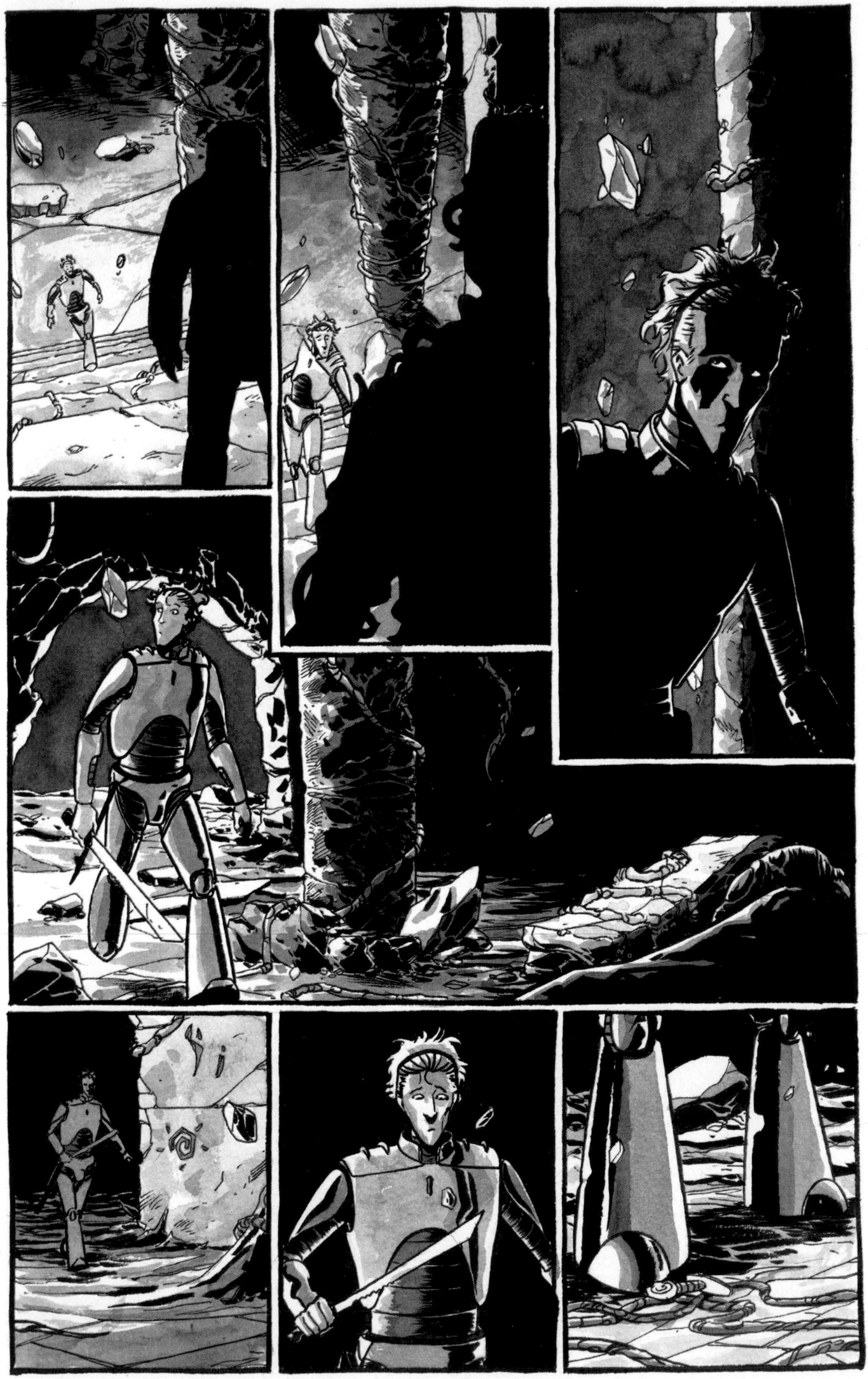

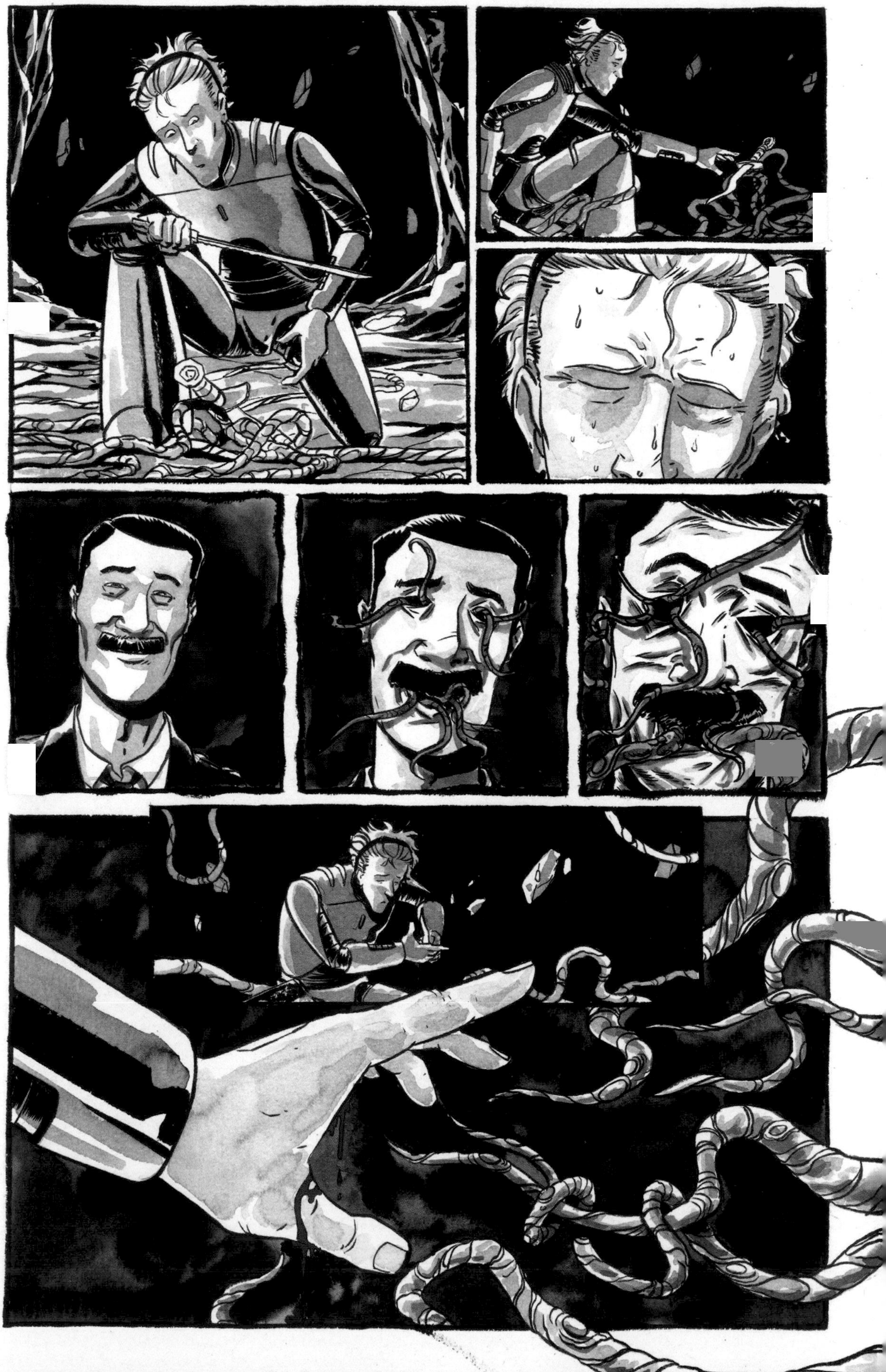

CREATORS

IVY NOÉLLE WEIR
WRITER

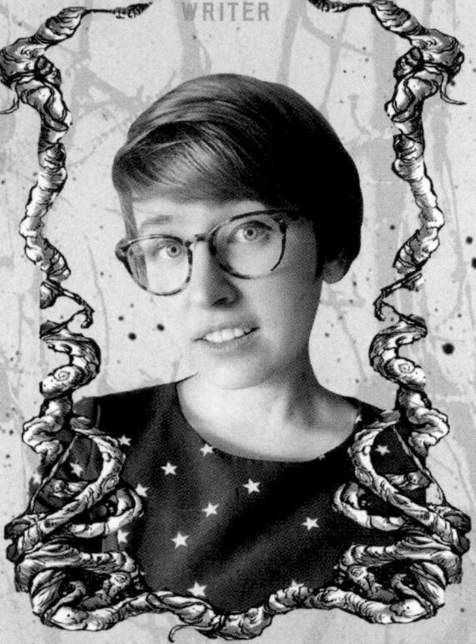

IVY NOELLE WEIR IS A WRITER OF COMICS AND PROSE LIVING IN THE GREATER BOSTON AREA. SHE IS THE CO-CREATOR OF THE DWAYNE MCDUFFIE AWARD-WINNING GRAPHIC NOVEL ARCHIVAL QUALITY (ONI PRESS), AND HER WRITING HAS APPEARED IN ANTHOLOGIES SUCH AS PRINCELESS. GIRLS ROCK (ACTION LAB ENTERTAINMENT) AND DEAD BEATS (A WAVE BLUE WORLD). SHE IS ALSO THE AUTHOR OF TWO UPCOMING MIDDLE GRADE GRAPHIC NOVELS FOR LITTLE, BROWN BOOKS FOR YOUNG READERS. THE SECRET GARDEN ON 81ST STREET (2021) AND A MODERN RETELLING OF ANNE OF GREEN GABLES (2022).

KELLY WILLIAMS
ARTIST

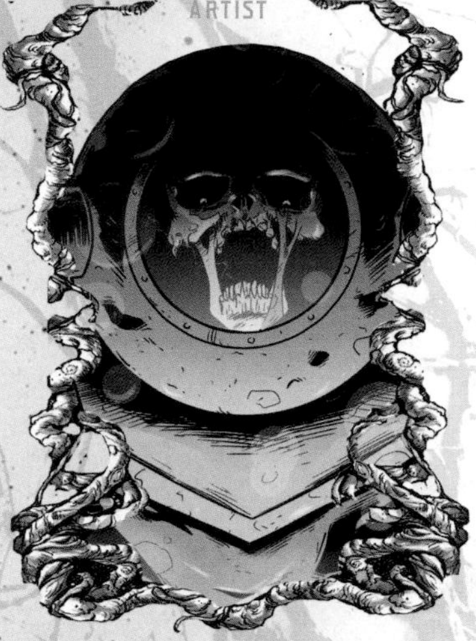

KELLY IS A COMIC BOOK ARTIST, WRITER, READER AND APPRECIATOR WHO HAS WORKED WITH PUBLISHERS LIKE DARK HORSE, IDW, BOOM!, MAD CAVE STUDIOS, TOP SHELF, AND MORE.

MOSTLY KNOWN FOR HIS WORK IN HORROR WITH CONTRIBUTIONS TO BOOKS LIKE CREEPY AND EERIE AS WELL AS CREATOR-OWNED BOOKS SUCH AS THE CABINET AND THE DARK, HE LIKES DOING SPOOKY STUFF.

GIORGIO SPALLETTA
COLORIST

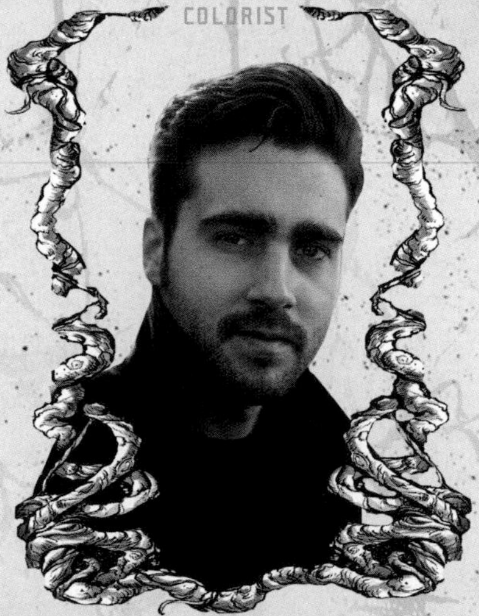

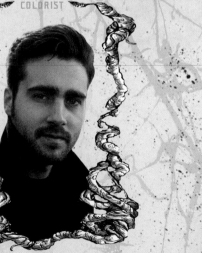

BORN IN ITALY 1989, GIORGIO SPALLETTA ATTENDED THE INTERNATIONAL SCHOOL OF COMICS IN ROME, WHERE HE IS NOW A TEACHER. HE LIVES IN ROME AND HE'S ONE OF THE MEMBERS OF STUDIO PANOPTICON. HE WORKED WITH BUGS COMICS, EDITORIALE AUREA, SERGIO BONELLI EDITORE, EDITORIALE COSMO AND IDW. HE COLLABORATES WITH MAD CAVE STUDIOS AS COLORIST.

JUSTIN BIRCH
LETTERER

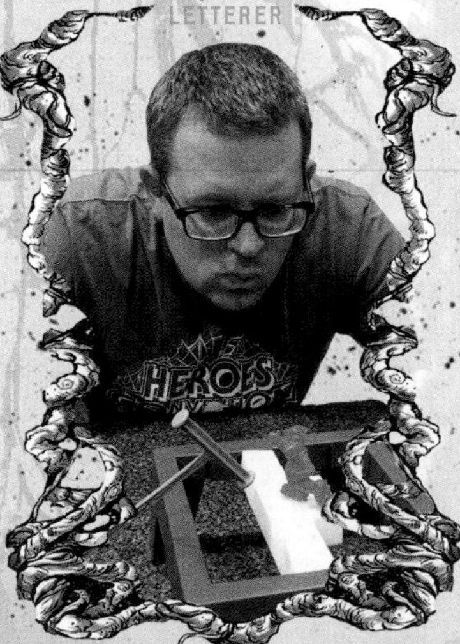
HEROES

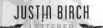

JUSTIN IS A RINGO AWARD NOMINATED LETTERER BORN AND RAISED IN THE HILLS OF WEST VIRGINIA. LETTERING COMICS SINCE 2015, HE IS A MEMBER OF THE LETTERING STUDIO ANDWORLD DESIGN AND HAS WORKED WITH NUMEROUS INDIE PUBLISHERS. JUSTIN STILL LIVES IN WEST VIRGINIA, ONLY NOW IT'S WITH HIS LOVING WIFE, DAUGHTER, AND THEIR DOG, KIRBY.

BOUNTIFUL™ GARDEN

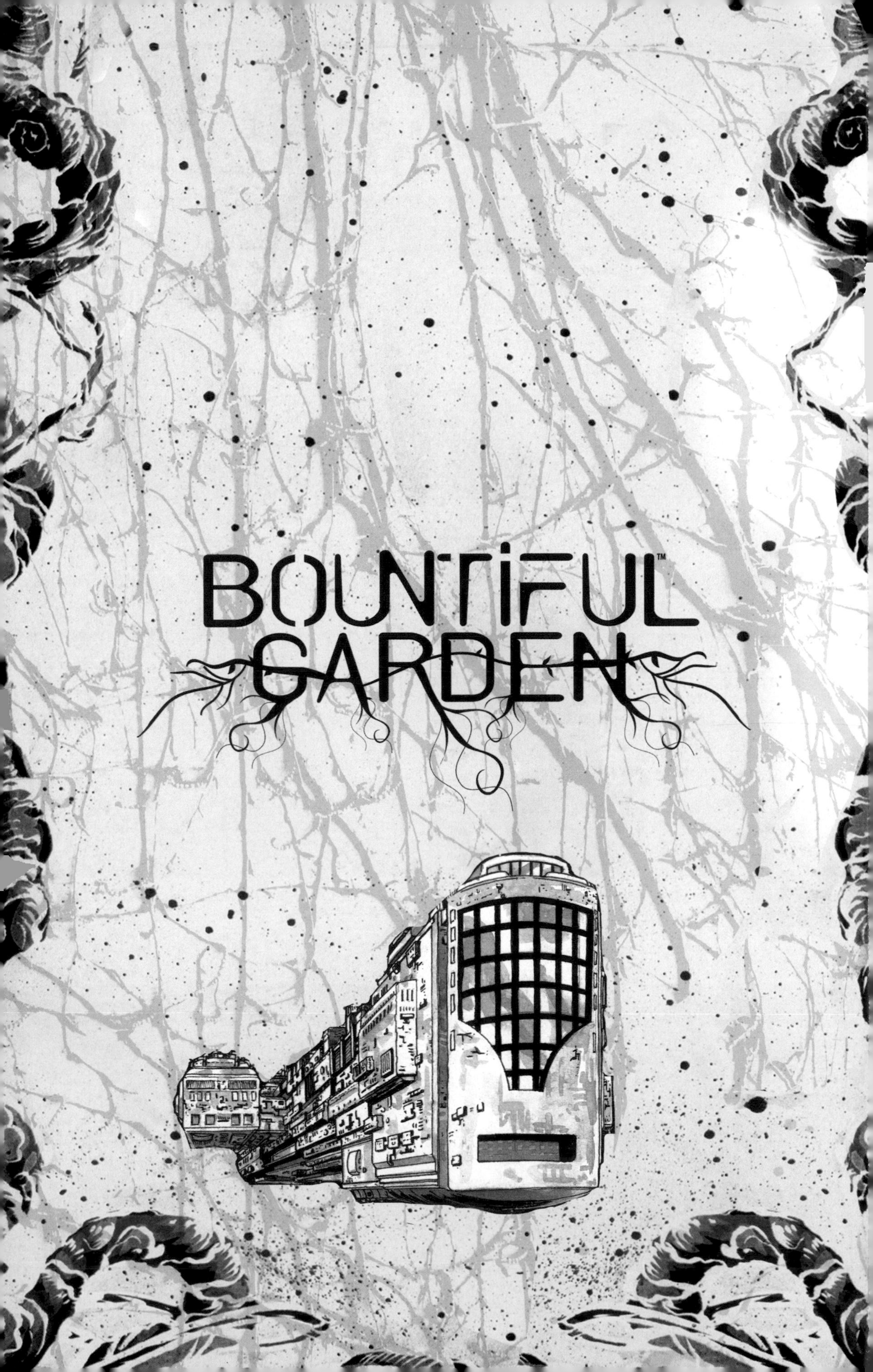

DISCOVER MAD CAVE

Nottingham Vol. 1: Death and Taxes
ISBN: 978-1-952303-14-2

Wolvenheart Vol. 2: A Tale of Two Wolves
ISBN: 978-1-952303-30-2

Knights of the Golden Sun Vol. 2: Father's Armor
ISBN: 978-1-952303-10-4

Battlecats Vol. 3: Hero of Legend
ISBN: 978-1-952303-12-8

Bountiful Garden Vol. 1
ISBN: 978-1-952303-17-3

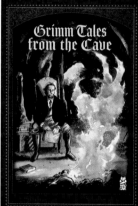

Grimm Tales from the Cave Vol. 1
ISBN: 978-1-952303-24-1

Becstar Vol. 1
ISBN: 978-1-952303-16-6

Honor and Curse Vol. 2: Mended
ISBN: 978-1-952303-11-1

SCAN ME